UNFORGETTABLE

Dean Hovey

ISBN: 1449927564
ISBN-13: 9781449927561

ACKNOWLEDGEMENTS

Like most endeavors, a book cannot get to final form without input from dozens of experts, editors, and proofreaders. Thanks to Julie for planting the idea that blossomed into this story. Thanks to Allen Solheid and Sue Downs who gave me the book's location where their cabin rests on the site of an old summer camp near Willow River. Thanks to the ladies at Dandelion Floral & Gifts for their support, enthusiasm, and the scene that became Pine Brook Floral. Thanks to my proofreaders, Fran Brozo, Nancy Mohr, Wendy Plauda, Lynn Hovey, Eleanor Rudin, Bil Brummund, Deb Brummund,, Mike Westfall, Natalie Lund, and Dennis Arnold, I can't imagine doing this without your support, ideas, and corrections.

Thanks for the support of the small booksellers like Once Upon A Crime, Lake Country Booksellers, Gordy's Gifts, Many Voices, and Valley Booksellers, who've been supportive and kept my books on their shelves. Thanks to the law enforcement officers of Carlton County, Pine County, and the Minnesota State Patrol who have provided insight and some detail. Thanks to the residents of Pine County who have been wonderfully supportive and supply me with dozens of new plots at every book event.

This book is a work of fiction, and any resemblance to events, locations, or people is coincidental. Restaurants, names, businesses, and locations are used fictionally.

☆ ☆ ☆

This book is dedicated to Verna and Oscar Mattson who exposed me to Minnesota/Scandinavian traditions and taught me to play cribbage. I'll skip the Lutefisk again this year.

CHAPTER 1

Thursday

"I'm just not sure what to do, Ginny. I can retire with a full pension. I'll be comfortable, but I don't know what I'd do with myself. That's probably the biggest problem." Floyd Swenson pulled up his jacket collar and turned his back to the biting April wind that moaned as it passed through a row of Balsam firs that lined the gravel driveway.

"Well, that's not the only issue ... I guess that I'm feeling a little useless. With all the young, college-educated deputies and the computers I feel a little like a dinosaur. I told you about that cute young deputy, Pam Ryan. Well, she had to show me how to access the BCA network so I could do a criminal background search. Sorry, I forgot you hate the acronyms; that's the Minnesota Bureau of Criminal Apprehension computer network. Anyway, it's kind of humbling. Not that the technology isn't great, we had a guy's file before he got comfortable in the holding cell, it's just that I feel...so out of it. Everything is computers, e-mail, faxes, electronics, digital cameras, and cell phones. Things happen faster than I can think them through."

Floyd pushed a newly emerged dandelion aside with the toe of his shoe, and then bent down to pull out a clump of brown grass that was infringing on the flat granite headstone. "I wish they'd trim a little better. I guess I could come out here more often and trim around the headstones and monuments. That'd be a useful retirement project."

Bent down, he stared at the engraving, tracing the letters in the gray granite with his fingers:

VIRGINIA SWENSON

1951 - 2007

On the other half of the granite he ran his fingers over the other name:

FLOYD SWENSON

1950 -

"It's really unfair that you went first," he said, wiping tears on the back of his hand. "There's so much that we planned to do. We would've gone to Hawaii and on an Alaskan cruise. Oh, I know that you told me to do all those things at the end, but it's just not the same without you."

He stood and wiped his nose with a tissue. "There is one more thing that I have to do. I don't suppose that you could've forgotten that little girl who disappeared from the Melody Pines Camp when I was a rookie. I probably told you about her a hundred times. Well, the sheriff got a call from the BCA – that's the same acronym. Anyway, Ramsey County got called about some bones that a guy found in the trunk of a car he'd purchased for restoration. The deputy who responded found out the car was from Pine County so he sealed it and had it shipped to the BCA lab in St. Paul. The deputy said there was a Melody Pines gray t-shirt with black lettering in the trunk with the bones. Dan Williams and I are driving down this morning to be there when they reopen the trunk."

"I sure hope that it's her. It's a shame that her family has gone all these years without closure. I can't think of anything worse than losing a child and never knowing what happened. At least we had twenty-nine years together before we had to say our good-byes and shed a few tears. Maybe this will give her parents closure."

Floyd started to leave, and then turned back to the gray granite headstone. "Maybe it'll give me some closure, too. I'll let you know how it turns out."

The sod, now wet and soft after the thaw and the spring rains, squished under his feet as Floyd walked back to the brown Crown Vicotria with the seven-sided star, the Pine County Sheriff's Department logo. He cranked the temperature setting to full heat to ward off the chill from the weather, the hole in his heart, and the impending resolution of a 35-year-old mystery, While he waited for the engine to warm his mind played through all the things that he and Ginny had planned to do in retirement as tears streamed down his face.

CHAPTER 2

Dan Willaims, the Pine County undersheriff, was standing next to an unmarked squad car in the Pine County Law Enforcement Center parking lot when Floyd drove up. "You're uncharacteristically late, Floyd." Dan said as Floyd climbed into the passenger seat of the unmarked car. At six-two, Dan was a couple inches taller than Floyd, retaining his high school fullback's physique. Floyd was slender and often described as wiry. As the undersheriff and chief investigator Dan wore casual clothes, a plaid shirt over khaki pants and his trademark buckskin jacket.

"I must've lost track of the time," Floyd said as he buckled the seat belt.

"Tell me more about the girl who disappeared from the camp", Dan said as he pulled out of the parking lot. "I was just out of high school in 1974, and I vaguely remember the fire department dragging First Lake."

Floyd looked at the Walmart as they approached I-35, trying to visualize the time long past. "There was never any evidence of foul play. The only things missing were the girl and a camp T-shirt she'd been wearing for a nightgown. I questioned every camper and staff member, but no one knew where she had gone. The rumors about skinny-dipping surfaced quickly and that seemed like such a natural answer that the sheriff called out the fire department." He paused as a dark image came to mind. "The worst part was the parents. They showed up about the time that the fire department started dragging the grappling hook through the swim area. The mother was absolutely wild, teeing off on everyone from the camp staff to the sheriff. The father was angry, but subdued."

"What leads came from the questioning?" Dan asked as they traveled past the Pine City Golf Course where it bordered the Interstate. Two hardy golfers stood in the brown fairway, contemplating their approach shots to a temporary green while the raw wind slapped at their wind shirts and pants.

"Not a one. It's like aliens had spirited her away in the night." Floyd paused, and then added, "But I was a dumb rookie. I wonder if I asked the right questions from the key people. I wonder if a more skilled interviewed might've got more out of someone. I wonder if I was too stupid to catch a look or body language that would've made me suspicious of someone's story."

They rode silently for a while until Floyd asked, "Can you tell me more about the BCA phone call?"

"Sorry," Dan apologized. "I was mulling over the history. The sheriff got a call from a Ramsey County detective. A homeowner called them to report the discovery of a human skeleton. When their deputy responded they found a skeleton in the trunk of a car. The caller had purchased the car from a farm near Hinckley where it was stored behind the barn. The detective said they took one look to verify that the remains were human, and then they closed the car up and delivered it to the Bureau of Criminal Apprehension for a complete investigation."

"How old was the car?"

"That's the strangest part," Dan said. "The license tabs expired in 1955. The Ramsey County guys assumed that the bones have been in the trunk since then. When they verified that the car had been purchased in Hinckley and that it wasn't their crime, they called us for follow up."

"When you called, you said there was a T-shirt from the Melody Pines Camp on the body."

"The shirt was with the body," Dan corrected. "with a pair of cotton panties and athletic socks. They didn't give me a lot of details, but it appeared that the clothing had been placed there alongside the body, although they said that everything was jumbled around because the car had been towed."

Floyd shook his head. "It doesn't make sense. The body couldn't have been there since '55. I was a counselor at Melody Pines back in the sixties and we didn't have printed T-shirts in those days. The body must've been tossed into the car years later, like in '74."

Dan shrugged. "I guess we'll see if the BCA has any way to determine that."

"Who was the last owner of the car?"

"The plates are so old the BCA had to look up the numbers manually," Dan replied. "They were registered to Herbert Benson. He had a post office box in Hinckley, but he lived east of town on the road the locals call Swede Alley."

"I don't recognize Herbert Benson's name," Floyd said. "Did Ramsey County say if the car had been purchased from Benson?"

"Apparently not," Dan replied. "A young couple bought Benson's farm. When the car collector approached them about selling a junker behind the barn, they jumped at the chance. Although they didn't have the title, they gave him a bill of sale and he said he'd be able to sort out the abandoned vehicle title with the state."

"So, this guy buys the car, shows up with a trailer, and drags it to the Twin Cities. He starts checking out his new toy and he finds a skeleton in the trunk," Floyd summarized. "Any chance he put the bones there?"

"The Ramsey County sergeant I spoke with said the purchaser was a basket case. They strongly doubted he had any involvement. Besides that, it sounds like the buyer wasn't born in 1955. He was looking for an old car he could customize into a hotrod."

Dan took the Maryland Avenue exit off I-35 and drove through the aging neighborhoods that had been filled with blue-collar families when the Whirlpool and 3M had provided hundreds of manufacturing jobs and Hamm's brewery had slaked the thirst of the workers. The once proud neighborhoods of Scandinavians in the mid-1900's had morphed into a melting pot of new immigrants who had turned the old neighborhood grocery stores into tortilla shops, Asian grocery stores, and an array of restaurants that represented Mexico, North Africa, and the Far East. Most of the houses looked like they were a few years past the need for a new coat of paint and the yards were littered with toys left on scruffy patches of brown grass.

They drove past a group of young men wearing dirty aprons and assorted baseball caps, with the bills worn at odd angles. They stood in the alley behind a restaurant, smoking cigarettes and giving the obvious un-marked cop car a hard glare. The houses started showing more care as they drove east, and at Arcade Street they passed the southern edge of Phalen Park Golf Course. The houses were now decorated with stone or brick facades, and the yards sported neatly trimmed lawns. When they arrived at the Bureau of Criminal Apprehension St. Paul offices Dan parked in a visitor's space off Maryland Avenue. Laurie Lone Eagle, Dan's former partner, now an agent with the BCA, was waiting for them at the security desk.

"I heard half the Pine County sheriff's department was on their way down." Laurie shook hands with both officers and gave them visitor badges. "Clip these on and follow me."

"I feel like I should be dropping bread crumbs so I can find my way back to the reception desk," Dan said, as Laurie led them through carpeted hallways winding between offices and labs. She wore a wool pant's suit with fine vertical stripes that were intended to make her look taller than her five-two stature. Her straight, black hair was worn short, not as much a style statement as a matter of convenience for someone who spent many nights in motels across the state in her search for information that might lead her to a missing child.

"The maze keeps the bad guys from stealing our secrets," Laurie said. "It sure beats our old building, over on University Avenue where everything was cramped, with poor ventilation, and in a deteriorating neighborhood. We don't even need a guard in the parking lot here." She opened a door that led to a huge garage. Inside, two men dressed in white coveralls were arranging high intensity halogen lights around the rusted body of a car. The walls were stark white and the spotless floor had a fresh coat of glossy urethane paint.

"If not for the Chrome Dodge nameplate," Floyd said, "you couldn't tell what make of car this boxy old hulk was."

"The guys who buy these things for hotrods amaze me," Dan said as he stood back and took in the scene.

"It's hard to believe that someone could take a rusting hulk with no windows and a mouse infested interior and turn it into something they'd be proud to drive around."

Laurie led them to the trunk. "Floyd Swenson and Dan Williams, I'd like you to meet Jeff Ness and Tom Class." Jeff was close to 50 with thinning sandy hair and a bit of a paunch. Tom Class was about the same age, with a little more hair and a little less stomach. Both were dressed in white Tyvek coveralls and wore white hair nets so they wouldn't shed lint, hair, or fibers while they investigated. A digital SLR camera dangled from a strap around Class's neck and he quickly returned to arranging halogen lights around the back of the car.

"Laurie says you guys are the A-team from Pine County," Ness said jovially as he shook Dan's hand. Even through surgical gloves, Floyd could feel that his hands were calloused and hard as horn, definitely not some desk-jockey who never picked up anything heavier than a pen. Class was turning on the lights, making the garage as bright as daylight.

"If we're the A-team," Dan said, "I feel sorry for the B-team."

"Could you all stand back for a few minutes while I capture this Kodak moment?" Class asked as he started taking pictures of the car from every angle.

"It's too bad that we couldn't have done this in-situ on the farm," Laurie said, "Who knows how much evidence has been lost or destroyed in the two trips that it's made over the past week."

Floyd watched mutely with a hollow expression as the camera clicked. "Are you okay?" Laurie asked.

Floyd shook his head. "I just had this terrible vision of an old horror movie. The police pull an old car out of a lake where college kids had pushed it decades before after they thought they had killed a girl. They'd sunk the car to hide the body. Well, when the movie flashed back to the car originally sinking, the girl had only been unconscious and when she got wet she woke up and it was too late for her to escape. When the car is pulled from the water fifty years later, one of the aged frat boys opens the door and the corpse falls on him, as if she were attacking him for abandoning her all those years before."

The others had all stopped to listen to Floyd's story. When he finished, the garage was silent.

Laurie put her hand on Floyd's arm. "Maybe you and I should get coffee."

Floyd stared at the trunk. "She had black hair and was about twelve years-old. The missing camp T-shirt was gray with black lettering spelling out Melody Pines Camp."

Jeff Ness looked at Floyd, then Dan. Seeing no indication he should wait any longer, he untied the yellow rope securing the trunk. The buyer had removed the trunk latch, and he carefully inserted a screwdriver in the hole, lifting the lid against the resistance of the rusty hinges that gave a complaining groan. When the trunk was fully open, Tom Class moved a set of lights close to illuminate the trunk enclosure and snapped six pictures from various positions, then stepped back so the others could see.

Laurie and Dan stepped forward, while Floyd hung back. She took a deep breath and recited what she saw, "Looks like a gray T-shirt on top of skeletal remains. The corpse had dark hair."

Floyd closed his eyes, turned away from the car, and uttered, "Sonofabitch," as his voice cracked. He walked away. "C'mon, Laurie, I'll take that coffee now."

CHAPTER 3

Floyd was silent on the return trip to Pine City, watching the passing patches of plowed fields and brown swamps interspersed with wood lots. The first light green sprouts were bursting from tree buds near the Twin Cities, but as the drove further north, and into Pine County, the buds were still hard brown scabs on the branches, the spring buds delayed a week by the slightly cooler temperatures fifty miles to the north.

He was staring out the window as they passed the Harris exit. "You know, First Lake is a stupid name for a lake."

Dan's thoughts had been on arrangements for examination of the remains and pursuit of the investigation. Floyd's comment caught him off guard. "What?"

"Melody Pines Camp was on First Lake," Floyd replied. "It's a stupid name for a lake. I mean, what kind of idiot surveyor names a lake 'First'?"

"Are you okay?"

Floyd shifted so he was looking at Dan. "What's wrong with calling a surveyor stupid for not having enough imagination to come up with a real name for a lake?"

"You haven't been able to talk about this case since we opened the trunk."

Floyd drew a deep breath and let it out slowly. "I'm okay. It's just a blow to finally find the remains after all these years." He sat in silence for a few more seconds then added, "I may have screwed up the investigation. If I'd asked questions differently maybe I would have turned up the key lead. Hell, if I had been sharper at following the leads, maybe I would have cracked the case and saved the kid?"

Dan shrugged. "It's a rhetorical question. There are a thousand Monday morning quarterbacks who can second-guess our actions. We all do the best we can in the heat of the moment; sometimes the results are great; sometimes the results are less than optimal."

"There's a big difference between less than optimal results and having a twelve year-old die in a trunk because you screwed up the investigation."

"You can't change the past," Dan replied. "Let's get on with the murder investigation and find out who did it."

"It's too late, Dan," Floyd said, shaking his head. "It happened over thirty years ago. All the people who were involved are dead or gone."

"It's out of character for you to give up without a fight."

Floyd ran his fingers through his thinning hair. "I don't know if I'm up for the fight anymore. I requested my retirement papers from the state yesterday."

Dan slowed the car and took exit ramp for Pine City. "You're getting your papers?" He stopped the car at the top of the ramp and stared at Floyd. "Really?" he asked.

"Really," Floyd said without emotion. "I'm over fifty-five. I collect a full pension and staying on longer doesn't give me anything but more frustration. Besides that, I'm tired."

A horn sounded and Dan glared in the rear-view mirror at the young driver who had the nerve to honk at what was obviously an unmarked squad car. He motioned the car to pass them and then flashed his badge as the male teen passed. The driver gave Dan a look of disdain.

"See," Floyd said. "That's exactly what I mean, no one respects us; not the kids, not the judges, not the little old ladies at the supermarket. We're busting our humps to protect them, and what do we get in return? I'll tell you. We get spit on and sworn at. The courts expect us to take it with a smile and reply, 'Yes sir. Have a nice day, sir.' When you give some asshole a ticket, he tells you to put it where the sun doesn't shine and all you can do is smile and tip your hat."

"So, when are you planning to retire?"

Floyd closed his eyes and thought. "Well, I've got about a decade of comp time coming, and a month of vacation on top of that. I thought maybe I'd work through this rotation of shifts, and then take accrued vacation until July first. I don't have to sign the papers until a week before the effective date."

"Won't you stay on and help us solve this murder?"

Floyd shook his head. "I put everything I had into this case thirty five years ago and it still gives me nightmares. I think a new set of eyes might see something I missed. You'd be better off putting someone else on it and letting me fill in on the road until you hire my replacement."

"You're the best investigator I've got."

"Bull," Floyd replied. "Sandy Maki has more energy than I do, and Pam Ryan is more analytical. Use either of them and you'd be ahead."

"I'll miss having you around."

Floyd smiled. "If you're buying coffee, I'm around."

"So, where are you going to start the investigation?" Floyd asked as Dan pulled off the exit ramp and drove past The Red Shed restaurant. It was late morning and the lot was about half full of mud splattered car and pickups that had migrated into town on the gravel roads leading from the farms that surrounded Pine City, the county seat of Pine County.

"I got the name of the couple who bought the Benson farm," Dan said. "I thought I'd go out there and talk to them about the history of the car. After that, I figured the courthouse clerk could look up the property abstract to see if Bensons owned the farm at the time of the murder."

"How long before the BCA will have a positive identification on the body?"

"They don't know," Dan replied. "It may take a while to track down dental records that old."

"Let's see," Floyd said as he did calculations in his head. "If the girl was twelve in '74, she was born in '62. The parents were probably around twenty or so when she was born, which would put them in their sixties. There's a fair chance they're still alive, of course who knows where they could be today. I'd give even odds that they're in Sun City, Arizona versus still in The Cities."

CHAPTER 4

Friday

"Hey Floyd, did you forget to go home last night?" Deputy Kerm Rajacich asked as he walked into the office area the deputies called The Bullpen. Kerm was a haystack of a man known for despising paperwork and relishing a 911 call to a bar fight. He shed his jacket and draped it over the back of a scarred desk chair near one of the half dozen desks. The hard upholstery on the chair arms had been repaired and held in place with black electrical tape. The chair paint was a slightly different shade of gray from the desk indicating that they'd probably been procured in different, long past decades, or possibly as surplus from some Federal Agency.

"Naw, I had something nagging at me and I wanted to dig through some old files." Floyd said looking up from pile of old reports and notebooks he'd stacked neatly on his metal desk in the furthest corner of the room. "Is it the end of the night shift already?" He asked, the chair creaking as he leaned back and stretched.

"Yeah, I came off the road early to write up a DUI." Rajacich leaned over Floyd's shoulder and looked at the report he was reading. "That's some ancient history. I was still in junior high in '74."

"Ancient and new," Floyd replied. "It appears the bones recovered from the Junker in St. Paul belonged to the missing girl in this old investigation."

"Yeah, I read about that in the early edition of the Minneapolis paper, "Rajacich said as he walked to the counter built into one wall of the bullpen. He poured coffee into a chipped green cup with a John Deere logo that he pulled off a drying rack behind the coffee pot.

"They mentioned the skeleton," Kerm said as he walked back to Floyd's desk, "but I thought they said something about Ramsey County. So, why are you digging into these dusty files in the middle of the night?" Kerm dragged his finger through the dust on the box top.

"It was my first investigation. I was digging through the old files to see if there were any items that I'd overlooked. You know, any rookie mistakes." Floyd held up a legal pad. "I'm trying to list all the people who were working at the camp that summer. I wonder if any of them might remember something now that they'd overlooked back then."

"Don't you mean," Rajacich corrected, "they might admit something now they were too embarrassed to say then?"

"That, too," Floyd said, leaning back and taking a sip of coffee from a stained cup with the logo of a long defunct real estate salesman. "I think I've got my work cut out until I retire."

Rajacich sat in metal guest chair. "You're actually going to retire?" he asked. "I mean, we're all going to retire sometime, but you're thinking about going now?"

"I requested papers from the retirement board Wednesday. I'm gone July first, maybe earlier if I decide to take some comp time and vacation."

Rajacich considered the piles on Floyd's desk. "It may take longer than that to read all these files and notes." He pushed himself out of the chair, shaking his head. "If it were me considering retirement, I'd definitely go before I had to read all those notes. Paperwork makes me crazy."

Floyd considered Kerm's comments about being in junior high school in 1974. Helen Smith would be Kerm's age if she'd lived. What would she have been like? Her parents were well off, so she probably would've gone to college and met a husband there. They'd have a couple children and be living in a suburban house, driving a minivan to little league games and chairing the PTA. But she never had the chance.

"Were you still alive when I was questioning the counselors, Helen? Could I have saved your life?" Floyd stared at the notes, waiting for something to jump out, hoping that something he'd missed would emerge and lead him to the killer. "Give me some help. Dear Lord, help me make this right."

✲ ✲ ✲

The lights were blazing through the kitchen windows of the Benson place when Dan pulled into the gravel driveway. A young woman opened the old farmhouse door cautiously and peered at Dan in the glow of the rising sun.

"Hi, I'm Deputy Williams, from the sheriff's department." Dan held his badge holder to the crack in the door so she could read the identification card.

The door opened quickly and the petite, raven-haired woman stepped back. "I'm sorry. Please come in." She looked like a very young teen, but was dressed professionally in wool slacks and a sweater. The greeting badge pinned to the sweater indicated she worked for one of the Pine City banks and was named Becca.

"I need to ask you and your husband some questions about the old car you sold a couple days ago," Dan said as he stepped into the entryway. It was cluttered with dust-covered mementos from the previous owners. A stuffed owl was perched high over the door, studying all who passed with dusty glass eyes.

The woman's face flushed. "Uh oh. Is this about the title? We didn't have one, but the previous owners left a lot of stuff behind, and we assumed it became our property after the closing."

"Cars have titles," Dan said, "and without a formal transfer of title a judge might say they still belong to the title holder. On the other hand, if they're abandoned, he might consider that differently. At best, I'd say the ownership is murky."

A young man stepped from the kitchen. He was dressed in a pinstriped shirt with an embroidered patch that said, BRIAN. "What's up?" He asked. He was lean, but had muscular shoulders. His hair was combed straight back, still damp from the shower.

"This deputy came to ask us about the junk car we sold that guy," Becca said nervously.

Dan held up the badge case again. "I'd like to ask you two a couple of questions."

Brian looked at his watch. "We've gotta leave for work pretty soon. Can you make it quick?"

Dan motioned them into the kitchen. The place was freshly scrubbed, but the buckled linoleum floor and the stained kitchen window shades told him that Brian and Becca didn't have the money to update any of the decaying problems in the old farmhouse, but were trying to keep the place neat and clean. The effort was like putting lipstick on a pig.

Becca noticed Dan's quick inspection and said, "It's his turn to wash dishes," nodding toward the two cereal bowls and spoons in the sink.

Brian waved an arm and said, "He's not the cleaning police."

Dan interrupted the bickering. "Tell me about the car you sold to the guy in St. Paul."

"It was behind the barn," Brian replied. "The previous owners left it there with a few others. This guy just drives up the driveway one day and asks if we're interested in selling it. I said, 'Sure, if the price is right.' So he asks if we'd let it go for three hundred bucks."

"But then we told him we didn't have the title," Becca added. "So, we walked out in the field and checked the plates. He said that since it hadn't been licensed since '55, he could get a title for it if we gave him a bill of sale. The woman who sold us the farm didn't seem interested in keeping anything around here, so I kinda assumed she'd abandoned the cars and they were ours."

"Did you ever move the car, or look inside it?" Dan asked.

They both shook their heads. "We've been too busy getting the house in shape," Brian said. "We haven't even been in the barn since we signed the mortgage."

"Please show me exactly where it was parked."

They walked across the scruffy tufts of brown grass, still laid flat by the snow, as the sun cracked the scudding clouds on the horizon. The windows missing from the hayloft and the open lower door made the barn look like Edvard Munch's The Scream, silhouetted against the rose tinted sunrise. The longer grass beside the barn sparkled with dew, and their pants were quickly soaked. Becca lagged behind, pulling the hem of her pants up in a futile attempt to keep her wool slacks from picking up burrs and moisture. Faint hints of red paint showed in some of the wood grain, but most of the barn siding was gray with weathering. A few boards were missing near the door at the end of the hayloft and a pair of pigeons flew out as they approached. A shabby streetcar sat on cement blocks behind the barn with the weather worn door hanging from one hinge and an aging outhouse listed to the east with collapsed roof boards showing through the doorway.

"It was sitting in that empty spot." Brian pointed to the vacant slot in a row of seven remaining cars where black earth showed in a hollow in the grass. "The grass is matted where the guy pulled the trailer in to load it."

Dan's mind spun with the possibility there might be a body in every trunk. The cars were a variety of American cars aligned in rough chronological order from oldest near the barn, to cars from the seventies furthest into the tall grass. "Have you actually looked closely at, or been in any of these other cars?"

Becca pushed up next to Dan so she could be part of the conversation. "No. But, why do you care? I mean they're all junkers." Suddenly she looked worried. "I get it! I got ticketed for not having current license tabs on my car. We're in trouble because these are way expired."

"You haven't seen the news or read the paper today?" Dan asked.

They both shook their heads. "We can't afford a television yet."

"There was a dead body in the trunk of the car you sold."

The grass rustled as Becca made a beeline out of the weeds. "I'm outta here!" she shouted over her shoulder.

Brian stared in disbelief. "A dead body?" he asked. "Really? Do you think it was here before the car was taken out?"

"It appears so. The car is at the BCA lab in St. Paul and they're going over it now to determine how long it's been there."

Dan looked at the other cars. All were rusted and sitting on flat tires. Most had broken windows and some of the car doors were tied shut with rotting twine, although it seemed unlikely that any of the hinges would open given the advanced state of rust.

Brian started to say something, and then his eyes went wide. "You don't think there're more bodies in these, do you?"

"Can we have permission to check?" Dan asked.

"Well, I'm not gonna look!" Brian replied. "Haul 'em all out of here and check 'em anyway you like. I just don't want to know if you find any more bodies."

An engine started in the yard, and the sound of spinning tires preceded the sound of gravel bouncing off the barn. Becca was accelerating down the driveway in an aging Honda on her way to work.

"We should probably check the barn to see if there is any evidence there too." Dan added.

Brian waved his arms. "You check wherever and whatever you want for dead bodies. There's that old streetcar next to the barn. It's kinda dilapidated, but you can check in there too. The previous owners told me they used to rent it out to an old hobo. He's maybe got all kinds of dead bodies in there, too."

"Who did you buy from?" Dan asked as they started back toward the house.

"Actually, it was an estate. It was listed through Lake Country Realty, but the old woman who lived here had died in a nursing home. Her daughter, Mary Jungers, was the one who signed the papers and represented all the siblings. She runs the flower shop in Pine Brook."

Dan sat in his squad car, pulled a cell phone out of his buckskin jacket and dialed the direct number for the sheriff's personal phone as Brian locked the house and drove off in a pickup. John Sepanen, the three term sheriff, answered, and after a short description of the barnyard and abandoned cars, he agreed to redirect all the day-shift deputies to search the barn and streetcar. "If there's a body in even one of those trunks," John Sepanen said, in a baritone voice made gravelly by years of bad cigars, "we'll have so many police agencies and news people here that we'll have to build another motel and restaurant."

☆ ☆ ☆

At two-thirty Pam Ryan came out of the barn pulling a dust mask off her face. "Dan, may I interrupt you?" Pam asked, as she wiped grime off her uniform pants with the surgical gloves she'd donned to protect herself from the dust and rodent droppings.

Dan removed the metal detector headset. "You look like you've been chasing spiders," he said, pointing out a cobweb in her short, blonde hair.

Pam brushed it aside and said, "I found an axe, a hatchet, several saws of various sizes and varieties. There are hay hooks hanging from the rafters and rusty pitchforks standing in the corners. There's a big steamer trunk in a corner that's filled with rusty hand tools. The hay loft has some moldy loose hay covered with pigeon droppings, and bats hanging from the rafters. I guess it looks like either a regular working barn, or a torture chamber, depending on your point of view.."

Floyd Swenson joined them, picking tiny two-pronged burrs, the size of grains of rice, from the legs of his pants. "I got through the interiors of the cars. There's nothing of interest inside or under the hoods.

Mostly, I found mold and mouse nests. Outside there's mostly these infernal stickers." He flung one into the air for emphasis. "All the trunks are locked, and there aren't any keys in the ignitions."

Sandy Maki rounded the corner of the barn with a smirk on his face. "You guys find anything interesting?" he asked as he stripped surgical gloves from his hands.

He joined the others, making complete the group who looked as mismatched as children at an orphanage: Dan, squarely into middle age, with a physique that still hinted at his years as the star fullback for the Pine City Pioneers, with a ruggedly handsome face. He'd been with the department for nearly twenty-five years, and had been appointed the chief investigator after solving a politically charged case that had secured the sheriff's re-election. Pam Ryan was the rookie, the youngest and shortest. Her blonde hair, worn short, and her fair complexion were inherited from her German mother with a bit of temper inherited from her Irish father. She was the one "outsider", with roots in the Southern Minnesota farm country. Sandy Maki was twenty-something, with a narrow face, solid build, and straight black hair from his Finnish roots. He'd grown up locally helping the family with their tree cutting business. Floyd had graying hair and a wiry build, only slightly taller than Pam, he was the training officer for every new deputy, and by virtue of that, he was also the father figure that they sought out for advice when they were reluctant to approach Dan or the sheriff.

Dan dug a hand into his pants pocket and pulled out a dozen coins. "About seventy-three cents and a thousand nails."

Sandy motioned with his thumb. "That street car is really something. They turned it into a regular apartment with a kitchen, living room, and bedroom all lined up single file. It's suffered a little from neglect, but aside from a few leaks it's in pretty good shape."

Pam had noticed Sandy's smirk when he'd arrived, and he often found mirth at her expense. "So, Sandy, what's so funny?"

"Well, it's like whoever lived there was a collector." Sandy paused to add to the suspense. "He had…"

"What makes you sure it was a he who lived there?" Dan asked.

"Well if you'll let me finish, he had about fifteen years worth of Playboy magazines."

Pam groaned.

"Hey!" Sandy protested. "There are probably some real classics."

"And I suppose you had to check every page of every one for fingerprints." Pam added with disdain.

"All right guys." Dan ended the discussion. "Were there any other items of interest in the streetcar?"

"Would you believe I found a pair of handcuffs under the bed? They're the only metal items in the place that aren't rusty, so they must be stainless steel." Sandy said.

Floyd looked at the line of cars and shook his head. "We'd better get a locksmith out here and get these trunks open."

Dan shook his head. "I've been thinking about that. The previous owners of the farm told the new owners they owned everything left behind. But, cars have titles, and if we happen to find evidence in one of them that ties back to an owner who didn't give us permission to search, the evidence might be thrown out in court."

"Search warrant?" Pam asked.

"We'd have to show probable cause," Sandy replied. "We might be able to argue that finding a body in one would lead a reasonable person to suspect there may be bodies in the others."

"They're abandoned cars!" Pam said. "Who in the world would object to the search?"

"The person who left the body or incriminating evidence in the trunk," Dan replied. "And that person's lawyer," he added. "Call out a tow truck and impound them until we can get a search warrant or permission from the owner," Dan said to Sandy.

"Geez, I'm glad I'm retiring," Floyd said.

As they walked back to their squad cars, Floyd pulled Dan aside. "I'd like to pursue the old aspects of this case."

"The old aspects?" Dan asked. "I thought all the aspects were old."

Floyd shook his head. “Not at all. There are all kinds of modern leads to follow up on; the forensic evidence with the body, the ties to this farm, and the car itself are all recent stuff. What I’d like to do is trek through all the old leads and try to turn over a stone that will tie to the modern stuff.”

“Why?” Dan asked. “Most of the people that were associated with the camp are gone or dead. You said that yourself. Even the camp is gone. What’s left to investigate?”

Floyd worked an agate loose from the gravel in the driveway with his toe. He picked it up and wiped the grit from it, exposing alternating layers of red, white, and pink stone. “Well, I think there is something I missed back when I did the original investigation. I’ve been digging through the file and my own notes. I can’t believe how little I recorded and how many comments I took at face value. I think there’s more there to be learned.”

“I think that would be a good idea,” Dan said, hiding his skepticism, but realizing Floyd’s need for closure. “I’ll talk this case around with the BCA and other agencies. You see if you can find some of the people who were originally involved in the camp and try to find a new thread to follow.”

Floyd’s eyes brightened. “Thanks.”

CHAPTER 5

Saturday

The back door of Pine Brook Floral was open a crack when Floyd arrived. "Anyone home?" Floyd called out, deeply inhaling the scent of fresh flowers.

"C"mon in!"

He walked down a narrow hallway lined with cardboard boxes, which opened into a cluttered work space arrayed with tables covered with flowers and brightly colored ribbons. At each of three tables sat a middle-aged woman cutting and arranging flowers. A fourth woman was moving quickly from one table to the next dropping off supplies and collecting finished white boxes with their attached billing statements. A light rock station was playing Billy Joel's Piano Man on a radio sitting on a stepladder.

"Hello," Floyd said, although everyone seemed too busy to notice him.

None of the women slowed a beat. "How can we help you?" The roving woman asked. She was full-figured and the flowered embroidery on her lavender sweatshirt was ringed by the works, BETHY'S

GARDEN. "You know we don't open for another hour." Floyd's uniform didn't seem to invoke the normal curiosity as the women worked methodically at flower arrangements.

"Janie," Bethy said to a slender woman who's hair was tied back in a tight bun, and who had a butane lighter sitting on top of a pack of Marlboros on the edge of her workspace, "Is that the corsage for Jake Buck?"

"I just put Jake's in the cooler," Janie replied. "I'm working on two for the Olson twins." Work went on as if Floyd was a shop fixture.

"Is Mary Jungers around?" He asked.

"Hey, Mary, there's a guy here to see you," the roving lady called to someone out of sight in an office.

Another middle-aged woman came out of an office looking haggard. "I'm Mary. Is there something I can do for you?" She said the words politely, but there was an obvious air of concern in her voice, having a uniformed deputy show up before the shop opened. Her blonde hair was a little frazzled, like she's run her fingers through it a few times. The dress code seemed to be the same for all the women - sweatshirts and jeans. Mary's sweatshirt was a little fancier, with an intricate flower arrangement embroidered across her chest. Floyd guessed she was about his age, but on second thought guessed that she was a little closer to forty, than fifty, her face aged by the strain and the early hour.

Floyd offered his hand. "I'm Floyd Swenson; we met a few years ago when I investigated your brother's diving accident. Could we talk for a second?"

Mary's hand went to her mouth, leaving Floyd standing with his hand extended awkwardly. "Something happened to one of my kids," she gasped. Activity stopped and someone turned off the radio.

Floyd shook his head and retracted his hand. "Nothing like that, I have a couple questions about your old homestead."

Mary quickly urged the other women back to work and led Floyd to a small office near the retail area in the front of the store. "Can we make this quick?" She asked. "Tonight is the Hinckley prom and we have about a thousand corsages to make before three this afternoon."

Floyd looked at the two chairs covered with components to make corsages. When Mary failed to offer to move the stock, he assumed her urgency was acute. "I assume you read about the skeleton found in the car down in the Twin Cities?" he asked as he stood near the door.

Mary nodded her head. "It was all the talk yesterday. It sounded pretty grisly. I'm glad we don't have much of that kind of crime around here."

"Actually," Floyd said, "the guy who bought the car lived in the Cities. He purchased it from a local farmer."

Mary's eyes grew wide. "Tell me it's not one of the wrecks from one of the local farms."

"It was a blue Dodge," Floyd replied. "The guy bought it from the young couple who purchased the farm from you."

Mary closed her eyes and took a deep breath. "Oh, God."

A round face, with braided pigtails, appeared around the doorframe. "Excuse me. We need the cranberry ribbon." Seeing Mary's obvious distress she asked, "Are you okay, Mary?"

"I'm fine, Bethy," Mary replied. "The ribbon is in the bag on the chair." She pointed the chair closest to the door. "Take the whole bag with you."

"I'm not much of a car person. Which one was the Dodge?" Mary asked as Patty disappeared with the bag of ribbon.

"It was the boxy blue one, about half-way down the line."

"Do you know who was in the car?" she asked.

Floyd hesitated. "We have some indication who it may have been, but no positive identification yet. It may take a while."

"So, are you thinking ancient history or recent?" Mary asked. "The house has been vacant since my mother died – maybe eight or nine months. Is it possible someone hid the skeleton there recently?"

"Probably not," Floyd replied. "But, you may be able to help us nail that down. That car was last licensed in nineteen fifty-five. Do you know if it's been sitting behind the barn since then?"

"It's been there as long as I can remember," Mary replied as she crossed her arms across her chest and shivered, "but I was born in sixty. I remember riding in some of the other cars, but not that one. You see my family was pretty poor. Dad used to buy old cars and he'd drive them until they died. It was usually more expensive to repair them than to buy another older used car, so we'd pull it home with the tractor and push it in the line behind the barn. When Dad died, the finances were even worse, so the tradition continued with mom."

Mary considered the implications of the question and her response for a few seconds. "So, do you think the skeleton has been there since '55?" she asked.

Floyd shook his head. "If the skeleton is who we think, it may have been there since '74."

Mary did the math quickly in her head. "I was like fourteen," she calculated. "That means that someone put the body there after my Dad died. He passed away in '65."

"Can you remember anything special that occurred in that timeframe?"

"Phew! That's a long time ago." Mary paused to think. "Well, other than being dirt poor, I don't remember much about those years. Things were really tough and we struggled to make ends meet. I remember that the banker used to come out and talk to Mom once in a while. Every time he showed up he was really apologetic."

"Do you remember the cars smelling really bad?" Floyd asked.

Mary shook her head. "No. I remember playing in them when I was really little. We used to take make believe trips. It wasn't as much fun when I got to be a little older. That and they were kinda creepy when I was older."

"Creepy how?" Floyd asked.

"I don't know. I guess I must've seen some horror movies and they just seemed creepy with all the mice running around in the upholstery and the cobwebs hanging from the ceilings." Mary paused as a thought struck her. "Well, there was something else too. When Dad died, the banker talked Mom in to moving that old streetcar next to the barn so she could rent it out to make the mortgage payments. Some of the hobos who rented were pretty creepy by their own rights. There used to be an old outhouse they used behind the barn and one of them surprised me when he came out of the outhouse in his underwear. I told Mom about it and she told me to stay away from the outhouse, streetcar, cars, and barn."

Floyd considered the expanding list of possible suspects to investigate. "Do you know where your mother's ledgers are?" Floyd asked. "I'd like to look at who was renting during the time period we think the skeleton was placed in the car."

Mary laughed. "You don't know my mother. She didn't write anything down. The renters would show up with a handful of cash and Mom would jam it inside her bra. It was spent on groceries before sunset."

The phone interrupted the conversation. "Pine Brook Floral."

"Uh huh. Yes." Mary sorted through the piles on her desk and retrieved a pen and order pad. "Go ahead."

She wrote out an order and added the name and phone number off the caller ID box. "We're really swamped right now, and the girls have been working since three this morning. You can plan to pick it up between two-thirty and three." Mary paused as she listened, then added, "I'm sorry, but we're only open until three, and I can't have it ready before two-thirty."

The conversation must have continued, because Mary listened intently. When she responded, she struggled to maintain her composure. "Of course you could go to Mora or Cambridge for the flowers. We try to meet our local customers needs, but we have orders for over three hundred corsages and another couple hundred boutonnieres. Most of them were ordered weeks ago. I will do all I can to accommodate you, but we are really busy with all the other orders, too."

There was another pause while Mary got another earful of the caller's thoughts. "All right then, we'll see you after two-thirty. The total will be twenty-two dollars, plus tax."

Mary made some notes on the order form after she hung up, and then turned back to Floyd. "Now, there's a motive for murder. A mother calls in before we're open to order a corsage for tonight's dance. She's ticked off that I can't have it ready when it's convenient for her to pick it up. Then, she threatens to order it from a different shop until she realizes they're too far away. To top it off, she's ticked because the price is too high!"

Floyd chuckled. "What's her name?" he asked. "In case she turns up dead, I'll come looking for you."

"Back to the skeleton," Mary said, her eyes wrinkling at the corners as she smiled. "I remember a bunch of old men living in the streetcar. They all smelled bad, and they all had wiry whiskers. Most of them only stayed a couple of months. I remember lots of first names; Don, Harold, Whiskey, and Pete all come to mind. I remember Whiskey especially well because his breath would have melted iron. I don't think he was around in the late sixties. I think he was one of the first tenants after Dad died."

"You said the banker suggested the rental idea to your mother. Do you think he might know who any of the renters were?"

"I don't know where Mom found the renters," Mary replied. "I think they found us by word of mouth - I don't think she ever advertised."

Commotion in the work area interrupted the conversation. "Bring a couple of those doughnuts in here!" Mary yelled over Floyd's shoulder.

The pigtailed woman showed up in the door with a white box and two steaming cups of coffee. "Clydie, from the bakery, just took these out of the deep fryer. You two looked like you could both use a cup of coffee too." She set the unmatched porcelain cups on the corner of Mary's desk and held out the box of maple-glazed cinnamon rolls.

"We don't get rolls like this at the courthouse." Floyd said, inhaling the warm maple scent and carefully plucking a roll from the box.

Mary smiled. "We only share these with our really good friends." She handed Floyd a tissue from her desk as the warm maple glaze started to ooze onto his fingers.

"Did your parents own all the cars behind the barn?" Floyd asked as he turned the roll to minimize the amount of frosting that would run onto his hand and smear on his face.

Mary wiped some maple frosting from her lip. "Mmm. A moment on the lips, a lifetime on the hips." Then she added, "But they're worth it. Anyway, back to your question. As far as I remember, they were all our cars. I don't remember anyone else ever bringing one to the farm to add to the line of wrecks."

"Are you the executrix of the estate?"

"Sorta," Mary replied. "Mom never had a will 'cause there really wasn't anything to her estate other than the farm. I was the oldest kid, so I made the decisions about selling the farm and disposition of the few things of value Mom had."

"Since the cars were probably last registered to your parents, I would like to get your permission to search the other cars."

Mary stopped in mid-bite and her eyes grew wide. "You think there might be more skeletons?" she asked.

"We don't know. It would be negligent not to check," Floyd replied. "We towed them all to the impound lot yesterday to make sure no one tampered with them."

The phone rang again. "Pine Brook Floral," Mary listened intently, quickly wiping frosting from her fingers before taking her pen to a post-it note pad that scooted around on a stack of papers as Mary tried to write on it. "Sure. We'll change the colors. Her dress is violet, not mist green. Got it."

"Another motive for murder," Mary muttered as she edged past Floyd into the work area. "Patsy, have you made up the Sean Cook corsage yet? His date's dress is violet, not mist green."

Mary returned to the office and fell into the chair. "I don't know how many more years I'll be able to do this."

"Is it like this before every formal dance?" Floyd asked.

"It's always absolute pandemonium. If it weren't for the girls pitching in, I couldn't do it. It's heaven and hell all wrapped into one. If not for funerals and formal dances we'd be bankrupt. On the other hand, we get a one or two day notice for funerals and the last minute calls for corsages before the dances are infuriating."

"It's kinda like being a cop," Floyd said. "Hours of boredom and seconds of terror."

"I like that," Mary said with a laugh. "At least ours isn't terror. It's only insanity." She handed Floyd another tissue as he took the last bite of the roll.

"That's all I need for now," Floyd said, wiping his fingers. "I'll stop by if I have any other questions."

"You will let me know if you find another skeleton, won't you?" Mary asked.

"Oh, yeah," Floyd replied. "You can count on seeing me again."

"Umm, Floyd," Mary said hesitantly, "I was kidding about those motives for murder."

Floyd's lips curled slightly. "I guess we'll see about that this afternoon when the people come to pick up the flowers."

✲ ✲ ✲

He was drinking coffee and reading the Saturday morning Minneapolis Star Tribune when a headline near the obituaries caught his attention. He folded the page and leaned back in the chair. The headline said, Skeleton Found In Car. The article explained that skeletal remains had been discovered in the trunk of an antique car purchased from rural Pine County. The victim hadn't been identified, and the Bureau of Criminal Apprehension was investigating assuming that foul play was involved. He read the article a second time and smiled.

"There can't be two bodies stashed in old car trunks," he said to himself. "It took them thirty years to find her. What a bunch of buffoons!"

He retrieved a scissors from a kitchen drawer and carefully cut the article from the paper. After pouring another cup of coffee he made his way to his private space. He took a plastic covered album from a drawer and opened the first page. He reread the headlines about the missing camper as he'd done a hundred times before, then he arranged the new clipping on the facing album page and attached it with strips of Scotch tape.

The chase had been off for decades, and now it was on again. There was no risk of capture - he was smart and the cops were stupid. He could feel the tingle of anticipation, the mild rush of adrenaline. Yes, it felt good and he had missed it. He went to his trophies and touched the one in the middle. The dark hair was dusty and the luster diminished. He closed his eyes and he could see that pretty face and the blue eyes. A smile came to his lips and his breath quickened.

There had been too many years of doctors and mind numbing drugs. What he needed was the adrenaline rush, not the drugs that evened everything out. He needed highs and lows, especially the highs. He missed the highs.

CHAPTER 6

Floyd sorted his list of people from his old notes into locals and others. He set aside the list of others, including the campers, reasoning that most were going to be hard to locate after thirty years, and focused on the locals. After a search of the phone book and a few dead ends with wrong numbers and families of camp employees who'd passed away, he came up with a number for Grace Palm, the cook at Melody Pines Camp.

Floyd remembered her as matronly at the time of the original investigation. She hadn't been in direct contact with the campers, but he remembered her as the hub of camp information and gossip. He guessed that she would be in her seventies or eighties now. The phone rang twice before a young, female voice answered.

"Hello, this is Floyd Swenson, from the Pine County sheriff's department. I'm trying to get in contact with Grace Palm."

"Well, aunt Grace doesn't live here anymore. Can I help?"

"I'm following up on an old investigation. Could you tell me where I might reach her?"

"Actually, she moved to the Riverview Nursing Home, in Mora. My husband and I are sorting through her belongings and consolidating. The house is for sale and we're arranging her stuff for an estate sale. Is there anything I can help with?"

"No, but thank you. I'll contact Grace at the nursing home."

Floyd contemplated the wisdom of interviewing a nursing home resident in a murder case, but had little else to go on. He stopped in front of Dan's open office and said, "I found the camp cook in Mora's Riverview Nursing Home. I thought I'd drive over and see what she remembers."

"We're going to open the trunks of all the old cars in a couple hours," Dan said. "Don't you want to be around to see what we find?"

"This trip isn't going to take a couple hours," Floyd said as he picked his jacket off the coat tree. "If she's got a little dementia or Alzheimer's I'm guessing that we'll have a very short interview."

The drive was quiet, even for a Saturday morning. The sprouts of new tree growth wouldn't start to show for weeks, and the fields were still too wet to plow leaving a landscape of varying shades of brown. Two farmers standing next to a pickup parked on the edge of a field waved as Floyd passed. A small pond held a half dozen Mallard ducks resplendent in their bright spring plumage. The spring rebirth of animal activity was in motion and there were assorted deer and skunk carcasses, called road pizza by the locals, dotting the shoulders of the road during the hour drive.

The interview notes from the old investigation were disturbing. He'd read the sketchy tidbits that he'd captured at the time and tried to picture the people and how they had acted. His memory was so hazy, and the notes so incomplete it was impossible to reconstruct what had been asked, or what the specific people had said. If he handed these files to a prosecutor today they would throw a proposed case out in a second. Life had been so much easier back then.

The nursing home was a one-story red brick building located on the edge of the Knife River, the lake behind a reservoir was called Lake Ann. During the summer the gardens along the shore were resplendent with flowers and benches were situated along the walking paths providing lovely views of the lake and of evening sunsets. Today, the lake was gray, and ominous, with rows of waves blown into white caps rolling down the length of the lake from the north.

The Riverview Care Center sign was on a brick monument and the entrance to a small parking lot. Floyd bypassed the signs reserving parking spots for residents and found a parking space at the end of the lot. He passed one of the sprawling arms of the building that spread like one-story brick tentacles from a hub that housed the visitor's entrance.

Floyd inquired about Grace Palm at the front desk which was located in an airy atrium and attended by a gray-haired, slender woman with a volunteer's nametag that said, Astrid. He was directed to a first floor room that Grace Palm shared, by an aging male volunteer dressed in a white shirt with a knitted brown tie. "She only moved here a couple days ago," the volunteer, whose nametag said BOB, offered. "But she's getting along with the folks pretty well. She won twenty cents at Bingo last night."

Floyd walked down the hallways that smelled gently of antiseptic and women's cologne, passing people in wheel chairs and walkers. He knocked gently on the door marked with Grace Palm's name and peeked in on the woman lying on the nearest bed. The room was light and airy, but with a hint of mustiness in the air. "Excuse me. Are you Grace Palm?"

The woman appeared to be at least eighty, and the skin drooped from her face, like she'd lost weight. Her gray hair was permed in tight gray curls and she wore a rumpled flowered dress. "Yes, I'm Grace," the woman said without sitting up. "Do I know you?"

Floyd fidgeted with his cap. "Well, yes," he replied. "We met a number of years ago. I'm Floyd Swenson."

Grace frowned. "I don't recall your name. But, please come in. I like company."

Floyd stepped in and pulled a straight-backed oak chair from the corner. "I have a few questions I'd like to ask you." He moved the chair so Grace could see him without turning her head.

"You have a uniform on. Are you a cop?"

"I'm a deputy sheriff investigating a crime," Floyd replied. "I have to ask you about something that happened a long time ago. Do you remember the summer you cooked at the Melody Pines Camp?"

There was no sign of recognition in the woman's face. "I think I cooked at a camp a long time ago. What did you say the name was?"

"Melody Pines. Does it sound familiar?" Floyd's hope for a meaningful interview was quickly fading.

"They had a lovely oven. I could make a dozen loaves of bread at a time."

"That must have been a lot of work," Floyd said. "Did you have any helpers."

"Two little girls were the kitchen helpers, but they were puny. I had to do most of the work myself."

Grace's current state was a contrast to what Floyd remembered of Grace Palm thirty years before. She had been a robust, big-boned woman who appeared to have been accustomed to heavy work. "Do you remember the names of your helpers?" Floyd asked, noting a picture on a nightstand of a middle aged couple standing next to Grace. The couple was smiling, and Grace looked sad.

"They were Janice Lund and Shirley Johnson. I think they came from some little town near Princeton."

Floyd pulled out his list. The names sounded correct, but he wanted to verify the information. "My notes say they were from Dalbo."

Grace smiled and said, "Yes. I remember them talking about the Day Fish Company. That's where they make all the lutefisk, you know. Day is the next town north of Dalbo just off highway forty-seven."

"How long have you lived here, Mrs. Palm?"

Grace looked around the room. There was an antique dresser in the corner and a cedar chest at the foot of her bed. On the other side of the room were an empty bed and a newer dresser. Grace's roommate apparently had a television.

"Oh, I don't live here," she replied. "I'm just visiting my friend. She lives here."

"I must have misunderstood your niece. I thought she said you had moved here."

"My niece?" she asked. "I don't think I have a niece."

Floyd tried another tack. "What did you have for breakfast today?"

Grace's look was vacuous. "I don't think I had breakfast today. Most days I make myself oatmeal. I suppose that's what I had."

"Who else worked at Melody Pines?"

Grace smiled. "That was a fun place, with all the children running around." Without hesitation she rattled off the names of most of the staff members from thirty years ago.

"Do you remember something bad that happened that summer?" Floyd asked.

Sadness swept the woman. "It was so sad. That girl disappeared. They thought she had drowned, but she didn't, you know."

"She didn't drown?" Floyd asked.

"Oh no!" Grace replied. "Those poor firemen spent all that time dragging the lake. And her parents! They were so sad. It's too bad they didn't know she didn't drown."

Floyd crossed his legs and leaned close. "What happened to her?"

"Why she ran off with that man." Grace the statement with such certainty that Floyd believed she knew what had happened to Helen Smith.

"I talked to you right after the disappearance. Why didn't you mention it then and save the firemen all that time?"

Grace leaned closer to Floyd and studied his face. "I didn't talk to you. There was a young cop who came around with some stupid questions about skinny dipping."

"That was me, a long time ago." Not seeing any recognition, Floyd decided to move the questioning along.

"The girl's name was Helen Smith," Floyd explained. "Did you see her leave camp with someone?"

Grace contemplated the question. "No. Someone told me they saw her leave."

"Who told you?"

"It was a secret," she whispered.

"Who did she run away with?"

"That was the secret."

"Was it someone at the camp?"

"Yes," she said with a conspirator's grin.

"You didn't seem to know that when we talked right after she disappeared."

Grace thought for a moment before answering. "I didn't know then."

The conversation was maddening, and Floyd was becoming unsure of Grace's credibility. She seemed to have little short-term memory, and he had to question her long-term cognitive skills as well. "Did you ever tell your husband?"

That question seemed to trouble Grace. "I don't think I can talk to you anymore. He'll be home from work pretty soon and I don't think he'd like me entertaining a man in the bedroom like this." Grace rolled on the bed so she was facing away from Floyd.

"May I come back and talk to you again?" he asked.

"Sure you can, Honey," she replied. "But next time we'll have to talk in the living room. We wouldn't want people to start rumors."

"Before I go, I need to know who the Smith girl ran away with."

"I told you," Grace said, looking irritated, "it's a secret." She folded her hands and closed her eyes without looking back at him.

Floyd borrowed an Isanti/Kanabec County phone book from Bob, at the reception desk, and looked up Lunds and Johnsons in the town of Dalbo. There were three Lunds and two Johnsons in the town of seventy-nine people. It took five phone calls, but he got married names and phone numbers for both Janice Lund and Shirley Johnson. He took the numbers and drove back to Pine City.

✲ ✲ ✲

Floyd met Pam Ryan and Sandy Maki at the impound lot on the northeast outskirts of Pine City. A ten-foot fence with razor wire circled the rows of seized and abandoned vehicles parked on the gravel. The five city snowplows stood near the gate, ready to attach to the sanding trucks if another ice or snowstorm hit. The odds were long that they'd be required, but July is the only month that Pine County had not recorded a measurable snowfall.

Floyd parked near the galvanized steel office building and walked down the muddy driveway that threaded through the rows of vehicles after waving to the caretaker, a paraplegic veteran who wielded his authority as the keeper of the keys with relish. A red Ford Probe, with a caved hood and the windshield smashed from the inside, stood in eerie testament to a deadly one-car accident the previous night.

The seven cars from the Benson farm were lined up in the back corner of the lot with their trunks toward the chain link fence. Sandy Maki was taking pictures of the cars where they sat, while Pam was recording the VIN numbers from doors and door frames that had been wrested open with a large crowbar that was lying across the hood of the last car.

"I got permission from the Benson family to open the trunks," Floyd announced as he approached the row of cars. "They're the owners of record."

Pam sat on her haunches beside the driver's door of the DeSoto, while trying to rub the accumulated crud from the VIN tag on the doorpost. "These cars must have been sitting there for decades." In frustration she spit onto the rag and rubbed harder, trying to discern some corroded VIN numbers.

Sandy Maki walked back from the end of the row, changing a roll of film as he walked. "We've got the locksmith coming in half an hour?" he told Floyd. "He had a lockout at the Hinckley casino and they pay faster and in cash."

Pam recorded the last VIN and joined Floyd and Sandy. "Why don't we just pop the trunks open with a crowbar?" she asked. "It's not like these junkers are worth anything."

Sandy and Floyd exchanged a look. Sandy answered, "Well, they may not look like much, but antique cars are skyrocketing in price. I'd hate to be the one who decided to punch the locks unless the owner told me it was okay."

Pam considered the lineup of rusting hulks. “These are valuable?”

“Beauty is in the eye of the beholder,” Floyd replied. “Some guy from The Cities paid several hundred dollars for the car with the skeleton in the trunk.”

“Too bad they didn’t leave the keys in the ignitions,” Pam said.

Floyd reached for the cell phone on his belt and dialed 411. “Connect me with the Pine Brook Floral shop, in the town of Pine Brook.”

Within a few seconds the phone was ringing. “Pine Brook Floral, this is Mary. How can I help you?”

“Mary, this is Floyd Swenson. I have another question for you. Where are the keys for all the old cars?”

“Umm, I don’t know. Aren’t they in the cars?”

“Not a one,” Floyd replied. “Do you remember them when you were a kid?”

“I’m not sure,” she said after a brief hesitation. “I thought I remembered them in the ignition.”

“Think hard. Are you sure they were in the ignition?”

“I’m not sure. If you can hang on a minute, I’ll call one of my brothers. They’re into car details like that. I’m sure one of them will know.”

Floyd gave her the cell phone number and waited. About three minutes later the phone buzzed.

“Floyd Swenson.”

“Hi, Floyd, My little brother, Robbie, says he thought the keys were in the cars. It’s not like we were trying to keep people from stealing them. They were already broken." Then Mary asked, "Is that good or bad news?"

"I don't know," Floyd replied. "It may mean that someone didn't want anyone else to get into the trunks because they hid something there."

"More dead bodies?" Mary asked, with a hint of anxiety in her voice.

"That's a possibility."

Mary sighed. "Keep me posted." Then she added, "I have another murder motive for you. A bride's mother just called and wanted to pick out flowers for her daughter's June wedding. We have enough books of arrangements to keep her busy reading for two hours, but we close in fifteen minutes. She was ticked off when I suggested we schedule a time during the week."

Floyd chuckled. "You better give me that name, too, just in case she shows up dead."

"I love gallows humor," Mary replied. "It fits so well with my mood at the moment. We are open for another fifteen minutes and we still have twenty corsages that haven't been picked up yet. Hey! There's another motive."

"Say, Mary. We're waiting for a locksmith to unlock all these trunks. Do you mind if we punch out the locks and open them with a crowbar? We've been hesitating because the cars may have some collector value."

"Oh, hell. Don't waste your time or the taxpayer's money. Pry 'em open and get it over with. The engines are all shot and most of them are so rusty you can't recognize what they are anyway. When you're done, have them all towed to the junkyard."

"Thanks!" As Floyd folded the phone he said, "Sandy, grab that crowbar, a screwdriver, and a hammer. Pam, have the dispatcher cancel the locksmith."

Sandy retrieved the tools from the office and set them on the hood of the first hulk. The first car was a Buick according to the chrome on the trunk, with three chrome ovals on the side of each front fender. The license plates were for nineteen sixty-two. Sandy put the tip of a large screwdriver into the lock and struck it with a hammer, easily punching the lock free of its rusty hole. With the lock punched out of the trunk lid, Sandy jammed the crowbar under the trunk lip and lifted until the latch yielded. Floyd caught himself holding his breath and inhaled deeply as Sandy lifted the lid against the rusted hinges. Pam stood at the corner of the car with the digital camera ready. Light flooded the trunk and exposed a rusted jack and a flat tire. Mice had ripped upholstery from somewhere and made a huge nest in the dark recesses behind the seat. Aside from that, it was empty. Pam took pictures from several angles while Sandy spread the contents of the mouse nest with the crowbar.

"Do you think we need to bag the mouse nest materials?" Sandy asked. "They probably have a little bit of hair and fiber from every recess of the vehicle."

"Sure," Floyd replied. "Bag it, although I doubt that we'll look at it again unless we start finding more bodies."

Pam took out a plastic bag and gingerly deposited the mouse nest into it with her latex gloved fingers. She noted the date, the car license, and the time before sealing it with tape, signing the tape with a *Sharpie* marker, and setting it into a Rubbermaid container they'd brought to hold the evidence bags.

The second car was a DeSoto with big fins in the back and red paint that had oxidized to a hideous pink. It had been licensed most recently, in nineteen seventy-one. Sandy had to work harder to punch the lock free from the less corroded trunk metal. With the latch broken the trunk sprung open, much to everyone's surprise. The cavernous trunk was empty except for a wool navy blanket. The white blanket was spotted with rust and moths had apparently eaten holes in every square inch of the fabric. Sandy reached inside the trunk gingerly and lifted the blanket with the crowbar only to uncover the rusting floor of the trunk.

"Are those rust stains, or blood stains?" Pam asked as she held a new bag open so Sandy could roughly fold the blanket and stuff it into the bag.

"They look like rust to me," Sandy said, trying to keep the dust and rust off his jacket as he maneuvered the blanket's tail into the bag. "But, I wouldn't bet my job, or a court case, on that judgment."

Floyd's cell phone buzzed as they walked to an old Chevrolet with fenders that sloped in every direction. "Floyd Swenson."

"It's Mary, from the flower shop. I just spoke with my other brother, Joe. He said Mom took the keys out of the ignitions after Robbie locked him inside one of the cars. They had to break the windows to free him. He didn't know where she put the keys."

"Can you guess when that happened?" Floyd asked.

"Phew. I didn't ask specifically, and I don't know if the guys would know either. They're both younger than I am, so it may not have been a concern for Mom until after the late sixties or early seventies, when the boys weren't more than ten years old."

"Thanks." Floyd glanced at his watch. "It's after three. Are all the corsages gone?"

Mary snorted. "No, I have two left. Luckily, the back room is such a mess that it'll take me another half-hour to finish cleaning. You don't have to worry about any other murders as long as the last customers aren't any later than that."

Dan Williams rolled into the parking lot in his brown unmarked car and parked near gate. "Any more skeletons?" He asked as he approached the Chev.

Nothing but mouse nests and a moth-eaten blanket, so far," Floyd replied.

Floyd nodded for Sandy to go ahead with the Chev. The plates said it had last been used in fifty-eight. The lock released easily and Sandy lifted the lid to reveal the ground under the car.

"The whole trunk floor is gone!" Pam said. "I wonder if we should go back over the road where the wrecker towed these things to see if anything fell out with the trunk bottom?"

Dan shrugged. "It's probably too late. If a bunch of bones had fallen out, I'm sure someone would have called and the sheriff would be chewing my butt."

Sandy moved to a Studebaker. "Weird car," he said as he inserted the jack under the trunk lid, "it looks pretty much the same from the front or back." The license plates said it hadn't been driven since fifty-seven. Sandy gave a quick jerk and the trunk popped open two inches. Skittering sounds came from somewhere inside the trunk and Sandy stood back.

"Geez, that scared me!" Pam yelped as a chipmunk raced past her feet.

Sandy tried to laugh it off, but he was uneasy inserting his hand under the lid to lift it open. The hinges creaked as it came open, but the interior was barren except for a chipmunk-sized nest of upholstery materials. Sandy poked at the nest with the crow bar, but nothing more emerged.

"Looks like the night Geraldo opened Al Capone's vault on television," Floyd said as Sandy gathered the nesting materials and put them into another bag.

"I must be too young to remember that," Pam said innocently. "Did they find chipmunks?"

"Mostly they found lots of dirt and a few empty bottles," Floyd said. "It was the non-event of the decade."

An old Ford, with chrome-plated hinges on top of the trunk, was next in line. The license plates showed that it hadn't been licensed since fifty-one. The lid released with very little effort and the interior was a watery, rusty mess. "Looks like a seal let loose somewhere and let the water run in here," Sandy said. "In another year or two this one would have been rusted through, too."

"Two to go!" Pam said. "It looks like we may not have any more bodies."

"We can only hope," Dan added.

The sixth car was a boxy Plymouth, last licensed in sixty-one. Sandy punched the lock several times before it let loose. Once the lock was gone he lifted on the crowbar, but the trunk refused to yield. He tried another purchase, a little deeper and gave a jerk, without apparent results.

Pam put her hand on Floyd's arm as Sandy strained against the crowbar. "Do you smell that?"

Sandy was sniffing too. He stepped back from the bumper. "What is it?"

"It's not carrion," Floyd said. "It smells more chemical."

Sandy tried another purchase with the bar and the lock yielded with a sharp, "crack." He carefully lifted the lid and stepped back as a wave of stink escaped from the enclosed trunk space.

Pam and Floyd stepped back too. The trunk was littered with metal and cardboard containers. Floyd took a handkerchief from his pocket and covered his face. After taking a deep breath he stepped up and made a quick survey of the contents. He blew out his breath as he stepped back.

Sandy peeked over the fender at the array of soggy boxes and rusting cans. "They appear to be cleaning chemicals and pesticides," He said. "I suppose Mrs. Benson must have stored them here to keep them away from the kids. We'll have to call the fire department Hazardous Materials Squad to clean this up."

They moved to the last car. It was an older Ford that had last been licensed in fifty-two. It had been parked next to the Dodge that had hidden the body. Sandy pushed aside a clump of brown weeks and punched the lock. He slid the crowbar under the lid and pulled. It released gently, but the trunk stuck after opening a few inches.

"I'm a little reluctant to stick my fingers under there," Sandy said, "if you know what I mean."

Floyd scanned the area and walked to where a car frame was sitting atop concrete blocks. He reached into the weeds and came back with a board in each hand. "Here are a couple short two-by-fours." He handed one to Floyd who inserted it under the lid. Sandy lifted with the wide end of the crowbar, while Pam stood by with the camera.

Together, the three of them lifted on the trunk lid until it felt like the rear wheels would come off the ground. With an abrupt *Bang!* the lid released and flew open so they almost fell into it. They all recoiled from the sudden release of resistance, and stared into the cavernous maw. Four pairs of beady eyes stared back from the deepest recess behind the seat. Sandy dropped the crowbar and drew his pistol.

"Just back away," Floyd cautioned. "A mother raccoon can be really nasty when she's cornered."

Sandy drew a bead on the largest animal as they backed away from the rear of the Ford. "Let's just ease away between these other cars and let her escape with her babies," he said, keeping the gun pointed at the trunk until they were standing in front of Dan's car.

Sandy holstered his gun. "That was way more exciting than Geraldo."

"And a lot less exciting than finding another dead body," Pam added.

Floyd's cell phone buzzed again. "Floyd Swenson."

"So, were there more bodies?" He recognized Mary Jungers' voice.

"We only found contaniers of old lawn chemicals, a chipmunk and a family of raccoons."

"Thank God!" she said. "At least I will only have nightmares about one skeleton in the trunk."

"Are you out of corsages now?" Floyd asked.

Mary laughed. "Actually, I'm delivering the last one on the way home. And believe me, they won't be happy about the delivery charges!"

"But it's not another murder plot?"

"Oh, no," Mary said, "Not when they pay an extra twenty bucks to drive two miles out of my way."

"Thanks, Mary. I'm sure we'll be back with more questions."

Pam gave Floyd an inquisitive look. "What's all this about murder motives?"

"Mary Jungers owns the Pine Brook flower shop," Floyd explained as he put the cell phone away. "Tonight is the Prom and she was giving me a list of murder motives related to late flower orders."

"Hey, Pam, is that creepy morgue technician still sending you flowers?" Sandy asked.

"He's not creepy," she said. "He's just from a different world. And, yes, he's still sending me flowers. Speaking of different worlds, are you still shacked up with the tattooed hooker?"

Dan motioned for them to follow him out of the impound lot.

"She's not a hooker anymore," Sandy replied, defensively. "She's working as a professional photographer. You should see some of her nature shots."

Pam snorted. "I've heard about her nature shots. Doesn't one of them include a tattoo that says, 'Property of Butch'?"

Floyd and Dan looked back at the two bantering deputies. "Sandy, are you blushing?" Dan asked.

"My home life is fine," Sandy said.

CHAPTER 7

Dan's cell phone buzzed as he got in the car. "Dan Williams." The John Sepanen's name flashed on the caller ID and Dan thought it odd that the sheriff would call on a Saturday.

"Dan," the sheriff's bass voice boomed over the phone. "I had a call from Washington County. They located Helen Smith's father and sent a deputy to tell him they may have recovered his daughter's body. He gave them the name of the family dentist and the BCA is trying to get in touch with him to secure dental x-rays."

"That was quick," Dan said, "considering the number of Smiths there are around the country."

"They asked if we would interview the father. The deputy who spoke with him said his reaction was…inappropriate considering the gravity of the news."

"Inappropriate how?" Dan asked.

"Well, I guess he seemed happy," the sheriff explained. "I'll leave the name and address with the dispatcher. Drive down and interview the guy. He lives in Stillwater, near the Washington County Courthouse."

"Sure."

Dan took a loop around town to gather his thoughts before returning to the courthouse. As he cruised through the deserted county fairgrounds he pondered the emotions that would make a father happy to hear that his long missing daughter's remains had been found.

"I'd probably be relieved," he said. "Or, maybe I'd be struck with grief again. But, I doubt that I'd be happy. I guess it takes all kinds to make a world, but I think this might be an interesting interview."

✲ ✲ ✲

When Dan got to his office there was a message on his desk with the name and address of Helen Smith's father.

"Floyd," Dan said as he poured coffee from a pot in a corner of the room, "I've got a few minutes if you want to talk."

Floyd set the report aside and followed Dan back to his office, which seemed tiny because of the piles of paperwork that filled every flat surface. Not one square inch of the desktop or file cabinet were visible, a strong statement about Dan's disdain for the office part of his job as the county's chief investigator. Dan lifted a pile of purchase orders from his guest chair and motioned for Floyd to sit as he relocated them to the windowsill.

"I made a list of all the people I interviewed right after the disappearance," Floyd said. "I can't find a lot of them and haven't even tried to find the campers. However, I did find the camp cook. Her name is Grace Palm."

Dan smirked as he settled into his desk chair. "Did you get any good recipes?"

Floyd ignored the comment and said, "She's in a nursing home, in Mora. I drove over and talked to her this morning. She's a little confused about recent events, but remembered a lot of the things that happened the summer she worked at Melody Pines."

Dan looked skeptical. "Does she remember the girl disappearing?"

"Very lucidly. She even felt badly that the firemen had spent all that time dragging the lake for the body when the girl had, 'run off like that'."

"She said that the girl had run off?" Dan asked. "Did she know where the girl went?"

"She told me it was a secret and she couldn't tell me who'd told her."

Dan swirled the coffee in his cup while shaking his head. "Does she have dementia?"

"Well, I think she has obvious short-term memory problems," Floyd said. "But, I think her memory of older events is pretty clear. For instance, she gave me the names of her two helpers in the kitchen that summer. They were Janice Lund and Shirley Johnson. She said they were both from Dalbo, over by Princeton.

I tracked them down, through relatives, and spoke with both of them on the phone. They both remember Grace, and they both remember the disappearance, although neither of them knew anything about the girl running away."

"Did they have anything else of interest?" Dan asked.

Floyd chuckled. "Well, it seems that Melody Pines was a church camp, run by some non-profit outfit in the Twin Cities. They had a chaplain and religious services every day."

"That's lovely, but what does it have to do with the investigation?" Dan asked impatiently.

"I'm getting to that. I couldn't remember how we got to the point of dragging the lake. It seems the staff used to sneak off Saturday evenings to skinny-dip. No one would admit it back then, but they laughed about it now."

"So, they thought that maybe the Smith girl had been skinny-dipping, and somehow they'd lost track of her."

"Well," Floyd said, "neither of the cook's helpers remembered anyone skinny-dipping that night. However, when I interviewed the staff right after the disappearance, someone let it slip that they'd seen Helen skinny-dipping with the staff that night. When I spoke with Janice and Shirley, they thought it was odd that we asked about that because the one hard and fast rule was that only the staff were invited, and only on Saturday nights between groups of campers who arrived Sunday afternoons and departed on Saturday mornings."

"You're thinking someone threw that in as a red herring?" Dan asked.

"I've been pouring through my notes trying to figure out who told me that story. It sure seems odd that the whole staff were sure about no one skinny-dipping that night except one person. I'm afraid my notes are too sketchy to give me the answer. It wasn't either of those two because I didn't interview them at the time."

"Have they stayed in touch with any of the other staff members or campers?" Dan asked. "Maybe they have a periodic reunion or something?"

Floyd shook his head. "This Janice and Shirley were friends before they worked at camp, and they've stayed in touch with each other. They've never seen any of the others since that summer."

"Did they have any speculation on what happened to the Smith girl?"

"Actually, Shirley had an interesting comment." Floyd pulled out a note pad and read it back. "It was odd that she remembered the Smith girl at all, since hundreds of campers came through during that summer, but something about her stuck out. She thought Helen Smith was a little flirt. In her opinion, a couple of the male staff members were giving and receiving undue attention. I think that there may have been a little jealousy involved because this little camper was getting more attention than the staff girls."

"Do we have any records of the employees and campers at the time of the disappearance?"

"I've been digging through the reports and we have some of it. We have full names of most of the staff members, but I don't have addresses or even hometowns. I have almost nothing on any of the campers."

Dan's eyes lit up. "Were any of the men named Benson? Maybe one of them was related to the Benson's who owned the farm where the body was stuffed in the car."

"There were a couple of Bensons," Floyd said, "Of course, considering this is Minnesota, there were also a couple of Johnsons, Petersons, and even a Sorenson. We didn't know about the link to the Benson farm at the time, so I don't have any information about that at all. I tried to find the camp records, but the camp was sold to a developer in the late seventies and no one seems to know if any of the records still exist.

"After spending the afternoon opening the cars from the Benson farm, with nothing much there except mouse nests, a chipmunk, a raccoon family, and a rusty wool blanket," Floyd said, "I feel a little deflated. We bagged all the contents, but I really don't think it's worth the time or money to do any analysis."

"The sheriff had a call from Washington County today," Dan said. "They located Helen Smith's father. They're trying to track down dental records so the BCA can have a forensic dentist do a positive identification."

"Who's going to do the post mortem on the skeleton?" Floyd asked.

"A forensic anthropologist from the University of Minnesota is going to examine the bones. Laurie Lone Eagle called and said anyone who was interested could come down Monday and watch his exam. They recovered a bunch of insect parts from the bottom of the trunk and they're going with the skeleton to have an entomologist examine them at the same time."

"An entomologist?" Floyd asked.

"A bug expert," Dan explained. "A forensic entomologist can look at the debris left by the bugs around the body as it decomposed and tell you things like what season of the year the body was decomposing, what region of the state or country the murder took place, what plants may have been nearby, and sometimes even what year."

"That's not going to happen until Monday?"

"Are you in a rush after all these years?"

"Did you forget? I'm retiring in a few weeks. Time is slipping away."

✲ ✲ ✲

Sally Williams heard Penny barking happy yips in the yard before the sound of tires crunching on the gravel driveway reached the kitchen. She met Dan at the door with a can of Michelob as Penny skittered in ahead of him.

"How goes the murder investigation?" She asked.

"We found the missing girl's father and he supplied the name of the family dentist," Dan said as he hung his buckskin jacket on a hook behind the door. "With any luck, we should have a positive identification tomorrow."

The house was small by country farmhouse standards. The kitchen barely large enough for the round table and four chairs that used to seat Dan, Sally, and their two daughters, Teresa and Emily. The girls were now off with their own families, their empty chairs pushed against the wainscoting and wedged behind the table. The evening news headlines were background noise on a television in the living room.

"But, you're already certain of the identity so this is just a formality?" Sally asked.

"Pretty much so," Dan said, "but there are always surprises that pop up."

"How's Floyd doing?" Sally said as she pulled sandwich makings from the refrigerator. "You said he was pretty rattled by the discovery of the skeleton."

"He's still depressed and is talking about retiring this summer. He's reading through his old reports over and over. Today he went to Mora and talked to a senile old woman who used to be the cook at the camp. Floyd was pretty sure that she had lucid memories about the summer of the disappearance, but I sure hope we don't have to pin our hopes for solving this on her. The county attorney would laugh us out of his office if we tell him our number one witness has dementia and doesn't remember where she lives or that her husband is dead, but she can still remember pertinent details of a crime thirty years ago."

"How bad is Floyd's depression?"

"I guess I'd hate to see him retire today," Dan said as he slipped off his shoes. "I think that he shouldn't be spending a lot of time alone right now. I hope we can bring the investigation to some sort of closure or I'm afraid that he's going to have some serious problems. We need him to go through the old information thoroughly, but I think he's consumed with it like a widow who can't do anything but look through old photo albums of dead relatives.

"The only high point today was that I heard Floyd laugh when he was talking to the woman from Pine Brook Floral. I think that's the first time I've seen him crack a smile since Ginny died."

"Do you think that you'll be able to recover enough evidence from the skeleton to lead you to a suspect?" Sally put the sandwich on a small plate and set in on the kitchen table. "I mean, there can't be much there after all these years."

Dan shrugged as he sat down and took a bite. "It's hard to tell what trace evidence might show up. In some respects, we may have a better shot at forensic evidence now than back then. The DNA technology and ability to identify trace fiber evidence has advanced so far that we might be directed to a specific suspect."

Sally sat in the chair across from Dan and leaned on the table. "If you don't solve the crime, what happens to Floyd?"

"He's been the department counselor and confessor for decades. When anyone needs a shoulder to cry on, or an ear to chew about the unfairness of life, Floyd's been the man. What do you do when the doctor needs a doctor?"

"I guess you'd better solve the crime."

"As if I didn't have enough pressure already," Dan said with a smile.

CHAPTER 8

Sunday

After attending the Lutheran nine o'clock service and ducking the pastor's offer of lunch, Floyd Swenson stopped for a caramel roll and cup of coffee in Hinckley, before driving the back roads across Pine County on his way back to the Mora nursing home. The cold clear skies of the previous day turned to drizzle as warm air swept across the middle of the country from the Gulf of Mexico. There was a small accident on a highway 23 bridge over the Rum River where the cold air had turned the wet surface to ice. He stopped to make sure no one was injured, and then called for the highway department to dispatch a sanding truck.

In Mora, he stopped at the nursing home, where friends and relatives were moving a dozen elderly people around the parking lot. It appeared that Sunday was the day to take grandma or uncle out for lunch and a drive. He waited briefly at the information desk while a young woman had a discussion with the receptionist about their dates the previous evening. When the finally realized there was a deputy standing at the desk, they quickly broke the discussion.

"Who would be the best contact for information about Grace Palm's medical condition?" He asked the young receptionist with red hair, freckles, and piercing blue eyes. Her nametag said she was Penelope.

"Um, I guess that would be the nursing supervisor, Deb. Would you like me to page her?"

After a few minutes an attractive middle-aged woman in a white uniform came down the hallway. A laminated card dangled from a lanyard around her neck and said she was Deb M. The picture looked like it was computer generated and somehow had managed to spread her face so it looked like she was much heavier and her face rounder.

"I'm Floyd Swenson, from the Pine County Sheriff's Department," he said as they met at the information desk.

"I'm Deb McIntosh, the nursing supervisor. How can I help you?"

Floyd guided her to a pair of empty chairs in the entryway. "Well, I have a problem, and I was hoping you could shed some light on it," He explained as a fifty-something man wheeled a gray-headed version of himself to the front door in a wheelchair. The son was burly and hearty, the father pasty and gray, but they shared the same facial features.

They sat down near an aviary where a pair of doves cooed. "I'm sure you know Grace Palm, who is a patient here. I interviewed her back in the nineteen-seventies about a girl who disappeared from a camp where Grace was working. At the time, we thought the girl had drowned in the lake. We recently found the girl's body and we are certain that foul play is involved. Grace seems to know more about the girl's disappearance or at least some information about the people who were around the camp at the time of the disappearance. The problem is that I don't know whether I can trust her memory."

Deb McIntosh listened politely through Floyd's explanation. "I see your problem," she said, "and I'm not sure I can do a lot to ally your fears. Grace is one of our moderately lucid residents. I find her interesting and polite, but I don't think I would rely on her memory to make a life or death decision."

"When I spoke with her yesterday," Floyd said, "she seemed confused about the present. But, I checked on a few things she told me about the past and she seemed to have the details correct."

The nurse smiled. "It's amazing isn't it? We see that happen so often. Patients have detailed childhood memories, but can't remember who their roommate is. There's a chemical component to long-term memory, and many of those memories remain etched in our minds. On the other hand, short-term memory is more electrical and as we age the connections get fouled up and we sometimes lose those memories quickly."

"So, Grace may have credible memory of old events, even though she's confused about today?" Floyd asked.

"Credible may be too strong an adjective for Grace's long-term memory," McIntosh replied. "Her memories might be founded in fact, but they may be clouded or enhanced to make them more…pleasurable."

"Or more palatable to her?" Floyd asked.

"I believe we all filter our memories to keep the good and set aside the bad," Deb replied. "It helps us stay upbeat and looking forward. People who dwell on the bad get terribly depressed and have a lot of problems moving ahead with their lives."

"So, Grace may remember the essence of things, but I should temper what she tells me with the knowledge that it might be tainted?"

"I wouldn't put Grace on a witness stand, if that's what you're asking," Deb replied. "On the other hand, she may have some very lucid visions of what was happening thirty years ago. If she offers them up with ease, I'd say that there is probably some thread of truth to what she's saying. I just wouldn't get too focused on the detail of what she says."

Floyd stood up. "Thanks for the perspective," he said. "I'd like to talk to Grace some more. Is there somewhere she and I could talk quietly for a while other than her room? She seemed a little uncomfortable being alone with me there."

"Lunch is over, so the dining room is empty. Why don't you sit at a table there, and I'll get you some coffee and cookies. Grace loves to talk over coffee."

Floyd was sitting at a table covered with a red and white checkered tablecloth, making notes when Deb McIntosh led Grace into the dining room. "Grace, this is Sergeant Swenson, from the sheriff's office. He said that he would like to treat you to a cup of coffee and some cookies."

Grace smiled politely and took the chair Floyd pulled out for her. "It's very nice of you to treat me to coffee," Grace said as she sat. She displayed no recognition that she'd ever met Floyd before.

"It's entirely my pleasure," he replied. "Deb told me that you used to be the cook at Melody Pines camp. I bet that was a lot of work."

Grace smiled as the memories of the camp came to mind. "It was a lovely place, but it was a lot of work. We baked bread every day and I've never prepared so many tuna fish hotdishes in my whole life. And back then we didn't use any of that Campbell's mushroom soup. We made it all from scratch."

"Now, there were a couple of girls who worked for you that summer," Floyd said. "Their names were Janice and Shirley. Were they much help?"

Grace shook her head while watching the nurse set cookies on a small plate and pour coffee into a carafe. "They were almost as much work at they were help. It used to take them hours to wash all the dishes.

Sometimes I swear it would have been easier to wash them myself."

"Now, Grace," Deb admonished as she set the cookies and coffee on the table, "you let this nice deputy have some of these cookies." She winked at Floyd and added, "Oreos are Grace's favorite." Then she left.

Grace picked up a cookie and dunked it in her coffee. Her fingers were frail and the skin translucent, lined with blue veins and little else. "Actually, I like Russian tea cakes best, but no one here knows how to make them." She bit off the soggy part of the cookie and washed it down with coffee.

"Did any of the boys ever help around the kitchen?" Floyd asked, taking a cookie for himself and setting it on a paper napkin.

"Not very often. One of them took a little shine to the Johnson girl, but she didn't return his interest so he didn't come around much."

"Do you remember the boy's name?" Floyd asked.

"He was tall and gangly. I think that she was almost a foot shorter than he was. I think that might have been why she didn't like him very well."

Floyd nodded asked, "Was he a local boy?"

Grace shook her head. "He was from St. Cloud," she replied. "His family was German." In a whisper she added, "I think he was Catholic, too."

"Did any of the boys like Janice Lund, the other girl?"

"She was a tomboy and skinny," Grace replied. "I think she could out run all the boys. They shied away from her."

Floyd watched Grace dunk a second cookie. "I forget which one ran off with that Smith girl. Was it the boy who liked the Johnson girl?"

"She was a flirt," Grace said with a mouthful of Oreo.

"But she flirted more with one of the boys." Floyd said trying to redirect the conversation as Grace smeared the black cookie on her fingers while turning it so she could dunk another piece of the edge.

"She ran off that summer," Grace stated casually. "Probably got pregnant and had to leave town."

"I can't remember the boy's name," Floyd said, pressing ahead subtly. "He was a bit of a troublemaker, wasn't he?"

Grace pushed the last of the cookie in her mouth, and then looked at her blackened fingers. "Oh dear, I think I've made a mess."

Floyd slid next to her and took a paper napkin from the table dispenser. "Let me clean up some of those crumbs," he said. He wiped Grace's fingers and then folded the napkin to get a clean surface before gently wiping her mouth.

"That boy who ran off with the Smith girl was some troublemaker, wasn't he?" Floyd asked again.

Grace reached for the last cookie and dunked it in her empty cup. "I seem to be out of coffee. Are you going to drink all of yours?" she asked.

Floyd slid his cup to her. "What was that boy's name anyway?" he asked.

Grace looked up as she took a bite off the cookie. "What boy?"

"The one who ran off with the Smith girl," Floyd replied.

"He didn't run off with her. She went on her own."

The conversation was infuriating, but Floyd persisted. "Well, he was the one who got her pregnant, wasn't he?"

Grace stopped chewing and stared at Floyd as if she were seeing him for the first time. "Is he in trouble?" she asked. Her eyes flicked to Floyd's badge for an instant.

"Oh, no," Floyd replied. "They're all grown up now and they have their own children. I was just trying to remember his name, that's all."

"She's just a little girl, that Smith girl." Grace said as she ate the last of the cookie. "But she's a terrible flirt. It's no wonder he couldn't help himself." She tipped the cup to her lips and sipped at the coffee while her shaking hands trembled.

Floyd sensed Grace's defensiveness, like someone who was hiding a criminal. "Was he a friend of yours?" he asked.

"It was her fault," Grace replied. "She was such a flirt, she got whatever she deserved." She pushed herself back from the table and reached for her cane, resting against a chair. "I have to take a nap. I'm very tired."

Floyd stood and took her by the arm. "Can I walk you to your room?"

"It's been very nice of you to visit," Grace said as they shuffled from the dining room. "I hope you can come some time when my husband is here. He really enjoys visitors. If you go out to the barn you can probably talk to him while he milks the cows."

"I think I'll do that."

Dan drove to the Smith address on Myrtle Street, in Stillwater. The street climbed a steep hill above the St. Croix River and Dan mused how many accidents the hill would cause with a heavy snowstorm. On the way into town he's passed a historical marker set where the logging companies has put a steel boom cable across the river to catch the logs that were floated to the sawmills in Stillwater. The downtown area was a menagerie of antique shops, bars, trendy restaurants, and shops set up in turn-of-the-century brick buildings. Even in the brisk spring weather, the sidewalks were lined with people making their way between the shops.

He found a parking spot on a side street and walked the sidewalk back to the address he'd been given for Michael Smith. The house was a two-story with a huge Victorian style porch across the front. It had been painted in subdued grays and white, with shutters that looked like they could be closed to brace the windows against a gale. A stone retaining wall, topped by a wrought iron fence, raised the lawn two feet above the sidewalk.

Dan knocked on the oak front door and watched the Sunday afternoon traffic pass as he waited. An oak swing hung from eye-bolts in the ceiling, and it swayed slowly with the breeze. Within a minute a neatly groomed man, with graying hair answered the door.

"Mr. Smith?" Dan said opening his badge case and showing his ID. "I'm Dan Williams, from the Pine County Sheriff's Department."

"Yes, I heard you were coming," the man replied. "I'm Mike Smith. Won't you come in?"

They shook hands and Dan was surprised that Smith's hands were calloused. Given his appearance, Dan had assumed that he'd had a leisurely retirement.

Dan walked into the entryway, which was flanked by a long staircase of dark wood. The house was brightly lit despite the dark wood, and it smelled of furniture polish. A living room off the entryway was filled with antique furniture that looked like it might've been there since the house was built. Not a speck of dust nor piece of clutter was visible anywhere.

Mike Smith was a few inches shorter than Dan with a slight paunch around the middle. His hair had thinned on the top and was gray at the temples. Dan guessed Smith to be about sixty. Although he was wearing jeans with his turtleneck sweater, they looked like they were fresh from the dry cleaner. His feet were bare inside tasseled brown loafers.

"Let me take your coat," Smith said as he closed the door. "I have a pot of coffee brewing if you'd care for a cup." Smith took Dan's buckskin jacket and hung it in a small closet tucked under the stairway, then led Dan to the kitchen in the rear of the house. The kitchen cabinets were finished in the same dark oak, but huge windows let early afternoon sun shine on pots of green plants hanging from wrought iron planters. Smith directed Dan to the kitchen table while he set out china cups, sugar, and cream.

"Was it you who contacted the local sheriff's department?" Smith asked as he poured coffee. "A Washington County Deputy stopped by and told me that Helen's body had been found."

"We're not sure it's Helen's body," Dan replied.

Smith sat in the chair opposite Dan and poured coffee for himself and Dan. "But you're reasonably certain or you wouldn't be here?" Smith asked.

Dan accepted the cup Smith offered. "I'd say there's a high probability, but we need to examine your daughter's dental records to be certain. I understand the Bureau of Criminal Apprehension has the dentist's name and he's looking for her records."

"You have to hedge," Smith said with a disarming smile. "I can respect that."

The man's smile made Dan uneasy. It did seem like an inappropriate response to the news. "You seem unusually happy about the discovery," Dan said.

"Don't misunderstand my response," Smith replied. "It's just that my ex-wife and I split up shortly after Helen's disappearance. Once we were sure Helen hadn't drowned, she felt that Helen's disappearance was a kidnapping. She held out for months waiting for a call requesting a ransom. I told her over and over to accept the fact that Helen was dead, and she was very bitter about my stoicism."

"What made your ex-wife think it was a kidnapping?" Dan asked.

"She was very uncomfortable with our financial situation," Smith replied. "She'd grown up in the poor part of St. Paul, called Frogtown. I grew up a few miles away in the Highland Park area. We met at the University of Minnesota and married before graduation. We lived like paupers in the married student housing, and limped along financially for a few years. I got a job with Honeywell, when it was hardly more than a startup operation and worked my way into an executive position in military avionics with five-figure stock options and a six-figure salary. The problem was that I was designing systems to make our warplanes more effective, and my wife was out protesting the Viet Nam war."

"So," Dan summarized, "your wife assumed that someone had noticed all your wealth, and kidnapped Helen to get a big ransom. She would have been happy to pay the big ransom because in her mind the money was all dirty anyway because it was made on military hardware."

"We argued all the time," Smith said. "I said it was more likely that Helen had been abducted because she was a cute little girl. My wife was absolutely convinced that Helen was still alive, and she was completely repulsed by the idea that someone might have taken her for other reasons."

"Where is your ex-wife now?" Dan asked.

Smith shrugged. "Last I heard, she took the divorce settlement and donated it to a homeless shelter in Minneapolis. She worked in their soup kitchen for a few years, but I haven't seen or heard anything from her since we signed the final divorce decree and my lawyer handed her lawyer the check."

"What's your ex-wife's name?" Dan asked.

"Colleen McCarthy," Smith replied. "She went back to her maiden name when we divorced."

"Did you have anything to do with your daughter's disappearance?" Dan asked casually, hoping to measure Smith's response.

"That's absurd!" Smith said.

"Not at all," Dan replied. "Murderers are known to most of their victims. Well over half of all murders are committed by immediate family members, lovers, or close family friends."

"I spoke with a deputy back at the time of the death, and I must have supplied them with an alibi."

"At the time your daughter disappeared," Dan said, "we thought she'd drowned accidentally. No one was looking for an alibi."

"Oh," Smith replied as his veneer of calm confidence peeled away. "I couldn't even guess what I might have been doing on any specific day thirty-some years ago."

"Can you think of any other suspects who would've known your daughter?"

"It happened a long time ago," Smith said. He took a deep breath and stared at a spot near the ceiling. "I can't think of anyone who'd want to harm my daughter."

"Did you have any family friends who were working at the camp, or who had a lake home near Willow River?"

Smith took a deep breath. "Look," he said, "I didn't know any perverts back then, and I don't know any now."

"Why did you say, 'perverts'?" Dan asked. "I didn't say that your daughter had been sexually assaulted."

"Well I assumed…" Smith backpedaled. "She was a cute teenager, why else would anyone kidnap her?"

"Do you know the Benson family?" Dan asked.

"I don't recall the name," Smith replied. "Did they mention me?"

"They owned the farm where your daughter's body was found."

Smith shook his head. "The name isn't familiar at all," he said. "I don't think I know anyone from that area near the camp."

"The car that contained the remains had been stored on property owned by the Benson family. Their farm is east of Hinckley, about twenty miles from the site of the Melody Pines Camp."

"You think someone drove a car with Helen in the trunk and abandoned it at this farm?"

"The car was abandoned behind Benson's barn in '55. We believe that someone used the abandoned car as a convenient place to hide her body. It worked well for thirty years." Dan finished his coffee and set the cup on the table.

"This is a lovely old house," Dan said as he stood and took in the kitchen and the view of the gardens in the back. The dead flower stalks in a flagstone tiered garden hinted at colorful splendor in the summer. "Do you do the gardening yourself?"

"I dabble at house restoration and gardening. I find pulling weeds and pruning roses quite cathartic. The house restoration, on the other hand, is painstakingly slow and sometimes infuriating when I'm constantly reminded that there are no square corners in these old mansions."

"Did you have many other children?"

"Colleen had a problem when Helen was born," Smith said as he escorted Dan to the front door. "She couldn't have any more children."

"Were you having an affair at the time of Helen's disappearance?"

Smith looked stunned. "Was I having an affair?"

"Jealousy is a strong motive for murder," Dan said retrieving his jacket from the closet. "If there were a jilted lover involved, he or she might seek revenge on you by hurting Helen."

"I can say unequivocally that I was *not* having an affair at the time of Helen's disappearance. I can't speak for my wife, and I suggest you ask her the same question."

"Did you remarry after the divorce?"

"I date some," Smith replied, "but I don't see the need to tie myself up like that again. They say that love is grand, but I know that divorce is a couple hundred grand."

"Thanks, Mr. Smith," Dan said. "I know it's difficult to reopen old wounds."

"Umm, Deputy Williams," Smith said as Dan walked through the door. "Was Helen sexually assaulted?"

"We don't know at this point," Dan replied. "But, like you said, why else would someone kidnap a cute teenaged girl?"

The color drained from Smith's face as he held the door. "Was she killed…I mean was she dead before the bastards put her in the trunk?"

"I don't know that we'll be able to determine the sequence of events surrounding Helen's death."

"I was out of line before," Smith said. "I was kind of pleased that I'd won. After all these years it was good to know that Colleen had been naïve about the disappearance, and that I had pegged it right. Now, to know that Helen may have been sexually assaulted and killed … well, it's disturbing."

"Yes, it is, Mr. Smith." Dan reached in his pocket and handed Smith a business card. "If you think of anything else, please call."

Smith took the card and read it quickly. "Do you think I'll remember anything new after all these years?" He asked.

"Sometimes a discussion dredges up old memories."

Dan popped two TUMS in his mouth and took a steep street down to downtown Stillwater and the St. Croix River. He drove north on highway 95, the river coming in and out of view, while he reflected on the strange conversation with Mike Smith. He seemed too smug and confident, and then started to melt down when the realization of the circumstances around Helen's death finally sunk in. He couldn't remember if he'd had an alibi for the night of Helen's disappearance, which led Dan to believe that he probably didn't need one. Most innocent people rarely supply an alibi a week after a crime unless they'd had a significant event, like a birthday party, on the date. Criminals tended to bind themselves up with an alibi that they think of as solid and can furnish it under questioning years after the crime.

He turned off Highway 95 drove into the little town of Scandia where he saw a brightly painted Swedish-style Dala horse near a business with a Swedish name on the corner of Highway 8. The horse was blocky, and nearly waist high. He'd seen knickknack Dala horses on shelves, but never one as large as this one. He paused at the stop sign and looked around and noted four more, all painted in bright blues, reds, or yellows like they'd just been transplanted from Upsala, Sweden.

He turned west and drove into the town of Lindstrom where he stopped for gas and a cup of coffee. Across the highway he noted the statue of a family in the city park. The marker said the statue was a tribute to the Swedish immigrants who'd settled the town in the late 1800's.

"It appears that there are a lot of proud Swedes here, but I wonder if the Norwegians, Germans, and Irish feel slighted?" Dan asked himself out loud.

A gray haired man walked up behind Dan paying for his coffee at the cash register and said, "We don't feel slighted," he said. "We just know that the Swedes are all crazy and we let them carry on."

Dan turned and the man pulled off his mitten and stuck out his hand and introduced himself "Hjelmer Bergen." His knit hat had the blue Norwegian cross outlined in white, on a red background. His voice had a hint of a Norwegian accent that came off like the movie, Fargo."

"Dan Williams," he said, shaking the man's hand.

"Looks like you're driving a cop car, and you're not from around here."

"I'm from Pine County."

"Ah, I've heard of Pine County. You got your own branch of craziness up there with all those jack pine savages who're trying to live off the land while escaping life in the Twin Cities."

Dan cracked a smile. "I guess I've got my challenges. I didn't know that Pine County had such a reputation."

"Oh, ya. We hear about you folks all the time. People commit a murder and they drive up to Pine County a drop the body because that's as far as you can get on a half tank of gas. Then they drive back and no one's the wiser because there's no paper trail of receipts, and no one's seen their face in a store or gas station."

"I'd think that Lindstrom would be prime for that, too. It's about the same distance."

"It's too settled here," Hjelmer said as he selected a caramel glazed cinnamon roll from a display on the counter. "Up in Pine County you've got fourteen hundred square miles that's half swamps and not so many people to see anything."

"It's only forty-nine percent swamp," Dan said with a wink.

Dan drove off and considered Bergen's comments about criminals from the Twin Cities. Hinckley was easily within a two-hour drive of either downtown St. Paul or Minneapolis, and Helen was from "The Cities". Were they looking too close to Pine County when there were another million suspects within a short drive?

Mike Smith said that his ex-wife was last living in Minneapolis. There was an old saying, "Go to Minneapolis to sin and St. Paul to be saved." Could Colleen McCarthy have been involved in something in Minneapolis that spilled over to her daughter?

CHAPTER 9

Monday

"You had any coffee yet?" Floyd asked, finding Dan at his computer desk typing notes. The computer was the one spot in Dan's office that wasn't crowded with paperwork.

"Yup," Dan replied, holding up a stained ceramic mug. "Grab a cup and then we can compare notes."

Floyd was back in less than a minute with his own cup sporting a logo from the Minnesota Drug Task Force.

"I don't know what to do with the camp cook," Floyd said. "I spoke with her again yesterday and she's so lucid at times I could swear that she is visualizing things clearly in her mind. Other times it's like she just fades away. At one point I was convinced she knew something about Helen Smith's abductor and was being evasive. A few minutes later she didn't know her husband was dead."

"Sounds like dementia," Dan said. "She has pretty good long term memory, but sometimes the old and new get mixed around. We would never consider putting her on a witness stand even if she named the murderer and claimed to be a witness."

"What did you find out from the girl's father?" Floyd asked as he moved the new pile of files from the guest chair.

"He wasn't much help either," Dan replied. "He and the girl's mother divorced shortly after the abduction. He said that once it was clear the girl hadn't drowned, the mother was convinced the girl had been kidnapped for ransom because they were rather well off. The father had argued a sexual predator took the girl, and the mother couldn't accept that. It seems the parents had grown apart about the time of the girl's disappearance. The father was designing hardware for military jets and the mother was an anti-war protestor."

"The ransom angle is new. There really wasn't any discussion about a kidnapping or ransom demands in any of my notes," Floyd said, mentally reviewing the file. "No one heard any commotion, and there wasn't any evidence of a struggle that would lead me to think that she'd been forcibly kidnapped."

"Mike Smith made me think that avenue was something that his wife had dreamt up, and he indicated that he never put any credence in the theory."

"Do you suspect that the father was involved?" Floyd asked.

"Not really, he seemed sincere enough about his concern," Dan said. "But, there is an undercurrent of hatred between the parents. He mentioned suspicions about the mother's preoccupation with the ransom. I don't know if that surfaced as a result of the bitter divorce, or if it was there before. He also suggested that we ask her if she was having an affair at the time."

"It's hard to believe two parents would hate each other so bitterly one would harm their child to spite the other," Floyd said.

"I don't know," Dan replied. "Remember the woman over in Chengwatana Township who was making her little boy sick?"

Floyd shook his head with disgust. "I still have a hard time with that," he replied. "She was injecting her own son with feces to make him sick so she could rush him to the emergency room and save him. Luckily, the doctor in the emergency room caught onto it after a couple incidents and called us in before the poor kid died."

"The psychiatrist said she couldn't help herself," Dan said. "He called it Munchhausen's Syndrome by Proxy. She was so desperate for attention that she was compelled to look like the doting mother who would give up the world to take care of her ill child."

"What happened to her?" Floyd asked.

"She was in the state hospital for a while," Dan replied. "The last I heard, the doctors had declared her cured and released her. The boy's grandmother had been granted custody when the mother was committed and grandma was fighting the mother over custody rights."

Floyd pondered Dan comments for a few moments. "I remember Helen Smith's mother was pretty frantic over the loss of her daughter. Her flaming red hair fit her personality well. She certainly wanted to be the center of attention with all her wailing and cursing. Knowing what I do now, I might be more suspicious of her."

"What do you recall about the father's reaction?" Dan asked.

"I think he was shell-shocked," Floyd replied. "Once he got over his initial anger it seemed like he couldn't grasp what was going on. He was hanging on the fringes and asking questions about the plans. He seemed more lost than distraught."

"Knowing what you know now," Dan repeated Floyd's earlier words, "how would you assess him as a potential suspect?"

Floyd leaned his elbow on the arm of the chair and cupped his chin in his palm. "Whew!" He replied. "At the time we thought the girl had drowned. His response seemed appropriate for a parent whose child was missing. He asked about dragging and how large an area we would search. I remember him asking why we weren't using divers right away and if we were searching the woods. It all seemed reasonable at the time, and I can't think of anything he did that was inconsistent with what I might have done myself. I don't see anything he did that would lead me to move him onto a suspect's list."

"How about the mother?" Dan asked. "You said she was making a ruckus."

"More than a ruckus," Floyd said. "She was a royal pain in the butt. She was screaming and yelling and swearing at people. I thought we were going to have to sedate her for a while. The husband tried to calm her down a couple times, and I thought she was going to punch him."

"Would you put her on a list of suspects?"

"Knowing what I do now," Floyd said, "maybe. I think that she'd be a long shot at best. I still think that the answer is right under our noses here and locked away in the cook's head."

"The wife went back to her maiden name," Dan said as he leafed through pages in his notebook. "Her name is Colleen McCarthy. The husband said she gave the divorce settlement to a homeless shelter in Minneapolis. Maybe she's still there somewhere. See if you can track her down."

"Track who down?" Pam Ryan said, sticking her blonde head into Dan's office.

"Helen Smith's mother," Dan replied. "In the meanwhile, Pam and I are going to watch a forensic anthropologist examine Helen Smith's remains."

"Cool!" Pam replied, stepping into the office. "What's a forensic anthropologist?"

"They look at bones and tell us what they reveal about the person and possibly the cause of death," Dan said has he hoisted his buckskin jacket from the coat tree. "This may be the only time in your career to see one in action."

"Cool!" Pam said, again.

Floyd rose from his chair, following Dan and Pam into the hallway. "I'll make a few calls to see if I can find Colleen McCarthy," he said. "It can't be any more frustrating than interviewing a senile camp cook."

☼ ☼ ☼

Pam rode with Dan in his unmarked squad car. As they passed through downtown Pine City Pam said, "Tell me more about the forensic anthropologist."

"His name is Craig Neilson, and he's a professor at the University of Minnesota. The BCA uses him when they're working with old remains. His expertise was developed in Mexican excavations, and he's done some work locally on some of the old battlefields from the Indian wars in the Midwest. He's testified in a few cases for the BCA and FBI, and everyone thinks that he's darned good."

"But, what can he tell from an old skeleton?"

"He can determine lots of things," Dan replied, "like the age and sex of the victim to start with. Then he can often give us some views on how strenuous the person's life was, how their nutrition was, and sometimes a cause of death."

"But how can he determine a cause of death from just a skeleton?" Pam asked. "I've seen the medical examiner take weeks to get toxicology results back and even then sometimes it's a judgment call."

"I should leave that to the anthropologist to answer," Dan said. "He seems to come up with some pretty plausible conclusions from the bones he examines."

It took over an hour to fight through the morning rush hour traffic in the 694/494 loop around the Twin Cities. They drove down highway 280 to the University Avenue exit, then spent another fifteen minutes working through the local traffic until they found the parking ramp next to the west-bank campus of the university.

"I couldn't live with this traffic," Pam said as they walked across the campus. Pam's brown uniform and gunbelt garnered a number of stares.

"I'd have some problems dealing with the traffic too," said Dan. "On the other hand, it's kind of nice to be able to go out for dinner and not run into three or four people you've arrested."

"You know," Pam said, "that's really a pain in the butt. I mean, I was eating supper at the steak house the other night and this guy I ticketed for a DWI gave me a look that made me wonder if I'd have four flat tires when I went out to my car."

"Welcome to small town Minnesota, and just be glad he wasn't the cook."

"Oh, God. I never thought about that. What idiot in the kitchen is putting something in my burger?"

Dan smiled. "You'll notice that I only eat at three or four Pine County restaurants, and every one of the owners is a personal friend. Now you know why."

They climbed the steps of an old brick building, and went past the Bell Museum of Natural History. Winding their way through narrow halls choked with students rushing to classes, they finally found a second floor room marked, "Anthropology Lab." Inside were two men standing next to an old table, drinking coffee. Jeff Ness, from the BCA, was talking to an older man dressed in a plaid wool shirt with a plaid tie that didn't match the pattern of his shirt. He looked to be a hundred years old, his apparent age accentuated by his emaciated face. Pam whispered to Dan that he looked like an undertaker.

The lab was lined with glass-fronted wood cabinets whose finish had darkened to teak. The bench tops were granite, arranged as two peninsulas extending into the room with a sink cut into the end of each peninsula. Every cabinet had bones, skulls, or fossils on display. A large chart near the door showed a human face and the thickness of the tissue at critical points over the jaw, cheekbones, forehead, and face. Twenty pictures of bones with striations were arranged at the end of one peninsula and under each picture was the description of the knife or saw that had caused the marks. A full anatomical skeleton hung on a stand in the farthest corner of the lab.

"Gentlemen," Dan said, "this is Pam Ryan, our just-past-rookie deputy."

In turn, each man shook Pam's hand. "Jeff Ness. Craig Neilson."

Neilson set his coffee on a desk near the wall and stepped up to the stone topped table located under a bank of fluorescent lights. On top of the table was a medium-sized cardboard box, sealed with blue tape. He turned on the lamps, bathing the lab in blue-white light, then inspected the tape sealed on the box.

"The seal is still intact," he said. "Shall we begin?"

Neilson opened a drawer and selected an exacto knife. He slit the tape across the cardboard seams, and put the knife away. Pam watched Neilson's face as he opened the box and moved the Styrofoam pellets aside. His eyes sparkled like a child opening a Christmas gift. He slowly removed the skull with the tips of his fingers, and set it gently on one end of the table. As each bone came out, he verbally identified it and then set it in its relative position to the skull. It took him nearly twenty minutes to remove all the bones and arrange them in their proper anatomical position. Only once did he move a bone that had been previously placed, and move it to the opposite side. When he was done, he set the box aside and stepped back to examine the carefully arranged skeleton.

"Well, I can observe a lot already," Neilson said. "The skeleton is not very old, in geological terms. It doesn't appear to have been in contact with the ground at all. The bones have been cleaned of all skin and tissue, indicating the body wasn't embalmed and was subject to bacterial decomposition and subsequent attack by insects."

Pam leaned close to Dan's shoulder. "Doesn't he know it was found in a trunk?" she whispered.

"No," Dan replied. "He likes to come in without any information to taint his views of what he observes."

"Kind of like one of our investigations," Pam said. "Collect the evidence and let it lead you to the conclusions."

Neilson looked up. "Exactly!" he said somewhat sharply. "Now please be quiet, or I'll have to ask you to leave."

Pam's face turned crimson. "Sorry."

Neilson turned his attention back to the table. "As I was saying, the skeleton doesn't appear to have been in contact with the ground." He moved a few bones and added, "as a matter of fact, it appears that it was lying on something made of iron or steel. There appear to be some rust stains on several of the bones." He looked up at Pam, "Which would correspond to the information that the body had been in a car trunk perhaps?"

Pam's crimson turned deeper, "Sorry again."

Neilson removed a small metal ruler from his pocket protector, and measured the openings in the pelvis. "The victim was female." He examined the ends of the long thighbones and added, "And the growth plates appear to be at or near the end of her growth period. The muscle attachments are not overly stressed and the overall skeletal development seems healthy."

Neilson stepped back from the table and looked at the skeleton in total again. "My estimate is that this skeleton belonged to a young woman, probably just past puberty. There are no signs of malnutrition or disease. She doesn't appear to have experienced much hard labor since the points where ligaments would have been attached are not stressed."

Neilson picked up the jaw and noted, "There are three amalgam fillings in molars. The twelve-year molars are fully in place but there doesn't seem to be any sign of wisdom teeth. That would be consistent with the age determinations from the growth plates on the femurs, and would also point to a death since the advent of modern dentistry."

"The skeleton doesn't show signs of mechanical dismemberment. So, I assume it was found intact. There are no signs of scavenging by wild animals, so I also assume it was in some sort of protected location." Neilson looked up at Pam again. "Like the trunk of a car."

He picked up the skull and noted, "The skull is substantially intact and shows no signs of trauma."

Peering into the opening at the bottom Neilson added, "Viewed through the foramen magnum, there are insect pupae casings inside the skull. The location wasn't totally without access to the outside world, but I would have to estimate that the body lay undisturbed during its decomposition."

Neilson removed a large magnifying glass from a drawer and started examining the rest of the bones slowly. After a few moments he picked up a rib and held it at an angle. "This may be significant. There's a small nick in this rib. There's no sign of healing, so this was made very shortly before the victim died."

He set the rib back and arranged it with the others. He picked up the one immediately above first. "There's trauma to this one as well. Based on my experience, I'd say a large knife was inserted between these ribs."

Next he looked at the vertebrae. "And here's a nick where the tip of that large knife struck the vertebra," Neilson said, pointing to a piece of the backbone. He picked up the ribs to align them as they would have been in life; he used his finger to align the knife marks on the ribs with the injured vertebra. "Estimating the angle of the insertion, it would appear that the knife pierced a lung and possibly the aorta with an upward thrust. The young woman probably bled to death rather quickly." Neilson removed the small metal ruler from his pocket again and arranged one rib over the injured vertebra as he measured. "I'd say the knife blade was at least fifteen centimeters long and about four centimeters wide." Seeing Pam Ryan trying to do conversions in her head he added, "six inches long, by an inch and a half wide. The knife was inserted with the sharp edge up, and judging from the nick in the vertebrae, at a slight upward angle. I would speculate that the attacker was right-handed and struck with a great deal of force."

Neilson examined the remaining ribs closely, turning each over in his hand under the magnifying glass. Next he did the same with each vertebra, and then each of the bones of the hands. He set two of the finger bones aside as he checked through all the others.

"I don't see evidence of trauma to any of the other ribs. With a crime a passion, we quite often see multiple knife wounds, as if the attacker were trying to exact retribution on the victim. This appears to have been a single fatal wound unless there were abdominal wounds that we wouldn't be able to discern from the skeleton."

Picking up the two bones he'd set aside, Neilson examined them again. "It appears the victim fought off her attacker. Two phalanges have apparent cut marks. They're on the right hand, so I assume your victim was right handed, if that's any help."

Next, he picked up the pelvis and examined it from all angles under the magnifying glass. "There's no evidence of penetration by a foreign object," Neilson observed.

Pam let out a sigh that caught Neilson's attention. "It's terrible that we even need to make this type of exam, but we occasionally find a sexual aspect in many attacks on women."

Pam nodded. "I know," she said. "But I'd like to believe that a youngster like this wouldn't be subjected to that kind of abuse thirty years ago."

Neilson glanced at Jeff Ness, the BCA agent who'd delivered the box of bones. "Last week Agent Ness brought in a box of bones recovered from an archaeological site near the Iowa border. It appeared that renegade Civil War soldiers had ransacked the house and killed the residents. There was evidence of a vicious sexual assault on a female child in those remains, and that site dated back over a hundred years. Mankind has been unkind to its children for millennia. Pedophiles are not a recent invention, but perhaps their crimes are more publicized recently."

"Can you tell how long ago the victim died?" Pam asked.

Neilson considered the question as he stood back and looked at the skeleton. "More than a year or two ago and less than fifty years ago."

Pam searched the man's face for a hint of mirth, hoping that he'd be able to narrow the span to a year or two. When there was no further information offered she asked, "Can you do carbon dating or something to narrow it down?" Pam asked.

Neilson smiled. "Carbon-14 dating is a very powerful tool for dating ancient bones," he said, "but it really isn't useful on modern remains. It gives us an estimate that is plus-or-minus a century. The clues that I see here are the dental fillings that tell me that the dental work is less than fifty years old. The complete absence of all residual tissue and the desiccation of the bones tell me that the victim has been dead for at least two years. Beyond that, you'll be better off finding other clues to pin the date of death down. Perhaps the age of the car the remains were found in, or the last time witnesses saw the victim alive would be better barometers of the date of death."

"Do you have some names to check the dental work against?" Neilson asked. "Or perhaps some identification that was found with the remains?"

"We have a good lead on the identity," Dan said, "and we're checking on dental records."

"Actually," Agent Ness said, "We got Helen Smith's dental x-rays from Stillwater this morning. They match."

Neilson stripped off the latex gloves he'd worn and dropped them into a wastebasket. "So," he said, "you're primary interest here was to determine the cause of death."

"That, and to see if there was anything else that might be unexpected," Dan said.

“Is this the body they found in the trunk of the antique car I read about in the *Pioneer Press* this past week?” Neilson asked.

“Yes,” Pam replied. “She disappeared from a Pine County church camp in the seventies without a clue.”

“Friends and family are the usual suspects,” the professor suggested.

Dan nodded. “We haven’t found a good suspect in those categories yet.”

“Then,” Neilson said, “you should be looking for someone who’s done this before or since. Do you have anymore young stabbing victims whose bodies are stashed in car trunks?”

“Not that we know about,” Pam replied.

“Then cast your net more broadly,” Neilson said. “If the person who did this enjoyed it, this probably wasn’t his first victim, and he didn’t quit after this one.”

Dan shook his head. “The farm where the car was stored has a rental property. It sounds like there were dozens of vagabonds who lived there over the years. It could’ve been any of them, or scores of others that passed through.”

CHAPTER 10

There was a knock on the anthropology lab door and a man stuck his head around the corner. "Excuse me, Craig," the man said to Neilson. "Is this a good time?" The visitor looked nervously at the law enforcement officers.

"David!" Neilson exclaimed. "Come in. Your timing is impeccable. Ladies and gentlemen, this is Doctor David Kramer."

Kramer had sandy brown hair that he combed straight forward to cover a rising forehead. He appeared to be in his fifties, with a weathered face that said he'd done a lot of field research over the years in addition to having credentials to earn the respect of the archeologist. He looked uneasy with the group assembled around the skeleton.

"Folks," Neilson said, "Doctor Kramer is an entomologist from down the hallway." Kramer shook hands as Neilson explained. "After I spoke with Agent Ness, I asked David to stop by for an entomological examination. He should add some data from the insect materials that were found with the remains."

Kramer smiled. "Craig…er, Doctor Neilson," Kramer corrected, "has asked me to identify insect parts in the past, but I've never had to be around any of his grisly skeletons."

Neilson smiled. "Dead bodies are no different than dead insects, David. Neither of them will hurt you."

Kramer stepped up to the table and looked at the skeletal remains. "That may be true," he said, "but my dead insects don't usually smell as bad as some of your clientele."

Jeff Ness handed Kramer a glass vial. "We collected these from the trunk of the car where the skeleton was recovered."

Kramer put on a pair of glasses from his pocket and broke the seal around the cap. He spread the contents on the tabletop and picked at the insect parts carefully. After a brief examination he said, "These are Nicrophorus americanus, known commonly as carrion beetles." He held up a medium sized beetle in the tip of a forceps that he'd removed from a pocket. Its body was black, marked with red on the head and shell. "I see some Nicrophorus pupae cases too."

"Is that significant?" Dan asked.

"It depends," Kramer replied. "Carrion beetles used to be terribly common. They were all over in nature and, in fact, most universities still maintain a colony of them. We use them ourselves to remove flesh from animal carcasses to get clean skeletons. In nature, there are three things that we can learn from this. First, the remains were moist, because the beetles are not effective at removing dried material. You can assume that the skeleton wasn't dessicated over a winter and then exposed to the beetles. Second, you can assume that when the beetles consumed this body it stunk to high heaven. I assume the skeleton was found in a remote location where there weren't many people around, because if someone had smelled the decomposition it would have sent them running for the police."

Kramer hesitated, and then pushed more of the insect debris into piles on the tabletop. "Third," he said, "the body was probably left to decompose over two decades ago." He looked up to see that the law enforcement people understood the gravity of his comments. "Carrion beetles have been undergoing a severe population crash for thirty or forty years. We're not sure of the causes, but they just aren't common anymore. Twenty years ago I would have expected to see a few carrion beetles cases at every fresh carcass I found. Now, I rarely see them.

"Craig, do you have a dissecting scope here?" Kramer asked.

Professor Neilson directed Kramer to a corner of the lab, removing a plastic dust cover from a microscope. Kramer pushed his glasses atop his head and spread some of the samples under the microscope.

"There are several species of insects represented in this debris," Kramer observed. "That's not surprising, but the mixture can tell us more than a layman might guess. In addition to the Nicrophorus debris there are shells and pupae cases from Dermestid beetles, too. That would be consistent with the late stages of decomposition. They eat the dried flesh and the skin.

"Interestingly," Kramer said, "I don't see any evidence of Calliphora vomitans, which would be an indicator that the body had been invaded in the spring. I do see a lot of Phaenica sericata pupae."

Dan looked over Kramer's shoulder as he separated the insect debris into five different piles on the microscope stage. "What's the significance of that?" He asked.

"Well," Kramer replied, "the presence of Calliphora, which is the genus of the blue bottle fly, would indicate the body decomposed in the spring. The Phaenica is the green bottle fly," he held up an iridescent green fly, "and they are a summer species that only lay eggs when the temperature is over seventy degrees Fahrenheit. There are several other fly species represented here, and most aren't particularly seasonal. The missing specimen is the carnivorous wasp. They're around late summer and early fall, so we can narrow the period of decomposition to the range of June to early August."

"That would be consistent with the victim's disappearance," Pam Ryan commented. "So the killer didn't keep her tied up somewhere for months. There are some insect parts that fell out of the skull when Doctor Neilson was doing his exam. Are they significant?"

Kramer walked to the exam table and looked at the insect debris that had fallen from the skull. He took a few pieces to the microscope and examined them under magnification.

"It's more of the green bottle fly pupa cases," Kramer said. "That's pretty common. They invade the orifices of the head quickly and tunnel up the spinal column into the brain." He hesitated then added, "Another factor to consider is that the victim may not have been dead when she was placed in the trunk. Green bottle flies often lay eggs in open wounds before death."

Pam grimaced. "I don't suppose that's an issue at this point."

"On the contrary," Neilson said. "If you find a series of similar crimes with the victims left injured to die, that might tie a serial killer to this case, too."

"Sorry I brought it up," Pam said.

"Most times," Kramer said, "the insect debris is left in layers, and some additional determination can be made about the course of decomposition by the order the species are deposited. If I could look directly at the site the skeleton was found I might be able to offer additional insights."

"The skeleton was found in the trunk of a car," Jeff Ness said. "By the time it made it to the BCA lab it had been trailered twice and the contents of the trunk were pretty well mixed. There is some evidence of the location of the body during decomposition, based on body fluid stains on the floor of the trunk. But the bones and insect matter were pretty well randomly distributed around the entire floor."

"That's often a problem we encounter with ancient sites," Neilson added. "The sites have been disturbed by animals or humans, and the remains are not usually complete or without depredation. At least this skeleton had all the pieces together, even though they may not have been arranged in their anatomically correct locations."

Neilson started to load the bones back into the box when he hesitated. "There is one other observation I didn't mention." He paused to make sure he had everyone's attention. "There are a few fibers attached to the skull where the jaw would normally articulate. I assume that you were already aware that there had been some sort of a cloth used to gag the victim, and that it hadn't been removed before decomposition."

Jeff Ness winked at Dan. "We found a long, cotton sock with a knot in it, near the skull. It looked like it might have been used to gag the victim, but the orientation was changed. One small piece of it had attached itself to the skull, apparently with the fluids from decomposition."

Neilson continued loading the bones. "So you were testing me?" He asked.

"You told us not to reveal anything about the skeleton, or the situation where it was found," Ness replied.

"Touché!" Neilson replied.

When the box was loaded, Ness sealed it with evidence tape and signed his name across the seal so that some of the signature extended beyond the tape, and onto the cardboard, on both sides.

"There," Ness said as he picked up the box. "If Doctors Neilson and Kramer could send me a report summarizing their observations, I will include it in the file." He turned to Dan and Pam. "If you two have a little time, we have a team sorting through the microscopic evidence in the trunk. They may have some additional information by now."

"Give me a second, Dan" Pam said as she pulled a cell phone from her pocket. "I promised Floyd that I'd call as soon as we had any information."

CHAPTER 11

After five telephone transfers around the Hennepin County Sheriff's department, Floyd Swenson was connected with a detective.

"Detective Kline, I'm Sergeant Floyd Swenson, from the Pine County Sheriff's department. We have a tentative identification of a homicide victim, and we're trying to locate her mother who was last reported living in Minneapolis."

Kline shifted in his chair to check the phone number on the caller ID box. Satisfied that the call was legitimate, he picked up a pen. "What is the mother's name?" he asked.

"Colleen McCarthy," Floyd replied. "We don't have an address, but her ex-husband reported that she had been working in some relief agency."

"Hang on," Kline said as he wrote the name on a note pad and picked up the phone book. "I don't suppose this will be one of those simple jobs where her name just shows up in the phone book." He flipped through the pages to the section of M's. "How long ago did she move to Minneapolis?"

"Some time in the seventies," Floyd said.

"Seventies?" Kline asked.

"That's the best estimate I can give you. She separated from her husband just after their daughter's disappearance and he said she moved to Minneapolis."

"How long ago was the homicide?"

"The girl disappeared in '74," Floyd said. "We just located her remains this past week."

"Well, I found the McCarthy's," Kline said as he flipped through the pages with both hands, holding the phone to his ear with his shoulder. "There's no listing for Colleen, but there are two with the initial C. Hang on. I'll pull up the reverse directory and put the phone numbers in to see what names come up." In the background Floyd could hear the computer keys clicking.

"You know," Kline said, "that she's probably moved or married or something."

"I know."

"Well, Sergeant, you are one lucky cop. I have a Colleen McCarthy living on Forty-second Avenue South. I'll dispatch a deputy to go over and break the bad news to her. Tell me the daughter's name and any other pertinent information."

"Actually," Floyd said, "I'd like to break the news to her myself. Can you give me the address and directions?"

"Tell me more about this thirty year-old homicide," Kline said.

"A girl disappeared from a camp on a local lake," Floyd explained. "We had some information that she may have drowned, so we dragged the lake and did all the drowning follow up. We never came up with a trace of her. Last week we got a call from the BCA saying someone had reported finding a skeleton in the trunk of an antique car they'd bought from a farmer twenty miles from the camp. I just got confirmation that the body was the missing girl."

"I read about the skeleton find in the *Strib* this weekend," Kline said, and then he paused. "Tell you what, if you can find the Government Center, in Minneapolis, I'll drive you over to this address. I think I'd like to hear the whole story."

"We swap prisoners once a week with you guys," Floyd replied, "so I know where you are. I can be there in about an hour."

CHAPTER 12

Monday afternoon

"What's the matter?" Dan asked Pam as he drove down University Avenue toward the BCA offices.

"I'm having a problem with the concept of teen-aged girls being kidnapped from rural church camps in the seventies," Pam replied. "I mean, what's safer than a church camp?"

"Who says she was kidnapped?" Dan asked. "Are you jumping to conclusions?"

"Like she'd run off with someone who killed her?"

"Keep in mind that most murderers are known to their victims. She may have wandered off with some-one she trusted only to have that trust betrayed."

"I have a hard time with that," Pam replied.

"How many cases of date rape are reported a year?" Dan asked. "And how many more aren't reported? Every one of those cases involved a rapist known to, and most often, trusted by the victim."

Taking Pam's lack of response as skepticism, Dan added, "Remember what Doctor Neilson said about the attacker possibly being a serial killer. We may be dealing with someone who is a master of gaining a woman's trust through lies and deceit. If the killer was someone in a position to gain the victim's trust, she may have gone willingly with her killer. You know, not all killers look like Freddie Krueger. There are many that look very disarming and they're usually the ones who are most successful. Look at Jeffrey Dahmer, he was a good looking, clean-cut guy who got away with murder for a decade."

"Okay," Pam said. "Let's hypothesize that the killer was someone Helen met at camp and trusted enough to leave with. Who would you put on the list of suspects?" She counted off suspects on her fingers. "The male counselors. The chaplain. Oh yes! He'd be at the top of the list," she quiped. "The other campers, and the other male staff members."

"Maybe you're thinking too narrowly," Dan said. "Her father and any male family friends were only an hour drive away. Is there a local delivery person she could have come in contact with? There are a number of other seasonal cabins on the lake. Could she have befriended someone from one of them?"

Pam shook her head. "It could've been anyone in Pine County!"

"No, probably wouldn't have been someone who just dropped by," Dan replied. "It had to be someone who knew about the junked cars behind Benson's barn."

"Like one of the transients who rented the streetcar," Pam said. "They had access to the cars and Mary Jungers told you that they were all creepy."

"That would contradict the theory that Helen Smith left with someone willingly. If it were one of the bums, they would have scared her to death and she wouldn't have left without a fight. Besides, no one at camp would have let any creepy old guy near the place. How would any of them known about Helen Smith?"

"Unless she was a random victim," Pam said. "Maybe a bum just snuck in and took the first girl he came across. He gagged her and tied her up, and dragged her off."

"Someone would've heard," Dan said as he turned the corner after passing the BCA building and pulled into a visitor's spot in the parking lot.

BCA agent Tom Class met them in the lobby and signed for their visitor's passes. "We made some discoveries while you guys were looking at bugs with Agent Ness," Class said.

He escorted them through the security doors and led them down the hallway to a brightly lit laboratory. In the center of the room was a large table covered in butcher paper. Two people dressed in white smocks and wearing surgical gloves, sat on stools examining lumps of material under magnifying lenses built into the centers of round fluorescent lamps.

While the two technicians continued their search Class explained, "We vacuumed the inside of the trunk and emptied the contents on this table. Now we're sorting all the particles into groups; Hair here, insect parts there, fibers there, and miscellaneous other things there." He pointed to small piles of debris set in locations on the white paper.

"You said you'd made discoveries?" Pam asked.

"I was waiting for Agents Ness and Lone Eagle," Class said. "They'll be interested too." Looking at Dan, the agent said, "I understand you and Agent Lone Eagle were partners in the sheriff's department before she became our expert in missing children."

"Laurie's come a long way since she was a rookie in Pine County."

"She's got a national reputation for tracking down missing teens," Class said. "She's been going through the database to see if she could identify any other missing girls who might have disappeared under similar circumstances to our victim in the trunk."

They stood watching the technician's meticulous efforts at sorting for a few moments until a door opened and Laurie Lone Eagle and Jeff Ness came in. As if on cue one of the technician's spoke up, "Tom, here's another one of the odd hairs." Class reached over and took the forceps the technician was using to hold the hair.

Class led the group to a microscope set on a bench top in a corner of the room. He set the hair on a glass slide and slipped it under the optics. After a few minutes of adjustment he stepped back and said, "Take a look."

In turn, each of the people stepped up to the microscope, starting with Pam Ryan. "It looks like a curly hair with bulges on it," she observed.

Dan looked next and stepped back without comment. Laurie Lone Eagle looked for a longer time. When she stepped back she was smiling. Class gave her a nod of agreement as Jeff Ness stepped up to the microscope.

"Either the victim or the killer had ring hair," Ness said as he adjusted the microscope. "I assume that since you're being so secretive that it's the murderer."

Tom Class was grinning ear to ear. "Bingo!"

"What's ring hair?" Pam asked.

Laurie stepped back to the microscope and adjusted it to view a different field. "It's a genetic anomaly that causes a person's hair to grow in spurts. The result is rings that bulge the stalk of each hair. I've read that there isn't one person in a hundred thousand that has ring hair."

"So," Dan summarized, "if we find a potential suspect who has ring hair, we can be pretty sure we've got the murderer. On the other hand, it'll be really easy to sort the non-suspects out."

"But there's no database that will give us that information," Pam said.

"There are all kinds of databases that will help us eliminate potential suspects," Laurie replied. "And if we find any mention of ring hair in any database we can try to match that criminal to Pine County."

Dan looked over at the piles of microscopic evidence on the table. "You said there were a couple of discoveries. What's the other one?"

"We found a pair of panties in the corner of the trunk," Class replied, as he took a microscope slide off the shelf and put it under the lens. "There was a dark hair stuck to the blood on them." After adjusting the slide he let each of them look at the magnified hair.

"It's different than the others," Pam said. "It's like it has a ladder pattern or something."

Dan looked and said, "It's not human, is it?"

"It's definitely not human," Tom Class replied. "We've also eliminated dog, cat, rat, mouse, cow, pig, goat, horse, and sheep."

"So," Pam asked, "what's the significance?"

"The killer may have had an exotic pet of some kind," Class replied. "I took a photomicrograph of the hair and e-mailed it to an expert at the University of Oregon. He's got a database of hairs from thousands of animals. I hope he'll be able to get to it quickly. Once we know what it is, we could get some quick leads. People tend to remember unusual pets and the people who own them."

"Laurie," Dan said, "Agent Class thought you might have been looking through the missing persons database to find some similar crimes. Have you had any luck?"

"Well, the lead on the ring hair will certainly help me focus. Until now the search criteria have been so broad that I got a thousand matches."

"What kind of search criteria did you use?" Pam asked.

"Criminals tend to chose victims in patterns," Laurie said, "especially serial sex offenders. I've been looking for young girls with dark hair. There are literally a thousand who have been missing since the time of this victim's disappearance."

"A thousand missing girls?" Pam asked.

"Sadly, that's about how many were abducted during that period."

"And they're all still missing?" Pam asked.

"Oh no," Laurie replied. "That's how many were reported missing. Many have been found alive or otherwise located. There are still a couple hundred unaccounted for. I've been looking for a pattern in the unsolved cases. Lots of them are runaways who turn up later and others are lured to the big city by some unsavory characters who befriend them. Many of them end up as prostitutes and they are identified the first time they get arrested. Mostly I've focused on the ones who are still missing, or the ones who were abducted and where the crimes involved resemble this case."

"I assume the Native American girl who disappeared up in Fond du Lac came up?" Dan asked.

"She fits the profile," Laurie replied looking somewhat shaken. "She was fifteen, with dark hair. She was walking or hitchhiking home from Cloquet and disappeared before she got there."

“Was she murdered, too?” Pam asked.

“We don’t know,” Dan said. “She’s never been seen again.”

“There were two girls canoeing on the St. Croix, too,” Agent Class said. “They dragged the river for days after their canoe was found by Stillwater. Neither of their bodies was ever recovered.”

“One was blonde, but the other had dark hair,” Laurie said.

“But they drowned, didn’t they?” Pam asked.

The others all looked at each other and shrugged. “We thought this girl had drowned, too,” Laurie said. “The bodies were never recovered, and most drowning victims eventually show up on a busy waterway like the St. Croix.”

“So, what’s next?” Dan asked.

“We search the National Crime Information Computer database for sex offenders with ring hair,” Agent Ness offered.

“And we wait to find out what kind of animal the odd hair belonged to,” Class said.

Dan nodded. “I’ll check with the family who owned the farm and ask if they had any renters with strange pets.”

CHAPTER 13

It took nearly ten minutes for Brad Kline to respond to Floyd's page from the lobby of the Hennepin County Government Center. Although they'd never met, Floyd recognized Kline in the busy lobby when he emerged from the elevator with a sports coat over one arm and a badge on his belt. A bit of paunch extended over the top of the badge, threatening to hide it from view if another five pounds joined it. Kline's appearance reminded Floyd of Bill Brown, a former running back for the Minnesota Vikings. His short-cropped hair was graying blonde and cut into a flattop with what had been chiseled facial features, that drooped slightly from an excess forty pounds of weight.

Kline walked straight to Floyd across the open atrium, "You must be Swenson." Kline said, extending his hand.

"You must be a detective," Floyd said with a smile. "You picked me right out from all the other Pine County sergeants in the room."

Kline shook Floyd's hand heartily. "I like a smart ass. You and I will get along just fine. My car is parked in the garage." He stopped for a second and added, "Unless you'd rather drive around Minneapolis."

Floyd put a hand on Kline's muscular shoulder and nudged him forward. "I don't drive here unless I use the red lights and siren," he said, "and then I'm lost most of the time."

The car was parked in a cavernous garage under the government center. Aside from a layer of grit from the garage, it was indistinguishable from any other unmarked police car in the state. They pulled into the relatively light midday traffic in downtown Minneapolis, and wound through the streets to the Interstate.

"I'd swear I've been in rush hour since crossing I-694," Floyd commented.

"Naw," Kline said. "In rush hour the traffic doesn't move. This is light."

"What do you do if there's an emergency during rush hour?"

"We drive on the sidewalk."

"Really?"

"No," Kline said, with a laugh. "We use the lights and sirens, then we swear a lot."

As they pulled onto I-35 West Kline said, "I ran a background check on Colleen McCarthy. She's been arrested a couple times."

"Let me guess," Floyd said, "anti-war protests and possession of a controlled substance." He hesitated and then added, "I looked at her record, too."

"She tried to sue the Navy reserve in seventy-three," Kline said. "The shore patrol turned a fire hose on a bunch of protesters who were climbing a Minneapolis Naval Air Station fence in January. She claimed they had violated her first amendment rights, had violated due process by punishing them without a trial, and had endangered their lives."

Floyd shook his head. "Did she win?" he asked.

"The judge laughed them out of the courtroom."

"At least there's one rational jurist in this state."

"She pleaded no contest to the trespass charges from the war protest," Kline said, "and was sentenced to public service. She did the hours at a homeless shelter in a Methodist Church. She was convicted on the possession charge and was fined three hundred bucks and was put on probation for a year. She talked to her probation officer regularly and continued to work at the shelter. At the end of the year she was clear and has kept her nose clean since then."

Kline exited the freeway and drove to a blue-collar neighborhood of nicely maintained bungalows. The house he stopped at was slightly smaller than the rest, with white stucco and brown trim.

"The last time I was in this area, I felt like I was driving through a tunnel," Floyd said as they walked up the sidewalk. "The elms met over the street and went on for blocks and blocks. Too bad the Dutch Elm disease wiped them out. These new ash and maples just don't have the character of the old elms."

"I called the shelter," Kline said. "She's off Mondays."

Floyd pushed the doorbell button on a modest house in a row of slightly dingy bungalows. Floyd looked at Kline with sadness in his eyes. "You know," he said. "This is the one part of the job I really hate."

The door opened and a short, slender woman with graying brass-colored hair tied in a ponytail looked at Floyd's uniform with surprise. The lines in her fair skin made her appear older than her sixty-odd years. "Yes?" She was wearing a gray sweatshirt over a pair of blue jeans. Judging from the smell of furniture polish in the air, Floyd guessed that her day off was cleaning day.

"Are you Colleen McCarthy?" Floyd asked.

The woman studied his face for a second. "What's this about?" She asked. Her body language said that she was not pleased to see police officers on her doorstep.

"I need to talk to Colleen McCarthy," Floyd said. "Are you Colleen, or is she home?"

The woman looked at Floyd's badge. "Pine County?"

Kline edged forward. "Excuse me, Miss McCarthy," he said. "I recognize you from your booking pictures. Sergeant Swenson needs to talk to you, could you let us in for a minute?"

The woman looked back and forth between Kline and Floyd for a second, then opened the door, and stepped aside. "You still haven't told me what this is about."

Once inside, Floyd took off his brown baseball cap and held it in both hands. He tried to remember Colleen Smith's face from his contact with her thirty years before, but all that came to mind was the blazing red hair, and that had apparently turned a brassy color with age or Clairol. McCarthy made no motion to invite them any further into the house than the entryway.

"I'm terribly sorry about the circumstances," Floyd said softly, "but I came to inform you that we have located your daughter Helen's body."

It took a few seconds for the information to sink in. When the meaning of the words hit, Colleen McCarthy sucked in a quick gasp. Tears glistened in her eyes as she asked, "You found Helen? Where? When?"

"You may have seen an article in the paper about a body found in the trunk of an abandoned car. The car was bought in Pine County and transported to the Twin Cities where the new owner found Helen's remains in the trunk. We made a positive identification over the weekend."

"Oh, God," McCarthy said as she covered her face with her hands. "I thought we'd never know what happened. This is so…so disturbing." She turned and walked toward an open doorway at the end of the small living room, pulling tissues from a pocket and holding them to her face.

The house was cluttered with furniture that looked like it had been purchased from the Salvation Army Store, or picked up from the curb on garbage day. Every piece was clean, but threadbare and all of the wood showed the scars of use. The floors were hardwood, but nearly black from a very old coat of shellac.

Colleen McCarthy walked to a chair in the small kitchen and sat down while she sobbed into the tissues. Kline and Floyd followed behind and stopped at the kitchen door taking in the old fashioned refrigerator with a domed top, and countertops covered with flowered linoleum that looked like it had been in place since the 1930's. They stood quietly until the sobbing stopped and the woman looked up. She seemed surprised to see them there.

"Is there anything we can do for you?" Floyd asked.

The woman's eyes were red and she blew her nose into the tissue and shook her head. "No."

Floyd took a business card from his pocket and walked across the kitchen. He set the card on the table. "If you have any questions, please give me a call."

"Where is she?" McCarthy asked. "Can I see her?"

Floyd glanced at Kline, then back to the woman. "The Bureau of Criminal Apprehension has her remains," he said. "There's really nothing much to see."

She searched Floyd's face for the meaning of his words. "Not much to see?" She asked.

"It appears she died shortly after her abduction," Floyd explained. "So, all that's left is a skeleton."

"A skeleton?"

"Yes, ma'am," Floyd said. "They identified her with dental records."

"But the kidnappers…"

"What about the kidnappers, ma'am?" Floyd asked.

"They would have kept her alive," she said, "or else they couldn't collect the ransom."

"We weren't aware there had ever been a ransom demand," Floyd said.

"I waited for them to call," McCarthy sobbed, again burying her face in the tissue.

"They never did call, did they?" Floyd asked.

"But we would have paid. I waited for them to call," she said, nearly pleading.

"We thought she had drowned in the lake," Floyd said. "What makes you believe she was kidnapped?"

"I just knew in my heart that she was alive. It had to be kidnappers."

Floyd knelt next to the table and took the woman's hand. "Is there something that happened since Helen's disappearance that makes you say that?"

"My ex-husband said that some sex fiend had taken her," McCarthy said, pulling her hand away from Floyd's grasp.

"You didn't believe that," Floyd said.

"Never!" She said, her face reddening with rage.

"If you're okay, we should be going," Kline said, giving Floyd a subtle nod toward the door.

The woman followed them to the door. "How do I arrange for a funeral?"

Floyd and Kline hesitated in the doorway. "I suggest you contact a funeral home. They can call the BCA to see when your daughter's remains can be released."

"Has anyone contacted my ex-husband yet?" she asked.

"He's been notified."

"I'll bet he was very smug," she said. "He always took great pride in being right."

"I think he was saddened by the news," Floyd said.

"He took great pride in killing babies," she said.

"Oh?" Kline asked, glancing at Floyd. "How's that?"

"He designed war plane stuff," she said. "He took great pride in how effective he could make it. I'll bet his planes killed a thousand children in Viet Nam."

"I was in Viet Nam," Kline said. "A lot of those kids tried to kill me."

McCarthy's eyes narrowed as she stared at Kline. "So," she said, "you're a baby killer, too. May God have mercy on your soul." The door slammed in their faces.

As they walked to the car a light drizzle started to fall. Kline started the engine and adjusted the heat. "You know," he said, "it's all Jane Fonda's fault."

Floyd gave a look of skepticism. "Jane Fonda?"

Kline put the car in gear and pulled down the street. "Yup. If she hadn't had her picture taken sitting in the anti-aircraft battery it wouldn't have been socially acceptable to be anti-war."

They drove a while in silence, then Kline added, "But I forgive her."

"Why do you forgive Jane Fonda?" Floyd asked.

"Because she's got a great body," Kline replied. "I saw her in Barbarella and she was really hot."

"You're a sick man, Kline." Floyd said with a smile.

"Hey!" Kline said. "Thinking about Jane Fonda's hot body is better than nightmares about dead bodies. Those are my only two memories of Viet Nam."

"What do you make of Colleen McCarthy?" Floyd asked.

"She's nuts. I think she may have dropped a few too many tabs of LSD during the protests, or maybe got her wiring messed up with some harder drugs. Most people outgrow the Don Quixote phase about the time they get their first real job and realize what it takes to put food on the table."

"I think you just answered the question. She's never had a real job."

CHAPTER 14

Tuesday

Floyd Swenson was sitting in the Sheriff's office updating him on the interaction with Colleen McCarthy when Pam Ryan stuck her head inside the sheriff's office, hazy with cigar smoke. The sheriff was a burly man with a gravelly baritone voice that played well on television sound bites. Although all public buildings were non-smoking by state law, the sheriff always had a cigar in his pocket and continued to smoke in his office.

"Excuse me," Pam said, "but we, on the day shift, are waiting for Floyd to send us on our assignments."

Floyd looked at his watch and realized that it was past seven o'clock. "Well," he said, "I think I'll check the names on the list of people I interviewed in '74 to see if any of them turned up in jail later."

The sheriff shook his head. "These cases out of the filing cabinet are tough. No one really expects us to crack them, but they expect us to put up a good effort." He stood and walked Floyd to the door and closed the door behind him.

As Pam and Floyd walked the hallway to the bullpen she asked, "Sheriff Sepanen doesn't really expect us to solve this case?"

"I don't see how anyone expects us to solve this," Floyd replied. "All the leads are cold and the people who were involved are hundreds of miles away."

"But we've got fresh leads," Pam complained. "Who knows, maybe they'll lead us in a different direction."

The hallway opened into the bullpen arranged with a dozen institutional desks, each with a computer. Deputies Sandy Maki and Kerm Rajacich were sitting with coffee cups in hand and their feet on desks. Floyd went directly to a table on the wall and poured himself a cup of coffee from a carafe that looked like it hadn't been washed in a decade.

"Okay," Floyd read from a clipboard and took a sip of coffee.

"This is terrible," he said pulling the cup from his lips. "It tastes like it was made with kerosene."

Sandy Maki leaned toward Pam, "Yesterday it tasted like pine tar, so I guess this is an improvement."

"Here are the assignments for the day. Hedvig Boquist called from Royalton Township and there is a sheep sitting on her doorstep that won't let her out of the house. I have a half dozen warrants and subpoenas to be served, and I have a list…"

At the word, list, Rajacich was up from his chair. "I'm on the sheep," he said. Being the most senior deputy, he had his choice of assignments. He grabbed his cap and stepped toward the door.

"I've heard that about you," Maki called after him. He stood up and put on his own cap.

Pam Ryan rolled her eyes. "Please, it's too early in the morning for sexual innuendo about farm animals."

"Since Pam is the rookie," Maki said, picking up the stack of warrants from Floyd's desk, "I'll let her take care of your list."

"Geez!" Pam protested, "Why do I always get 'the list'?"

Maki was gone and Pam found herself alone in the bullpen with Floyd. "So, what's the list?" she asked.

"I went through the notes I made when we interviewed all the people at the camp," Floyd replied. "I want to check every male name to see if they have a criminal record."

"Ah," Pam said. "The BCA suggested they may have continued a pattern of assaults."

"Violent people don't tend to turn into church secretaries," Floyd replied. "If they commit one crime, they usually commit more, and they trend toward increasing violence."

He picked up two sheets of paper from his desk and gave a page of handwritten names to Pam. "I'll split it with you," he said. "You get the first part of the alphabet and I'll take the last."

Dan Williams walked into the bullpen and poured himself a cup of coffee. “Floyd,” he said, “did you locate Colleen McCarthy?”

Floyd and Pam both rolled desk chairs back from their computers and stretched. “Hennepin County loaned me a detective,” Floyd replied. “We drove over to her house and told her the bad news.”

“How’d she take it?” Dan asked, taking a seat at an empty desk and drinking coffee with a grimace.

“About how you’d expect,” Floyd replied. “She shed a few tears and it took a while for her to get composed enough to talk. She had some interesting comments, like she thought that the girl had been kidnapped, and she’d waited for the kidnappers to call with a ransom demand.”

“Her ex-husband had mentioned that,” Dan said. “He had suspected foul play all along and even mentioned something about perverts and a cute kid. He said the wife had held out that the girl had been kidnapped and hoped for the call demanding a ransom.”

“The McCarthy woman sure had a lot of residual animosity for her ex-husband. She mentioned specifically his job working for a company making baby-killing aircraft for the Viet Nam war. She even got on the Hennepin County detective for being a Viet Nam vet.”

“Yup,” Dan said, nodding agreement. “The husband even mentioned that. He said she’d felt all the money he made was somehow dirty and she would have gladly paid it out in ransom. He said that she got half of it in the divorce settlement and thought she'd given it to a homeless shelter.

"What are you two doing today?" Dan asked.

"Pam volunteered to help me check the list of people I interviewed at the camp."

"Volunteered, my ass," Pam said. "Your other macho deputies bailed and left me stuck with a list of names to check for criminal records."

"That's very nice of you to volunteer," Dan said with a smirk.

Pam glanced at the computer screen and turned quickly to face it. "Hey! I got a hit." She punched a few keys, and then looked deflated. "Oh, this one's a big time criminal. He has three whole speeding tickets and a DWI."

"Perseverance pays," Floyd said.

"You know," she said as she entered another name, "this is not what they teach in criminology at college or the state patrol academy."

"Did Pam tell you about our visit with the forensic anthropologist and the entomologist?" Dan asked.

"No. We've been too consumed with our computers to get into much small talk."

Pam rolled her eyes. "It's more like my brain went numb with this mindless computer search."

"Anyway," Dan said, "the victim was apparently stabbed once with a fairly large knife by a right-handed assailant. The bugs in the trunk indicate the body decomposed over the summer. It probably smelled very bad, and the smell didn't go away for a couple months. Then we went over to the BCA. They had vacuumed the debris from the trunk. They found a couple of hairs that may be significant. One was a human pubic hair with an abnormality called 'ring hair'. That should help us narrow the field of potential suspects significantly. The other hair was from an animal, and it was something exotic. The BCA contacted an animal hair expert in Oregon and they were waiting for him to tell them what type of animal it belonged to."

"The agent said," Pam added, "that if the hair was from something exotic it may help us. People tend to remember exotic pets and their owners. Laurie Lone Eagle said she would run through the sex offenders on the computer on see if she got any matches for ring hair."

"I'm sure all that will be in your report," Dan said.

"Of course it will be," Pam replied, "as soon as I get a break from 'the list' to write it."

"Write while it's still fresh on your mind," Dan said as he got up from his chair. "I'll have Floyd go over to Pine Brook to see if Mary Jungers remembered anything new."

CHAPTER 15

The sign on the front door said Pine Brook Floral was open, but there was no sign of customers inside. A small bell rang over the front door as Floyd opened it. By the time Floyd walked past the rows of gifts, cards, and china cups, Mary Jungers was peeking out of the office, wiping crumbs from her chin and holding a sandwich in the other hand. She looked less haggard now that the rush of Prom had passed, and she wore an Eddie Bauer sweatshirt over blue jeans. On Saturday she had her hair tied up, probably to keep it out of the way as she and the others made corsages. Today she wore it down and the little bit of makeup she wore made her look younger, healthier, and far less frazzled.

"Hi, Floyd," Mary said. "You caught me sneaking an early lunch." She motioned for him to sit in the cramped office. "Let me get you a cup of coffee."

The office was much tidier than on his previous visit. The chairs had been cleared of supplies, and it appeared that Mary was working on financial accounts on the desktop computer. She joined him carrying two mugs emblazoned with the Teleflorist logo.

"You take it black," she said, "if I remember."

"Black is fine," he replied. He took a quick look at her ring finger as she handed him the cup.

"I'm a widow," Mary said.

Floyd felt his face flush, but realized the Mary was smiling.

"It's your memory that brings me back," Floyd said, trying to redirect the conversation.

"And I thought it was my fine coffee," she said playfully.

"We have a positive identification of the remains from the trunk. It was the girl who disappeared from the camp in '74."

Mary turned very sober. "I'm sorry to be flippant. I was just trying to be a good hostess."

"I know," Floyd said. "I hate to keep bringing up this morbid case." He took a sip of coffee and explained. "We got more information yesterday, and I'd like to ask some more questions now that I know more. I have to ask you not to share this information."

"Sure," Mary said, "I understand that you need to keep some details from the general public."

"The body was in the trunk of that car a long time. She might not have died there, but she certainly decomposed there, so the skeleton wasn't moved there any time recently." Floyd made sure Mary understood what he was saying, and then said, "So, there was a period of weeks or months where there would have been a terrible smell coming out of the trunk. Do you recall that at all?"

"I really don't," she replied. "The old outhouse is there too, and that was pretty ripe in the summer months. Do you think we would have noticed it over that?"

"Definitely," Floyd replied. "This would have been very strong and much different from the smell of an outhouse."

"I guess I just wasn't out there much. That area behind the barn and around the old cars was pretty spooky at that point in my life. My brothers might remember more, but they were even younger than I was. I doubt they would remember much."

"Can you remind me of their names and give me phone numbers?" Floyd asked. "I can call them and follow up directly."

"Sure," Mary said, grabbing a yellow pad of Post-it notes. She wrote out two names and put phone numbers next to them.

"There was one other interesting thing. They vacuumed the trunk of the car and sorted through all the fibers, hairs, and bug parts. They found an odd hair they couldn't identify. It wasn't human, and it wasn't from the normal range of household pets or barnyard animals. Do you remember that any of the boarders in the old streetcar ever had an unusual pet?"

"I guess I wouldn't know if any of them had any pets at all," Mary replied. "Like I said before, Mom didn't let me hang around the people who rented there. I never saw any big pets, like a tiger or llama. But, one of those guys could have had a small pet that didn't roam the yard, and I wouldn't have known."

Floyd finished his coffee and stood. "Well, thanks for the coffee and your time."

Mary walked Floyd to the front door. "You know," she said, "not all of the renters were old men. I'd forgotten, but there were a couple of young men who stayed there over the years. Mom made extra sure I stayed away from the barnyard when they were renting."

"Do you remember anything specific about them?"

"Well," she said, "what I remember most is that they were just as scary as the old ones. The best description I could offer was that they remind me of the guys who work at the carnival. You know the type, a little lean, like they haven't had a square meal in a while, and uneasy when you look at them too long. Their clothes are a little worn and maybe could use a wash."

"Do you remember any of their names?"

"Sorry," she said, "I know a million and none. Who knows if any of them gave us a real name anyway?"

"Are these home or work numbers?" Floyd said, looking at the phone numbers she'd written on the note.

"Robbie is always home," she said. "You remember him, he's quadraplegic."

"Yup. He was in the diving accident," Floyd said. "Is he doing okay?"

"He married his home health aide and now he writes children's books using a stick he holds in his teeth. I guess he's okay. Joe's number is his work number. He's married and his wife doesn't like our close relationship, so I call him at work."

"Thanks," Floyd said as he opened the door.

"The last number is my home, just in case you need to get in touch when the shop's closed." She hesitated, and then asked, "Do you think the girl died in the trunk?"

"There's not enough evidence to say."

"What do you think?" Mary asked.

"We can't be sure."

"I understand that you can't be sure," she said. "But, what do you *think*?"

Floyd stared at the note and considered his words. "I think that she was killed before she went into the trunk. The car was just a convenient place to hide the body."

"But, she probably died on the farm."

"Probably, but I doubt we'll ever be sure."

A shudder ran over Mary's body. "It's so sad." She quickly reached out and pulled Floyd into a hug. "I'm sorry, but I really need to hold someone right now."

"Yup," he responded, not trusting his voice to utter another word without breaking. Floyd gently patted her back as he felt the spasms of sobs wrack her body and as tears welled in his eyes.

✲ ✲ ✲

"Doesn't anyone eat lunch around here?" Dan asked as he walked into the bullpen, breaking Pam and Floyd's concentration on their computers.

"Is it finally that time?" Floyd asked as he rolled his shoulders.

Pam was up and putting on her jacket before Floyd finished his response. "Where are we going?" she asked. "I'd be willing to eat sawdust rather than enter another name in the computer."

They drove to Nichol's Café, across the street from the old courthouse and took a booth in the corner. Pam hung her jacket on a peg next to the booth and announced, "Order me a diet Coke," as she headed for the rest room.

"How's it going?" Dan asked as he slid into the bench across from Floyd and pulled the laminated menus from a slot behind the sugar container.

"Slow," Floyd replied. "We're almost through the list and we haven't hit any pay dirt yet."

"Did you think you would?" Dan asked, slowly looking around the restaurant, scanning faces and nodding to a few local businessmen. He noted a lone stranger, who appeared to be a salesman reading a newspaper by himself. He relaxed, a bit, confident that none of the patrons appeared ready to assault them physically or verbally.

"You never know what'll pay off. Sometimes you get answers in the most unlikely places."

"Speaking of unlikely places," Dan said, "are you going back to the nursing home?"

"I was hoping to narrow the list down to a couple of names and then I thought I'd drop them to see how my old friend reacted."

"What old friend would that be?" Pam asked as she slid in next to Floyd. She squirmed to adjust the bulletproof vest worn under her uniform shirt.

"The cook from the camp is in a nursing home," he said. "I've talked to her a couple times, but she's been either confused or evasive."

"Take me along next time," Pam said. "Little old ladies like me."

Floyd and Dan exchanged a glance. "Little old men like you, too." Dan added.

"What's not to like?" Floyd asked. "You're young, cute, polite, and bright."

Pam decided it was better to change the direction of the conversation, judging by the smirks on Dan and Floyd's faces. "Floyd, what did you find out from the flower store?"

Pam waved at someone, and Dan turned as John Sepanen, the sheriff, made his way around the tables filled with the lunch crowd. The sheriff was a consummate politician, shaking hands and joking with everyone who looked old enough to vote. Dan slid over to make room on the bench next to him.

"So," the sheriff said as he slid into the booth, "all the troops sneak out for lunch and leave the old man sitting at his desk reading budget requests."

"Sorry," Dan said. "We were caught up in the discussion of the Smith investigation. You slipped my mind."

"What's the latest?" the sheriff asked.

Dan reviewed the investigation while the sheriff read the menu. The waitress interrupted the discussion while she took their orders.

"Any possible suspects?" the sheriff asked as the waitress walked away.

"We're checking through the list of people we looked at when the girl disappeared," Floyd said. "Pam and I are more than halfway through the list, but no one jumps out so far. I spoke with the camp cook, and she seems to know something, but she's a little confused and she hasn't named any names. She's hinted that the girl may have left with someone willingly."

"Laurie Lone Eagle," Pam said, "is going though the database of sex crime offenders to see if she can find any references to convicts with ring hair."

They stopped talking as the waitress delivered three cups of coffee and a Diet Coke. "The kitchen's backed up a little," she said. "But, I moved your orders up in the pile. I know you guys sometimes don't get a lot of time to eat."

"Thanks," Floyd said. As the waitress left he went on, "I spoke with Mary Jungers, from Pine Brook Floral. Her family owned the farm at the time of the disappearance. She didn't have much to add, other than the fact that they rented out an old streetcar to transients after her father died. She said most of them were scary, and she didn't know any names. The one thing she added today is that there were a couple of younger men who rented too. She didn't remember the exact timing of them being there, but she said they looked like carnival workers; kind of lean and mean, with straggly hair."

The sheriff pondered the information as he took a drink from his coffee. "So, what happens next?" he asked.

"Pam and I," Floyd said, "will finish cross-checking the list of people I interviewed with the criminal database to see if we find anyone who is a sex offender. Then we'd talked about going back to talk to the cook again in the nursing home tomorrow. We thought maybe she would open up to Pam better than she has to me."

"I can't go tomorrow," Pam said. "I've got three days off, then I rotate to night shift."

"I'll authorize the overtime for you to come in tomorrow," Dan said. "Then if we hit something hot, I'll swap you onto days for a while. I think Floyd should call Mary Jungers' brothers to see if they remember anything about the rotten smell in the car, or any of the men who rented the streetcar. We should search the streetcar on the Benson farm for ring hair and exotic pet hair."

The waitress was back with their sandwiches. They were silent while she delivered the plates, but it was obvious that something was on the sheriff's mind. He looked over his shoulder to make sure she was out of earshot.

"It's great that you guys are fired up about this," he said, "but this is a thirty year-old murder. Most of the suspects are long gone, and the chances of getting enough evidence together to get a conviction after all these years are almost nil. I don't know that I want to pay overtime and sink a lot of additional effort into an investigation that's got no chance of leading anywhere."

"How bad is the budget?" Dan asked reading between the lines of the sheriff's expressed concerns.

"We're about eleven thousand over," Sepanen replied. "We had to add another deputy to security after we moved to the new courthouse."

"But we cut back on all kinds of stuff," Floyd protested.

"And, that's why we're only eleven thousand over," Sepanen said. "If not for the economization everywhere else we'd be a hundred and eleven thousand over."

"We can't ignore this," Dan said, almost in a whisper. "This is a murder investigation. We have to put everything we can into it, and we have to pursue every lead."

"Let me lay it out from my perspective," the sheriff said. "There is a county board member who lives in Sandstone – I won't name any names – but, that person has served notice that if this department is one dollar over budget at the end of the fiscal year, heads will roll."

Dan and Pam smiled, aware that only one county board member lived in Sandstone so the sheriff had effectively named names. "Surely, that won't be an issue if we solve this murder?" Pam asked.

"Would you care to bet your job on solving this murder?" the sheriff asked. "Because that's what it will come down to. We would have to cut some jobs. You're the least senior road deputy, Pam, so you could probably bump one of the lower seniority bailiffs. But, you'd have to move into the courtroom."

"That sucks," Pam said.

"That's politics," Dan said.

Floyd had been quiet through the whole discussion. He leaned forward and said, "I'll bet my job on it. I had the pension board send retirement papers last week. If we don't solve this before the end of the month I'll sign the papers for an immediate retirement. That'll give you eight months without my salary to get the spending in line."

Sepanen looked surprised. "You're going to file for retirement?" he asked Floyd.

"Like I said, if we don't solve this before the end of the month I'm outta here."

Pam put her hand on Floyd's. "Don't do that," she said. "I can work as a bailiff until another road position opens up. It's not a big deal."

"No," Floyd said, shaking his head, "I've been haunted by this crime for over thirty years. If we can't crack it in a couple weeks, I don't want to hang around."

"But, you'll stay on if we solve it?" Dan asked.

"I'll be open to discussion," Floyd replied. "Let's see what happens with the investigation, and how the county board responds to the results. This opens the possibility that I can be the scapegoat if the investigation goes down the tubes. I'll retire and leave with all the blame."

The sheriff's face remaining impassive, but Dan could see that he liked the concept of having a budget out and a scapegoat if the investigation bore no fruit. "I don't like this arrangement," Dan said. "We're all in this together. I don't want the whole thing dumped on Floyd's shoulders."

"No, Dan," Floyd said emphatically. "I feel like I screwed up the original investigation. I left too many leads dangling without follow up, and took too many statements at face value when I should've been digging for deeper answers. It's only fair that I take the fall if we can't wrap it up now. Besides, it's not much of a fall. I was going to retire anyway. What am I losing?"

They finished their lunches in silence and the sheriff picked up the bill. "You folks wrap up the investigation like you think it should be pursued," he said. "We'll deal with the fallout later."

Dan heard the words, but knew the political pressure that could be brought to bear on the sheriff could be merciless. Someone would have to take the fall if they didn't bring a murderer to trial after spending a small fortune on the investigation.

CHAPTER 16

Tuesday afternoon

Floyd went to his desk and took out the Post-it note with the phone numbers for Mary Jungers' brothers. He dialed Rob's number first. When a woman answered the phone, he asked for Rob Benson.

"Hello."

"Rob, this is Floyd Swenson, from the Pine County Sheriff's Department. I'd like to ask you a couple questions."

"Hi, Floyd. Mary said you'd be calling." Floyd had been the investigator assigned to Rob's diving accident, which had caused his paralysis. Floyd had spoken to Rob several times in the hospital and again at home shortly after the accident.

"I assume that Mary told you about the remains we found in the car trunk. I need to know what you remember about that specific car, and the person who was living in the streetcar the summer the girl disappeared."

"You know," Rob said, "I was in grade school when the girl disappeared and I didn't pay much attention to the news as a kid. I can't really recall anything specific about things that happened then."

"Do you remember a summer when there was a terrible, rotten smell coming from one of the cars?"

"I don't know," Rob replied. "There was always something spooky about them. I guess I always thought they smelled kinda rotten. Lots of the windows were broken and the insides were rotten and smelled of mold. I remember mice running out of the upholstery when we'd sit on the seats."

"This would've been stronger than rotten upholstery," Floyd said. "This would have turned your stomach and driven you away."

"I guess I don't remember anything smelling that bad," Rob replied, "But there were a couple of the renters who were pretty spooky even to Mom. There were times when she wouldn't let us go out to the barn or play in the cars."

Floyd drew an image of a mother so desperate for money that she had to take in character's she was afraid to have her children around. As Floyd remembered it from his visit after the diving accident, the Benson house had been net as a pin, but with the house in need of paint, and every piece of furniture distressed and unmatched. He had a vague memory of a fund-raising dance that had been held to pay off Rob's medical expenses. The family didn't have insurance, and they had no way to ever come up with funds to cover the doctor and hospital bills. They'd set Rob up on a bed in the living room and had volunteers from the March of Dimes come out for his physical therapy.

"Do you remember any names of the spooky ones?" Floyd asked.

"There were so many of them," Rob said. "Most were there a couple months and left. Some just disappeared. I remember that Mom made them pay in advance because they were all pretty seedy. I remember a few names. I heard Jack, Carl, and Albert, but I can't tie any of them to a face or a particular year."

"Do you remember any of them having an unusual pet?"

"Whew!" Rob said. "I don't remember any of them having a pet at all. I don't think there was ever a dog or cat around. We had a few barn cats, and they didn't tolerate strange animals very well. On the other hand, if any of them had a pet inside the streetcar we would never have known. We were strictly forbidden from going inside the streetcar."

"Well, if you think of anything, please give me a call at the sheriff's department," Floyd said. Then he asked, "How are you doing? I haven't seen you in a few years."

"I'm okay," Rob replied. "I appreciate you asking. I got married a couple years ago, and now I spend the days writing. I've got a couple children's books in print, in case you need reading materials for a grandchild."

"No grandchildren," Floyd said, "But I'll keep that in mind if the day comes." He hesitated, and then added, "I was worried about your state of mind after the accident. I was afraid you'd given up."

"I had for a while. Then, I met Marge, and she got me focused on making plans and moving ahead instead of grieving over what I'd lost."

"That's great, Rob. If you think of anything else, please call."

Pam Ryan was standing at Floyd's desk when finished the phone call. He could see by the expression on her face that she was pleased about something.

"We have a suspect!" she announced as she walked to Dan's office. "His name is Ryan Martin."

"Is he off the list of people Floyd interviewed?" Dan asked.

"Floyd never actually spoke with him," Pam replied. "He was off for a couple days when the girl disappeared, but he was on the list of employees. C'mon, you've got to see his rap sheet."

"He's got quite a court history," Floyd said as he pushed back from the computer screen. "Take a look."

Dan sat at the desk and read through the list of charges and convictions that Ryan Martin had amassed in his forty-nine years of life. He had turned eighteen in the spring of '74, so any criminal activity before that was in sealed files in the juvenile courts. He'd been charged with assault and burglary in St. Louis County the November after Helen Smith's disappearance. After that his crimes had become increasingly violent including numerous assaults, and two rapes. One of the rapes had been apparently plea-bargained down to third-degree sexual contact, and the other had been dropped. Most recently, he had been serving a four-year term in Wisconsin for attempted murder. He'd been released in the previous few weeks.

"We can find him," Dan said as he pushed away from the computer and wrote the name on a note pad. "I'll put a call in to Wisconsin Corrections. He should've registered as a sex offender, so they should know exactly where he lives. With any luck, he's got a diligent parole officer who's keeping close tabs on him."

Floyd picked up the Post-it note with the Benson brother's phone numbers. He dialed Joe Benson's number and waited as it rang six times. A woman's electronic voice announced that Mister Benson was away from his phone. Floyd left his name and phone number on the recorder.

Pam was back at her computer again. "Looking for more suspects?" Dan asked, as he looked over Pam's shoulder

"We only had half a dozen names left," she replied. "We might as well check all of them, just in case we had another with a record."

"You said you hadn't interviewed the Martin guy back in '74," Dan said to Floyd as he popped two Tums into his mouth to counteract the heartburn from the lunch. "Why not?"

"I looked at the notes, and he was off for a few days. I think there was some sort of disciplinary problem, but I really can't recall the details. My notes said that he wasn't around the camp when I was interviewing people."

"That might be a topic for Grace Palm," Dan suggested. "She might have a clear memory of that if there was something significant involved in his absence."

Floyd wrote a note to himself. "There might be a number of people who could remember Ryan Martin, especially if he were a troublemaker. I'll call the two kitchen helpers and run the name past them, too."

The dispatcher's voice paged Floyd over the intercom. He picked up the flashing line at the end desk in the bullpen. "Sergeant Swenson."

"Deputy Swenson, this is Joe Benson. You left a message for me to call."

"Yeah," Floyd said, shifting mental gears. "I wanted to ask you some questions about the junk cars behind the barn at your old farm."

"Mary has called me a couple times about them," Joe replied. "I told her most of what I remember, but I'd be happy to answer your questions, too."

"I assume you know that we recovered human remains from the trunk of the blue Dodge," Floyd said. "We believe that the victim was killed and her body put into the trunk to decompose and that probably happened soon after her disappearance in '74. The experts said that would have caused a terrible smell as the body decomposed. Do you remember that?"

"Well," Joe said, "I would have been eight years-old in '74. So, I suppose that was between second and third grade. What I remember is that we used to play in the old cars a lot. But Robbie and I got in trouble when I got locked inside one of them. Mom took all the keys and put them up so we couldn't get to them anymore.

"You know, there's one funny thing about that blue car," Joe said. "The keys weren't in it. I remember playing in all the others, but we never played in the Dodge because the trunk was locked up and there weren't any keys for it. No, there were keys when I was really little, but then they were gone when Mom took all the others. I remember her yelling at us, because she thought we'd hidden the Dodge keys. They disappeared before Mom took away the other ones."

"That's interesting," Floyd said, as he made notes. "How about the smell?"

"I don't remember a bad smell. But there was one year Mom didn't let us play out there."

"Do you remember why," Floyd asked.

"Too well!" Joe said, with a chuckle. "There was a guy staying in the old streetcar. Mom caught us peeking in the windows when he had a girlfriend over. Mom tanned our hides, then forbid us to go anywhere near the barn, the streetcar, or the old cars."

"One of the old transients had a girlfriend?"

"He wasn't old," Joe replied. "I'd guess he was maybe twenty. He was different from most of the other guys who rented. Most were like hermits and didn't have cars or friends. The young guy drove a beat up Chev and there seemed to be too many people who visited him at all hours of the day and night."

"I'm surprised Mary didn't mention him," Floyd said. "That seems like something a young girl would remember."

"Huh," Joe said, "That's an interesting point. I guess it was because Robbie and I shared the bedroom that faced the streetcar, and her bedroom was on the other side of the house. We could hear all the cars come and go, and all the people laughing when they were standing around outside." He paused, and then added, "It must have been summer. I remember it vividly I slept on an old rollaway bed under the open window, so I heard a lot of what was going on."

"Tell me about what kinds of things were going on."

"I learned a lot of four-letter words!" Joe replied. "I also learned about Viet Nam, and dodging the draft. There were some girls over one night who didn't like the streetcar because it smelled and was kind of messy inside. The guys seemed to think it was cool. I learned that Buckhorn beer was cheap, and that there was a liquor store on highway twenty-three that sold to minors. I learned that Marlboros caused impotence, although I didn't know what impotence was for another ten years."

"Did you ever hear names?" Floyd asked.

"Mostly nicknames. Things like, shit head and asshole."

"I'll bet there were a few more choice than those."

Joe laughed. "Not that I care to mention from my cubicle with three female coworkers within earshot."

"The remains in the trunk belonged to a girl named Helen Smith," Floyd said. "Is that name familiar?"

"I think so." Joe said, after a pause, "But I don't know why."

"How about Ryan Martin?" Floyd asked. "Is that name familiar?"

"I think the guy who rented the streetcar that summer might've been named Ryan. I think I remember that name when the guys were talking outside. Yeah, I think one of the guys told Ryan that he had a real sweet setup in the streetcar."

"Did you know that Ryan worked at Melody Pines camp?" Floyd asked.

"I don't know," Joe replied. "I might have known that, but it's not jumping out at me."

"Can you remember any other names," Floyd asked. "Do you remember if any of the other people you heard were local?"

"I was a kid," Joe said, "and the people who were partying there were a lot older. I doubt that I would have known any of them."

"I can't think of anything else to ask right now," Floyd said. "If you think of anything else, give me a call at this number."

Floyd dialed Rob Benson's number and was surprised when Rob answered the phone himself. "Rob, this is Floyd Swenson again. I have some new information and a couple new questions for you."

"That was quick."

"Sometimes things come up," Floyd said. "Do you remember the summer a young man, named Ryan, lived in the streetcar?"

"Wow!" Rob said, "That's a name from the past. I recognize it now that you've mentioned it."

"Besides getting in trouble for window peeping, what else can you tell me about Ryan's time in the streetcar?"

"There were lots of parties," Rob said, "and Mom was really pissed about all the people coming and going. Actually, I think Mom was pissed at all the girls coming and going and all the commotion late at night."

"Do you remember any of the people who partied with Ryan?"

"I think most of them were strangers. I don't remember many names being said unless someone was swearing at someone else. Joe had the bed under the window, so I don't remember looking at the people. Besides, that old streetcar is like fifty yards from the house. I don't think we could see many faces."

"Who was the girl with Ryan when you peeked through the window?" Floyd asked.

"It wasn't a girl," Rob replied. "I didn't see her face, but she was definitely an older woman."

"Did she drive her own car in?" Floyd asked, "Or, did she ride in with Ryan?"

"I don't remember."

"How did you know that there was something to see?"

"I don't remember," Rob said. "Wait! We were playing outside and we heard noises inside the streetcar."

"And you're sure it was an older woman?"

Rob chuckled. "Oh, yes. I'd never seen a young woman naked before, and it took a few years before I realized that his partner was probably in her forties. Let's say her figure was more matronly than a teenaged girl. Her drooping breasts are etched in my mind."

"I'll bet getting caught by your mother was a real surprise."

"She snuck up on us and dragged Joe and I back to the house by our ears. When we got home, she found dad's old belt and beat the curiosity out of us. That was a pretty high price for a glimpse of boobs and wide hips."

"Did you get a look at the woman's face?"

"I don't know. I think I was so shocked at seeing all that flesh that it never occurred to me to look at her face."

"That happens a lot when people are exposed to unexpected nudity," Floyd said with a laugh. "There was a guy robbing Twin Cities stores in the nude, and no one could describe his face. They only remembered that he'd been circumcised." Floyd paused, and then added, "The girl whose remains were found, was named Helen Smith. Does that name sound familiar?"

"I can't say it does."

"Do you remember if Ryan had an exotic pet of some kind?"

"I really don't remember anyone in the streetcar having a pet."

"Think about this some," Floyd said, "and see if anything else comes to mind. Give me a call."

Floyd dialed the flower shop and Mary Jungers answered on the second ring. "Hi, Mary. It's Floyd Swenson with more questions."

"I thought you ran out," she said. "Actually, I kinda hoped that you'd run out. Every time you call it dredges up all kinds of gruesome images of skeletons in car trunks."

"Sorry about the gruesome mental images. Every time I talk to you I think of people being murdered for screwed up flower orders."

"You know, this is kind of like Columbo. You get all the answers, then call back a little later with one more question that came to mind." Mary paused, "Does this mean that I'm a prime suspect and you're just waiting to slap the cuffs on me?"

"I've never been compared to Columbo before. That's quite a compliment because he always solved every crime and did it in an hour. And don't worry about being accused of the crime, I've never arrested a woman who runs a floral shop for murder. They all feed me coffee and rolls, and no one who buys me rolls is a murderer."

"I wouldn't be so sure about that! I might be on the long-term plan to kill you off by raising your cholesterol leading to a heart attack. You'll never suspect it because you'll be on a sugar high."

"Actually," Floyd said, "I thought I'd run out of questions, but we've got a couple more leads. I spoke with both your brothers, and we may have a thread from them. Do you remember a young man who rented the streetcar named Ryan Martin?"

"The name Ryan sounds familiar," she said. "But I don't remember the last name, and I can't tie it to a face."

"He rented the summer the boys got punished for peeking in the window when Ryan was entertaining a lady friend. Does that sound familiar?"

"Sorry," she said, "I don't remember that."

"Do you recall an older woman visiting Ryan in the streetcar?"

"I remember cars coming and going, but most were older cars with teenaged boys and girls. I don't remember anyone I would call an adult hanging around."

"The boys said he threw a lot of noisy parties that summer. They learned a lot of four-letter words and how to use them in proper context."

Mary laughed out loud. "I always wondered where those words came from. But, I don't remember the parties or Ryan."

"The boys said you were all forbidden from going near the streetcar, barn, or old cars that summer. Does that jar your memory?"

"There was a scary, young guy who lived in the streetcar one summer," Mary said as the memories slowly returned. "He was really skinny, and kind of mean. He had really long brown hair, and he wore a beaded headband. I remember that he used to leer at me in a way that made me scared. One time he offered me a cigarette. On the days when it was too hot to be inside I remember seeing him leaning against the side of the streetcar smoking cigarettes. He'd watch me mowing the grass, and he'd smile a kind of wicked grin when I noticed him watching. The problem was, every time I was outside and happened to look his way he was watching me. I remember hanging clothes on the line one day when two of them were watching me. They kind of leered at me and talked back and forth. They started to walk over and I ran in the house and locked the door."

"You were about fourteen that summer?"

"I don't know for sure. I'd guess I was somewhere between fourteen and fifteen," she said. "And he wasn't that much older, but somehow I knew he was a dirty old man. On the other hand, there were a bunch of men who lived there and I caught most of them staring at me when I was in the yard. It was a kind of scary place to live for a few years. I used to lock my bedroom door at night." As she spoke, her voice lost its confidence.

"Are you okay?" Floyd asked.

"Like I said, it was a sad and scary part of my life. I'm glad it's behind me. I'm a lot happier as a successful adult than I ever was as a timid teenager."

"Did you know any of the people who came over to party with Ryan?"

"I didn't even realize there were parties going on," she said. "I'm sorry but I can't help."

"Please give me a call if you think of anything else."

"I wish you'd stop telling me that. I'd rather forget about the dirty old men in that streetcar than try to remember anything more."

CHAPTER 17

Wednesday

The morning editions of both Twin Cities newspapers carried a small article about the identification of the Pine County remains buried near the obituaries. The killer found that terribly insulting. He threw the papers in the wastebasket, then reconsidered and retrieved the papers so he could cut out the articles. He turned on the light and admired the shrine and his trophies from his loves. When he walked around the room they swayed as his motion disturbed the still air.

Opening the top drawer and taking out the album brought a tingle of excitement like he hadn't felt in a few years. He opened it to the page with the articles about Helen Smith as he felt a little rush of adrenaline. He re-read all the accounts before putting the new clippings into the album. He hadn't realized how much joy reading those old articles would bring until years later. By then, the newspapers were long gone and he's had to steal them from the library. Back in the eighties the libraries actually kept old newspapers instead of putting them all immediately onto microfilm.

He read through all the articles, from the first, when they thought that poor Helen had drowned, to the later ones where they speculated on kidnapping. Then, the articles stopped. The stupid cops didn't know what had happened, and after a few days there were bigger news items to grab the interest of the fickle public. Helen disappeared from the headlines, and then from the inside pages. The cops moved on to other things, but felt a certain passion linger for her. She'd been so young and naïve, believing all that he told her. Right up until… His heart was pounding and he felt a stirring. Finally, the drugs were wearing off. Finally, he could feel happiness, sadness, hunger, and passion without the moderating effect of the drugs. They brought everything to a nauseating and boring middle ground where he could function as *they* thought he should be. Day to day humdrum with nothing to look forward to but a meager check that paid the rent and bought groceries. He craved more, and now, drug free, he could pursue it.

He put the album away, then reached up, and touched his trophy from Helen. He closed his eyes and he could bring back the memories of her face, her dark hair, her creamy skin, her tiny breasts with the hard nipples, the athletic sock tied behind her head to muffle her screams, and the fear in her eyes when he drew out the knife.

CHAPTER 18

"Why'd you decide to wear the party dress?" Floyd asked after picking Pam up at the courthouse for their drive to the nursing home. She'd curled her hair and wore a yellow sundress with a pink belt. The white sandals and polished, pink toe nails were a far cry from the black oxford shoes she wore with her uniform.

"I thought it might seem less threatening than a uniform," Pam replied as she slipped into the seat and modestly tucked the hem of the dress under her legs before buckling the seat belt. "You said that she's been keeping a secret from the cops, so maybe I'm not a cop today."

"Seems unfair to trick a confused old woman. I like it!"

"What's Dan doing today?" Pam asked as they started through Pine City as the business day started. Shop owners were opening their doors, and there was a line of cars at the Holiday gas station where people were waiting to buy a newspaper, doughnut, and cup of coffee. Two men were having a quiet conversation that they interrupted to give Pam and Floyd a wave as they passed the A&W. One was dressed in the farmer's uniform of denim overalls over a plaid short-sleeve shirt. He wore a green John Deere cap. The other was the county farm agent, dressed in jeans and a denim shirt. He had a clipboard and was taking copious notes about the conversation.

"Dan's calling Laurie Lone Eagle to see if the BCA can push Wisconsin on Ryan Martin's current address. Then, he was going to start picking the streetcar apart."

"It seems strange that we wouldn't get a quick response on an inquiry on a convicted felon."

"We usually do," Floyd replied, "if we have a warrant. If we're just interested in talking to them, or knowing their whereabouts, the response isn't as fast. I think it's all the cutbacks. Everyone in law enforcement is too busy to deal quickly with anything that's not life threatening these days."

"Now that you've been in Pine County a year, how do the Jack Pine savages compare to Blue Earth farmers?" Floyd asked after a few minutes of silence.

"It's a little strange to be hemmed in by all the trees here," Pam said. "In Blue Earth, you can see for miles in every direction. And it's pretty strange having a swamp no more than a couple hundred yards in any direction. In Blue Earth, they were drained to make more farmland. Up here, no one seems to care if there's a swamp on their land."

"Are the people any different?"

"Are they ever," Pam replied. "In Blue Earth, the farmers all try to get along with each other. They share farm equipment, and they help each other during harvest. Up here, the people are so independent. I guess that the Jack Pine Savage image really fits some of the rural folks. The downtown people are really nice, but a lot of the people out in the boonies moved here to get away from civilization. It's kind of creepy to walk up to some of those old farmsteads, say nothing of the hunting shacks with tarpaper siding never knowing who or what's inside."

"Now," Pam said, "It's your turn. Are you really going to retire?"

"I thought I would. Aren't you planning to retire someday, too?"

"You're avoiding the question, Floyd. Maybe I should have asked why you're going to retire *now*?"

"I don't get any more pension by staying on longer. There's nothing here to keep me around anymore. I'm getting cynical and tired. Those are three good reasons."

Pam considered Floyd's comments for a few miles. "You've never been in this job because of the salary, pension, or the glory. I can see that you do it because you love the job and the people in the department."

"I'm obsolete and I want to get out before I'm incompetent. I screwed up this investigation thirty years ago, and now it looks like it's too late to retrieve it and find the murderer."

"You weren't the only person investigating the murder in '74, and it's not your personal responsibility that it wasn't solved. Besides, everyone thought it was a drowning, not a murder!"

"I don't see it that way," was Floyd's reply.

Floyd drove past highway sixty-five and turned onto Main Street in Mora. After a few blocks he pulled into a parking spot in front of the bakery.

"We're picking up baked goods?" Pam asked.

"Grace likes Russian Tea Cakes," he replied as he exited the car. In three minutes he was back with a white bag.

Pam and Floyd asked for Deb McIntosh at the front desk, and waited patiently while the high school aged receptionist paged her. It took almost ten minutes for the head nurse to come to the entry.

"Hello, sergeant," the nurse said. "I see you brought a friend along today." She was wearing aqua surgical scrubs and had her graying hair pinned back tightly. Her smile was broad and her handshake solid. Everything about her was disarming and non-threatening; the perfect persona for the nursing home setting.

"Deb McIntosh, this is Deputy Pam Ryan. We're hoping Pam might be able to break through the ice with Mrs. Palm."

"I see you brought your own cookies," McIntosh said, nodding to the white bag while shaking Pam's hand. "I suppose you'd like to meet with Grace in the dining room over a cup of coffee." Deb led them through a wide hallway with handrails attached to both sides. The décor consisted of jigsaw puzzles that the residents had solved and then glued to thin sheets of cardboard. The subject matter varied from flower gardens, to puppies, to maps.

The kitchen staff were setting the tables for lunch, but had left a corner table clear. Smells of roast pork and cherry glaze emanated from the kitchen along with the clattering of pots and pans. Floyd hung his jacket over the back of a chair and went to the kitchen to find coffee and cups. Before he returned, the head nurse walked into the room with Grace Palm, who was using a cane for support as she walked with caution. She was more stooped and seemed to study the floor before taking each step. She wore dark blue slacks and a print blouse with large red flowers. Her orthopedic shoes seemed too large for her feet and she seemed to struggle to get them firmly planted before taking her next step.

"You must be Mrs. Palm," Pam said, as she pulled a chair back for Grace.

Grace smiled cordially. "It's nice of you to visit," she said. "But I don't recall your name. Have we met before?"

"My name is Pam Ryan, and we haven't met before," Pam said as she helped Grace get settled in her chair. "But, I have a friend who's met you before and he invited me along. We would like to talk about the summer you were the cook at Melody Pines Camp."

Grace appeared to miss most of Pam's introduction, having been distracted by the bakery bag. "Are those cookies?" she asked as she lowered herself into the chair slowly.

The head nurse waved a discreet goodbye as Pam slid the bag over. "I believe they are," Pam said. "Would you like one?"

Grace was totally focused on the cookie bag. "Yes," she replied, "I would like a cookie. What kind are they?"

"Well," Pam said, "I don't know. My friend bought them downtown and he didn't say." She looked into the bag and didn't recognize them. Taking one out, she handed the small ball, dusted with powdered sugar, to Grace. "I don't know what they are called."

"I think it's a Russian Tea cake," Grace said, accepting the cookie from Pam. "They're my favorite," she said as crumbs dribbled off her lips.

"We were talking about Melody Pines, and we came across the name of a man that you might know," Pam said as she rolled the top of the bakery bag down so she could reach in more easily. "Do you remember Ryan Martin?"

Grace finished the first cookie and rubbed her bony fingers together, effectively spreading the powdered sugar evenly over them. The skin on her hands appeared to be paper thin and blue veins protruded in wandering trails "He was a stinker," Grace replied. Her focus again went to the bag. "May I have another cookie?"

Pam pushed the bag across the table, so it sat in front of Grace. "Why do you say he was a stinker?" Pam asked. Out of the corner of her eye she could see Floyd standing at the door holding cups and a carafe of coffee. He nodded and motioned for her to go on.

Grace tipped the bag to look in. When she did, two cookies spilled onto the table. "Oh my, I've spilled sugar on the table," she said. Then she picked up a cookie and put the whole thing in her mouth. She swept the spilled sugar into her hand with painful deliberation, and the rubbed her hands clean over the floor.

Pam repeated the question, "You said Ryan Martin was a stinker. Was he a troublemaker?"

"He got in a lot of trouble," Grace replied, fumbling the other cookie in her fingers until it was oriented with the top up. "He got fired, you know."

"No, I didn't know that," Pam replied. "Why was he fired?"

"He was bad," Grace said, "and the camp director told him to stay away." She took a bite that removed half a cookie and chewed it, obviously savoring the flavor. "Russian tea cakes are my favorite cookie," she mumbled while chewing.

"What bad thing did he do?" Pam asked. Seeing Grace looking for something to wipe her fingers on, Pam reached over to the next table and took a paper napkin from the dispenser.

"We never heard," Grace replied as she wiped her fingers on the bunched napkin. "But, those girls who worked with me said they caught him smoking dope." She dug in the bag and took out two more cookies. One fell from her grasp and rolled off the table.

"Was he in other trouble too?" Pam asked as she knelt down to pick up the errant cookie.

"Of course he was," Grace replied. "That's why he stayed out on Benson's farm. They wouldn't let him stay with the campers like the rest of the counselors."

"Did he do something at camp?" Pam asked. "Is that why he had to stay at Benson's?"

Grace wiped her fingers on the napkin and reached into the bag for another cookie. "Oh no," she said. "He was in trouble at home. That's why he had to work at the camp for the summer."

"Do you know his family?"

Grace stopped, with a cookie halfway to her mouth. "I think so," She said. "I think his auntie worked at the camp. Didn't Mary Martin work in the laundry? She was a big, hard woman, but she had a heart of gold when you got through the crust."

Pam had been so focused on finding a male suspect that she didn't recall the names of any female camp employees. "Why yes," Pam said, bluffing, "Mary worked in the laundry. She was pretty upset with Ryan, wasn't she?" She said it loud enough that Floyd could hear one side of the discussion from several feet away.

"Mmm," Grace mumbled. "I would have been too if my nephew had been in trouble like that."

"Did you know Mary Martin well?"

"We weren't close friends," Grace replied, "but we were the only older women working at the camp, so we talked a lot."

"Did Ryan get in trouble because of the Smith girl?"

Grace stopped chewing and rolled her tongue around the inside of her teeth while she studied Pam's face. "You're the same age as those campers. Were you there?"

"No," Pam said, nodding. "I just heard about it lately."

"Ryan's friend," Grace said. "He got that Smith girl pregnant and they had to run away to do the right thing."

Pam motioned for Floyd to join them as Grace continued to talk. "Mary never knew the other boy's name, but Ryan told her about it. I think Ryan stole a boat from the beach house to take the Smith girl to visit his friend. I remember that the head lifeguard was really mad that Ryan took a boat out in the middle of the night, especially when he wasn't supposed to be at the camp at night."

Floyd set the coffee cups on the table, and caught the end of Grace's conversation. He poured three cups of coffee and set cups in front of each of them.

Grace looked up at him without recognition in her eyes. "You're a cop," she said.

"Actually, I'm a deputy sheriff," Floyd said. "We spoke earlier this week and you told me you liked Russian tea cakes."

"This girl brought a bag of them," Grace said, reaching for another cookie. "Do you know her?"

"Yes," he said, "We've known each other for a long time."

"Grace was just telling me that Ryan Martin stole a boat from the camp after dark and took Helen Smith to meet a friend of his. She said that the Smith girl was pregnant, and that Ryan's friend was going to marry her."

Grace gave Pam a furtive glance. "That's supposed to be a secret," she said. "The cops weren't supposed to know."

"Oh. Sorry."

"Is that why we had all the firemen dragging the lake for a body?" Floyd asked. "They thought Helen Smith might have fallen out of the boat?"

Grace pondered the question. "I don't think so," she said. "Mary said that Ryan told the lifeguard about the people skinny dipping when he brought the boat back. Mary didn't know about Helen running away until later, after Ryan got fired."

"Who is Mary?" Floyd asked.

"Mary Martin," Pam said, "worked in the camp laundry. She was also Ryan Martin's aunt." Pam addressed Grace, as she was digging the last cookie out of the bag. "Did Mary know the name of Ryan's friend, the one Ryan took Helen to?"

"Mary never knew," Grace replied. "I don't think that Ryan ever told her his name."

"Do you know if he was local," Pam asked, "or maybe someone from the Twin Cities."

Grace wiped her hands on the napkin and then picked up the coffee cup in both hands to take a sip. Her hands trembled and it was an effort for her to get the cup to her lips without spilling. "That was part of the secret."

"What secret?" Floyd asked, as Grace sipped from the cup.

"If I told, it wouldn't be a secret." Grace looked around the room like she was expecting other visitors. The sound of clattering pots and pans emanated from the kitchen and Grace was distracted by the noise. "I hope we have chicken for dinner," she said, changing the topic. "We had pork for lunch yesterday and my piece was from a boar. It was so strong I couldn't eat it. They shouldn't serve boar meat. We used to make boars into sausage when I lived on the farm."

Pam glanced at her watch, reassuring herself that it was almost noon and that Grace wasn't confused.

"Does Mary Martin still live in the area?" Floyd asked.

"I don't think she ever did," Grace said, shook her head. "She lived in Cloquet."

"Have you seen her since you worked with her at camp?" Pam asked.

"I remember her funeral," Grace replied. "She committed suicide. Turned the car on and sat in the garage. I think her husband found her when he got home from work."

A plump young woman dressed in a white uniform with a white hair net and a blue-checked apron approached the table and put her hand on Pam's shoulder. "Excuse me, Grace," she said, "but we've got to have you and your friends move to the lobby so we can set up for lunch."

"I think we're done visiting for the day," Floyd said as he stood up. "Maybe we can visit you another day, Grace." He helped Grace get up from her chair, and Pam handed her the cane.

"That would be nice," Grace said, "especially if you bring more cookies. You know, Russian tea cakes are my favorite."

Pam smiled, noting the powdered sugar that dotted the red flowers on Grace's blouse and her dark slacks. "We'd heard that you liked them."

As they walked to the lobby Pam asked again, "Who was Ryan Martin's friend, the one who got the Smith girl pregnant? I forgot his name."

Grace stopped and looked at Floyd's uniform, then turned back to Pam. "It's a secret, we can't tell the cops."

CHAPTER 19

The dispatcher's page broke Dan's concentration as he reviewed a budget proposal from the sheriff. The budget was dismal, and he was happy to have an excuse to pretend they wouldn't have to make the cuts the sheriff had outlined to balance the rising gas prices.

"Dan Williams."

"Deputy Williams, this is Jerry Schwab, I'm a parole officer from Burnett County, Wisconsin. I understand that you're looking for Ryan Martin. Can I ask why?"

Dan glanced at the caller ID and verified that it said Burnett County. "We have an old murder case, and Ryan was one of the people associated with the investigation. We'd like to talk to him about the case."

"A murder?" Schwab asked.

"A very old murder. The girl disappeared from a camp in the summer of '74 and we just found her remains in the trunk of an abandoned car where Ryan rented."

Dan could hear papers shuffling. "I've got Ryan's file in front of me," Schwab said. "He has no criminal record before November of '74 although there's a note about a sealed juvenile file in Hennepin County. Since then, he's been a guest of a county or state facility about half of the past three decades. Were you able to determine a cause of death from the remains?"

"The only remains we found were skeletal," Dan replied. "A forensic anthropologist analyzed them and the injuries are consistent with a knife wound to the chest."

"Ryan likes knives," Schwab said, reading through the files. "He has two assault convictions and a third where the charges were dropped. It appears that his weapon of choice has been a large hunting knife. We both know that once a criminal finds something that works for him, he tends to stay with it."

"Were his victims male or female?"

"One assault occurred during a burglary," Schwab said. "In that instance, he assaulted a couple who were living together. They had some minor cuts, but he used the knife to scare them into submission. The other cases were both bar fights with men, where there was some question about who the aggressor may have been. That's why the charges were dropped in one case - Ryan's attorney was able to argue that it was self-defense."

"We saw a conviction for third-degree sexual assault on his record," Dan said. "What are the details on that?"

"I take it you have reason to believe your victim was sexually assaulted?" the parole officer asked.

"We can't say definitively, but there was other pubic hair with the remains and she was only twelve at the time of her disappearance," Dan said. "Here's an interesting bit of trivia I wouldn't like shared publicly; the foreign hair we found, had a condition called ring hair. Do you know if Ryan has that?"

Again, Schwab shuffled papers. "I don't see anything in his file, but I don't know why that would show up here. You asked about the sexual assault charge. It was immediately after his release from prison. He picked up a prostitute and forced her to have sex with him, or stiffed her on the payment, depending on which story you believe. The motel manager heard the yelling and called the police. They arrested Ryan, for rape, but the prosecutors and public defender plea bargained the charges down third degree sexual contact."

"Since most criminals tend to stick to patterns," Dan said, "is there any chance the prostitute was young, with dark hair?"

"She had dark hair, as in African-American," Schwab replied, "but she was over forty."

"I'd like to talk to Ryan, to see what he remembers about our victim, and what he may have for an alibi."

"Sure," Schwab replied. "He was due to contact me this week, and I haven't heard from him yet. We can catch up with him at his duplex in Rice Lake."

Dan reached for a Wisconsin map. "Is that close to Spooner?" he asked.

"Rice Lake is about twenty miles south of Spooner, on highway fifty-three."

Dan ran his finger across the map. There were no highways running east and west across the two states in that area. "Are you free this afternoon?" he asked. "I can drive across some back roads and be there by two o'clock."

"There's a Country Kitchen just off the highway, south of town. Take the south exit and turn left. I'll be drinking coffee."

Dan made notes on a Post-it note pad as Schwab gave directions. "How will I recognize you?" he asked.

""Oh, you'll recognize me," Schwab said. " I used to be a defensive tackle for the Houston Oilers."

CHAPTER 20

"Grace Palm seemed very lucid," Pam said as she slid into a booth in The Sportsman's Café, a small brick building with parking for a couple dozen cars, which overlooked the traffic on highway 65 in Mora. "She seemed to have a clear memory of a lot of those events." A truck full of cattle rumbled past on their way to the auction barn about a half-mile down the road.

"She didn't remember me," Floyd countered, "and I've been there twice in the past week."

"Do you remember a laundry worker named Mary Martin?" Pam asked.

Floyd shook his head. "Not really," he said. "I'll look through my notes. If I questioned her she didn't offer much. Of course, if she was Ryan Martin's aunt and was trying to keep his involvement under wraps, she might just leave a few things out of her statement. I feel like such an idiot, not realizing that the two Martins at camp might be related. That's a real rookie mistake."

"What do you think about the suicide?" Pam asked. "Do you suppose there's any connection with Helen Smith's disappearance?"

"You know Dan's famous quote, 'There are no coincidences in police work'."

"I'd like to track down the lead on Mary Martin," Pam said as she reviewed the Grace Palm discussion in her head. "I'll see if I can find an obituary in the Duluth newspaper. Maybe it will list her husband's name. Then I can track him down and see what he remembers."

"What did Grace tell you before I walked over?" Floyd asked.

"Oh," Pam said. "I'm sorry. I'd forgotten that you didn't hear the whole discussion. Grace said that Ryan was a stinker. He couldn't stay at the camp, like the other counselors, because of some trouble he'd been in. As a matter of fact, she said that's why he was working at the camp, and staying at Benson's. He'd been in some trouble at home and someone made arrangements for him to work at the camp and live at Benson's. That would be a great question for Mary Martin's husband."

"She mentioned him stealing the boat," Floyd said. "Did she mention other trouble that he'd been in?"

"She thought that the two girls who worked with her that summer said he'd been fired for smoking dope."

"That'd be a pretty big deal back then," Floyd said, "especially at a church camp. I think I'll call Grace's helpers and ask a few more questions. If Ryan was a real troublemaker, they'll certainly remember him."

"Have you tried to find the lifeguard?" Pam asked. "It would be interesting to know if he remembers the stolen boat incident the same way Grace does."

"I'll give you his name when we get back to the courthouse. That can be your backup project."

"Me and my big mouth," Pam said, shaking her head. "You'd think I'd learn."

Maddie, round and smiling, delivered their burger baskets and set a squeeze bottle of ketchup on the table. "Is that all for today?" she asked.

"I think so," Floyd said as he opened his burger and doused it with ketchup. They ate in silence for a while. Floyd noticed Pam staring out the window at the passing traffic.

"What's wrong?" he asked.

"Do you think Ryan really had a friend who was involved? My first thought was that he'd made that up as a cover story and that he was the only person involved. But, if there really was another person, that would certainly put a different spin on the investigation." Pam paused, and then asked, "Why would he take Helen to his friend in a boat?"

"Because he didn't want his car seen at the camp after he's been fired or suspended," Floyd said. "Maybe his car wouldn't start. Maybe his friend lived across the lake. Maybe he'd killed her and he couldn't risk putting her in the car at the camp. He took her across the lake to a deserted spot and moved the body later."

Floyd ran out of ideas, and then added a final thought, "Maybe Grace doesn't remember any of this at all."

"Suppose," Pam said, "that he did have a friend across the lake. How could we find out?"

"I suppose someone might remember," Floyd said. "We could pull all the abstracts for the properties around the lake and run the owner's names from '74 against the NCIC computer database of criminals."

"That might take the two of us months!"

"Yup," Floyd said, "and we don't have months. The other way would be to do like the FBI and put a couple dozen agents on it."

"Where would we get a couple dozen people to dig through property abstracts on the outside chance we might find someone with a criminal background?"

"We won't," he replied.

Pam sat silently for a few seconds. Suddenly, she sat up straight with her eyes wide. "Why would Helen Smith go quietly with Ryan Martin on a late night boat ride?"

"Who said she went quietly?"

"If Helen had resisted, someone would've heard the commotion in the cabin. Grace said she was quite a flirt, so maybe she was sneaking off to neck with him. I'll bet that a boat would be about the only private place around the camp for a romantic interlude."

"Since I have little perspective on the mind of a pubescent girl," Floyd said. "Maybe you could tell me if, or why a girl Helen's age would go for a late night boat ride with an eighteen year-old ne'er-do-well."

"Well, girls that age have a warped view of romance, and are flirtatious. Bad boys are always a turn on because they're a little mysterious and forbidden. On the other hand, 'tweens tend to hang around in groups just to protect themselves from getting in a bad situation. It's rather like teasing a flame with your finger. They want to feel the heat, but they're afraid of getting burned."

"If I distill that down to a yes or no answer, you think she wouldn't go off alone with Ryan."

"Not from a romantic standpoint. At least I wouldn't think so. On the other hand, I was a farm girl and a precocious city kid might be braver than I ever was."

CHAPTER 21

Wednesday afternoon

Dan found the restaurant in Rice Lake easily, and parked in the rear, near two other police cars. He walked in the restaurant, and nodded to two uniformed Rice Lake police officers who were eating lunch. He didn't know them, but they'd seen his unmarked car drive through the parking lot. The informal fraternity of law enforcement officers required that he introduce himself.

"Hi guys," he said. "I'm Dan Williams, from Pine County, Minnesota."

The officers shook his hand and introduced themselves as Young and Bishop. "What brings you to Rice Lake?" the older of the two asked.

"I'm supposed to meet Jerry Schwab."

A smile crept across both officers' faces. "You don't know him," the younger officer asked, "do you?"

The older officer pointed to a window table where a giant man was reading the newspaper and drinking coffee. "Jerry's hard to miss."

Schwab sat at one of the few tables, apparently because his girth wouldn't fit into any of the booths. Dan took the chair across from Schwab. "I made it," he said. "I'm Dan Williams."

Schwab folded the paper on the crossword puzzle and shook Dan's hand. "Call me Jerry." He was dressed in a tweed sport coat that looked like it might have fit him about twenty pounds earlier. He wore a white shirt that strained at the buttons. In addition to being physically large, his neck appeared to taper up to his bullet-shaped, clean-shaven head.

"What can you tell me about Ryan Martin?" Dan asked as he signaled the waitress for a cup of coffee.

"He's a cocky little twerp," Schwab said. "He's got more mouth than good sense, and when he shoots it off he gets himself into trouble."

"He's been in more trouble than you'd expect from a big mouth."

"He doesn't know when to quit," Schwab replied. "He's got an attitude as big as his mouth, and he won't back down. He likes to carry a big knife to back up his attitude."

Dan waited as the waitress poured him a cup of coffee and then topped off Schwab's cup. "I take it you don't like him much," Dan said as the waitress retreated.

Schwab looked out the window and shook his head. "I don't like many of the people I deal with very much. They're the scum of the earth. They don't like me, and I return the favor."

"Why do you stay in the job?" Dan asked.

"What else is a former football player supposed to do with his life?" Schwab said. "I wasn't good enough to make the big bucks, and I blew what I did make on women and booze. The county needs someone who can intimidate these creeps, and that's the one thing I do pretty well. It came down to a choice between being a bill collector or a parole officer and I decided it'd be easier to tell my mother I was checking up on parolees than to tell her I was busting heads to collect car payments."

"I can believe that," Dan observed.

"So, tell me more about your murder. I read about the body in the trunk earlier this week. Do you think the body has been there all this time?"

"It appears so," Dan replied. "This isn't on the record anywhere, but it appears that the body went through decomposition in the trunk. The t-shirt the girl had been wearing when she disappeared was in the trunk with her."

"Where was this car stored that no one smelled the body rotting?"

"On a farm," Dan said, "right behind the streetcar Ryan Martin was living in."

"No one else on the farm noticed the smell?"

"Turns out that Ryan had them pretty well spooked. The mother was widowed, and had a girl who was about thirteen and two younger boys. The girl said that Ryan used to stare at her when she was in the yard in a way that made her skin crawl. The mother got after the boys and didn't let them near Ryan either, especially after she caught them window peeping to watch him get it on with some older woman."

"Well," Schwab said, "based on what I've seen of Ryan Martin, nothing that you've told me is a surprise. He likes girls, and most of them seem to find him kinda creepy." He folded the rest of the newspaper neatly, drained his coffee cup, and dropped a five-dollar bill on the table. "Follow me."

Ryan Martin's apartment turned out to be half of a duplex in an area of Rice Lake that looked like it had been developed in the sixties. All of the houses looked the same, and the trees were mature. They parked at the curb in front of a house with two front doors that looked like one side had once been a garage that was remodeled into living space. Without speaking, Schwab led Dan to the front door and knocked hard on the storm door. Behind the door, Pink Floyd's *Off the Wall* blared at a volume that would deafen the listener after a few years.

"I'll bet," Dan said, "the people in the other half of the duplex just love him."

"He's an asshole," Schwab said, "and he does nothing to soften that image." Schwab banged on the storm door again, this time with more vigor. "Open up! This is your parole officer!"

Failing to get a response, Schwab opened the storm door and pounded on the inner door with his fist. "Open up!"

The front door on the other half of the duplex opened, and a young man stuck his head out. All that showed was a mussed head of brown hair and a Green Bay Packers sweatshirt. "Hey, are you guys cops?" he yelled over the music.

"Yeah," Schwab answered. "Why?"

"I was hoping somebody would call," the man said. "I'm working nights and that goofball's stereo is keeping me awake."

"Does he do this all the time?" Schwab asked.

"Not usually," the man replied, "but he parties a little. I don't mind that so much because it's in the evenings. But this daytime stuff is killing me. I've got to get some sleep."

"How long has the music been this loud?" Dan asked.

"I don't know, maybe a couple hours or so. It's all been this same sick group, I think he must have a five CD set of this crap. You know, he might not even be home. I heard a car door a while ago. It was out back about the time you guys showed up."

Schwab pounded on the door again and tried the knob as Dan hustled around to the rear of the duplex. The back yard was enclosed with a white picket fence in need of paint. Dan pushed through the gate, and noticed another open gate along what appeared to be an alley. He ran up the back steps, and stopped at the open kitchen door. There was dribble of blood on the cement steps, and the metallic odor of blood was strong inside the kitchen.

"Hello!" Dan yelled, to be heard over the music. He drew his Smith & Wesson as he stepped carefully around drops of blood on the kitchen floor. Moving to the doorframe leading to the next room, he stepped across the threshold, leading with his pistol.

The living room was pounding with the rhythm of Pink Floyd adding to the surreal scene of mayhem. A middle-aged man was bloody and bound to a kitchen chair set in the middle of the room. His unseeing eyes stared at the ceiling, his t-shirt cut and soaked with blood. Dan reached behind the entertainment center and pulled the stereo plug. In the silence, he yelled, "Jerry, this is a murder scene. Call the police!"

Dan retraced his steps back through the kitchen, carefully avoiding the blood on the floor and not touching anything. At the back door he drew a deep breath of the crisp spring air, leaving his gun hanging at his side. The neighbor walked around the back of the house in the same outfit, with a pair of plaid flannel pants showing below the green Packer's sweatshirt.

"Wow!" the neighbor said, "Did you say there's a murder?"

Dan avoided the question. "You'd better go back inside until the cops show up. They'll want to talk to you."

The man frowned. "I thought you guys were cops."

"We are," Dan replied, "But from the wrong jurisdiction."

"Wrong jurisdiction?"

"Minnesota," Dan said. "I drove over to talk to your neighbor."

"Who's dead?"

"I don't know the man," Dan said truthfully. "Go back in the house. The murderer may still be around."

The neighbor was suddenly aware that Dan was still holding the pistol at his side, and appeared to be hiding beside the doorframe. "Right! I'm in the house when they want me."

Sirens started to wail in the distance just before Schwab came through the gate. "The locals are on the way," the parole officer said. "I called the county, too. They have more investigative resources." He was carrying a chrome-plated revolver with a short barrel in his left hand. "Who's the victim?"

Dan shrugged. "I've never seen him before. It could be our man Martin. Either that, or I'd say Martin is the chief suspect."

"Martin is middle-aged," Schwab said, "with long brown hair, usually in a ponytail. He's skinny and kind of reminds me of Willie Nelson."

"I'd say you have one less parolee to worry about."

Jerry stared at the back door for a few seconds, as if considering a look inside, but then he stepped back. "I'm not sure I need to see this scene."

A siren stopped in front of the house, and Schwab went back through the gate. A second siren rounded a corner nearby. Within a few seconds the second Rice Lake squad drove down the alley.

Suddenly aware that he was an unknown person, holding a gun, Dan fumbled to open his badge case with his left hand. He held the badge high as the officer stepped out of the squad. The officer was the older of the two officers he'd seen at the restaurant, and the man waved as he came around the front of the car.

"Did you call this in?" the officer asked as he drew his pistol and pressed his back against the door opposite from Dan.

"I think Jerry Schwab did," Dan replied. "I was holding down the fort back here."

"Your name is Williams?"

"Right."

"Are you sure it's a murder?"

"Yup," Dan said. "No doubt at all. The neighbor said he heard a car door slam before we got here. I'd guess that was the murderer leaving, but I'm not willing to bet my life on it."

The younger officer ran through the gate with is gun drawn. "Jerry's got the front door covered. What's up?"

"Deputy Williams says there's a dead body inside, and probably no murderer." The older officer motioned for the younger man to come to the door. "You and I are going to check the place to make sure there's no one hiding under the bed." He looked at Dan and asked, "You're okay holding down the back door?"

"Sure," Dan replied. "Be careful. There's a lot of blood on the floor, so there might be some footprints from the murderer. There's also a blood trail leading through the kitchen and out the door." He pointed his gun toward the drops on the steps.

More sirens wailed in the distance as the two officers stepped into the kitchen, one covering the other as they moved cautiously ahead. Dan watched them pause at the living room door.

"Holy shit!" the younger man uttered. "What a mess."

They disappeared, and Dan stood at the kitchen door surveying the scene. Opposite the cupboards was a Formica table surrounded by unmatched vinyl chairs. To the side of the table was a door, which probably led to the basement. There was a brown smear above the handle, indicating that the murderer, or someone with bloody hands, may have gone to the basement.

It took the two Rice Lake officers almost ten minutes to check the house. By the time they came back to the kitchen, Schwab had been relieved at the front door, and he reported an ambulance crew was waiting in the front yard.

"Did you look in there?" the older officer asked Dan. "It's terrible."

"Guys," Dan said. "Someone may have gone through the basement door." He pointed to the blood smeared on the basement door.

The older officer pushed the door open with his shoe and peeked around the corner. When he stepped back he said, "That's a hell of a place to check. If anyone is downstairs, they'll see our feet coming before we can see anything."

The younger man pushed past. "I'll go down fast and cover you as you come down."

They disappeared through the door and the sound of running feet resounded through the basement. The footsteps returned slowly. The younger officer returned first, shaking his head.

"What a mess," he said.

"Another body?" Dan asked.

"Bloody towels in a wash basin."

It took the coroner almost a half-hour to arrive at the duplex. He showed up driving a BMW sedan, and Dan's first impression was of a self-important rich doctor with little interest in solving crimes. Dan watched through the front window as the man dressed in a sport coat and dress slacks, opened his trunk, and dug out a black bag. The coroner stripped off his coat and laid it neatly inside the trunk. Then he pulled out a white coverall and pulled it over his pants and shirt.

Dan guessed that he might be close to forty, with a trim build and thinning brown hair.

The two Rice Lake officers, and two deputies from the Burnett County Sheriff's Department, had taken pictures of every room and had dusted for fingerprints by the time he'd arrived. Dan was relieved that the coroner couldn't screw up the investigation terribly, as the old Pine County coroner had done at times.

Dan met the coroner at the door. "I'm Dan Williams, from Pine County, Minnesota."

"Richard Drew," the man said, shaking Dan's hand. "I'm the coroner for Burnett County. Why are you here?" he asked Dan.

"I had planned on interviewing the victim about an old murder in our county. By the time I got here with his parole officer, the man was already dead."

Drew looked past Dan's shoulder into the living room. "I suppose someone checked his pulse?" the coroner asked.

"It was pretty evident that he was dead when we found him," Dan replied. "But one of the paramedics put a stethoscope on his chest just to be sure."

"I take it you've seen a few dead bodies?" The coroner asked as he set his bag down and took a pair of purple surgical gloves from the pocket of his coveralls.

"A few," Dan said. "Enough to know that this guy was dead the first time I saw him."

Another unmarked police car stopped across the street from the duplex. A very thin man, wearing a sheriff's department uniform, got out and immediately lit a cigarette before crossing the street.

"The sheriff's here," Drew said loudly. "Everybody act professional!" The coroner winked at Dan. "It's a standing joke. A couple of us were laughing at a murder scene a few years ago because a deputy had taken like forty pictures before he realized there was no film in the camera. You know how you have to break the tension sometimes. Anyway, the sheriff pulled up just then and hit the ceiling. He told us that it was unprofessional to laugh while the body wasn't even cold yet."

The sheriff stopped at the bottom step, and took a long drag on his cigarette. He exhaled slowly as he ground the butt out under the toe of his shoe. He walked up the steps and shook the coroner's hand.

"Hi, doc." He turned to Dan and asked, "Who are you?"

"Dan Williams, Pine County, Minnesota," he said, showing his badge. "I'm the undersheriff and chief investigator. I came over to interview the victim about a homicide."

"Sven Jacobson," the sheriff said, shaking Dan's hand. "I think I've heard about you. Didn't you crack the case with the murder-suicide that turned out to be a double homicide?"

"That was me," Dan replied. "Luckily, we caught the mistake before the coroner issued his report."

Drew gave Dan a skeptical look. "You had a coroner who couldn't tell a double murder from a murder and suicide?" he asked. "Where did he get his M.D., at the University of Mail-order Diplomas?"

"He was just senile and arrogant," Dan replied. "He's not the coroner anymore."

"Speaking of that," the doctor said, "I should get to work. Is everything dusted and all the pictures taken so I can touch stuff?"

"In there they are," the older Rice Lake officer said, looking in from the kitchen. "We're still working on the kitchen and basement."

Dan and the sheriff watched the coroner make his preliminary inspection of the victim and surrounding area. The coroner took out a small thermometer, and Dan felt the sheriff touch his arm.

"C'mon," the sheriff said, "I need a smoke." As they walked down the sidewalk he asked Dan, "What do you think, Williams?"

"I think the victim suffered a lot before he died. Whoever did this was either terribly sadistic, or wanted something from Ryan that he wasn't offering willingly."

"Drugs," Jacobson said. "They're behind so much of the crime we see. The gangs get involved and they get pretty violent."

"Ryan was a little old for the gang and drug scene." Dan thought for a second, and then added, "Although he may have been a dealer. He hasn't been out of prison long. Maybe he developed some contacts inside."

Jerry Schwab walked around the corner of the house and saw Dan and the sheriff talking. He walked to them and said, "The guys in the back found some tire marks. They're not deep enough to cast, but they think they can get a picture with lighting from the side that will show enough contrast to visualize the tread pattern."

"Did you see the mess inside, Jerry?" the sheriff asked.

"Yeah," the parole officer replied. "I've never seen anything like that in person before."

"What's your take on the possible motives?"

Schwab stood next to the sheriff while he considered the question. The parole officer's size was a stark contrast to the sheriff. Schwab was nearly a foot taller and nearly two hundred pounds heavier. Dan considered himself a big man, having played high school football, but next to Schwab he felt puny.

"Well, sheriff," Schwab said, "I would have said drugs if I didn't know Ryan better. He was a boozer from way back and he's never had a drug charge of any kind. He's always thought of himself as a ladies man, and I'd be more inclined to look for a jealous husband than a druggie looking to score a hit."

"Did you guys notice," Dan asked, "that there is not a sign of forced entry? I checked both doors and the windows, and everything is locked or intact. Ryan must have left a door unlocked, or willingly let the murderer into the house. If there was a jealous husband involved, I wouldn't think that Ryan Martin would have invited him in for coffee."

"Actually," Schwab said, "what I find interesting is that someone could get the drop on him. He's an old scrapper and bar fighter. He's used everything to assault people with his fists, to beer bottles, and the big knife that he carries." Schwab snapped his fingers. "We've got to tell the guys to look for a knife. It's got a four-inch blade, and the handle is ivory colored. Martin didn't leave the house without it, and he always had it within reach inside."

"Yeah," Dan agreed, "you don't get a convict to sit down in a chair and let himself be gagged and tied up like that. We see that all the time with homeowners where burglars break in. They let themselves be bound and gagged to keep the burglars from hurting them or their families. But cons are natural skeptics. They know every trick and aren't willing to play along without a fight."

"So, you think that maybe there were several people who broke in and tied him up?" The sheriff asked.

"I don't know," Schwab replied. "I can't see him letting a group of people he doesn't trust into the house. Maybe he was drugged, or drank so much he passed out."

"The furniture is still pretty much in place, too," Dan added. "It doesn't look like there was a big fight."

The coroner stepped out the front door and saw the informal gathering on the sidewalk. He stripped off the surgical gloves as he approached the group.

"Lots of homemade tattoos, I take it the victim was a convict?" Doctor Drew asked.

"He was on parole," Schwab replied. "I talked to him last week, and he had a job hanging wallpaper for a local paint store a couple days a week."

The sheriff gave Schwab a glare. "He was working at a job where people let him into their houses?" he asked. "Do you think that was wise?"

"Hey!" Schwab said, defensively, "He's never had a burglary on his record. Mostly he likes to get drunk and beat people up. We've had a real tough time finding anyone who would hire him. We were both happy that he'd found this."

"What do you think, Doc?" Dan asked, trying to redirect the conversation.

"I appears that he died less than an hour ago," the coroner replied. "The body has only lost a couple degrees of temperature, and the blood hasn't started to dry yet. I want the ambulance crew to take the body to the hospital. I'll do an autopsy tomorrow morning, after I get a few other things cleared off my platter."

"Preliminary cause of death?" the sheriff asked.

"Blood loss," the coroner replied. "There are a lot of superficial wounds that look bad, but weren't life threatening. Then, there's a deep puncture wound to the chest. My guess is that someone tortured him for a while, and then ended it with a stab wound to the chest."

"Would you say it was a vicious attack?" Dan asked.

"Oddly," the coroner replied, "I would have to say no. Normally, when there's a crime of passion or hatred, we see the murderer flailing away with his or her weapon. That leaves a pattern of spray, where blood flies off the weapon and leaves spatter patterns on the surroundings and multiple stab wounds. There's no evidence of a spatter pattern here that I could see and there doesn't appear to be more than one deep stab wound. In fact, it appears that the superficial cuts were made almost methodically or ritualistically. I wouldn't rule out some sort of a cult ritual."

"Nah," Schwab said emphatically, "cons aren't into cult stuff. They're too skeptical unless they're the leaders. I can't imagine him letting anyone in the house who could get the drop on him. It's totally out of character for him to trust anyone."

"I think it was someone who knew him pretty well," the coroner said. "There's a bag of new CDs on the floor by the entertainment center. The wrapper off the one in the player was on the floor. They're all hard rock music from the seventies. I saw Pink Floyd, Procol Harem, Jimmy Hendrix, and Joe Cocker. There's a receipt from Music City, in Superior, in the bag."

"There's an open liter of Jack Daniel's on the counter," Schwab added. "It looks like there may be about eight ounces gone."

"That would explain the broken glass on the floor, next to the entertainment center," the coroner said. "That would be an opportunity to, 'get the drop on him.' If the victim turned away and bent over to put a CD in the player would certainly offer the opportunity for someone to knock him out or to pounce on him."

"I have a hard time imagining Ryan trusting anyone that much," Schwab said.

"Unless it's someone from his distant past," Dan said. "Perhaps someone he used to drink and listen to music with in the old days."

"I'll have to check his toxicology," the coroner said. "There isn't enough booze gone from the bottle to get him drunk. I suppose that the murderer could have slipped something into the bourbon to knock him out. That might explain how he was able to subdue the victim."

The sheriff was shaking his head. "We still don't have a motive," he said. "You don't kill an old buddy for no reason. Someone went to great lengths to set this up. He picked up CDs, he bought a bottle of booze, he somehow planned to torture the guy, but for what? You don't do that just for kicks. There has to be a motive somewhere."

"What if," Dan said, "you had killed someone a long time ago, and thought the body would never be found. Then, the body is found, and you have this convicted criminal who might be able to connect you with the crime. I think that would be a great motive."

"I don't buy it," Schwab said. "If Ryan Martin had known something about an unsolved murder he would have said something years ago to get a reduced sentence."

"Maybe not," Dan said. "Maybe he didn't know where the body was. It's hard to convict someone without a body."

"I can't buy it either," said Jacobson, the sheriff. "I think its drug related."

"Did your investigation find any drugs?" Dan asked.

"No," Jacobson replied. "They tortured the poor guy until he told them what they wanted to know and then killed him and ran off with the drugs. Did you look at him? He's a mess. Could you have kept a secret under that kind of abuse?" The sheriff paused. "Besides, let's say your murderer comes here to knock off Martin. Why bother cutting him up like that? Why not just kill him and be gone?"

"Maybe the murderer had to know who else Martin may have told," Dan replied. "Or, maybe he's just a sadistic son-of-a-bitch."

"The person who did this is a psycho," the coroner said. "You'd better get on the system and start looking for crazy killers. Everything I've read says no one starts with a killing like this, they build up to it."

"He didn't start here," Dan said. "He started thirty years ago in Pine County." He snapped his fingers and turned toward the coroner. “Check all the microscopic evidence. Our killer has an unusual condition called ring hair. See if you can find a strand of it somewhere in the house or on the body.”

CHAPTER 22

When they returned to the courthouse, Pam went to the Internet and searched for a listing and address for the name Martin, finding seven Martins in Cloquet. She wrote down all the numbers and started calling each of them, trying to find Mary Martin's widower. After seven calls she had left four messages and spoken with three people who knew nothing of Mary Martin except in a Peter Pan context.

Next she called the *Duluth News Tribune* and spoke with a young woman in the archives. The woman quickly scanned the database of old newspapers and found an obituary for Mary Martin. The date of death was listed as March fifteenth, nineteen seventy-five. The death was listed as sudden. It also listed Mary's husband as Arthur Martin, of Cloquet. A brother-in-law, Gary Martin, in Minneapolis and a sister, Robin Peterson, in Williston, North Dakota were also listed. Her parents were both dead, and there were no children listed. None of the names in the Internet search were Arthur, Art, or listed as the initial A.

The dispatcher paged Pam to pick up line one. It was Frances Martin responding to a voice mail she'd left earlier in the day. Fran didn't know either Mary or Arthur Martin. Scratch another lead.

Next, Pam called Carlton County, and checked with the clerk of court to see if Mary Martin's estate had been through probate. It took the clerk almost twenty minutes to find the probate records for seventy-three, and another few minutes to find Mary Martin. The estate was minor, and all real estate and monetary property went to Arthur, with the exception of a small bequest to the Cloquet Evangelical Lutheran Church.

"Does it list an address for Arthur Martin?" Pam asked.

"He had a P.O. box and an address on highway thirty-three," the clerk said. "I think it is somewhere north of town."

"Who filed the probate?" Pam asked. "Was it Arthur Martin?"

"No, it was filed by an attorney," the clerk said. Without waiting for a response she added, "The lawyer was Arlyn Prokop. His address is on highway sixty-one, in Willow River."

Floyd Swenson had been working on his own calls at a desk in the other corner of the room. When Pam hung up on Carlton County she walked to the coffeepot and poured a cup as Floyd hung up.

"Making any progress?" she asked Floyd.

"That was Janice Lund, one of Grace Palm's helpers. She remembered Ryan Martin as a slimy troublemaker. Janice said that she remembered his firing, but didn't really know why."

"Did she remember anything about the boat being stolen the night of Helen's disappearance?" Pam asked.

"No," Floyd replied, shaking his head. "It seems like camp was pretty quiet that night as best she can remember. She didn't know where the story about Helen disappearing while skinny-dipping had come up either. She just knew that it was bogus."

Pam was about to mention the Willow River lawyer when the dispatcher paged Floyd to answer line two. He picked up the phone and listened for a moment. "Hang on, Dan," he said. "Pam's right here. Let me put you on the speakerphone."

"I found Ryan Martin," Dan said. "He was living in Rice Lake, Wisconsin. When his parole officer and I went to the house we found him dead."

"So much for our prime suspect," said Pam.

"Yeah, maybe," Dan replied. "Someone killed him brutally. I think it looks like a gang style torture and execution. He's not into drugs, and there are no signs of forced entry, so we're operating under the assumption that he knew the killer. As a matter of fact, it appears the killer may have brought some CDs and a bottle of booze. The house has the appearance they were planning to party."

During the conversation, Sheriff Sepanen walked into the bullpen and listened to Dan's report. When Dan finished he said, "Dan, this is John. Did I understand correctly that your top suspect was killed?"

"Yup," Dan replied. "I'm sitting in the Rice County Sheriff's Department answering questions and filing reports. I hope I will be able to wrap it up in another hour or so." He paused, and then added, "Floyd, would you tell Sally I'll be late for dinner?"

"Sure," Floyd replied, "like she ever expects you to be on time."

"I assume this wraps up the investigation?" Sepanen asked. "Suspect identified, and later dies a brutal death. Case closed."

Pam gave Floyd a furtive look. "Umm," Pam hesitated, trying to judge if it were her place to bring the topic up. "We talked to someone today who thought that Ryan Martin had a friend who took the Smith girl."

"What do you think about that, Dan," Sepanen asked.

"Well," Dan replied, "it seems like there is something else going on here. The killing here was strange, and doesn't seem related to anything else Ryan Martin was into. He had a new job, and he wasn't into drugs. You know how I feel about coincidences."

"There are no coincidences in law enforcement," Pam said. "Speaking of that, we tracked down the laundry worker from camp. She was Ryan Martin's aunt. Oddly, she committed suicide the winter after the Smith girl disappeared."

"I'll add another to the pile," Floyd said. "We found out that Ryan Martin lived in Benson's streetcar because they wouldn't let him sleep at the camp even though he worked there. It seems that he had a sealed juvenile file in Hennepin County, and somehow his aunt managed to get him a camp job to get him out of the Cities."

"Well, he must have been an interesting guy," Floyd said. "The Benson boys told me that he had wild parties in the streetcar, and they caught him having sex with a woman who was visiting. The bottom line is, that he made a lot of friends quickly for an outsider. Who knows what local connections he may have had."

"Who was the woman?" Sepanen asked.

"The boys saw her naked," Floyd said with a chuckle. "They didn't notice her face."

"I guess that's a normal reaction for a teen-aged boy," Sepanen said as Pam shook her head in disgust. "So where do you take the investigation from here?"

"I've left a few messages for people who used to work at the camp," Floyd said. "I've had one call back, and she remembered Ryan, but not any of his friends or the circumstances of his departure from the camp."

"I'm trying to track down more information about the aunt, Mary Martin," Pam said. "It appears her widower has either moved, or is dead. I tracked down the probate records of her estate. An attorney in Willow

River, named Prokop probated it. I was just going to call him to see what he remembered about Mary's death. She committed suicide and our source indicated that her death may have been linked to Ryan Martin somehow."

"Okay," Sepanen said. "You've convinced me that you have enough to justify making more calls. Please take a rational view of this. We can't keep this investigation going on for years. We've got to wrap it up and stop dumping overtime into it."

"Right, sheriff," Dan said as Pam and Floyd nodded assent.

After Dan hung up and the sheriff left, Pam asked, "Have you ever seen a law office in Willow River, or is this another of those dead ends from thirty years ago?"

"There's a little sign on a building across the street from the fire department. I've never run across Prokop in court, so I'd guess that he doesn't do much litigation. Probably specializes in real estate and probate."

Pam found a number for Prokop & Prokop, Attorneys at Law, in Willow River. She dialed and got another recorder. She left her name and the sheriff's department number on the machine, requesting a return call on Thursday. When she hung up she looked at the clock, then at Floyd.

"I'd better call it a day before I rack up anymore overtime," she said.

"Me, too. I think this has been a hell of a long day."

"So, Floyd, what are your supper plans?" Pam asked as they walked out of the courthouse.

"I've got a little squirrel belly right now, so I thought I'd pick up a can of chicken soup and some saltines."

"Squirrel belly?"

"It feels like a couple squirrels are chasing each other around my stomach."

"My mother always fed me ginger ale when my stomach was upset," Pam said. "Why don't you ride with me to the drive-in, and I'll buy you a ginger ale?"

"Has Dan assigned you baby-sitting duties to keep me out of trouble?" Floyd asked as he stepped into Pam's Sunfire.

Pam gave him a confused look. "No, I don't understand why the case isn't closed now that we've found Ryan Martin dead, and I want you to explain it to me."

"Ryan didn't act alone."

"How do we know that? Helen was killed with a knife and Ryan was into knives."

Floyd thought about how to best frame his thoughts. "Let's start with some basics: One. Ryan was slashed and killed shortly after Helen was discovered. That leads me to believe that there was someone else involved who wanted to make sure Ryan couldn't rat him out. Two, Ryan was gregarious, and partied with a whole bunch of people at Benson's farm. He wasn't a loner. Three, killers don't start out killing, but they escalate to it from assaults and other lower crimes. Ryan was always a petty crook who seemed to peak with some assaults, but stopped short of killing anyone. Fourth, and finally, the camp cook told us that Ryan was picking up the girl for someone else."

"I don't put a lot of faith in what Grace Palm told us," Pam said as she parked at the A&W and locked her car. "Her memory is shaky, and she's being evasive. That's a bad combination."

"I agree, but if you weigh her comments with the other pieces, it sure doesn't make me fell comfortable pinning the whole thing on Ryan Martin."

Pam stood at the counter and ordered a chicken sandwich and a root beer. Floyd ordered a burger basket and a root beer.

"I thought the squirrels weren't happy?" Pam asked as they sat in a booth overlooking Main Street.

"They seem to have settled a bit, so I decided to chance a burger."

"You think that Ryan had an accomplice?"

"I think Ryan was a patsy for someone who had the brains to pull this off and keep it hidden for a couple decades."

Pam shook her head. "I may be a rookie, but I see these guys come through jail and they can't help bragging up all the crimes they've pulled so the other prisoners are afraid of them or hold them in awe. Why wouldn't Ryan rat out an accomplice? Isn't it more likely that he was involved somehow and that someone else killed Helen?"

"That's an interesting thought," Floyd said, pausing as a teen girl delivered their meals, "although I don't see how they could pull off dumping a dead body in Ryan's backyard without his involvement. I think that it's more likely that someone put the fear of God into Ryan and he decided that he was more afraid of this person's retribution than whatever came up in prison."

"There are some really scary people in prison. The person who scared him would have to be a very imposing person."

"Not necessarily physically imposing, but perhaps someone who was just crazy enough to keep Ryan watching his back for thirty years."

Pam squirted ketchup onto her plate and plucked a fry from Floyd's basket. "Someone crazy," she said as she swirled the fry in the puddle of ketchup, "and someone who kept on killing? Why aren't we finding a trail of dead bodies?"

"Give Laurie Lone Eagle a little time," Floyd said as he pushed the basket away.

"The squirrels are unhappy again?"

"I think I may have moved from squirrels to ferrets."

A grin crept across Pam's face. "I had a friend who had a pet ferret who pooped in every corner."

"Exactly!" Floyd said as he slipped out of the booth and moved quickly toward the rest room sign.

CHAPTER 23

Wednesday evening

After cleaning up the cut on his arm, he considered going to the emergency room to have a few stitches put into it. He pinched the edges together and watched the blood ooze from the long gash. It was a long cut, but probably not deep enough to need stitches. Besides, the people in the emergency room would ask questions, and maybe even call the cops. It was best just to close it up as best he could with band-aids and hope the bleeding would stop soon.

Ryan had been such a jerk. Why couldn't he just accept that he was going to die and go with dignity? Even in his drugged state Ryan pulled the stupid knife from the hidden sheath and sliced his arm open before he could get Ryan's second arm tied to the chair. It must be the animal instincts that prison brought out that put a man so on edge he'd try to defend himself even when his mind was hazed with drugs and death was staring him in the face.

After several one-handed attempts, he managed to get two strips of tape attached to a Telfa pad, and then smoothed the whole bandage onto his arm. He added an Ace bandage wrap to keep the bandage in place and to put additional pressure to stop the bleeding. He looked at the injury in the bathroom mirror and decided that wearing a long sleeve shirt would nicely hide the damage. It was spring, and everyone wore long sleeved shirts this time of year. He was just lucky that he'd deflected the blade with his arm. Ryan had swung the blade at his face when he made his last desperate flail, and that wouldn't have been a wound he could've hidden.

He looked over and saw his white shirt, in a pile next to the sink, splattered with a bloody mixture from himself and Martin. It was cold out, and a good night for a fire in the stove. To be safe, he reasoned that he should throw his whole ensemble into the fireplace – it was stupid to save an eighty-dollar pair of bloody shoes that the cops could DNA test for Martin's blood. Tomorrow morning he would have to take out the ashes and dispose of them. There would be zippers, snaps, buttons, and eyelets from his shoes that wouldn't be consumed by the fire. If the ashes were dumped along the road no one would ever suspect they were anything more than the detritus from the world's decadent lifestyle.

It took a few minutes to get the pieces of cedar and pine crackling in the cast iron stove. Once they were roaring, he put on a pair of split oak logs and carefully draped the shirt over them. Within minutes the flames consumed the cotton. Next, he put the wool slacks on the fire. The socks weren't as cooperative and they seemed to melt rather than burn, and the leather of the shoes just seemed to smoke. He threw more oak on top of the shoes, and closed the cast iron stove doors.

He checked the wrap on his arm again and saw no signs of seepage. Although the cut was painful there was a certain amount of satisfaction in the sensation. He liked the *edge* that had returned to his life. He slipped into the tired recliner across from the stove and watched the flames dance through the blackened window in the door. The years of living in shades of gray were gone and his life had regained bright reds and oranges.

CHAPTER 24

The lights were still on in the house when Dan pulled into the driveway. Penny ran from a doghouse under the wooden steps and raced to his door. He bent down and petted as she circled his legs her before going to the house.

Sally Williams was sitting on the couch, reading *Glare Ice,* by Mary Logue. She set the book on the end table and took off her reading glasses. "Have you eaten already, or should I warm something up?" she asked.

"I grabbed a burger on the way," he said as he hung his buckskin jacket on the coat tree.

"Then," Sally said, "I'll just make you a salad." In response to the grumbling from the kitchen she added, "if not for me, you'd probably have scurvy."

"If not for you," Dan replied, "I'd eat things that tasted good." He popped two Tums in his mouth to counteract the coffee and greasy hamburger he'd eaten in Spooner, on the way home.

Dan walked to the bedroom as Sally set out a bowl and ripped lettuce into it. "How'd your interview with the convict go?" she asked. When he didn't answer, she assumed he hadn't heard her, and she asked it louder. Dan surprised her when he walked into the kitchen.

"It didn't go well," he said quietly. "He was dead when we got to his house."

Sally tried to read his reaction. It was too subdued. "From natural causes?" she asked, half afraid she already knew the answer.

"He'd been stabbed," Dan replied. "From what I could see, it happened only minutes before we arrived." He hesitated, and then added, "If I hadn't had a cup of coffee with his parole officer before we drove to the house, we might have stopped the murder. At a minimum, we might have seen the murderer."

"You can't stop, or even solve every crime," she said, running her fingers through his hair. "You aren't Superman, Supercop, or even Bruce Willis." Dan poked at his salad as she spoke.

"I know," he said, "but sometimes we come so close."

"How bad was it?"

"I asked for my hamburger well done," he replied.

"That's bad. Maybe you should become a vegetarian. They're rarely victims of violent crime."

"I told you that Floyd's requested his retirement papers," he said, pushing the salad away. "Maybe it's time for me to retire, too. I get more personally involved in each of these cases. One of them is going to push me over the edge and I'll do something stupid."

Dan ran his hand over his face. “I think it’s time for someone young to take this over, and for old horses like Floyd and I to be put to pasture.”

“You and Floyd solve all the crimes,” Sally said. “If both of you retire at the same time, who would teach the young deputies?”

“Why should I care?”

“Because you still live in this county. Because you can’t help caring.”

“Maybe,” he said, “I’m just not smart enough to walk away.”

“You’re smart enough to do anything you want,” Sally said. She picked up the bowl of greens and dumped them into the disposal. “You dwell on the negative too much. Think of all the good things that have happened, and all the crimes you’ve solved.”

“There’s an old saying, ‘It’s hard to fly with eagles when you work with turkeys.’ Most of the criminals I deal with would have to move up the ladder several rungs to deserve the title, ‘turkey’.”

Sally put her hand out to him. “C’mon. It’s time for bed.”

“I don’t think I can sleep yet,” he replied.

“That’s okay. I just wanted someone to warm me up,” Sally said taking his hand and leading him down the hallway.

✲ ✲ ✲

With the ferret belly subsiding, Floyd spread peanut butter on a slice of toast. The 13" television on the spotless counter was recounting news headlines about unrest in the Middle East, followed by a breaking story about a murder in Rice Lake, Wisconsin, which the sheriff's department spokesman said it might be drug related. He switched the channel in time to see Vanna White illuminate four "E's", which allowed the contestant to solve the puzzle. He took a bite of toast and switched to an infomercial about an amazing exercise machine that strengthened every part of your body, but stowed out of sight in your hallway closet.

Giving up on the television, he moved his toast to the living room and picked through several old issues of magazines before giving up in disgust. He stared at the empty recliner across the coffee table and pictured Ginny. Every evening she'd talk for a couple hours about things that interested her, or that she'd heard around town. He never needed to say a thing, because she could carry on both sides of a conversation, and in his mind, that was fine.

Maybe things would be different if they'd adopted a child. He'd have some tie to another human being, someone who could bridge the hole in his heart. Maybe he could call…who?

He washed the toast crumbs down the disposal and washed the knife. He put the peanut butter in the cupboard and braced himself on the counter top while he contemplated the pistol on the closet shelf.

"I'm sorry, Ginny. I can't keep doing this," he said as tears streamed down his face. "You told me to be strong and move on, but I miss you too much. I just don't think I can do it anymore. I'm not much of a church person, that was always you, but, Lord give me strength."

CHAPTER 25

Thursday Morning

It took Pam Ryan almost ten minutes to scrape the frost from the windows of her squad car after the calm night left a glazed deposit. Even with the defroster roaring, the windows seemed to prefer their frosty state, the white quickly reappearing on the recently clear surfaces. Waiting for the windows to clear gave her the perfect opportunity to think about the Helen Smith case, Floyd's four reasons why Ryan Martin didn't act alone, and the sheriff's request that they wrap it up.

Grace Palm was a less than credible source of information. On the other hand, she seemed quite lucid about her days at the camp, the people, and the events. When they had been able to find witnesses, they had corroborated Grace's observations. Grace thought Ryan Martin had a friend, and that stealing the boat was a link to the friend. She kept coming back to the same question, "Did Helen Smith leave the camp with Ryan Martin willingly?"

When the windows cleared, Pam drove the five miles to the courthouse and parked in one of the many spots reserved for sheriff's deputies. She passed the dispatcher's glassed-in cubicle, and started down the hallway.

"Pam," the dispatcher called after her. "I have a stack of messages for you."

Pam leafed through the pink message slips as she walked the hallway back to the bullpen. All the office doors were closed, and no lights shown under them. It was very unusual for the day-shift deputies to beat Dan to the courthouse. By the time she'd hung up her coat and made a fresh pot of coffee Kerm Rajacich and Sandy Maki were arguing about the day's assignments.

"Hey!" she interrupted, "would either of you care to trade your subpoenas and court paper deliveries for the messages I have to return and the calls I have to make?"

Rajacich made a face and took a pile of subpoenas. "Nah," he said, "I'd rather have a root canal."

Sandy pulled a chair next to Pam's desk and sat leaning over the back. "I heard you lost your top suspect yesterday."

"He wasn't really the top suspect," she replied. "But we think he knew the murderer."

"So, if he wasn't the murderer," Maki asked, "what are you doing today?"

"Calling people," Pam said, holding up the pile of message slips, "then waiting for people to call me."

"Sounds about as boring as watching grass grow."

"It was pretty exciting when we found the Martin guy's name in the NCIC database. It was kind of like finding the prize in the bottom of the Cracker Jacks. You know it's somewhere inside the box, but you feel kind of good when you finally lay your hands on it."

"Better you, than me," Sandy said, pushing the chair back. "I can't handle sitting around that much."

"That's why you'll never be an investigator," Floyd said, as he walked into the room.

"You're right, Floyd. If that's what it takes, it's not what I want out of life. Leave me on the road chasing down speeders and feeling the adrenaline flow through my veins when I'm driving a hundred miles-an-hour."

"I kind of like that, too," Pam said, putting on her best pout.

"Make your calls and stop your whining," Floyd said, with a grin.

"Are the squirrels behaving this morning?" Pam asked as Floyd poured coffee from the stained carafe on the counter.

Floyd sipped the coffee and grimaced. "They were pretty quiet, but I'm not sure they'll like this coal tar mixture that the night shift left in the coffee pot for us."

"Do you think they actually sabotage it, or is it just that they make it badly and it sits on the warmer for hours?"

"Personally, I think that they have no idea how much coffee it takes to make a batch," Floyd said as he emptied a package of powdered cream into his cup and stirred. He considered the color for a second, and then added a second package. "Then, it tastes so bad that they just leave it on the warmer where it burns down and gets thick."

"Why don't you dump it out and start a new batch?"

He sampled a sip and nodded his head. "The problem is that the swill I make really doesn't taste any better."

Pam made calls to all the Cloquet Martins, and hit pay dirt on the fourth call.

"Yeah, I knew Art and Mary," the older woman said. "Art was a shirt-tail relative of my husband. We didn't know them well, but I met them a couple of times at weddings and funerals."

"I understand that Mary died in '75," Pam said. "Did you know if she committed suicide?"

"It was the talk of the family," the woman replied. "We all heard about it, and everyone said it was a shame. She was a nice woman who tried to do right by folks. I think that was her downfall. All the good things she tried to do never seemed to turn out for her."

"Do you know about a cousin named Ryan Martin?" Pam asked.

"Hmph!" the woman snorted. "He was the black sheep. Last I heard he was still in jail somewhere."

"I heard that Mary got him the job at Melody Pines Camp one summer."

"I knew it was some sort of camp for city kids," the woman said. "Yeah, seems to me it was Mary who got him that job. I heard he got in trouble there too, and they fired him. That was another one of Mary's do-gooder projects that went down the toilet."

"You said he got in trouble there too. Was he in trouble before that?"

"You betcha he was in trouble," the woman said. "We knew Ryan's Dad better than Art and Mary. Ryan was trouble from the day he was born. His mother died in childbirth, and it's been downhill from there. By the time Mary got him that job at the camp, he'd been thrown out of his daddy's house because of the things he'd done."

"What things would those be?" Pam asked.

"Well, he got caught up in some anti-war protest thing and got himself arrested. While they were trying to arrest him, he pulled a knife and cut some cop pretty bad. He was a juvenile back then, so the court didn't do much, but I heard that the other cops had a talk with him, if you know what I mean."

"Somehow Ryan doesn't seem like the war protest type of guy."

"Oh," the woman said, "he's whatever kind of guy he needs to be to get around girls and booze. I imagine there was some cute thing who whispered in his ear and he followed her to bed or to a protest, not necessarily in that order. His daddy told my husband that Ryan had been fired from a job once for necking with the boss's wife in the back room. He was always trying to get into somebody's pants, and he wasn't too particular either. I guess the boss lady was in her forties at the time, and Ryan must have been all of sixteen."

"Do you know if he had any friends locally?" Pam asked.

"I wouldn't know. We had kids the same age and I tried to keep them as far from Ryan as I could. All I ever heard about him was secondhand hearsay."

"I tried to locate Arthur Martin," Pam said, "but he isn't in the phone book."

"You'll need a medium to contact Art. He died a couple years ago of lung cancer. He was a big time smoker, you know."

"I imagine that Mary might have left a suicide note," Pam said. "I would like to know what it said."

"I never heard about a suicide note," the woman said. "I imagine that Art kept that to himself. I suppose the police might have seen it, though. Maybe they have it in a file or something. Art and Mary lived up north of town and I think it was the Cloquet cops who came to the house after Art found her with the car still running in the garage."

"Normally," Pam said, "we don't pass information like this over the phone. But since you aren't a close relative, I'm probably safe informing you that Ryan Martin died yesterday."

"You make that sound like I should be sad," the woman said. "I don't think we'd go to the funeral, and I don't think anyone will shed any tears."

Pam brewed a fresh pot of coffee and was filling her cup when the dispatcher paged her to pick up the phone. She punched the third button as she sat down in her chair. "Deputy Ryan."

"This is Arlyn Prokop. You left a message on the law office answering machine yesterday while I was away. How can I be of service?"

Pam had to mentally shift gears after her conversation with Mrs. Martin. "Thanks for calling me back Mister Prokop. We are following up some leads on an old case, and I understand that you filed probate papers for Mary Martin in nineteen seventy-five. Is that correct?"

Prokop laughed. "I'm afraid you're looking for my father. I was in college in seventy-five. I joined my father's firm here, in Willow River, in nineteen-eighty, after I finished law school and passed the bar exam."

"Could I speak with your father?"

"I'm afraid that he retired about ten years ago and moved to Florida. He hasn't been interested in talking law when I've spoken with him. If you could tell me what you're looking for, I might be able to look it up in the archives. We never throw things away."

"Well, Mary Martin committed suicide," Pam said. "We were hoping to find some information about her death, and maybe a suicide note."

"Whew!" Prokop said. "I've never dealt with a suicide note or anything like that when we've gone through probate. We get a certified copy of the death certificate, and that lists the cause of death, but I'm really afraid I'd be wasting my time searching for that old file to see if there's a suicide note." He paused, then added, "I think you'd do better checking with the coroner's office. If they ruled the death a suicide, they must have read any suicide note, and probably have a copy of it in their files."

"That's a good thought," Pam said as she wrote herself a note. "Thanks. By the way, I don't think we've ever met, and I don't even know where your office is."

"My office is in downtown Willow River, across from City Hall on old highway sixty-one. It's not much of a place, and I don't spend a lot of time there. The reason we've never met is probably because my father steered his practice away from criminal law. I haven't done much criminal work except for a rare stint as a public defender, so I don't meet many of the people in law enforcement unless they come to me to have a will drawn up, or to check on a property abstract."

"Interesting," Pam said. "I wouldn't have guessed there was enough of that type of business to make a living in Willow River."

"Who said I make a living at it!" Prokop said with a laugh. "My parents gave me their house, and the building the law office and a real estate office share. Beyond that, I keep my tastes simple and I get by."

"Well, thanks. If I ever decide to have a will drawn up, I'll think of you."

"I appreciate that. Most of my new business is through referrals."

CHAPTER 26

Pam was starting another fresh pot of coffee when Laurie Lone Eagle walked into the bullpen. Laurie hung her tan overcoat on the coat rack and ran her fingers through her short black hair to straighten the mess that the wind had made of it.

"So," Laurie said, "They still make the woman brew the coffee."

Pam looked at Laurie and shook her head. "Whoever drains the pot makes coffee." Laurie was wearing a lavender blouse that nicely complemented her native complexion. The holster on her belt seemed too large for her small stature.

"What brings you to Pine City," Pam asked as she wiped spilled coffee grounds.

"I heard you were running a little short on manpower," Laurie replied. "I got permission from the director to give you a hand on the Helen Smith case for a few days. He was especially interested because we'd done the original forensic work on the car, and it would look bad if we didn't find the murderer."

"You heard about Ryan Martin?" Pam asked.

"I heard that Dan was a little too late. Not that it makes a whole lot of difference in the case because a hardened felon like Ryan isn't going to be brimming with information."

"So, what are you going to do?" Pam asked.

"What do you need done?" Laurie asked. "I've been a deputy, and I've run a few investigations of my own out of the BCA. I suppose you've got hundreds of documents to read and dozens of phone calls to make. I can handle any of those tasks."

"Really?" Pam asked. "You're willing to sit here and make phone calls with me?"

"Why not? That's sometimes what it takes to break a case so we can make the glamorous arrest on television." Laurie paused. "You know, it seems like the television cameras never show up when we're on the phone, only when we've got our guns drawn or when we're standing on the courthouse steps."

"The guys are all out on the road, chasing down speeders and handing out subpoenas. They don't want to sit here and make phone calls."

Laurie smiled. "It takes patience to break a murder investigation open. Most cops don't have the patience to sit on a phone for hours. It takes a lot of perseverance to pursue a lot of little leads and put it together in a way that makes sense to a prosecutor. If you're like a bull in a china shop you often overlook subtle evidence and ruin other evidence. It takes more finesse than testosterone."

"So says Pastor Laurie in her recent sermon." Floyd's voice startled them both. "So," he added, "I don't have enough testosterone anymore, and that's why I can solve crimes? That sounds like age discrimination."

"Laurie was just trying to energize me for spending another day on the phones," Pam said as she got up to pour a cup of the fresh coffee dripping into the carafe. "She volunteered to help us for a couple days."

"Great! We'll take all the help we can get, especially since the county board is pinching the budget and we're fighting to authorize overtime."

Laurie shook her head. "Some things never change," she said. "Back when Dan and I were partners, we spent a week trying to track down a guy who'd walked away from the minimum security part of the Sandstone Federal Penitentiary. The old sheriff was on us every day to find the guy and quit spending all the money on overtime."

"Did you catch him?" Pam asked.

"Yes," Dan said, as he walked into the room. "I chased him into a swamp and tackled him when he stumbled on a root." He walked to the coffee pot and poured himself a cup.

"I remember it differently," Laurie said. "I thought it was you who turned his ankle on the root, and I had to help you out of the swamp after I chased the escapee down."

Dan hid his smile by taking a sip of coffee. "I suppose I could've been confused about some of the facts."

The dispatcher paged Floyd, temporarily interrupting the banter. He went to a desk and picked up the phone.

"I don't know if Laurie heard," Dan said. "We lost our suspect yesterday. Ryan Martin was killed in his Rice Lake, Wisconsin duplex yesterday."

"Too bad you never got a chance to interview him." Laurie asked.

"He was dead when we arrived," Dan said solemnly. "So, what's the plan for today?"

"Well," Pam said, "Floyd was going to try to find the lifeguard, and he had calls in to the girls who helped the camp cook. Because of the lead about the boat, we'd talked about looking at the property abstracts for all the lots around the lake. Then, we were going to check the names of the owners in '74 against the NCIC database to see if any of them were convicts then, or were convicted of a crime later."

Floyd's whistle broke up the conversation. He waved them over to his desk and pressed buttons to open the speakerphone.

"Hello, Shirley," he said. "I have a number of colleagues who will be interested in what you just told me. I've put you on the speakerphone. Please repeat what you said."

"Well," the female voice started, "it's a long time ago, but I remember a little about Ryan Martin. He was a little bit of a troublemaker, but that appeals to a lot of teen-agers. He was always stirring things up, and

I remember that he got in trouble several times for fairly minor things."

"Please tell us about his friend, from across the lake."

"He came over a couple times, in a canoe. I thought he was kind of geeky. Actually, he reminded me of Harry Potter, or the drawings of Harry Potter on the jacket of the books. He had sandy hair that was kind of straight and combed to the sides. Mostly, I remember his glasses. They had round wire rims, and they were always sliding down his nose. He had this nervous habit of pushing them up on his nose, even when they hadn't slipped down."

Dan leaned close to the phone and asked, "How old do you think this guy was?"

"Oh, I'd say he was in his late teens or maybe twenty. Somebody said he was in college, but I don't think anyone that old would be hanging around with a bunch of high school aged camp counselors. He was sort of tall, but he was so socially awkward that I think he was just tall for his age."

"What do you mean by socially awkward?" Pam asked.

"You know how teenaged boys can be. He would blush when anyone mentioned any sexual innuendo. He didn't talk a lot. He seemed to enjoy being around other kids, but he seemed like he didn't know what to say."

"Do you remember his name?" Dan asked.

"Phew! That was so long ago. I remember Ryan riding him about a lot of stuff. He'd always say things like, 'can't you get anything straight?' and 'you're such an idiot.' Wait! His name was Earl. I can almost hear Ryan saying, 'you're such an idiot, Earl'."

"Do you remember him doing anything social at the camp?" Floyd asked.

"There was a group of local teenagers who came around on Saturdays sometimes. Saturdays were our days off. The new bunch of campers would come at noon on Sunday, but the other group would leave at noon on Saturday. We used to go into town for movies, and then play football and stuff we couldn't do when the campers were around."

"Is that the day the counselors went skinny-dipping?" Floyd asked.

"We couldn't risk doing anything like that when the campers were around. So, the few times we did skinny-dip, it was on a Saturday night." Shirley paused, then let out a sigh, "Wow! I'd forgotten about the night that Earl came over to skinny-dip. Ryan brought few people over in his car and Earl paddled his canoe to the camp in the dark. We sat around shore, you know, trying to get our courage up. Finally, Ryan stripped down and made a run for the water. Pretty soon, there were five or six of us in the water, with Earl standing there watching. Ryan really laid into him about being chicken and a prude. I think he got fed up and paddled away in his canoe without joining in."

"You said something about the night that Ryan took the boat," Floyd said.

"Yeah, it was a big deal for the lifeguards. Two of the lifeguards shared a room over the boathouse. They kept an eye on the equipment, and were also the first aid experts. That night, they got called to the most remote cabin because someone called in on a radio to report that a camper was sick. They ran all the way to the cabin with their first aid kits but everyone was asleep when they arrived."

"When they got back to the boathouse they put the first aid stuff away, but were too wound up to go back to sleep. After a while, they heard oars creaking, and the sound of a boat sliding on the sand. When they went down to the shore they caught Ryan running away. He got in his car and drove away before they caught him, but they told the camp director about him and she was going to fire Ryan."

"You said she was *going* to fire Ryan like she didn't do it." Laurie said.

"You know, that's funny. I think Ryan didn't show up the next day, so there was some big stink, and then it all got sidetracked."

"What sidetracked it?" Laurie asked.

There was a long pause. "That was the day that Helen Smith disappeared. Janice and I were in the kitchen with Mrs. Palm, so we didn't get all the gossip immediately because we were cooking, but I think they discovered that Helen was gone and everyone forgot that Ryan was in trouble. I don't think I ever saw Ryan again after that. I assumed that he'd been fired, but he may have just decided to stay away knowing that he didn't have a job anymore."

Floyd leaned close to the phone and said, "no one ever mentioned Ryan stealing a boat the night Helen Smith disappeared back then. That seems like it would have been pretty important to the investigation."

The line was silent and Floyd asked, "Are you still there, Shirley?"

"Yeah, I was just trying to remember. I guess I didn't hear about the stolen boat at the time. It must've been gossip I picked up later."

"I checked my notes," Floyd said, "and the lifeguard was the one who suggested that Helen Smith may have drowned while she was skinny-dipping. He didn't mention Ryan or the stolen boat. I wonder what would make him bring up skinny-dipping and a possible drowning?"

"He probably didn't mention the boat being gone because the grapevine said Ryan was naked when they saw him running away from the beach. It was Ryan who usually instigated the skinny-dipping parties."

Pam, Floyd, Laurie, and Dan all stared at each other without saying a word. Finally, Floyd leaned to the phone.

"Thanks a lot," he said. "You've been a great help. You have my number and I'd appreciate a call if you remember anything else." Then he pushed a button to disconnect the speakerphone.

"If you're naïve, and you think of Ryan as a mischievous kid," Laurie said, "you could extrapolate that a nude boy had been skinny-dipping. If you think of him as a felon, you could come to other conclusions."

"So," Pam said, "the next step is to find a geeky guy named Earl."

CHAPTER 27

"Okay, folks," Dan said as the others gathered desk chairs around Floyd's desk, "Let's recap what we know. Ryan Martin is dead, and he appears to have been a link somehow, although I'm more and more inclined to think he wasn't the killer. He lived in Benson's streetcar, and he used to host some wild parties. Martin was probably killed by someone he knew based on no sign of forced entry, and it appears he died from a stab wound to the chest after being tortured. His arrest record is lengthy, and he liked to intimidate people with a knife." Dan paused, and then said, "Pam, you go next."

"Well, I know that Ryan's aunt worked in the camp laundry. She apparently rescued Ryan from some problems he was having in the Cities while living with his father. According to another, distant relative, Ryan had stabbed a police officer at some protest march when he was a minor, and the aunt thought spending a summer working at camp would help. Based on what we've heard, it doesn't seem to have done much other than provide him with another set of contacts."

Pam shrugged, "I guess that's about it. Laurie, you go next."

"You all know about the forensic evidence we found in the trunk. It appears the Smith girl's body was deposited there soon after her disappearance, and she decomposed in the car. We found some microscopic evidence in the trunk including some hairs that didn't belong to the victim. Two of the hairs appear to be pubic hairs, and they exhibit a genetic abnormality called ring hair, which is pretty rare. We found one odd animal hair, and we just heard back from the University of Oregon yesterday that it appears to be from a ferret."

"The hair was from a ferret?" Dan asked. "They're not uncommon, but I wouldn't expect to find a hair in the trunk of a car."

"The ferret hair is an odd twist, although it may be something that got carried in at some other time." Laurie said. "We also know the victim probably died from an upward thrust single knife wound to the left side of the chest. That might indicate that her assailant was right handed. Based on what Dan said, that cause of death would be consistent with Ryan Martin's history."

"I'm the last one," Floyd said. "You all heard what Shirley Johnson had to say about the stolen boat and Ryan's friend, named Earl. Beyond that, I guess the thing that bothers me the most are the victim's parents - they seemed to be very antagonistic. I can understand that, in the context of a bitter divorce, but they seem to have gone way past that. I think the mother is disturbed, and actually took her divorce settlement and gave it to a charity that she knew her ex-husband would detest, just pissing him off. That's really cutting off your nose to spite your face, and I don't think a rational person would do that.

"The mother was also terribly hung up on Helen's disappearance being a kidnapping, and both she and the father mentioned how she waited for weeks or more for a ransom note to show up. I can't see why, unless she was just a little mentally disturbed, and was grasping at straws." Floyd paused. "I guess that's about it for me."

"Okay," Dan said, pulling a legal pad from the desk. "What do we need to do?"

When he didn't get an immediate response he said, "We need Ryan Martin's autopsy results. We need to know if there are any ring hairs in the microscopic evidence, and I think that his assailant was also right handed. I'll follow up on that. I'll contact Wisconsin Corrections Department and have them fax a list of Ryan Martin's visitors while in prison. Maybe Earl will show up there."

"I can run a search for sexual offenders named Earl," Laurie said. "There's probably not much use going through the property abstracts since Earl was probably someone's son, and not the owner of record. But, I can check Department of Motor Vehicle records for people named Earl, getting driver's licenses in the early seventies. I'll narrow the search to Pine and Carlton Counties."

"I know a detective in Minneapolis," Floyd said. "I'll see if we can get Ryan Martin's juvenile file unsealed, now that he's dead. Maybe it will lead us to some associates from the Cities prior to his move. Maybe he had a friend named Earl before he moved up here."

Everyone looked at Pam. "I've left a message for the Carlton County coroner to see if they have Mary Martin's suicide note," she said.

"Why don't you look up the court records from all of Ryan Martin's arrests after '74," Dan suggested. "Maybe Earl will show up again, or maybe one of his buddies will know Earl." Dan looked at the other three and said, "Let's get back together at four o'clock to see what we've uncovered."

CHAPTER 28

Dan went back to his office and called the hospital in Rice Lake. It took almost ten minutes for Doctor Richard Drew to answer the hospital pages. When he did answer the phone, he sounded breathless.

"Doctor Drew, this is Dan Williams from Pine County."

"I remember you," the coroner said. "I suppose you're looking for autopsy results."

"I really didn't expect that you'd have them yet. I thought maybe I could come over and watch."

"Well," the coroner said, "you're right that I haven't gotten to it yet. You can come over if you want. Most of the local police wait for the pictures and the report. They should be available in four or five days. If you'd like, I'll take your address and send them to you."

"If it's okay with you," Dan said, "I'd like to come over and watch. I promise to stay out of the way."

"Watch if you want, but an autopsy is a bloody mess. It's not a scene for weak stomachs."

"I've seen a couple dozen," Dan said. "I promise to clean up if I throw up."

"Fair enough. I was planning to finish up some histology reports, then I thought I'd start the murder victim about ten o'clock."

"I'll be over," Dan said, thinking about all the things that he had to accomplish.

"If you're not here, I'll start without you."

* * *

Pam Ryan started searching for Ryan Martin's arrest records. It promised to be a tedious day of finding records, then calling the counties and having copies faxed to her. As she waited for the computer to make its search for Ryan Martin, she watched Laurie Lone Eagle unpack a laptop computer, string the power cord, and satellite card.

"Laurie," she said, "You can use one of our computers to access the state database."

"Thanks," Laurie said, "I can get quicker access through my computer. We have a special search engine that goes through the database quicker. It also allows me to narrow the searches and come up with fewer extraneous hits."

Ryan Martin's arrest records popped up on Pam's computer, and she scrolled through it. Luckily, most of the counties were adjacent to Pine County, making the contacts easier because they would recognize her name. His later arrest records would be harder to get, having been mostly in Northwestern Wisconsin. Somehow, sharing records across state lines was difficult, even when the counties adjoined across the St. Croix River, like Pine and Burnett Counties did.

She started grouping the records by county as Floyd made contact with Brad Kline, the Hennepin County detective in Minneapolis.

"Brad, this is Floyd Swenson, from Pine County. I need some more help."

"You know," Kline replied, "I have other things to do. I am not the personal liaison to Pine County."

"You might as well be. Yours in the only name I have in Hennepin County."

"I try to be a nice guy once," Kline said, "And it turns out to haunt me until I retire. Just goes to prove that old saying, 'No good deed goes unpunished'."

Floyd laughed. "We tracked down our prime suspect, and found him dead. His name was Ryan Martin."

"And that affects me how?" Kline asked.

"We think he had a juvenile arrest record in Hennepin County," Floyd replied. "We have a good tip that says he was arrested in Minneapolis as a minor. We also have a good tip that he had a friend named Earl, who may be an accomplice in this murder. I was wondering if you could pull his juvenile file and check for accomplices?"

"Juvenile files are sealed," Kline said.

"He's dead."

"If you fax me a death certificate, I can see about opening the file."

"He only died yesterday," Floyd said. "I'm sure they haven't done an autopsy yet, so they won't file the death certificate until they determine a cause."

"Hang on," Kline said, muffling a conversation in the background. "Is he the guy who was stabbed in Rice Lake, Wisconsin yesterday?"

"He's the one," Floyd replied. "Our chief investigator found the body."

"I'll bring the newspaper down to the clerk's office and see what he says. I know he won't like it, but he owes me a couple favors. I'll call you in a bit if I make any progress."

Pam printed out the five pages of Ryan Martin's adult criminal record. He'd been arrested in Carlton County, immediately north of Pine County, twice. She called the courthouse and explained her need for Ryan Martin's files, and was asked to fax a formal request to a clerk who agreed to pull the records while he waited for Pam's fax.

Pam had barely poured herself coffee when the fax machine chirped, indicating an incoming file. It spit out dozens of pages before it quit. She was typing a request for St. Louis County, in Duluth when the fax stopped printing. She sent the fax to Duluth and arranged the many pages of the Carlton County reports while the fax machine sent her request over the phone wires.

At her desk she started scanning the reports for anyone named Earl, when another name caught her eye. “Hey, Floyd!” she said. “Guess who represented Ryan Martin in his first Carlton County trial.”

Laurie looked up from her computer and listened to Floyd’s reply. “Since you asked it the way you did, I expect it’s a name I’ll recognize. Most of the people practicing law around here have all started since the seventies, so it has to be one of the few old timers. I suppose it may have been Stan Ward, up in Moose Lake. He used to do some court work and picked up a few public defender cases, too.”

“Would you believe it was Arlyn Prokop?” Pam asked. “I think it’s ironic that he was also the person who probated Ryan Martin’s aunt’s estate.”

“There’s nothing ironic about that,” Laurie said. “There were only a dozen lawyers around the region back then. And, they tended to do a lot of business with the same families. You find someone you trust, and who seems reliable, and you stuck with him.”

“It would be interesting to ask him about that,” Pam said

“Go ahead and ask,” Floyd replied.

“I can’t. I spoke with his son, and the senior Arlyn Prokop moved to Florida several years ago. He apparently doesn’t discuss old legal cases anymore.”

“I don’t know what he could tell you anyway,” Laurie said. “All the public information about the case should be in the court records. The lawyer’s notes and conversations are privileged and he couldn't share that with you anyway."

"There's no one named Earl anywhere here," Pam said as she dropped the file on top of her desk with a plop.

"I have several Earls here," Laurie said as she slid the laptop onto Pam's desk so they could both look at the screen. "The first cut of sex offenders named Earl gave me about forty hits. I narrowed it to people born between forty-nine and fifty-seven. I assume that should be broad enough, in '74 they would have been fifteen to twenty-three years old. From the way the Johnson woman spoke, I can't imagine he would have been anywhere outside that range, even if she were a really bad judge of age. That leaves me with six sex offenders named Earl."

"I assume," Laurie added, "that she would have mentioned if he'd been any race other than Caucasian, and that drops us to two Earls. One is from Olmstead County, by Rochester, and the other from Lake of the Woods County, near Baudette. Neither of them has an arrest before seventy-five, meaning Helen Smith would probably have been his first victim, and neither of them has a murder conviction."

"Most criminals escalate their violence over a career," Floyd noted. "I rarely hear about someone murdering their first victim, and then getting less violent in subsequent crimes."

"Neither of these guys even have an assault charge against them," Laurie said. "The one in Rochester was a college student who was charged with date rape. He has no other arrests on the record. The other was a high school teacher who was convicted after having a sexual affair with one of his students. I think we can safely cross them both off the list."

The fax machine chirped, announcing the arrival of the St. Louis County records, as the dispatcher paged Floyd.

"Sergeant Swenson."

"I got the clerk to do me a favor," Kline said, "but technically, we're not supposed to open these files without a court order or a death certificate."

"So," Floyd said, "is there anything in the files about a friend or co-conspirator named Earl?"

Floyd could hear pages turning among the cacophony of sounds around Kline's desk. "Oh boy!" Kline said, "You're going to love this. Have you got a pencil?"

"I'm ready."

"Ryan Martin was arrested with a group of anti-war protestors. They were blocking the road into the Minneapolis Air National Guard terminal, and the police started to remove them physically. When they grabbed the woman next to Ryan Martin he pulled a knife and cut the cop's arm. They dropped the woman, and subdued him, but another cop caught her and they were booked together."

"I'm a little confused," Floyd said as he hastily wrote notes. "What's the significance of that? We're looking for a man named Earl."

"The woman arrested with Ryan Martin was Colleen McCarthy."

"No shit!" Floyd said. Both Pam and Laurie turned to see what he was excited about.

"It's the real thing," Kline said. "She apparently has a separate file somewhere, but they mention her by name in Martin's court files."

"Hang on." Floyd put his hand over the phone and said, "Ryan Martin was arrested for assault for apparently protecting Helen Smith's mother during a war protest."

"Brad, what year was that?"

" '73," Kline said, "when the Viet Nam war was ending, and the year before your girl was murdered. It's a little bit of a coincidence, isn't it?"

"What are you doing for lunch?" Floyd asked.

"Nothing, if you're buying."

"I'm buying," Floyd said, "then we're going to pay Colleen McCarthy another visit. I wonder what she'll have to say this time."

Floyd was out of his chair before Laurie announced, "I got one hit on sex offenders with ring hair. He was arrested in '69 for raping a little girl he kidnapped from a church in St. Paul. He's been jailed, or in prison ever since."

"Couldn't have been our killer in '74," Floyd said as he put on his jacket.

"So, Laurie," Pam said, "what do we do now?"

"Let's get a cup of good coffee in town." Laurie emptied her borrowed cup into the sink with finesse and hung it on the rack.

CHAPTER 29

The drive from Hinkley to Rice Lake took Dan through an area dotted with idled farms and empty vacation cabins. As he drove the narrow two-lane highways he wound his way through small towns that would soon be filled with summer residents. A small bar with a "Hamm's Beer" sign had three pickups in the parking lot. In July, the parking lot would be overflowing, with cars parked on the grass.

Dan's mind wandered through the scraps of information that they'd pulled together in a few days of investigation. The link to Ryan Martin was intriguing, but it didn't feel right. Ryan was a bully and a tough guy, but his ire was usually focused on other men. His criminal history made no mention of violence toward women or sexual assault. At any other time, Dan would've discounted his involvement, but it was too coincidental that he'd been killed as soon as Helen's remains were found. Somehow, his sudden departure from the camp was tied to Helen Smith's disappearance, but how?

It was five minutes after ten when Dan drove into the Rice Lake Hospital's parking lot. He found a parking spot in the employee's lot behind the hospital and walked in through a loading dock bustling with people unloading a food delivery truck. An aging janitor looked at his buckskin jacket and gave him a frown.

"Where's the morgue?" Dan asked as he flashed his badge.

"Bottom of the stairs, then right."

Walking the silent, brightly lit basement hallways, Dan followed the hallway signs and found the door marked "morgue and pathology lab". Drew looked up from the naked body on the stainless steel exam table when Dan entered the autopsy room. The room was cold and smelled of disinfectant, and the intense lights over the table made Ryan's naked body look chalky white. The multitude of bleeding cuts that had looked so gruesome at the murder scene were now pink slashes on waxy skin.

"I was starting to think you'd chickened out," Drew said. He was dressed in blue surgical scrubs, wearing green gloves, a cone-shaped surgical mask, and glasses with side shields. A middle-aged woman, also dressed in scrubs, stood alongside Drew with a tray of specimen jars and bags, and a black permanent marker.

"I didn't chicken out, it just seems like no one wants to run a straight road between central Minnesota and here."

"Angie," Drew said, "Meet Dan Williams, from Pine County, Minnesota. Dan, this is Angie Plum, my histologist. She bottles and examines tissue samples for me."

"Nice to meet you, Angie," Dan said as he hung his buckskin jacket on a rack behind the door, and selected a surgical mask from a box on the counter. "Did I miss much?" he asked as he approached the stainless steel table.

"I've been making notations about the general condition of the corpse. I was just about to do a microscopic exam." Drew pulled a lighted magnifying ring over the body and lit the fluorescent light around the lens. He started his exam at the feet and moved up each leg slowly. "Angie, tell Dan about the preliminary toxicology results."

"I took a blood sample as soon as the victim arrived, and ran a gross scan on it." She flipped a few pages of notes over and read from them. "There was a moderate level of blood alcohol, but I picked up a foreign chemical. I took it up to the lab, and they ran a quick scan for the usual drugs. The screening ruled out THC, methamphetamine, cocaine, morphine, heroin, speed, and LSD. So, they ran it through the gas chromatograph and FTIR. The peaks they picked up match with Rohypnol, the date rape drug. We sent a sample to the state crime lab, in Madison, for verification."

"Date rape?" Dan asked. "I don't understand."

"He wouldn't take it himself," Drew said. "So, I had the Rice Lake cops bring in the bottle of booze from the kitchen. It was loaded with it. My guess is that the killer knew that the victim was a street-smart con, and that it would be very difficult to subdue the victim. He doped the booze bottle, knowing that the victim would partake willingly, and that the Rohypnol would incapacitate him. I would even hazard a guess that he's used that technique before on other victims."

"One more thing to keep in mind," Dan said.

"The Rice Lake cops said that there wasn't a fingerprint in the house that didn't belong to the victim," Drew said as he picked a piece of lint-like material off the corpse and placed it on a stainless tray. "It appeared that the booze bottle and the CD covers had been wiped clean of fingerprints. Most of the blood in the living room was from the victim, but the drops in the kitchen and a lot of what was on the towels was different leading me to believe that our victim got a piece of his attacker before he died."

Drew stopped at the victim's right hand. "Angie, bring me some test tubes and a spatula. There's blood here, and no corresponding injury." After scraping some of the dried blood from under the victim's fingernails, he handed the test tubes to the histologist. "Run a blood type on these and see if it's the same as type as the samples from the kitchen."

Drew continued his examination as Angie brought the samples to a bench where she marked them, and then treated them with blood-typing antigens. "One interesting thing," Drew said. "When we removed the victim's clothing, we found a sheath for a knife strapped to his right calf. The knife was gone, and the Rice Lake cops said there was no sign of anything but kitchen knives in the house. The killer must have taken it with him."

"These samples are O-positive, same as the drops on the floor," Angie announced. "The victim is A-positive."

"Well," Dan said, "Remind me, O-positive is a common blood type, right?"

"Common as grains of sand on the beach," Drew replied. "Depending on ethnicity of the person, it makes up as much of sixty-percent of some populations. It's not going to narrow your search much."

"Did the victim have ring hair?" Dan asked. "We found a few hairs with our skeletal remains."

"You told me that at the house,"Drew said, "so I checked that first thing. No, he didn't have ring hair. I haven't found a ring hair on his body either, just a few cat hairs on his clothing and his own hair."

"These cuts were really cruel," Drew said, pointing to cuts running parallel to the victim's ribs. "The murderer cut the intercostal muscles. They run between the ribs, and they tighten and relax with every breath. It's painful as hell when the cuts are made, then it was painful with every breath the victim took after that."

Drew stopped over one of the cuts and picked up a forceps. He carefully freed a hair that was stuck to the blood along the wound. He held it up to the magnifying glass and examined it closely.

"This looks lighter than the victim's hair," Drew said, "and it's not a cat hair. Let's take it to the microscope and take a closer look." He mounted the hair on a microscope slide and placed it on the stage. After a few adjustments he stepped back. "Take a look. I think you just got the link you were seeking."

It took Dan a second to focus his eyes on the dark stripe, running across the field of the microscope. Once he was focused on the hair strand, the rings on the hair jumped out at him.

"Bingo!" Dan said, "We've got a serial killer."

When Dan looked up from the microscope the first thing he saw was Angie's frown.

"Sorry," he said, "It's not good to *have* a serial killer. However, it is good to link a serial killer to more than one victim."

"Oh," she said, "I can accept that."

"I'll get in touch with the Minnesota Bureau of Criminal Apprehension," Dan said. "They can work out the logistics of matching this hair to the one we found with the skeleton." Dan slipped off the mask and walked toward the door.

"You're leaving before we get to the gruesome part?" Drew asked.

"I've got the information I needed to know."

"Chicken," Angie added.

Dan turned back and saw the crinkles around her eyes, giving away her smile even though her mouth was covered with a surgical mask. "You're right," he said, "I probably couldn't take it."

She shook her head. "You're too cool. You hung around this dead body like you were examining meat at the store. The one's who chicken out are the one's who keep staring at them like they're going to come back to life."

"They only come back in my nightmares," Dan said as he slipped on his jacket, "never during the autopsy."

CHAPTER 30

Pam and Laurie sat in a booth drinking coffee and commiserating. Nichol's Restaurant was almost empty between the breakfast crowd and the lunch rush. The afternoon sun shone through the south facing windows glaring off the Formica tabletops. The cook sat on a vinyl-covered stool at the counter reading the newspaper and drinking coffee while the one waitress worked her way from table to table filled sugar containers.

"I get really irritated at the guys sometimes," Pam said. "It's like I'm the flunky who gets all the jobs that no one else wants. Even Dan dumps on me, and I have a lot of respect for him."

"They're not dumping on you," Laurie said. "You're the junior deputy, and the prime jobs are scooped up based on seniority. Your day will come."

"But, I get all the phone calls, the paperwork, and the grunt work. They are out driving around, chasing speeders, and racing to fire calls. That's a whole lot more interesting than sitting at a phone all day and reading reports."

"Listen," Laurie said, "I've been in your spot. I've driven the roads, I put up with the petty bullshit the guys were always pulling. I put up with what would be called sexual harassment today. At that time it was the good old boys letting off steam and joking around. Things are a hundred times better today than they were twenty years ago. You're treated pretty much the same as any rookie."

"But, I'm not a rookie anymore! I want to be a full deputy, respected for my actions and my position."

"You're the rookie, until a new rookie is hired. At the rate budgets are getting cut, and how few people are retiring, you may have to fill that role for another year or more. Besides, it's really not so bad. You're learning a lot of investigative techniques that most of the men have never mastered. You're good at the details, and that's what catches criminals."

"It's more exhilarating to chase speeders."

"Tell me how much gratification you get from handing out a speeding ticket," Laurie said. "Then, compare that to the sense of accomplishment you get when you nail a criminal after a long, tough investigation. I don't think there's any comparison."

"Well, that's true," Pam conceded. "But, it's so boring in between."

"Have you ever been in front of a news camera?" Laurie asked.

"No."

"It's a real rush," Laurie said. "Reporters are calling out questions, and you suddenly realize that you are the expert. You're the one who cracked the tough case. They're calling out your name because you did something remarkable in the public's mind. How many cops even get their pictures in the paper for handing out a speeding ticket? Do you get a plaque for serving more subpoenas than anyone else?"

"Is that why you moved to the BCA?"

"That's part of it," Laurie replied. "There aren't many television interviews, but that seems pretty insignificant when you can hand a kidnapped child back to a loving parent. Life doesn't get much better than that. And, you don't do that by chasing speeders. You spend hours, or days, or weeks, making phone calls and tracking down leads. I don't get many of the missing kids back, far too few, as a matter of fact. But, when you get one it's worth all the pain, boredom and hours.

"Did anyone ever tell you that you were getting a special opportunity in pursuing these investigations?"

"Dan tried to butter me up by selling me on the value of what I'm doing," Pam said. "I think he was just trying to sugar coat a bitter pill."

Laurie reached across the table and put her hand on Pam's arm. "Dan is a real gem of a guy. It took me a long time to realize that, but it's true. He respects you, and your diligence in working on these investigations.

He's told me that there isn't another person in the department with the possible exception of Floyd who can do what you're doing. Both Dan and the sheriff believe you have a special ability, and they're trying hard to help you develop that talent." Laurie paused, and then added, "I know this sounds corny, but trust me. You're a good investigator, and they're trying to make you a better one. Stick with it, and start finding the positive side of this instead of being swayed by the guys who'd rather be driving the roads anyway."

"But it's so slow, and so boring. How can you find the positive side of boredom?"

"Grab milestones," Laurie said. "The final one is arresting the bad guy and seeing him convicted. But, there are a whole bunch of little bits of progress that you need to recognize and savor. Look at how excited Floyd was when he found out that Ryan Martin had been arrested with Helen Smith's mother. That's a big deal! That's a milestone! Celebrate!"

"That's Floyd's milestone. What have I accomplished?"

"Pam, this is a team. The right fielder on the World Series winning team gets a championship ring, too. He may not catch more than one ball the whole series, but he played a critical role by being there. You're a part of this investigative team. The whole team passed a milestone when Floyd got that piece of information. When you get one, the whole team will celebrate with you, too!"

"Really?"

"Who was left out when you guys arrested the killer at the Frank House last year? Didn't the Rush City policemen get some credit? You risked your neck to cover Floyd, and Dan risked his neck to cover you. Sure, that was an adrenaline rush, and everyone was keyed up. But, what do you think happens when the Treasury agents bust a counterfeiting ring? It all goes down very quietly, and they party like there's no tomorrow. They hardly ever get to run around with red lights and sirens, but they grind out all the evidence, and make a quiet arrest of some guys in a smoky back room."

"Okay," Pam said, "I'm sold. What are we doing next?"

"Back to the computers. It'll be fun.

"Yeah, right."

CHAPTER 31

Floyd parked in nearly the same spot in the Hennepin County justice center ramp and wound his way through the mass of diverse humanity in the lobby. A man from India, wearing a turban, glared when he caught Floyd staring at him as they rode the elevator. The sea of detectives working at their desks and wandering the aisles with files underarm was astounding compared to the limited resources of the Pine County Sheriff's department. Two brown-uniformed jailers were putting a handcuffed man into a holding cell, while a Minneapolis officer, in a blue uniform, was talking to a detective in an alcove near a bank of vending machines.

Floyd walked down a long aisle separating dozens of desks before seeing Kline on the phone near the back of the room. One wall of the office was lined with windows that overlooked downtown Minneapolis and brightened the workspace. Kline spotted him about the same time and waved him over. The conversation was heated, with Kline arguing about the plea bargain that the prosecutor's office had offered a criminal he'd arrested.

"If that's the best you can do," Kline said, "then you'd better take it. But, you're the one who's going to tell her son that the bastard who attacked his mother is getting off with a slap on the wrist while his mother is still recuperating in a nursing home. Personally, I think it sucks. We put three weeks into finding the son-of-a-bitch, and then two uniforms chased him through downtown traffic on foot to arrest him. I kind of expected that maybe the prosecutor's office might put at least as much enthusiasm into the case. I guess I overestimated your capabilities and commitment to punishing crime."

Kline listened for a few moments, and then interrupted the lawyer. "Listen, I prefer to have my whine with dinner. I don't need it from a lazy lawyer," he said with vehemence before he slammed down the phone. "Let's go to lunch before that lazy, slime-sucking bastard calls back to apologize."

As if on cue, the phone started to ring. Kline glared at it and said, "Screw him. Let's go."

"I take it you don't agree with the plea bargain your county attorney negotiated?" Floyd asked.

"That guy is a lazy bastard," Kline said, "more worried about his case closure rate than serving justice. It sticks in my gizzard when we work our tails off to investigate a crime and arrest the perpetrator only to have someone like him negotiate it down to some petty offense that doesn't show up as a felony with real jail time."

They walked a few blocks to a small bar with a Grain Belt beer sign in the window. The inside was dark and smelled like beer and fried onions. Before Floyd's eyes adjusted to the dark, Kline was walking toward an empty booth in the rear of a side room. After they slid into the booth Kline held up two fingers to the bartender. Mounted above the bar was a smashed car door with a Minneapolis police logo. Further down the bar was a cork board with the shoulder patches from several dozen police agencies.

"I take it you're a regular," Floyd said. "What did you order me?"

"Half the cops in Minneapolis are regulars here," Kline said. "And I ordered you the house special."

"I hope I like it."

"You will," Kline said confidently, "it's the only thing on the menu. A half-pound of ground chuck with fried onions served on homemade bread."

"Can I get something to drink?"

"Your Coke is coming with the burger," Kline said with a grin. "Tell me what we're going to do with the McCarthy woman."

"I thought I'd just tell her that we'd had linked her to Ryan Martin and see what she says."

"When she says, 'so what', what's your come back?" Kline asked as the burley bartender set two monster hamburgers and two bottles of Coke on the table.

"That's eight bucks," the bartender said.

Floyd dug a ten out of his wallet and handed it to the bartender. "Keep the change," he said.

"I planned to," the bartender replied as he pulled yellow and red squeeze bottles from his stained apron and set them on the table. He hesitated, staring at Floyd's shoulder. "Got no Pine County patch on the board, bring an extra next time you come 'round."

"I'll send one down to Kline. He can drop it off."

"Means more if you put it up yourself," the bartender said. "A cop from Chicago flew up one weekend just to bring me a patch. He was real proud to put it on the board."

Floyd looked carefully at the board and the wall around it. Not only was Chicago there, but NYPD, New Orleans, and San Francisco were also represented with either patches or emblems.

"See that NYPD patch?" the bartender asked, pointing to a patch in the upper right corner of the corkboard. "The cop that put it up died 9/11. I'd rip a guy's arm off if he tried to take that one down."

"I'll put one up myself," Floyd said, "the next time I'm in Minneapolis."

The bartender nodded. "Be careful about Kline, he can be a real pain in the ass."

Kline was squeezing ketchup onto the burger before the bartender left. "My reputation precedes me," he said. "I'd like to say it's a lie, but I can't."

"What do you do that makes you such a pain in the butt?"

"I take great pride," Kline said with a mouthful of burger, "in getting people to reveal secrets that they don't want to tell other people."

Floyd lifted the half-inch thick, hand sliced piece of bread that covered the burger, and put mustard on the pile of fried onions. Kline had already finished half his burger by the time Floyd got the first bite. The noise level in the bar rose as more people pressed into the limited space. Floyd noted that each customer got the same burger, and he also noticed that each of them either had a visible badge or the bulge of a hidden holster.

"Lot's of cops here," Floyd said.

"If it weren't for cops Arnie would be out of business. Bad guys don't like to hang out with cops anymore than cops like to hang out with bad guys."

"So, tell me Kline, how would you approach the McCarthy woman?"

Kline took the last bite of hamburger and wiped his mouth with a paper napkin from the dispenser. "Well," he said around the mouthful of burger, "I'd go in soft. I'd tell her how badly we feel about the loss of her daughter and how hard we're working at solving the case. Throw her a few bones, like some of the leads that we've got. Ask her if there is anything at all that she can remember that could help us out. If you've got a list of witnesses, ask her if she recognizes any of them, and bury the Martin guy's name in the middle of the list. If she doesn't speak up right away when you throw it out, keep reading names, but note how she reacts. Let her get upset, and a little weepy. Then ask if she's sure she doesn't remember the Martin guy. Then you drop the hammer on her - you tell her we found his arrest record, and we know they were arrested at the same time. Then ask her to explain why she didn't tell us about that, and then we're silent until she starts blurting out information."

Floyd was able to finish all the burger he could eat during Kline's monologue. He wiped his mouth, and took a drink of Coke. "And you think that she'll give up something she didn't intend to if we do that?" He threw his paper napkin on top of the burger remnants.

"If she's got something to hide," Kline said, "we'll know it when you mention Ryan Martin's name. From there, she either comes clean right away, and it looks like she's clean, or she plays dumb, and we know she's got something to hide."

"What do you think she's got to hide?"

"I don't know," Kline replied, "but she's already had one chance to tell us about Martin, and she didn't. I suppose she may not have known he was working at the camp, but that would be pretty surprising."

Floyd pushed the plate away. "Are you ready to roust her?" he asked.

"I love this part of my job," Kline said with a smile as he slid out of the booth.

☆ ☆ ☆

They walked back to the Government Center and Kline checked an aging Crown Victoria out of the motor pool. It looked like it had been in a dozen wrecks and was only partially repaired after each. The heater threw out air that smelled of smoke, and the seats were dotted with fluids that Floyd preferred not to consider. Kline drove through the noon downtown traffic like a Tijuana cabbie, darting in and out of lanes and pushing through all the yellow lights. Kline took a cell phone out of his sport coat while at a stoplight, and he dialed a number written on the palm of his hand. The light turned green, and he continued to listen without an apparent answer for the next two blocks.

"She's not home," he said, pushing the off button. "That's actually a little easier, because the shelter where she works is just over on Franklin."

Franklin Avenue was a wide thoroughfare, with brick-fronted stores lining both sides of the street. The neighborhoods on the blocks behind the stores seemed to be filled with bungalows that were all in need of paint, and/or repairs of some kind. Gang graffiti adorned some of the alleyways, and teens, who looked like they should be in school, stood on the corners glaring at the unmarked car as they passed.

"If this is a good part of town," Floyd said, "I'd hate to see the bad parts."

"Lots of Indians move off the reservations and end up here. There's been a real infusion of cash since the casinos started making quarterly payments to tribal members, but instead of elevating the community, the money seems to have generated a lot more crime and drug use."

Kline pulled into a bus stop and put down the visor so the *Police Vehicle* sign showed through the windshield. They carefully locked the car, and walked down the block, filled with shops guarded by barred windows. There was a group of gaunt men smoking in front of a store halfway down the block, and they stepped aside as Kline led Floyd through the door.

The old store had been converted into a soup kitchen, with plywood tables and plank benches filling the area closest to the door. Hardened men and women dressed in ragged clothing sat at tables drinking coffee from porcelain mugs that may have been rescued from garage sales. Every set of eyes followed them as they walked to the rear of the building. When Kline opened a door into the kitchen the smell of yeast and cooked vegetables masked by the smell of soap and disinfectant assaulted their noses. A commercial dishwasher roared in the corner as three women and a man washed pots in a large stainless steel sink, yelling to be heard over the dishwasher.

Colleen McCarthy, wearing a white apron over a plaid flannel shirt and jeans, was drying a huge aluminum pot while holding a conversation with another woman. She saw them before they got half way past the racks of cooling bread loaves. Recognition quickly drained the color from her already pale complexion.

She set the pot and the dishtowel down, tucked a stray gray lock behind her ear, and directed the two officers out the back door, into a narrow alley. All activity stopped as the other dishwashers watched her disappear with Floyd and Kline.

"I'm surprised to see you," she said. "I really don't have anything new to tell you, if that's why you're here." The wind whipped through the alley and tugged at McCarthy's apron as they spoke.

"We've made some progress on the investigation," Floyd said, using the tactic suggested by Kline. "I've been working under the assumption that your daughter may have known her assailant, and I have some names I'd like to see if you recognize." Floyd took a slip of paper from his pocket and started reading. As he said each name, Colleen McCarthy shook her head. Ryan Martin's name got the same response. He read off three more then stopped.

"Did you say, Ryan Martin," Kline asked, acting if he'd had a sudden inspiration.

Floyd looked down at the list. "Yes, he worked at the camp the summer Helen disappeared."

"We just had a request to unseal his juvenile file after he was killed in Wisconsin last week." Kline snapped his fingers. "That's it! He was arrested at an anti-war rally. He stabbed a cop."

Colleen McCarthy's jaw tightened as she watched Kline's act in silence. "Miss McCarthy, didn't you tell us that you had been involved in the antiwar movement while your husband was busy making more effective ways of killing? Is there any chance that you might've met Ryan Martin at some antiwar protest?"

"I suppose it's possible," she replied curtly, "but I don't really remember him. Is he the kind of character who would stand out for some reason?"

Kline shot Floyd a furtive glance. "He probably would," he said. "He was sitting next to you. When the cops tried to carry you to the van he stabbed one of them. The police report said you tried to run away, but the other cop tackled you, and both you and Ryan were taken into custody."

"What are you insinuating?" she asked, as tears formed in her eyes. "Are you saying that I was involved in my own daughter's death? Is that what you're saying?"

Floyd and Kline stood silently, waiting for more to come. McCarthy stuffed her hands into the pockets of her jeans and broke into tears. No one moved. After a few seconds, she pulled a tissue from her pocket and blew her nose.

"Well!" she said, "If you two have nothing else to ask, I have work to do inside."

As she took a step, Kline put a hand on her arm. "How well did you know Ryan Martin?"

"I...I'd never seen him before that day," she said emphatically. "I don't recall seeing him since. That's why the name didn't mean anything to me. I don't remember the name of every person I've ever met for an hour or two. There were hundreds of protestors arrested that day. I didn't know most of them!"

The man who'd been washing dishes stuck his head out the door. His face was gaunt, and he was lean, like he'd led a tough life. "Everything okay?" he asked McCarthy.

Kline pulled his sport coat open so the badge on his belt showed. "Everything's just fine," he said.

At the sight of the Minneapolis detective's badge the man looked at the ground. "Sorry," he said softly as he withdrew through the door.

"You testified in Ryan's juvenile hearing," Kline said. "The transcript said you'd testified that he was just a misdirected teen, who reacted with too much exuberance at the wrong time. The court transcripts left me with the impression that you knew him pretty well."

McCarthy pushed Kline's hand from her arm. "You're mistaken. If you haven't noticed, I like to be an advocate of the impoverished and downtrodden. He was someone who seemed to need some words of encouragement and I offered them in his behalf. I don't know what happened to him after the trial."

"You never saw him again?" Floyd asked.

"Not that I recall. Now I really don't have any more time for your Nazi tactics. I'm going to go back to work and do something meaningful. I suggest that you two do the same. For that matter, why don't you police do something to help the people in this neighborhood instead of arresting them for drug use and throwing them in jail?" McCarthy paused, "Of course you won't, if they weren't criminals, you'd be out of jobs." She stormed away and slammed the door behind them.

Kline led Floyd down the alley. "Methinks the lady doth protest too much," he said.

"Shakespeare?"

"I think so."

They drove back to the government center in the mid-day traffic. Most blocks they covered in one stop-light change, and the most exciting thing they saw was an old guy pan-handling from a group of executives in front of an office building.

"What did you make of the guy who checked on us in the alley?" Floyd asked.

"He was an ex-con," Kline said. "Did you notice how he couldn't look us in the eye? That's typical for a con that's been conditioned by some heavy-handed guards in a maximum-security prison. I noticed the prison tattoos on his hands. They looked like they'd been done with pen ink."

"So, Kline, what do you suggest I do about McCarthy now?"

"Find evidence that she's had other contact with Martin. When you do, we confront her again. This time, I suggest that you bring her in wearing handcuffs. That has a huge psychological effect on people."

"My experience is," Floyd said, "that it makes them want to call a lawyer."

Kline chuckled. “Thank God for Miranda. If not for him, all those struggling lawyers would be out of business. Wouldn’t it be a shame if they all had to go out and find jobs instead of just being pains in the butt and producing heartburn?”

CHAPTER 32

Floyd was the last person to show up for the four o'clock meeting in the Pine County bullpen. He hung his jacket on the coat rack and joined the noisy group gathered around Pam's desk.

"So," Floyd said, "who cracked the case today?"

"We were hoping you had," Laurie Lone Eagle said. "Pam and I have worked our fingers to the bone with computer searches, and we've come up pretty much dry. If I try to track down one more felon named Earl I think that I'll gag."

"What did Colleen McCarthy have to say?" Dan asked.

"Well, first she said that she didn't know anyone named Ryan Martin," Floyd said as he took a chair. "Then we confronted her with the information that she'd been arrested with him, and she said she'd known lots of people at protests, and didn't recognize the name. Kline, the Hennepin County detective, pointed out that she'd testified at his trial, and she went to pieces. She started yelling and told us that we should solve the world's real problems and stop harassing the poor drug dealers and downtrodden people."

"She never saw him again?" Dan asked.

"She said the last time she saw him was at the war protest trial."

"Well," Dan said, looking at the faces around the desk, "does anyone have any ideas on how we might prove that she had contact with him after that?"

"I've been through the court records for five of his arrests," Pam said, "and there's no mention of Colleen McCarthy in any of them."

"She wasn't mentioned anywhere else in his juvenile records," Floyd added. "We read through all the files after we got back to the government center."

Pam snapped her fingers. "The two Benson boys saw lots of people coming and going from the streetcar. We could show them a picture of McCarthy they might recognize her."

Floyd took out a notebook and quickly flipped through the pages. When he found the one he wanted he picked up the phone and dialed.

"Who are you calling?" Laurie asked.

Floyd held up a finger. "Joe Benson please." He pushed the button for the speakerphone while he waited. "Hi, Joe, this is Floyd Swenson again. I recall you telling me about getting punished for peeping into the streetcar. You said there was an older woman there with Ryan Martin."

"Yeah," Joe said, "I remember saying that. I told you I didn't recognize her face when you asked who it was."

"Let me try something else on you." Floyd said, "I think you saw the face, but it was someone you didn't know. Does that sound plausible?"

"I don't know, Floyd. I might have seen a face, but I don't remember it and I don't know who she was."

"Do you remember what color her hair was?" Dan smiled and looked at the nods of recognition around him.

"I hadn't thought about it." There was a pause. "I think it was red. I don't know why I remember it, but I'm sure that's right."

"Thanks, Joe. That may help us."

"How would that help?" Joe asked.

"We have a red-headed female suspect."

"Cool!"

Floyd shut the speakerphone down, and then quickly dialed another number. He switched the speakerphone on as a male voice answered. "Hello."

"Rob, this is Floyd Swenson. I want you to think back to the day your mother spanked you for window peeping at the streetcar."

"I'd rather remember something more pleasant," Rob said with a laugh. "That's a rather painful and embarrassing moment in my life."

"Think about it and try to picture the woman you saw. You told me you didn't recognize her, but do you remember what color her hair was?"

"It was red," Benson replied. "The color of a new penny. That's really weird, because I don't know why that stuck in my mind. Is that significant?"

"It might be. It gives us another suspect."

"You think a red-headed woman killed the girl. That seems unlikely."

"We don't think the redhead killed the girl," Dan said, "but she might know who did."

"I always thought it was odd that someone that much older than Ryan was there with him. It didn't seem right somehow."

"How did you know she was old?"

"You sound like you're on a speakerphone."

"Yes, but I'm the only one here," Floyd said, looking sternly at the others.

"Well, she had droopy breasts," Benson said softly, like someone may have been listening on his end. Then he added, "and she had freckles on her chest, too. I was kind of awestruck by the sight."

Floyd shook his head, and Laurie stifled a laugh. Pam had a big grin and let out a snort as she tried not to laugh.

"Thanks, Rob. I think this will help."

"So," Floyd said as he turned off the speakerphone, "it looks like we have two witnesses who spotted McCarthy with Martin."

"Someone please tell me you're not going to take droopy boob casts to show the Benson boys," Pam said as she shook her head.

"No," Floyd chuckled, "we'll have to get a picture of the freckles and see if they can identify the pattern."

"I can almost see the two little boys peeping through window at a naked woman and then getting caught by their mother," Laurie said. "I'll bet they peed their pants."

"What do we do with that tidbit?" Floyd asked. "I can't see questioning her again tomorrow."

"Let's see if anything else comes up," Dan said.

"You could arrest her for obstructing a murder investigation," Laurie said. "Putting someone in cuffs and dragging them in for questioning sometimes yields unexpected results. She might get very talkative, especially if she can implicate someone else to free herself."

"Kline would love that!" Floyd said with twinkling eyes.

"Give him a call and see if he can sell that to his captain," Dan said. "What else can we do tomorrow?"

"I started through the property abstracts around the lake this afternoon," Pam said. "Laurie was checking the last names of the '74 owners against the database. It's actually going quickly, and I can probably get through the rest in a few hours tomorrow."

CHAPTER 33

Friday

Pam went through the stacks of property abstracts and handed Laurie a list of names to check every fifteen minutes. By ten-thirty, they had finished off all the properties, except three.

"Laurie, I have three properties in a row with the owner listed as Arlyn Prokop, the lawyer. Obviously, he didn't live in three houses at once, so I assume he either built them as spec houses, or he was renting them out."

"Let's see where the son lives," Laurie said. "He told you that he bought the practice and his parent's house when they moved to Florida." Laurie flipped through the phone book until she found the name. "It shows two addresses, one is the law office and the other is on McCormick Road. I think that's the gravel road that runs along the north side of McCormick Lake."

Laurie picked up the phone and dialed the number for the house, the recorder kicked in and she hung up. "He must be at the office," she said. "Let's take a drive to Willow River. We can get lunch along the way."

Downtown Willow River wasn't a bustle of activity on a busy day, and aside from the few cars at the Squirrel Cage Bar and the Laundromat, the town seemed pretty much deserted. A red Lexus sedan and a green Explorer were parked in front of the building that housed the *Prokop and Prokop Law Office* and *Willow River Realty* and lights were on inside both halves of the building.

Laurie led the way to the front steps, and knocked once before opening the door. There was no entryway, and when Laurie and Pam walked in together, they filled the area in front of Arlyn Prokop's desk. He looked up like he had been expecting them.

"Good morning, ladies," Prokop said. "What can I do for you?" He smiled at Laurie, showing a row of even, straight teeth, and then leaned to the side to smile at Pam Ryan standing behind Laurie. He stood to shake their hands and wasn't a large man, probably no more than six inches taller than the two women who were both five-three. His shoulders were broad, but when he shook hands the softness of his palms said that he wasn't accustomed to manual labor.

"I'm Agent Lone Eagle, from the Bureau of Criminal Apprehension, and this is Deputy Ryan, from the sheriff's department."

"Where are my manners?" He said as he took off his glasses and moved a stack of files from one of the two guest chairs. “Please have a seat while we talk. I believe I spoke with Deputy Ryan yesterday or was it Wednesday? She was asking about a case my father represented a long time ago.”

“We’re still working on it,” Pam said. “I’ve been trying to track down the ownership of the properties around First Lake. The records show that Arlyn Prokop owned three adjacent houses on the north side of the lake. I assume that your family didn’t each live in your own house.”

“Not at all,” Prokop said, the engaging smile spreading over his face again. “We lived on McCormick Lake. The cabins on First Lake weren’t houses, at least not in the seventies. My father built them as seasonal cabins that he rented out to tourists during the summer. He sold them about fifteen years ago, and the new owners winterized them and turned them into year-round housing.”

“Do you still have the rental records?” Laurie asked. “We’d like to know who rented the summer that Helen Smith disappeared.”

“Whew!” Prokop said as he leaned back in his chair. “That could be tough. I assume that Dad kept those records for tax purposes. You know, we lawyers get audited about ten times as often as the average person so we tend to keep meticulous tax records. On the other hand, the only things that can result from keeping old tax records past the mandated retention period are bad. I'm sure my father purged those records after seven years."

"Could you check?" Laurie asked. "We've been through all the plat books and we've identified every other resident around the lake without identifying another suspect."

"You think that someone who lived on the lake might be a suspect in the Smith girl's death?"

"We had a report that our prime suspect had stolen a boat from the camp the night she disappeared," Pam explained. "We're chasing down every possible lead, and there's a chance that he may have had a accomplice living on the lake."

"Let's see," Prokop said, "They'd be in the back room. Hang on for a minute." He opened a door that Pam had assumed to be a rest room and disappeared inside. While he was gone, Pam surveyed the inside of the sterile office. The walls were white plasterboard, and the woodwork was dark oak, which matched the featureless oak desk. There were no pictures or personal touches on the wall, except for a framed certificate declaring Arlyn Prokop a member of the Minnesota Bar Association. The desk had one file open on top of it, but there were several small piles of manila folders stacked on the credenza and a small table. An older IBM computer sat behind the desk. It was on, but a filter covered the face of the monitor so only someone sitting directly in front of it could see the display.

The front door opened quickly, startling both the officers. A middle-aged man, wearing a gold sport coat with a realtor's association pin stuck his head in the door and looked surprised to see the visitors. He had a toupee that looked like it was made of yellow polyester, its color contrasted against the graying hair on the rest of his head.

"Sorry," the man said, "I was looking for Arl to see if he wanted to go to lunch."

Prokop stepped out of the back room and waved the man off. "Not today, Jerry. I've got to help these ladies with a problem."

Jerry waved and was gone as quickly as he'd shown up.

After a few minutes Prokop emerged from the storage room with a dusty cardboard box. "It looks like my father may have kept some of the rental records after all." He set the box on top of the desk and took off the lid. The interior was filled with rows of manila folders, each with a carefully lettered tab sticking up. Pam stood to look at the tabs and Prokop carefully laid his hand across the files.

"I'm sorry," he said, "but there are a bunch of legal records in here, too. I really can't let you look through them." He looked at his watch and added, "And I don't have the time to do it at this moment either. Can you give me a couple days? I promise to make it a priority after I wrap up a couple of real estate matters."

Laurie stood. “We’d appreciate it if you’d check them within the next day or so.”

“Give me until Monday,” Prokop said. “The murder is thirty years-old, I can’t believe that a couple more days will make a lot of difference.”

Pam gave Laurie a pleading look. “Monday will be fine,” Laurie said.

“I think he’s stalling,” Pam said as they walked to Laurie’s car.

“He’s a businessman,” Laurie replied, “and he’s right. A couple days won’t make any difference at this point.”

“He was too smooth and too relaxed,” Pam said. “There’s something about him that makes me uneasy.”

“Let’s take a drive out past his house,” Laurie said. “I’d like to see what it looks like. Maybe we’ll talk to a neighbor.”

McCormick Lake Road was a single lane of gravel cut through a hay field. It disappeared through a veil of pine trees, and opened onto a beautiful, albeit small, lake. There were three houses on the road before it hit a dead end. A mossy bog covered the opposite shore of the lake until it turned into a Tamarack forest in the distance. All three houses fronting the lake were large, year-round homes with natural cedar exteriors. Each house had a mailbox along the road, and the second mailbox said Prokop in small block letters. Laurie stopped the car, and took a plat map from the back seat.

"What are you looking for?" Pam asked.

"I was wondering how far this is from First Lake," she replied as she flipped through the pages. "Look at this," she said, pointing to a blue line that meandered between two larger blue spots. "This creek connects First Lake with this lake. I wonder if someone in a canoe could paddle between the two lakes?"

"Didn't one of the camp cooks say that Earl wore glasses?" Pam asked.

"What?"

"Don't you remember?" Pam asked. "The Johnson woman, Shirley, said that the guy who wouldn't go skinny dipping wore wire-rimmed glasses that he kept slipping down his nose."

"He does wear glasses," Laurie said. "I guess I could be swayed."

Pam's eyes grew wide. "It's him!"

Laurie turned her head to see who had come up behind them. "Who?"

"Prokop!" Pam said, putting her hand on Laurie's arm. "Don't you see? He wears wire-rimmed glasses. What did the realtor call him when he stuck his head in? Arl! It sounds just like Earl! Prokop is the guy who wouldn't go skinny-dipping at the camp!"

Laurie ran through all the information in her mind and said, "It's awfully coincidental, isn't it?" Everything that Pam mentioned fit. "I might be able to buy that he's the kid who met Ryan Martin at the beach, but I have a hard time thinking he's the murderer, even if he is the *Earl* we've been looking for."

"Let's look in the windows of the house," Pam said.

"What will that tell us?" Laurie said. "I think we need to run this past Dan and the sheriff. I don't think there's enough probable cause based on what you've pointed out to get a search warrant for the house."

A red Lexus, which had been parked in front of the law office, came through the trees as Prokop's garage door opened. "Oh, no!" Pam said, "He's here!

"Aren't you glad you aren't peeking through the windows?" Laurie whispered.

Prokop pulled into the garage, and then walked down the driveway toward Laurie's unmarked state car. She rolled down the window.

"Fancy meeting you two here!" he said. "Is there something more I can do for you?"

Laurie held up the plat map. "We were looking at the plat map," she said. "We didn't realize that McCormick Lake was so close to First Lake." She pointed to the blue line linking the two lakes. "It appears there's a creek connecting them. Is it big enough to take a boat through?"

"Not a boat," Prokop said. "We had a canoe when I was a kid, and I used to canoe over there to go fishing. This lake is so small and shallow that the fish freeze out every few years."

"You have a beautiful view from here," Laurie said as she put the plat map back in the rear seat. "I'd have some huge windows overlooking the lake if I lived here."

"I do," he said. "Would you like to come in and see them?"

"I don't think…" Pam started to say before Laurie cut her off.

"We'd love to see the view," Laurie said, opening the car door and motioning for Pam to join her.

Pam walked beside Laurie and whispered, "I have a bad feeling about this."

Prokop held the door through the garage open for them, "After you."

They walked into an immaculate kitchen with beautiful knotty pine cabinetry and windows looking out over the lake. There was a small breakfast nook that opened into a living room with a vaulted ceiling and windows that reached from the floor to the peak of the roof. The view was breathtaking, with the calm, blue waters of the lake giving way to the dark green bog moss, then brilliant gold of the Tamaracks in the background.

"This is fabulous!" Laurie said, with awe. "I have never seen a more beautiful view!"

Pam hung back and kept her arms crossed over her bulletproof vest. "It's great," she said, "But we were going to grab a bite to eat, and I'm getting a little hungry."

"Yes," Prokop agreed, "I need to be on my way, too. I just ran home to grab a file I'd been working on last night. I have a client meeting me in ten minutes."

"Thanks for the tour," Laurie said starting for the kitchen door.

Prokop smiled. "You'll have to come back some time to see the rest of my house."

Laurie let out a gasp as an animal skittered across the kitchen floor.

Prokop spun, and then started to laugh. He bent down next to the kitchen table and reached under a chair. When he turned back, there was a ferret in is hands. "This is Kitty. Sometimes he can be a little unnerving when he sneaks around. He's not much of a people ferret. He's a little shy." Prokop held the ferret close to his chest and stroked its gray fur. "He's also a little temperamental. Sometimes he feels that he's not getting enough attention and he will sneak up and bite your toes. Then we play hide and seek. The one thing he doesn't like at all is getting put into the car carrier. He knows it's time to go to the vet for shots then."

Laurie ran a finger over the pointed head. "His fur is bristly. I thought it would be soft."

"They have long guard hairs that are stiff," Prokop explained, "with under-hairs that are soft. The biggest problem is that they tend to be a little musky smelling. Kitty's been descented, and if he doesn't get a bath every week he gets a little gamy."

"Would you like to pet him, Deputy Ryan?" Prokop asked, holding the ferret out.

"He reminds me of a granary rat," Pam said as a shiver ran over her body. She kept her arms folded.

"He's not a rat," Prokop explained, as Pam edged further into the garage. "He's a close relative of the weasel."

"I think he looks more like a cat," Laurie said, "although he's a little long for a cat."

"Actually, I feed him cat food. However, ferrets and cats are mortal enemies, and a cat would kill him in a second if it could."

Pam stepped further away from the door, waiting for Laurie to catch her unveiled hints about leaving. Her shoulder bumped into a long rusty saw with large wicked teeth that shifted on its mounting pegs and rattled like it was about to fall. It was almost four feet long, and it had a handle on one end that made a "T" with the blade. She put a hand on it to stop its swinging.

Prokop noticed Pam appraising the saw. He said, "It's an antique ice saw. Before refrigeration, the ice-men would go out on the lakes and cut huge ice blocks with that saw. They'd haul them onshore and store them packed under sawdust. In the summer they'd travel around and sell the blocks for people to keep in their ice boxes."

"It looks wicked," Pam said. Looking at Laurie she added, "I need to eat lunch. Are we done here?"

"Sure," Laurie replied. "Thanks," She said to Prokop.

"I think he's creepy," Pam said as they walked down the driveway. "He makes my skin crawl."

Laurie started the engine and turned around in Prokop's driveway. "All lawyers are a little creepy," she said. "I think it's their first class in law school."

"I think," Pam said, "that the whole story about picking up a file for a client meeting was an easy way to shoo us out."

"That'll be easy to check," Laurie said. "Let's eat lunch at the Squirrel Cage and see if his car comes back to the office in a few minutes."

They ate their lunches, had extra coffee, and talked for forty-five minutes. "He didn't come back," Pam said as they walked across the parking lot.

"I see that," Laurie conceded. "I'm going to call on something else that may be interesting. We found an odd hair with Helen Smith's body and an expert in Oregon said it was from a ferret."

Pam shook her head. "I doubt that ferrets live thirty years."

CHAPTER 34

Pam and Laurie knocked gently on Dan's doorframe. "Got a second?" Pam asked.

"I've got to make the hair call," Laurie said. "You update him."

Pam explained her observations about Arlyn Prokop and his ferret to Dan. He listened intently while Pam explained each of her points in great detail culminating with a description of the antique ice saw that was probably used to cut up dead bodies. She summarized by suggesting they go to a judge for a warrant to search Prokop's house.

"What's on your shoulder?" Dan asked.

Pam picked the piece of green off and squinted at it. "It's some of the mold that fell off the antique saw when I brushed against it."

Dan reached out and took it between his fingers. "It doesn't look much like a bloody body part to me," he said. "As a matter of fact, I think it's a bit of moss." He reached across the desk to a wastebasket and dropped the moss into it. "What other bodies would he have cut up with that saw?" Dan asked. "We only know about the Smith girl, and her body appeared to be intact. The forensic anthropologist would have noted any saw marks on the bones if they'd been cut."

"There must be others," Pam said. "Why would he kill just one person and quit?"

"Most murderers only kill once," Dan replied. "Most murders are acts of passion or hatred, and the murderer kills the source of his irritation and is done. Serial killers are really rare, and they react to social stimuli rather than personal hatred. I don't think that Prokop fits the serial killer profile."

"Maybe he killed the Smith girl for some reason," Pam said, after pondering Dan's words. "Maybe he isn't a serial murderer, and Helen Smith is his only victim. No, he had two victims. He had to kill Ryan Martin to keep him quiet. So there are two victims."

"Did you notice any cuts or bandages on his body? Ryan Martin's killer was bleeding when he left the murder scene."

"I wasn't looking for any, but I didn't notice any either. Maybe he got cut somewhere out of sight, like on his leg."

Laurie stepped into Dan's office and took the other guest chair as Floyd Swenson and Sandy Maki stepped in and leaned on either side of the doorframe. The two men were in uniforms that looked like they'd been rolling in rust.

"There is the ferret hair from the trunk," Pam offered, "and creepy Prokop does own a ferret."

Dan smiled and shook his head. “So much for the search warrant for Prokop’s house,” he said. “Besides, it’s a little hard to come up with evidence of a thirty year-old murder during the search of a house, assuming a murder occurred there. I am more inclined to check the streetcar to see if there’s any evidence we can glean from it.”

“Heaven knows,” Pam said, “that no evidence in that streetcar has ever been destroyed by cleaning. It looks like no one has laid a broom or dust cloth to it in the last century.”

“Speaking of not having been cleaned recently,” Dan said, looking at Floyd and Sandy, “what have you two been up to?”

“We,” Floyd said, “went through all the junk cars with a magnifying glass to see if there was anything that we might have missed. Sandy found a used condom jammed between the back and the seat of the DeSoto. The problem is there’s no way to know how old it is. It might have been there since someone drove it to the prom in fifty-one.”

Pam screwed up her face at the mention of the used condom. “Yuk!”

“Send it to the BCA,” Laurie said. “They may be able to estimate the date of manufacture. If there’s any recoverable DNA they might be able to run it against the sex offender database.”

“Was anything else interesting?” Dan asked.

"Not unless you're into mouse nests and dead flies." Sandy replied. "We took all the mouse nests out and bagged them. It looked like the mice had scrounged some human hair for nesting materials. I'll send them with the condom to the BCA."

The dispatcher paged Laurie to pick up line three. Dan pushed his phone across the desk and punched the flashing button.

"This is Inspector Lone Eagle."

Laurie's face suddenly got a smirk, as she looked at Dan and Pam. "Nothing that I can think of at the moment," she said. "I'm probably free from here anytime now."

She listened again then said, "Tell you what, I'll meet you there in half an hour. That way you won't have to go out of your way to take me back to the motel." After listening a few more moments she said goodbye and hung up.

"That was Arlyn Prokop," she said. "He's taking me out for dinner. He just finished reviewing a will with an elderly nursing home patient, which is why he didn't come back to his office after we saw him at the house."

Dan started to laugh. "I guess that lets him off the hook. I can't think of a single murderer brazen enough to ask the investigator on a date!" He stood, signaling the end of the conversation. "Let's meet here tomorrow morning and we'll do a thorough search of the streetcar."

"I still think Prokop is slimy," Pam said as she walked out the door.

"Of course he's slimy," Dan replied. "He's a lawyer."

CHAPTER 35

Friday evening

The red Lexus was parked at the steak house near the Pine City freeway exit when Laurie arrived. The crowd was sparse, but the beer signs and collection of televisions tuned to assorted sporting events portended a busy trade with a younger generation later in the evening. Prokop waved to Laurie from a corner table in the dining room.

"I haven't been asked out for dinner in years," Laurie said as she sat at the table. "Thanks for the invitation."

"I don't have much social life myself," Prokop replied. "I've dated most of the divorcees and widows in the county, and I find that we don't have a lot in common. Most of them are into either drinking or gambling as a primary pastime, and I value my brain cells and money too much to indulge in either of those activities heavily."

The waitress came to the table carrying a bottle of red wine and held it out so Prokop could read the label. The windows overlooked the freeway and the buzz of traffic was steady. The dining room was a rustic motif with knotty pine walls and huge pine logs that ran the length of the ceiling. A few stuffed deer heads, geese, and a huge Northern Pike decorated the walls.

"That's fine," he said to the young waitress. "I eat here quite a bit," he explained to Laurie, "and I talked the owner into stocking an Australian Zinfandel/ Shiraz blend that I like. I'd love to share the bottle with you, or feel free to order whatever else you'd like."

"I really don't drink much," Laurie said as the waitress pulled the cork from the bottle. "But, I'm not above having a glass of wine with dinner. I don't think I've ever had an Australian wine."

The waitress poured a sample into Prokop's wineglass. "Most of our customers prefer beer or sweeter wine than this," the waitress explained as the lawyer swirled, and then sipped the wine. "Mister Prokop showed me the proper way to open and sample the wine. I have surprised a few of the people from the Cities with my technique. It's got me a few nice tips."

"It's as good as usual, Jenny."

The waitress poured Laurie's glass full, and then topped Prokop's glass. "Are you ready to order?" she asked.

"I haven't even looked at the menu yet," Laurie replied. "Give us a few minutes." She took a sip of the wine and smiled. "It's a little dry for my tastes, but I like the fruitiness."

"Trust me," Prokop said, "It will be perfect with dinner."

After ordering dinner and exhausting the topic of weather, Laurie asked, "What inspired you to ask me out?"

The same engaging smile he'd shown in his office crossed the lawyer's face. "I thought you were bright and attractive. I didn't see a wedding ring on your finger, and I was tired of eating by myself." He paused and then asked, "Why did you accept?"

"You were charming," Laurie replied. "You treated me with respect and dignity, and you didn't have a wedding ring on your finger."

"Touché!" Prokop said, lifting his wine glass and touching it to Laurie's. "So, are you widowed or divorced?"

"Neither," Laurie replied. "I'm married to my job, with crummy hours and too little time for a relationship. And you?"

"When I was young," Prokop said, "I was too shy to date. Then I was too timid to stand up to my mother, and there was no one who could meet her standards. By the time she was gone, I was too set in my ways to ever find someone who would put up with me."

"So, you gave up?"

"Not really," he replied. "Like I said, I've dated most of the single women in the county, and we just have such different values that I find it hard to see them as soul mates."

As their salads arrived Laurie said, "You know that we're trying to find out who murdered Helen Smith at the Melody Pines Camp. We were told by a person we questioned that there was a local kid, named Earl, who hung around the camp with one of the maintenance guys that summer. Pam Ryan thinks that kid was you."

A smile spread across Prokop's face. "I was wondering if that would come up." He took another bite of salad. "Deputy Ryan is pretty sharp, for a young investigator."

"So, it was you?"

"My friends have called me Arl for years. To the untrained ear, it sounds a lot like Earl."

"You didn't answer my question."

"It was me," Prokop replied. "I hung around with the camp counselors for a few summers. It was one place I could meet some kids close to my own age, and hang around with some girls in a non-threatening environment. Like I said, I was terribly shy back then."

"But in '74 you must've been in college or law school. Most of the campers were teens and grade-school aged."

"Ah, I see your concern. I socialized with the camp staff when they were off on Saturday evenings. Most of the staff were high school students, and the directors, like the head lifeguard and the resident director, were college-aged. Sadly, I had a domineering mother who suppressed my social interaction for my teen years, and I was closer to the high school students in terms of social development. In a lot of respects I'm still the social outcast I was back then."

"You aren't alone," Laurie said with a smile. "Do you remember Helen Smith?"

"I don't remember many of the names of the camp staff, and, as I recall, she was a camper," Prokop replied. "It was thirty years ago, and I kind of hung around the periphery with the staff. I remember the girl disappearing, and the firemen dragging the lake. I don't know that I ever met her. Like I said, I hung around with the counselors. I'd canoe over on Saturday nights, and socialize with them when they were off duty. I don't recall ever being at the camp when the campers were there during the week."

"Did you know Ryan Martin?"

"My father defended him the fall after the girl disappeared."

"You didn't answer my question," Laurie said.

"I was being evasive," Prokop said. "I met him the summer he worked there. I guess you might say he used me. I was naïve, and hungry for interactions with people my own age. I brought him over to our house, and he stole some money my mother had stashed away in the cookie jar. My father caught him, and really raised holy hell with us. I didn't see Ryan after that, but he called my father when he got arrested. I don't know if it was because he respected my father for treating him squarely, or if Dad was the only lawyer he'd ever met and he needed someone to defend him."

"Do you think Ryan Martin had anything to do with Helen Smith's disappearance?"

"I honestly can't say," Prokop said. "He was certainly a social outcast and capable of criminal acts. I found him electrifying at the time. I'd had such a sheltered life until then, and he was definitely on the fringes of society. He'd done all the things a teenaged boy dreams about; he drank, he chased girls, he challenged authority. I don't know that he was capable of murder."

"You could have told us all this when we were at your office," Laurie said, the judgment thick in her voice.

"I didn't have anything to do with the girl's disappearance or her death," Prokop said. "I didn't think my relationship with the camp staff would be anything more than an unnecessary diversion for you."

Laurie smiled. "You know, cops are like lawyers. We like to have too much information and do the sorting ourselves. Is there anything else you know about that might be an unnecessary diversion, but that I might like to know anyway?"

"Is there a redheaded woman involved?" Prokop asked.

"The victim's mother was a redhead," Laurie replied. "Why do you ask?"

"A redheaded woman," Prokop said, "contacted my father after the girl disappeared. She showed up at our front door and wanted him to negotiate with some kidnappers. I was in the living room when they were talking and I caught some snippets of the conversation. I didn't hear the entire conversation and I don't know if my father actually got involved. I mostly recall that the woman was very agitated." The revelation came just as the waitress delivered the dinner entrees.

"You didn't think that was pertinent?" Laurie asked.

"Hey!" Prokop protested, "I just remembered it, and I never thought of it in the same context as the Smith girl's disappearance before. It hadn't thought about this whole thing in decades. As we talk, things come back."

Laurie waited for the waitress to leave. "Apology accepted. What happened?" She asked. "Had she actually been contacted by the kidnappers?"

"I don't know. I was a student, so I wasn't a formal part of the discussion. I remember the redheaded woman coming to our house and pleading with Dad in the kitchen. He took her into the den and closed the door when he realized that I was listening to the conversation."

Laurie quietly considered the new information as she ate. She made a mental note to talk with Floyd Swenson about Colleen McCarthy. They'd have to add this to their discussion with her the next time. She even wondered if it might be wise to have one of the BCA interrogation specialists join them on the next visit.

"Laurie."

"Sorry," she said. "I get off on tangents."

"This is going to sound a little out of place," Prokop said. "This is one of the most interesting dinner meals I've had in years."

"What do you mean?"

"You're the brightest woman I've ever met. This has been delightful! I mean most people I go out with talk about local drivel and gossip. You've actually challenged me to use my mind."

Laurie smiled. "I was feeling a little guilty about being asked out to dinner and then interrogating you. I thought you'd probably walk out at any minute and stiff me with the bill."

"Oh, quite to the contrary," Prokop said as he refilled their wineglasses. "I find most of my life quite dull and lacking in challenges. Dinner with you is a treat. Do you work out of the St. Paul BCA office?"

"That's where I have an office," Laurie said. "I travel about fifty percent of the time. I'm the missing child specialist, and every time there's a kidnapping outside the Twin Cities I pack up my bags and spend a week or two with the local investigators. Most of the time we're investigating a parental abduction or runaway, but occasionally there are some stranger kidnappings. In general it's very frustrating work, but when we return a missing child it's a world-class high.

"Do you find many missing children?"

"Twenty or thirty a year are located with non-custodial parents or relatives and another twenty or thirty are runaways that either call home, or are arrested somewhere and eventually make it back home. But, the real gems are the one or two a year that we find out of state with a stranger."

"I could see how that would be a gratifying experience," Prokop said. "You invest a month or two tracing leads and then you break the case open."

"How about you, Arlyn, you seem rather unhappy with Pine County life. Why do you stay here?"

"Please call me Arl. Everyone who knows me well calls me that. I suppose I stay here because it's comfortable. I have the house, the practice, and a fairly steady business. I make enough to get by, and I have enough flexibility to do as I want, when I want. I travel to interesting places on my vacations, and I indulge in some simple pleasures, like this wine. If I moved to Duluth, or the Cities, the pace would be grueling, and I'd have to live in the suburbs somewhere. I just don't see that as a reasonably attractive alternative to the quiet boredom of Pine County living in a house with a world-class view. Besides, there is a little excitement occasionally. I've had a few stints as a public defender, so I get to put on a suit and spend a few days in court."

"Where have your travels taken you?"

"Everywhere!" Arlyn said with sparkle. "I've been to every island of the Caribbean, and most of the countries in Central America. I've gone on safari in Africa and climbed to the top of Mount Kilimanjaro. I've gone scuba diving on the Australian Great Barrier Reef and caught trout on sparkling streams in New Zealand. I've gone to a few places in Asia, but I find the food and the culture…uncomfortable."

"I've heard that places like Bali are lovely."

"They are, but if you don't feel comfortable eating almost every variety of seafood, most of it raw, the trip looses a lot of luster."

Laurie laughed as commotion at the front door interrupted the conversation. They watched a group of musicians wrestle two large speakers and some electronics through the front door. Laurie looked around the dining room from their corner table and realized that most of the tables were now filled.

"Wow!" Laurie said, looking at her watch. "I didn't realize it was getting so late. I haven't had an evening fly by like this in a long time."

"I hope it was the company," Prokop said, signaling the waitress for the bill. "This has been the most enjoyable evening I've had in months. You know, it's Friday evening. We could grab a cup of coffee across the street. Neither of us has to be at work early tomorrow morning."

"Actually," Laurie said, "I do have to be at work early tomorrow. We're going to search the streetcar at the old Benson farm in the morning."

"Too bad. I really enjoy your company." Prokop helped Laurie put on her coat, then picked up his own. As they walked to the door he asked, "Are you going to be in town for a while?"

"It depends on how the investigation goes," she replied. "I think I'll be around for a few more days unless we get an unexpected break in the case."

Prokop walked Laurie to her unmarked squad as a light drizzle fell. He took her hand after she unlocked the door. "Would you consider dinner tomorrow night?" he asked. "I haven't been to the lodge on Hanging Horn Lake in a couple years. They have good food, and I like the homey atmosphere."

Laurie felt like an awkward teen waiting to see if her date was going to kiss her goodnight. The pulsing bass from the band added a surreal quality to the intimate moment in the parking lot. "That would be fun, if you can be flexible about the timing. I don't know what time I'll get free from the search."

"That's not a problem," Prokop replied. "I've got a pile of property abstracts to read before some real estate closings next week." He took out his wallet and handed her a business card. "Call my cell phone number when you get done." He leaned close and kissed her gently on the mouth.

Laurie felt the blood rush to her face as the sweet smell of his after shave lotion filled her nose. "Thanks for dinner," she said softly as she tried no to look at his face. "I'll treat tomorrow night."

Prokop stepped back, still holding her hand. "No, you won't." Her hand lingered in his for a second then he let go and left.

"What are you doing?" Laurie asked herself as she started the car. "You've been on two dates in your whole life, and both were set up by friends. Suddenly you're going out two nights in a row with a backcountry lawyer. This can't be right. What's he looking for?"

CHAPTER 36

Sally Williams met Dan at the door with a can of Michelob as Penny circled his feet, whimpering with excitement. "How was your day, any progress on the unsolvable old mystery?" She stood on tiptoes to peck him on the cheek. She'd changed from her medical transcriber's white uniform into jeans and a heavy sweater.

Dan patted the dog and slipped off his buckskin jacket, shaking off a few raindrops. "A few leads are starting to show up. There's nothing that points to a particular suspect, but the trail isn't completely cold. As a matter of fact, Pam Ryan thought she had the murderer identified this afternoon. She thought it was Arlyn Prokop."

"Arlyn Prokop?" Sally asked. "You mean the geeky lawyer from Willow River?"

"That's him. She thought he was being overly evasive. She also found a big saw in his garage and she was sure he used it to cut up dead bodies."

"Was the kidnapped girl's body cut up?" Sally asked as she set a roasted chicken on the table.

"No," Dan said with a laugh. "It appeared to be totally intact before decomposition."

"So, what made her think that Arlyn was the killer?"

Dan sat at the table. "She said he was slimy," he said as he dished up fried potatoes, and took a chicken thigh.

"I'd call him more geeky than slimy," Sally said. "But, that's just an opinion. I have a hard time seeing him as a killer."

"Mmm," Dan said as a reply. "He called just as we were leaving, and asked Laurie out for dinner."

"Arlyn Prokop asked Laurie out on a date?" Sally asked. "I kinda thought he was gay."

"Everyone assumes unmarried guys over forty are gay," Dan replied. "Sometimes, they're just weird, or picky."

Sally smiled. "I remember what Garrison Kiellor said about the Norwegian bachelor farmers. 'If a guy is unmarried after fifty the odds are good that the goods are odd'. I think Prokop would fit that pretty well."

✲ ✲ ✲

The clock said it was after three AM when Dan reached for the ringing phone.

"Dan, this is dispatch. Sergeant Thompson asked me to call and tell you there's a fire at the law office in

Willow River. He said you'd been working on an investigation that involved the lawyer."

"Have you dispatched the fire department?" Dan asked trying to clear the cobwebs from his mind.

"They're on the scene," the dispatcher replied. "You know, the fire department is only across the street."

"Was anyone hurt?"

"They haven't requested an ambulance."

"Call Floyd and the sheriff and ask them to meet me at the law office. Better get hold of Laurie Lone Eagle, too. I think she's in the motel by the freeway. I'm on my way."

Sally rolled over and pushed herself up on an elbow. "Am I dreaming, or did you say a law office was on fire?"

Dan was pulling on his pants and searching for a shirt in the drawer. "Yup. Dispatch said it was the law office in Willow River. Prokop's is the only one there."

"It's pretty strange it would start on fire now, isn't it?" Sally asked with a sleepy voice.

"It's more than strange."

By the time Dan got to Willow River the flames were extinguished, and the firemen were hosing down smoldering embers in a light rain. The streetlights illuminated what had been a law and real estate office, now nothing more than a charred hole across the parking lot from the Squirrel Cage restaurant. The heat had been so intense that the green paint on the restaurant had blistered and blackened.

Sergeant Tom Thompson broke away from the fire chief and met Dan in the driveway. “Some kids called in the alarm. They were driving home from Duluth and the building was already engulfed in flames. By the time the firemen arrived there wasn’t much they could do except save the restaurant. We’re lucky it was raining or some of the embers from the fire might’ve set the restaurant roof on fire before we got here.”

The Willow River Fire Chief, Glen Munson, joined them. “The place was a tinderbox. The smoke smells like the old pine and cedar and I suppose the lumber was seventy-five years old, still full of pitch, and dry as kindling. Kinda ironic that we couldn’t save the building right across the street from the fire hall, but by the time the volunteers arrived the roof had already caved in.”

“It seems unlikely,” Dan said, “that a downtown building would catch fire and no one would notice until it was engulfed in flames.”

“We found a kerosene can floating in the basement after the floor joists collapsed,” said the chief, “So I assume it wasn’t an accident. We’ll get the fire marshal out in the morning to look things over.”

“It’s awfully coincidental,” Dan said, “that we were waiting for Prokop to check some records for us. Has anyone called him yet?”

"I sent Jack out to his house a little while ago," Tom Thompson said.

There was commotion among the firemen looking into the burned out foundation. "Hey chief, take a look at this."

Dan, Tom, and the fire chief walked across the lawn, then into the charred grass near the foundation. They approached a group of three firemen who were staring into the basement where a fourth fireman was squatting in several inches of water while being pelted by raindrops. When the fireman stood they could see glimpses of ivory among the charred wood where he pointed.

"It looks like there was someone in the building when it burned. When we doused the last hot spot we washed the ashes off these bones."

CHAPTER 37

Saturday - early morning

Laurie was disoriented when the phone jarred her from deep sleep in her Pine City motel room. By the time she located the light, and then the phone, it was the fourth ring. "Inspector Lone Eagle," she answered.

"I'm sorry to disturb you," the female voice said, "This is Pine County dispatch. Dan Williams asked us to contact you. He's at a probable arson scene in Willow River and he would like you to join him."

"Arson in Willow River?" Laurie asked as her foggy mind rushed through possibilities. The only thought that came to her sleepy mind that would prompt a call from Dan was Arlyn Prokop. "Is it the lawyer's office?"

"Yes," the dispatcher said with surprise. "There's a body in the ashes."

"Do they know whose it is?"

"No one has said."

Arlyn Prokop's red Lexus was parked prominently among the emergency vehicles when Laurie arrived.

The area around the building foundation had been secured with yellow crime scene tape and a number of firemen and deputies were milling around the area under the bluish glow of the fire department Klieg lights as a moderate rain pelted them. Prokop was standing near the front of the burned out building with Dan Williams, Floyd Swenson, and John Sepanen, the sheriff. Prokop looked surprised to see Laurie.

"It's a total loss. Everything is gone," Prokop said waving his arm across the scene. He wore a teal colored slicker over a pair of jeans, and his brown hair looked like he had purposely stirred it randomly before the rain had plastered it against his skull. His face looked tired, and his eyes were rimmed with red. "And they found a body in the basement. What a mess."

"Do you have any idea who it is?" Laurie asked, directing the question to Dan.

"The remains are badly burned and we haven't found any clothing or identification. We secured the area and we're waiting for the medical examiner."

"They haven't been able to find Jerry," Prokop said. "He wasn't at his house and his vehicle isn't there either. They think it might be him."

"Jerry?" Laurie asked.

"The realtor," Dan explained, "who shared the building."

"He worked late sometimes," Prokop said. "It looks like the bones are in his half of the building." The lawyer turned away and started to sob as he walked toward the Lexus. Floyd walked with him, and spoke softly.

"He's taking it pretty hard," Laurie said.

"He was doing okay until we couldn't locate the realtor," Sepanen said. "He told us he could replace all his current records, but when he realized that the body might be his officemate he started to crumble."

The rain turned to drizzle, making the area under the bright lights look hazy. The fire chief, wearing a white helmet, walked over to the sheriff. "It's strange," he said. "I've been to a few fires where we've had a roaster, and you can smell 'em cookin'. They kind of smell like a pig roast. This just smelled like burning wood."

"A roaster?" Laurie asked.

"You know," the chief replied, "a body that gets burned up in the fire. It's tough when you get called to a fatal fire when you know everyone in town. It's easier for the firemen to talk about them in terms like that rather than to refer to them as human remains."

"You're right," Dan said, sniffing the air, "I don't smell any burned meat. I have the medical examiner on the way from Duluth. He'll be able to tell us for sure."

Tom Thompson joined the group. "I called in for Jerry Workman's license number. He owns a green Ford Explorer. It's not parked anywhere in town, and it's not at his house. We contacted his wife, Janet, who was staying at a friend's house, and she didn't realize that he wasn't home. She said he'd met with a customer from The Cities to show them a seasonal property this evening."

Laurie walked to the Lexus where Prokop and Floyd Swenson were talking in the drizzle. The lawyer seemed to have regained his composure, although the rain had left his hair matted with droplets running down his face. Prokop wiped his glasses with a sodden handkerchief to remove the gathering droplets of drizzle.

"They don't think the body is Jerry," Laurie said.

"How can they be sure at this point?" Prokop asked. He appeared to be totally deflated, and the news had little cheering effect on him.

"The deputies said that Jerry's Explorer isn't around town. They checked with his wife, and she didn't know where he was either. She said he met someone to show a property this evening."

"I probably shouldn't bring this up," Prokop said quietly, "but given the circumstances I suppose its best. Jerry's wife moved out of the house a few months ago. She still takes messages for his business, but he has a girlfriend who lives by the golf course. Maybe the sheriff could have someone drive by the girlfriend's house to see if his truck is there."

Floyd nodded. "I think we can handle that. What's her name?"

"Jenny Parkhurst. She's got a little, red, two-bedroom house that's next to the tee box for the fifth hole."

Having dealt with Jerry's whereabouts, Prokop looked suddenly confused. "If it's not Jerry, who's body is in the basement?" A shudder ran over his body. "This is too strange."

The drizzle evolved into a sprinkle and eventually became a light rain by the time the medical examiner's Suburban arrived. The eastern sky was still leaden, the Klieg lights offering little illumination beyond the basement, but illuminating the driving raindrops as the passed the metalized light reflectors.

Tony Oresek, the St. Louis County Medical Examiner, and his assistant, Eddie Paulson, stepped out of the black Suburban in their yellow rain slickers. Dan Williams met them at the rear of their vehicle as Eddie Paulson was removing a large, plastic box that would pass for a tackle box in a fishing boat. Oresek's slender frame was hidden under the raincoat, although nothing could disguise his six foot-four frame towering over everyone. Eddie Paulson was shorter, and older, his face was hardened by a tour of duty as a navy corpsman in Viet Nam. A salt and pepper ponytail hung from the back of a black Goretex baseball cap with CORONER emblazoned in white letters across the front.

"What have we got?" Oresek asked Dan.

"It's an apparent arson fire. The only thing the fire department could do was save the restaurant across the parking lot. After the building collapsed, the firemen found a body in the basement under all the charred timbers."

Oresek looked across the street. "The building must have been really burning by the time the call went in. The firemen only had to travel about fifty yards."

"It was," Dan replied. "Plus, it's an all volunteer fire department, so the first responders didn't get here for five or ten minutes after the call went out. A house fire doubles in intensity every two minutes, so even an extra four minutes can turn a minor fire into an inferno."

The threesome walked to the edge of the basement, and after consultation with the firemen, Eddie took a few pictures, and then descended a ladder into the watery mess of ashes, charred paper, and soot.

Eddie and two firemen consulted in the basement as the others stood around the rim, watching the conversation. After a few moments, they started to carefully pick pieces of charred wood out of the water, laying them aside near the wall. After nearly half an hour of work they stood back and surveyed the progress.

"The body surface is totally charred," Eddie announced after climbing out of the basement. "The joints are still articulated and most of the flesh is still intact, although the fire burned through to the bone in a few places. I'd say the body was on an upper floor and fell into the basement when the flooring collapsed."

"Are you sure the body fell into the basement?" Oresek asked.

"There are fragments of linoleum melted to some of flesh, so I'd say it was lying on the floor before it collapsed." The raindrops were falling full force now, and the surface of the water in the basement roiled in the deluge. They watched a fireman stumble on something submerged in the water as he moved around some debris. "Can we get a pump hooked up to lower the water level down here? I want to get pictures of the body as it lies before we attempt to move it."

The fire chief spoke to two firemen who retrieved a portable pump from the nearest fire truck. Dan Williams leaned close to the medical examiner as Laurie approached on his other side. "Repeat what Eddie said," Dan asked, "in layman's terms." Laurie pointed to the protected entryway of the restaurant, and the three of them walked away from the fire scene, followed closely by the sheriff.

"The remains are of a complete body whose joints are still connected," Oresek said as they stepped out of the rain and into the small roofed area over the restaurant entrance. "It was probably upstairs when the fire started and fell into the basement when the floor collapsed. We can tell that because of the linoleum flooring melted to the surface of the body."

"There wasn't any linoleum on the law office floor," Laurie said. "It was hardwood. I remember a big Oriental rug on the floor."

"I guess," Dan said, "that means the body was on the realtor's side of the building."

A small gas engine on a portable pump sputtered to life and the group watched the firemen feed a hose into the basement. Within seconds, a stream of water poured out of the pump and pushed in a narrow stream toward the street. The flow quickly disappeared in the rush of rainwater flowing down the street.

"At the rate the rain is falling," Dan said, "the basement should be empty in about three days."

"I was hoping we could get the remains out of the basement before the news people showed up," Oresek said. "Carrying bodies out of burned buildings makes great ratings, but it tends to put a lot of pressure on everyone to resolve the case quickly." He cast a questioning gaze at the sheriff.

"Dispatch called WDIO an hour ago," Sepanen said. "It usually takes the night editor a few hours to find a cameraman and get him into a van with a reporter. Add another hour for the drive from Duluth, and they'll probably show up around sunrise."

"Since Laurie is here," Oresek observed, "I assume that you have some other case going that might tie to this one. Do you have any idea whose remains these might be?"

Laurie looked at the red Lexus. "Well," she said, "we know it's not the lawyer and it's probably not the realtor, who had their offices in the building. Tom Thompson talked to the realtor's wife."

"How about the lawyer's wife?" Sepanen asked.

"Not married," Laurie and Dan said in unison.

"Arlyn Prokop said that the realtor was having an affair and that his wife has moved out. Floyd is on his way to the realtor's girlfriend's house. If he's not there..." Laurie let the words dangle.

"Or, if she's not there," the sheriff added.

"Our prime suspect in the Helen Smith investigation was killed a couple days ago." Dan said to Oresek as he dug under his raincoat for a roll of Tums. He pried two off the end and popped them in his mouth. "I wonder if someone else knew too much."

Thunder rumbled through distance clouds and the rain pelted harder. A shiver ran over Laurie's body.

"Just when you think it couldn't get worse," Laurie said, "it does." After a pause she added, "I wonder how many missing bodies are around here?"

Sepanen started to silently count on his fingers. "I think about eleven."

"Really?" Laurie asked.

"Most of them," Dan said, "are missing hunters or people who've had mental problems and wandered away from home. They're probably in a swamp somewhere they'll never be found."

"Yeah," the sheriff agreed, "and there was the drunk that walked away from his truck after an accident and the guys working on the power line found his body next to a pole in the swamp the next summer."

"There have been a few runaways," Laurie said, "and the two canoeists who disappeared on the river. None of them have ever been found."

Firemen gathered around the top of the ladder coming from the basement, and helped a person in a yellow slicker step away from the top. They directed Eddie Paulson to Oresek and the others standing in the restaurant entry. He reached the protection just as an Explorer roared to a stop behind the fire trucks. Floyd Swenson's squad followed the truck, and he rushed to the side of the man who flew out of the SUV. The man was extremely animated as he ran to the edge of the basement. The pounding rain covered his words, but his motions told all anyone needed to know. A fireman and Floyd subdued the man and walked him back to the Explorer as the realtor tried to keep his soggy toupee arranged on top of his head while he ranted.

As Floyd got the realtor to return to his vehicle, Eddie Paulson pulled a charred piece of flesh from under his rain slicker. He handed it to Oresek, who held it away from his body to catch the light from the fixture over the door. Laurie looked away when she realized Oresek was examining a charred human hand.

"I took this one out to show you," Eddie said. "It was ripped free of the body when something fell on it."

Oresek turned the hand and examined the arm where the wrist had been broken free from the rest of the arm. He turned it end for end and repeated the process.

"I'd say this has been buried for years," he said. "I wonder if someone pulled it out of an old grave somewhere." He ran his finger over a pattern on the edge. "It looks like it was against some sort of plant matter that stained it after it was embalmed. Discoloration like this is often due to the remains being in leaves. The tannins in decomposing leaves discolor the skin and then the tissue. There's a funny irregular pattern in the muscle and the discoloration is starting to penetrate the bone."

"Could the fire have done that?" Laurie asked.

"The fire causes the cracks like those you can see here in the fingers where all the flesh is gone. If there'd been more heat for longer, the bone would have broken into chunks. The fire causes a different kind of discoloration."

"How long does a bone have to be in the ground to get this discolored?" Dan asked.

"You get a little in a few months, and we won't know the depth of the coloration until we do more examination, but I'd say you're looking at a body that's been buried for several years."

"Dead hunter?" the sheriff suggested.

"I doubt it," Oresek said. "A body that hasn't been embalmed decomposes leaving only skeletal remains."

"Who would dig up a body and dump it into a burning building?" Dan asked.

Another shiver ran over Laurie. "Someone creepy," She said.

"A lawyer?" Dan asked with a smile. "They're creepy."

The whole group chuckled at the gallows humor.

"Uh oh," the sheriff said. "Everyone sober up, the news van is here. It looks bad when they see the cops laughing at a murder scene." Sepanen stepped between the others and moved quickly to catch the news crew before they got set up.

Oresek watched with amusement. "He's quite the camera hog, isn't he?"

"Better he," Dan said, "than me. I have a tendency to speak my mind and that tends to cause friction at times."

"I remember the time Dan told the news guy to take a flying leap," Laurie said. "Just because he was in the middle of a stand-off with a deranged gunman, Dan thought it wasn't an appropriate time for an interview."

"It was a woman, not a guy," Dan corrected. "And, I didn't tell her to leap. I suggested she do something anatomically impossible."

"Shh! You're doing it again." Oresek said turning to block them from the view of the camera crew as Laurie and Eddie started to laugh. He discreetly gave the charred hand back to Eddie, who slipped it under his raincoat. "Let's see if the water's down enough to take some pictures and see how the remains are arranged."

The news crew set up the camera and lights under a protective awning that extended from the side of their truck. By the time Oresek and the others were back at the basement, they became a backdrop for the reporter interviewing the sheriff.

CHAPTER 38

The rain let up a little and the water level in the basement dropped enough to show piles of charred rubble, although much of the debris was still submerged. A few lighter colored pieces were visible on the west side of the basement and Eddie Paulson pointed them out from ground level as the gas engine on the pump hummed behind them. Dan noticed the reporter stepping back and letting the cameraman zoom in on Eddie as he pointed into the basement. He supposed that the reclusive Eddie Paulson wouldn't relish center stage on the early morning news.

"I think we should take a few pictures now," Eddie said, "and then video the actual excavation of the debris. That way we'll have a record of the exact location of the body."

The fire chief approached the group and tapped Dan on the shoulder. "Excuse me, but the owner just opened up the restaurant and invited all the firemen in for coffee. Why don't you guys move inside where you can warm up?"

"Thanks," Dan said, ushering the group inside.

Marge Patterson, middle-aged and lean from working hard at managing the restaurant for twenty years, was carrying a tray of coffee cups to a table of firemen who were stripping off their helmets and bunker gear. “Grab a table boys,” she said to the deputies, “the coffee will be perked in a minute or two.” She passed the cups around the table of firemen and brought the remainder to Dan’s table. “Here you go. Anyone take cream?”

“This is awfully nice,” Laurie said, shaking the water off her coat.

Marge shook her head. “What’s nice is a dozen volunteer firemen dragging their butts out of bed in the middle of the night to make sure my restaurant doesn’t burn down. I’m just making a small payment on what I owe.”

Floyd and Eddie joined the group of law enforcement officers as Marge served the coffee. Eddie explained his excavation plan and was about to go back to check on the pumping progress when the mayor of Willow River, a stocky man dressed in a plaid flannel shirt and blue jeans, came out of the kitchen carrying a platter of caramel rolls.

“Hey boys, I got the first batch of Tobie’s rolls. Help yourselves while Marge cuts up some more.”

Dan watched as Floyd bit into one of the monster rolls, still warm from the oven. “Floyd, remember when you told me that you’re retiring because no one appreciates us anymore? I think Marge and the mayor appreciate us."

On cue, Marge came out of the back with another platter of rolls. She leaned past Floyd to set them on the table, and then pecked him on the cheek as she stood up. "Oh Floyd, I not only appreciate you, I love you."

Floyd smiled and said, "Prokop and Workman are sitting in the Explorer. They're kind of shell-shocked right now, but I got them to speculate on who might want to destroy their offices. Workman thought it might be his wife's doing, assuming she's upset about his girlfriend. Prokop didn't have a suspect to offer."

"Prokop was going to look through old rental records for us," Laurie said. "He'd located a box he thought might contain them, and he set it out before we left his office. If there were records someone didn't want reviewed, and somehow they heard that Prokop had them sitting in the office, they might be inclined to touch a match to them so their name wouldn't come up."

"Prokop mentioned that," Floyd said, "but he also said the only person he's spoken with since he pulled the records out is you, Laurie. He said you two were out for supper, and he went directly home from the restaurant."

"The restaurant?" Dan asked. "Not your motel room?"

The punch landed on Dan's shoulder so quickly he didn't have time to dodge it. "There are enough rumors flying around without you adding to them," Laurie said curtly.

"Ouch!" Dan said, as the others smothered laughter.

"I wonder if either of the businesses are having financial problems?" Tony Oresek asked. "It seems like insurance figures into half the arson deaths I've investigated."

"Prokop says he owns the building outright," Floyd said. "He says his parents gave him the business and the house when they retired to Florida."

"That matches what he's told me, too," Laurie said. "That leaves Workman with no motive, since he didn't have a financial interest in the building. He lost a bunch of paper and that's about it."

"All that's fine," Dan said, still rubbing his shoulder. "But you're forgetting the body. There's more to this than a simple arson for property insurance case. Sometimes a person gets killed by accident, or on purpose, in an arson fire. But, not many people throw an old body into a building before the light it on fire. Why do that?"

"What old body?" Floyd asked.

"While you were talking to the Prokop and Workman," Oresek explained. "We determined that it wasn't a fresh body."

"Maybe it was literally the skeleton in the closet," Eddie offered. "Someone had an old body hidden away in a closet that had been boarded up, or maybe they'd stored it in an old trunk or something."

"I think either Prokop or Workman would have mentioned it," Floyd said. "Both of them seemed pretty freaked by the thought of a body showing up in their offices."

Eddie stood up, signaling that he was ready to start his excavation project. The others put their coats on and finished off the last of the coffee.

The lights from the camera crew blinked out, and the reporter shook hands with the sheriff. As the news crew stowed their gear in the van, the rain lessened to a mild drizzle again. Red and blue lights flashed between the buildings as another emergency vehicle drove into town from the freeway. Pam Ryan's squad pulled to a stop behind the news van as the cameraman stowed the last case in the back. The reporter waved to her from the passenger's side as she walked to the edge of the basement.

"Dispatch told me you were all here when I came in to search the streetcar," Pam said, looking into the basement. "She also said that you'd found a body in the basement of the burned out building."

Watching the news truck pull away, Eddie Paulson pulled the charred hand from under his raincoat. "It's an old body," he explained. "No one died in the fire."

His faint smile hinted at his attempts to cultivate a relationship with Pam. "Most of the body is buried under the rubble. We're waiting for the water level to get pumped down so we can get some pictures and then take a video of the recovery."

"I'll grab the video camera from my squad," Pam said.

"You guys sort this out," the sheriff said to Dan. "I'll send the lawyer and realtor home, and then go back to the courthouse."

The clouds thinned, and started to lighten as Floyd Swenson took still pictures of the entire basement. After taking a dozen pictures, Eddie Paulson climbed down the ladder and pointed out exposed portions of the body as Floyd shot pictures, capturing the location and orientation of the evidence. When he was done, Floyd and Tony Oresek joined Eddie in the basement while Pam Ryan perched halfway down the ladder with the video camera. They slowly removed charred debris from the scene, leaving the body undisturbed, until the remains were totally exposed.

The basement crew stood back while Floyd took another set of still pictures from the ground level. It appeared that the body was complete, with the limbs somewhat jumbled, but in nearly anatomically correct position. The leg bones were broken and Tony Oresek examined the remains briefly in situ.

"It appears," Oresek observed, "this person was just a teenager, or a very young adult." He searched further and knelt near the remains. After a close inspection and some quick measurements of the pelvis he stood. "The deceased was female."

"We'll have to take her back to the morgue for a closer look," Oresek said, "but I can make a few observations. The deceased had an apparent wound to the left side of the chest, so we may be looking at a homicide victim. This is not an ancient body. She had amalgam fillings, which date it to the last fifty or so years, and there are remnants of a plaster orthopedic cast on the left arm, which means that it's prior to the middle eighties when everyone switched to lightweight fiberglass casts. I'll need to make some measurements in the lab, but also think that the deceased was Asian or an American Indian, based on the geometry of the face."

Dan felt Laurie's grip on his left arm. Her eyes were closed and she was grimacing. She took a deep breath and knelt down to the edge of the basement blocks.

"Tony," she said softly. "Did you say the cast was on her left arm?"

Oresek looked up at Laurie's somber face, and then moved to the left side of the skeleton. He brushed ashes away from left arm, and then looked back up at Laurie.

"It wasn't entirely healed," he said.

Tears welled in Laurie's eyes and Dan put his arm around her, helping her to her feet. She buried her face in his shoulder and pulled it tight against her. After a few seconds she stepped back and dug through her pockets. Dan handed her a sodden handkerchief as the men climbed out of the basement.

"You think this is the missing Fond du Lac girl you told me about?" Dan asked softly.

"Angie Little Bear," Laurie said, wiping her nose. "She disappeared on her way home from Cloquet about twenty years ago. She was in her early teens. The last time anyone saw her, she was walking along highway 210 on her way back to Fond du Lac. Carlton County investigated, and they've always suspected foul play, but no one ever found evidence. The media downplayed it as another Indian runaway. The deputies thought someone probably picked her up and raped her. We'd assumed the body would show up during hunting season or in a ditch somewhere, but it never did."

"You weren't working for the BCA then," Oresek said. "I'm surprised you know so much about the case."

"She was my baby sister's best friend," Laurie replied.

"Tony says it looks like the body had been embalmed and buried," Dan said. "Why would someone kill her, embalm her, bury her, then dig her up now and put them in this fire? I think it must be someone else."

"Why would a thirty-year-old murder victim suddenly show up in the trunk of a car?" Pam asked.

Laurie wiped her nose again on Dan's handkerchief. "I think someone is either trying to send us a message, or mess with our heads."

"Leaving the body on the doorstep of the murderer?" Pam asked.

"Maybe leaving someone a message to keep their mouth shut," Floyd said. "I wonder if Colleen McCarthy is home?"

Dan pulled a cell phone from his pocket and handed it to Floyd. "Let's see," he said.

Floyd dialed the number Kline has given him for McCarthy's home. He listened with all eyes on him for a few seconds. After nearly a minute of connections and ringing, he got a recorder.

"This is Floyd Swenson, from the Pine County Sheriff's Department. Please call me when you receive this message."

CHAPTER 39

Tony Oresek and Eddie Paulson carefully loaded the remains into a body bag. They were climbing the ladder out of the basement when sunlight brightened the clouds enough to say it was morning. Two news vans, one from Duluth, and the other from Minneapolis, who had missed their early morning news, but were recording footage for the noon and evening news, greeted them. Oresek patiently explained to each of the neatly groomed female reporters that it was too early to make any determination about the remains, other than to say that the victim had not died in the fire. That led to strings of additional questions that he deftly deflected. With the interviews done, Dan met Tony at the suburban as Eddie put the last of the medical examiner's gear into the back, next to the remains.

"Did you learn anything else?" Dan asked quietly, making sure the news people were busy packing up their vans, and safely out of earshot.

"It wasn't an accidental death," Oresek replied, "whenever it happened. There's a large post-mortem gash on the left thigh that might've been made when the body was removed from wherever it has been. There are wounds that look like a stabbing from a right-handed assailant. Would that be consistent with the body that was found in the trunk?"

"The forensic anthropologist said there appeared to be one knife wound in the first victim that nicked a rib and plunged all the way to the spine. If this victim was killed later, multiple knife wounds would fit with a killer who was becoming more aggressive and sadistic."

"I haven't dealt with a lot of serial killers," Oresek said, "but the literature says they trend toward greater violence. They get satisfaction from the kill, and it takes increasing brutality for them to get high."

Laurie and Floyd joined them as Oresek made his observations. She listened and then added, "If this is a serial murderer, he hasn't killed for a few years. Otherwise, there would be more bodies showing up."

"Maybe they're still buried somewhere, like this one," Dan said. "What if we have a very smart and careful killer. He may have killed several times, like this victim, and stashed the bodies away."

"That would be contrary to most of the serial killer cases," Oresek observed. "Most of them relish the discovery of the bodies and the apparent ineptitude of the law enforcement people in their efforts to solve the cases."

"We're only aware of the ones who get caught," Laurie said. "There may be dozens of them out there who are never caught because they were smart enough to hide the evidence. There are scores of people who disappear every year without a trace. Who's to say that many of them aren't crime victims whose murderers are never caught. There was the guy arrested in Michigan a couple years ago when a cop stopped him because he spotted blood on his car bumper. When they searched the car there was a body in the trunk, and the guy led them to dozens of graves in Georgia and Florida. If not for the one traffic stop, another serial killer might have been free for many more years."

Dan ran his hand over his face. "So," he said, "We may have a graveyard full of dead bodies somewhere?"

"That's got to be a possibility to consider," Oresek replied. "There's a strange pattern to the hand Eddie showed me. Maybe we'll be able to get some clues about location by examining the skin under a microscope."

"Why," Dan asked, "would anyone dig up an old dead body and throw it out for the cops to find if they'd literally gotten away with murder for years?"

"I've got a theory on that," Floyd said. "The whole thing had been laid to rest, and the murderer was satisfied with having fooled us all these years. Then, we find the body in the car trunk and he gets a kick out of all the publicity and the commotion. I think that seeing the discovery of this body on the news will be a real high for him."

"Oh, God," Laurie said, her face turning ashen. "I'd never considered that possibility. Sometimes the discovery of an old murder spurs the murderer back into action. Like Floyd said, the murderer had this warm fuzzy feeling about having kept this away from us all these years. Now, with the spotlight on him, the feelings get more intense and he's spurred to act on them again. I hope this doesn't lead to another kidnapping and murder."

"Are we sure he ever stopped?" Dan asked. "You mentioned the canoeists who disappeared on the St. Croix. Are there others we're ignoring or don't know about?"

"Serial rapists and murders tend to pattern their victims," Laurie said, squeezing her eyes shut in an effort to focus her thoughts. "Helen Smith was a teen, with dark hair. But, this victim was Native American."

"Also a teen with dark hair," Oresek noted.

"Yes," Laurie conceded. "There were two girls in the canoe. They were too young to drive, so early teens. I think one was blonde and the other had dark hair. I'll check the database when I get back to my motel room."

"Floyd," Dan said, "Get back to the office and send a fax to all the neighboring counties alerting them to this possible pattern. Ask them to search their missing persons files for the last thirty years for unsolved cases involving dark-haired teen girls."

"Do you remember the fax we got from Missouri about five years ago?" Floyd asked. "They asked us to watch for a teen girl who might be hitchhiking to Canada, up I-35. She was like fourteen, with raven hair and blue eyes. I don't recall hearing she'd ever been located.

"Would everyone who was kidnapped and killed by the Pine County psychopath please raise her hand," Floyd said softly.

Everyone turned to look at him, and Dan asked, "What do you mean?"

"You can't count people you don't know about. They're not here to tell you that they're missing. The missing girls are like drops of rain hitting the surface of a lake. It makes a ripple as it hits, but it's consumed by the water around it and as soon as the ripples die out, the evidence is gone forever."

"It's more like God is crying," Laurie said. "They're not drops of rain, they're heaven's tears being swallowed by the torrent."

CHAPTER 40

A broad smile spread across the killer's face as he watched the Duluth reporter interview the Pine County Sheriff. In the background firemen and deputies stood around the basement where the remains had been found. After the interview, the reporter speculated that the fire may have been set to hide a murder.

Was it possible that the cops were so inept that they couldn't tell a thirty year-old corpse from one that had been consumed in a fire? Maybe the fire had damaged the body so badly that they couldn't tell how old it was. How badly would a house fire damage a body? When a body was cremated the family got an urn of ashes. Would a house fire be hot enough to reduce the remains to at least a bare skeleton?

The broadcast showed two men lifting a body bag out of the basement. It appeared to have some mass and length to it. From that perspective, it appeared that the body may have survived somewhat intact. Maybe the fire department had squirted enough water on the fire to keep the remains from being totally consumed.

The question was, "What could they tell from the body?" Would it be a red herring, or would it be a clue to his identity? The new corpse would certainly be a diversion from the bones in the trunk for the sheriff's department. Now they would have two murders to investigate, and that would certainly tax their limited resources and brainpower.

Better than that, they wouldn't know that they'd been fooled twice. If only he could tell them how many times he'd slipped past them. If only they knew how many little girls were missing. They'd feel the fools. And having them feel the fools was so much more rewarding than just him knowing they were fools. Maybe he'd have to add to their misery again. Maybe knowing that they'd missed three, or even four murders would be sweeter. Maybe worth all the time and effort it took to recover that molding corpse and drop it in the realty office. He had been surprised that there was anything more to it than bare bones, that he could recover anything substantial enough to make it identifiable. He wasn't even sure which one he was recovering, but that rotting plaster cast ought to give them a twist. He thought about discarding it when he brought the body out, and decided to leave the sloppy mess that it had become as one more thing to tease them. Even if they could identify that little Indian girl they wouldn't ever tie that to him. Not even if they got close to him with the other remains.

He'd shut off the television and gone to his shrine. The candlelight in his private memorial was subdued, just bright enough to leave the room with an aura of reverence. He closed the door, and went through, touching each of his trophies, and picturing each lovely girl who had provided it, savoring the memories of their raven hair and their lean teenaged bodies. Too bad they had to die, but he had been meticulous in eliminating witnesses and that had paid off in over thirty years of freedom while less brilliant men had been caught and now languished in prisons. He touched the trophy from the one blonde victim. Too bad she'd been a complication, but he had to eliminate witnesses, and she had been almost as beautiful as her black-haired friend. She was almost as nice, but not quite as luscious.

CHAPTER 41

Dan, Laurie, and the day shift deputies met in the bull-pen after clearing the Willow River fire site. Usually barren at mid-day, the room was a hum of activity as a deputy sat at every one of the gray, industrial desks while phone calls were made, and new tidbits of information were shared over thick bitter coffee. Even Kerm Rajacich was phoning leads happily and jotting sloppy notes as the desk chair creaked under his substantial mass.

Laurie took a sip of the vile brew and grimaced. "Floyd, I think this coffee could eat stainless steel."

"Why do you think Dan eats Tums like candy? He drinks too much of this coffee."

"Maybe," Laurie said, "I'll buy some good coffee and brew a pot after lunch."

Floyd looked at her skeptically. "I think it's the pot. You know, it's never been washed."

"Maybe I'll buy a new pot and some bottled water, too."

"Listen up!" Dan yelled to get everyone's attention. "We're going to let the streetcar sit while we follow the leads on the Willow River fire. Let's get on the same page of information here and then we'll decide how to divide up the jobs. We've got a lot of phone calls to make."

"I'd rather have a phone jammed up my butt than sit with one jammed in my ear another minute," Kerm Rajacich whispered a little too loudly to Sandy Maki. Dan heard the comment and glared at Rajacich, the most senior deputy on duty.

"Kerm," Dan said, "we'd prefer to have this be a team effort. But if you'd rather have a phone jammed up your butt, I'm sure we could arrange that." The admonition brought a round of chuckles that helped break the ice.

"Floyd," Dan went on, "update us on your contacts since the fire."

"I sent a fax to all the northern Minnesota law enforcement agencies requesting information on any dark-haired female teen disappearances. So far, I've had about eight negative responses and three positives that I've turned over to Laurie for further investigation. I called the Hennepin County Sheriff's Department and asked them to locate Colleen McCarthy and question her about her activities of last night. They haven't located her yet." That revelation brought a round of raised eyebrows. "I think we should have another discussion with the old camp cook to see if any of the new information connects with her feeble memory."

"I can do that!" Pam said. "She likes me."

"So do a lot of men and stray dogs," a muted male voice whispered from the back of the room. Dan glared at Rajacich and Maki, assuming one of them had made the comment. Both put on their best innocent faces.

"I rechecked the database of missing children," Laurie said, changing the topic. "There are over a dozen missing girls that fit the rough profile I searched, including the ones that Floyd got return faxes about. One of the two canoeists that disappeared on the St. Croix had dark hair and the other was blonde. The murderer may have taken them both, focusing on the dark-haired girl. The others are spread all over the place, and heaven knows how many of them may be shooting up, turning tricks in Chicago, Las Vegas, L.A., or in a shallow grave elsewhere. There's just no way to know."

"Anyone else have something to share?" Dan asked. When no one responded, he said, "All right then. I want Sandy and Kerm to canvass all the houses in Willow River to see if anyone saw any unusual activity around the law office last night. Pam's is going to Mora to talk to Grace Palm. Floyd, I want you in Minneapolis with the Hennepin County guys. If they find Colleen McCarthy, I'd like to have her brought in for questioning. She's just too fishy to let her sit out there without answering some hard questions. Laurie, you follow up with the lawyer and realtor to see if they have any ideas about what might have happened now that they've had a chance to settle down. See what Workman's wife has to say about the fire since he thought she might be jealous enough about his girlfriend to try and get even with him."

"Any questions?" Dan asked.

"What are you going to do?" Rajacich asked impertinently.

"I thought I'd answer the phones. If you have a problem with that, I'd be happy to swap."

✲ ✲ ✲

Arlyn Prokop was a mess when he answered the door. He was unshaven, making his face look gray, and his hair was still matted to his head from the rain. He'd changed into a flannel shirt and dry jeans, and answered the door in bare feet.

"I thought I'd stop by and see how you were doing," Laurie said.

"I know you have to question the most likely suspects," Prokop said, pulling the door open and stepping back. "C'mon in. I've got coffee brewed if you'd like some."

The pristine kitchen from the previous visit had turned into a jumbled mess. The kitchen table was littered with mail that had been opened and carelessly discarded. Wet clothes hung from the chair backs, and the counter was littered with Prokop's breakfast. He took the wet rain slicker from the back of a chair and motioned for Laurie to sit at the table.

"What can I tell you?" he asked as he set a cup of steaming coffee in front of Laurie. He scooped the mail into one pile and set it on the counter, then sat in a chair with a wet sweatshirt draped over its back.

"I was wondering if you could think of anyone who was so upset with you they might burn your office down?"

Prokop ran his fingers through his matted hair, making it an even bigger mess. "I've wracked my brain trying to find one person who might do this," he said, shaking his head. "But, I really can't come up with a single name. I do mostly family law and real estate transactions with a rare stint as a public defender. If I were into more criminal cases I'd say there are always people who think you treated them badly, or who think you could have gotten them off. With my practice, there just aren't that many disgruntled customers."

"Do you think that someone your father represented might not want some records opened?" Laurie asked. "We've been stirring in some old ashes and maybe someone got worried about something that might turn up."

"That thought ran through my mind, too. I called Dad last night and asked about the old rental records. This morning I called again and told him about the fire, and then I asked about the criminal files."

"And."

"The box of records I found probably had the rental information in it. The criminal records are all locked in the row of steel file cabinets that were stored in the basement of the office." Prokop paused. "You know, the ones in a foot of dirty water. The fire probably didn't destroy them, but I doubt if many in the bottom drawers survived the water."

"You left the rental records on the desk," Laurie said, "So they were destroyed, too?"

"Oh no," Prokop said. "I put them into the trunk of my car before we went out for dinner."

"Really!" Laurie said. "Can we look at them?"

"I was just looking at the ledger when you rang the doorbell," Prokop said, rising from his chair. "I've got it in the living room."

Prokop had arranged the records into a neat pile on the floor next to a coffee table. On the table were several piles of papers, and atop them was a green-bound ledger book. They sat on the couch and he pulled the ledger to the edge of the coffee table and leaned over it.

"It goes back into the sixties," he said, "and I was working my way up to '74. It looks like a lot of the same people rented the same weeks year after year. Some would just rent a week, and others rented for a month at a time." He pointed to receipts for June of '74. There's a Mattson who rented the first cabin for the whole month, and paid in advance. The other two cabins were rented by the week."

Arlyn Prokop senior had noted the last name and form of payment for each rental with the neat strokes of a blue pen. On the next page were the July rentals. Laurie noted the three names recorded for the week of Helen Smith's disappearance. The entries were simple – a name and address with the amount of rent paid. There were no notations as to the gender of the occupants, how many people occupied the cabin, or their ages. The names weren't noteworthy – Thomas Anderson, Russell Watkins, and Douglas Rivers.

"I'm going to check these names for criminal histories," Laurie said, making notes as she spoke. "But these names are about as common as straw and I don't expect to have anything jump out."

Prokop flipped forward a few pages. "If it's any help at all, here are the people who rented the same week the following year. I assume that if one were a killer they wouldn't be back."

The same names were back the following year. Flipping back, they found the same families renting at the same time for several years before. Laurie leaned back and shook her head.

"It was a long shot," she said. "I'll still run the check, but you're right, I don't think anyone's brazen enough to be involved in Helen Smith's killing and come back to vacation in the same cabin the following year."

"If I need an alibi for last night," Prokop said, closing the ledger, "check my long distance phone records. I spent the evening at home after our dinner, but I called Dad about nine-thirty. After that, I was in bed until the dispatcher called me about the fire. I'm afraid it's not much of an alibi."

"Most innocent people don't have good alibis," she said. "You're only worried about beefing up your alibi if you think like a criminal."

The room brightened noticeably as the sun broke through the clouds for the first time in half a day. The lake was covered with ripples, and as the cold front that caused the showers pushed past. Mist rose from the lake as the cool air condensed the moisture-laden warm air above the water.

"This is really a lovely view," Laurie said.

"I mostly ignore it," Prokop said, closing up the ledger. "After living here for most of my life I tend to take it for granted."

"Could we walk down by the shore?" Laurie asked.

"Sure," Prokop replied. "Let me find some dry shoes and a jacket that's not dripping."

They walked onto a massive cedar deck through the living room doors, and then went down a short set of steps to the lawn. The grass was still wet from the rain, and their shoes were quickly soaked. A pair of mallards quacked their displeasure at the company, and swam away from shore.

"Do you put out a dock in the summer?" Laurie asked, her breath condensing in the cool air as she spoke.

"We used to when I was a kid. The last few years I haven't been on the water enough to make it worth the effort." Prokop walked with his head down and his hands jammed in his jeans pockets. He seemed to be in a faraway place.

"It seems like a shame not to take advantage of the water right at your doorstep," she said. Looking back at the house she added, "At least you have a canoe so you can go out and paddle around."

Prokop looked up at the house. "It's left over from the days I was a kid. As a matter of fact, you'd better not look too closely at it because I think the license probably expired about a decade ago. I wouldn't want you to ticket me." A frown crossed his face, "I guess the wind must've been pretty strong here. The canoe is usually up under the deck and it looks like it got blown down."

They walked back to the deck and Laurie helped Prokop turn the canoe to empty it of water. Together they pushed the aluminum canoe under the deck, exposing two wooden paddles whose varnish had long ago been peeled away by the weather. He pushed the paddles under the canoe.

"Maybe the neighbor kids have been using it. I told them they could whenever they wanted, but I also told them to put it back under the deck when they were through." He picked up a piece of moss that had fallen out of the overturned canoe and threw it toward the lake. "They like to paddle over to the bog and mess around. Personally, I find it kinda creepy, but the kids think it's an adventure."

They walked around the attached garage at the end of the house and Prokop escorted Laurie to the door of her car.

"I hope you don't mind," he said, "but I don't think I'm up for dinner tonight. I probably wouldn't be good company."

"It's been a tough day," she said. "I'll probably be in bed early tonight, too. I'll take a rain check for another night."

Prokop brightened. "Really? You'd consider a second dinner with a murder suspect?"

"I think your suspect status will change after things settle down a bit."

✲ ✲ ✲

Jerry Workman lived in a three-bedroom rambler between Willow River and Sandstone. Wood smoke was curling from the chimney when Laurie pulled in the paved driveway. He was in about the same mental state as the lawyer. It took him almost three minutes to answer the doorbell, and he looked very surprised to see Laurie. He appeared to have recently showered, and hadn't had a chance to put on his cheap toupee. He was wrapped in a blue terrycloth robe and bare feet. The entryway of his house was filled with wet clothes hung over a kerosene space heater.

"I can't really let you in right now," he said, looking furtively over his shoulder. "We're having a discussion about where I was when the cops came looking for me. Is there something specific I could answer for you?"

Laurie thought about Jerry being found at his girlfriend's house after his wife informed the night deputy that she hadn't seen him. She could well imagine that things were not all bliss at the Workman house.

"I was just wondering if you had thought of anyone who might be upset enough with you to burn down your office?"

Walker answered quickly with an emphatic, "No." Then he added, "There really aren't many real estate transactions that bring on that kind of anger."

"May I speak with your wife?"

Jerry gave another furtive look over his shoulder. "Actually, she's not living here right now. She's been staying with a girlfriend for a while."

"I hear someone in the other room," Laurie said. "That's not your wife's voice?"

"The woman in the living room is the reason my wife is staying with a friend."

"I'd still like to talk to your wife. Do you know where I might reach her?"

"She works at the dry cleaners in Pine City when we're not doing open houses and showing properties. I imagine she's there now."

Laurie thanked him, and then returned to Pine City where she found Mrs. Workman behind the counter at the dry cleaners. She was a matronly woman with salt and pepper hair tied in a ponytail. The nametag on her denim jumper said, "Janet."

"I'm Inspector Lone Eagle from the Bureau of Criminal Apprehension. I understand one of the Pine County deputies spoke with you about the fire at the real estate office last night."

"Someone called an office phone that I had rolled over to Celia's house, and I told them that Jerry had an appointment with some clients early in the evening."

"We suspect that arson may be involved, and I was wondering if you could think of anyone who might want the building burned down?"

Janet Workman's eyes went wide. "Arson? Someone burned down the office on purpose?"

"We think so. Can you think of any disgruntled clients or former employees?"

"Jerry and I are the only employees, and I'm not really salaried. As far as disgruntled clients, I guess I'm not aware of any, well other than me. Jerry might have a better idea about that." After a pause Janet added, "I'd think that Arlyn would be more likely to have a disgruntled client that us. I mean, aren't lawyers always on the outs with someone?"

"I understand that you and Jerry aren't living together. Can you tell me where you were last night?"

Janet Workman's face turned crimson. "We're having a little problem, so I've been staying with my friend, Celia Quist, here in town. We went to bed after the news and I slept until the deputy called to ask where Jerry was."

"How unhappy are you with Jerry?"

"I assume you're asking if I'm mad enough to burn the office down. The answer to that is, 'no.' The real estate office still pays all the bills, and my job here provides a little spending money. As you may recall, I still take the calls for the office, and I have a working relationship with Jerry around the office. Burning the building down wouldn't gain me anything but an empty checkbook."

"Do you have any idea whose body was in the office when it burned?"

"God, that's terrible," she said, shaking her head. "I just saw the news and they said the coroner removed a body from the building. I couldn't even guess who it might be. I mean, there's Jerry, and Arl, and I, and we're all the employees there are."

"Were you unhappy when you found out it wasn't Jerry who died in the fire?"

Janet hesitated for a fraction of a second. "Not entirely. But, like I said, I'd have some serious financial problems if Jerry died."

"Do you know anything about the insurance situation?" Laurie asked.

"Um," Janet hesitated. "We didn't own the building, so we didn't have property insurance, if that's what you're asking. I guess we have some renters insurance or something. I mail a check to State Farm quarterly, but I don't know just how much coverage we have."

"And, Arlyn's insurance?"

"I have no idea. I assume that he had the building insured, but I really don't know."

☆ ☆ ☆

The sheriff was sitting in Dan's office when Laurie walked down the hall. She stopped at the open door, and listened to the conversation.

"I want every resource applied to the arson investigation," Sepanen said to Dan. "Let the Smith investigation sit while you go after the arsonist."

"We already diverted everyone from the streetcar search," Dan explained. "I know we have to jump on the arson while it's fresh, and that's exactly what we're doing." He looked up and saw Laurie leaning on the doorframe. "Laurie, did you get anything of interest from Prokop or the Workmans?"

"None of them could come up with a motive for burning down their offices. The realtor was totally baffled, and the wife had no ideas either. Workman and his wife were each staying with girlfriends when the fire broke out.

"Prokop does mostly family law and real estate these days and there really isn't much there that would lead to arson either. The only thing that might tie in at all to the old murders was the fact that his father used to do more criminal work and someone may have been concerned about something in his files. If that were the case, they may have effectively ruined that evidence because all those files were in the basement of the building and they're all flooded now. Prokop said he spoke with his father last night, and again this morning. He found the rental records on the cabins across from the camp and he removed them from the office in his car before the fire. We looked at them this morning, and there doesn't appear to be anything of interest there."

"We should check his long distance records," Dan said. "He keeps saying his father is in Florida, but I don't think anyone has ever checked that out. Wouldn't it be interesting if he's been telling people that his parents gave him the house and business all these years when they were just gone?"

"Wouldn't that be clever?" Laurie said with a chuckle. "We can check that with one call and that would also verify his alibi for late last night."

"Are you two thinking that Prokop might have killed off his parents?" The sheriff asked. "Wouldn't that be something! Prokop kills off his parents, takes over the house and the business, and tells everyone they've moved to Florida. He could easily falsify all the papers and transfer all the assets to his own name with no one ever being the wiser."

"He told us a few days ago that his father didn't like to discuss old cases anymore," Dan said. "That may have just been a ruse to keep us from calling him."

Dan pulled out a phone book and looked up the area code for central Florida. He put the phone on speaker and dialed long distance information. They had a listing for Arlyn Prokop, in Naples, and the operator connected him to the number. After three rings, a man's voice answered.

"Mister Prokop, this is Dan Williams, from the Pine County Sheriff's Department. I'd like to ask you some questions about your old clients."

"Dan, what I surprise. I haven't had three calls from Minnesota in the past month, and you're the third one in two days. What can I do for you?"

The sheriff and Laurie were both smiling about how quickly their dire suspicions had been quelled.

"I take it that Arlyn junior has already told you about the fire at the law office. Now that you've had a little time to think about it, I was wondering if you can come up with any reason someone might want to destroy any of your old files?"

"Arl told me about the fire," the senior Prokop said, with the happiness drained from his voice. "That's really a shame. I've thought about it, and I really can't come up with a single motive. Arl is doing mostly real estate and wills these days and that sure wouldn't cause enough enmity in anyone to do something like that. I haven't practiced up there for over a decade, so I can't believe anyone's concerned about anything that happened that far back. I'm at a loss for an explanation.

"Arl mentioned that you'd found a body in the rubble," Prokop continued. "That must tie into this somehow too. I don't suppose it was one of Jerry Workman's girlfriends, was it?"

"It appears to be an old corpse," Dan replied. "That makes it all the more confusing."

"Mister Prokop, this is Laurie Lone Eagle. I'm an investigator with the Minnesota Bureau of Criminal Apprehension. You made an interesting comment about Jerry Workman's girlfriends. I take it that he's not been the model of marital fidelity?"

The old lawyer laughed. "If Jerry were the model of anything, it would be marital infidelity. I can't count the number of times he's been on the outs with his wife over a one-night-stand. The only reason she continues to put up with him is because he makes so darned much money and she loves spending it." The old lawyer paused, and then added. "I suppose I may have spoken out of school a little bit there. I really don't have first hand knowledge about Jerry's indiscretions, but they are pretty much legendary around town. On the other hand, if you're looking for a murderer, I don't think Jerry has caused much damage other than some broken hearts and homes, that and some horrendous marriage counseling bills. I think he was spending a couple afternoons a week in Duluth trying to patch things up."

"Has Jerry ever had any legal problems that you've represented?" Dan asked.

"I think that would be covered by lawyer-client privilege," Prokop replied. "You can ask him, if you'd like."

"I take that to mean yes," Dan said.

"If the answer were no," Prokop replied, "I would have said no."

Laurie leaned close to the speakerphone and asked, "Do you know that Ryan Martin was killed in Wisconsin?"

"I'd read that in the local paper," Prokop replied. "I suppose you are asking about that because I represented him a few years ago."

"Tell us about your dealings with Ryan," Dan said.

"There's a name from the past," Prokop said. "As I recall, he was an amoral little shit."

"He had been arrested once in the Cities with a woman named Colleen Smith," Laurie said. "Your son said she contacted you about negotiating with the kidnappers after her daughter disappeared. Do you have any recollection of her?"

"Colleen Smith was the stereotypical redhead. She came to the house and demanded that I negotiate the release of her daughter. It was one of the most bizarre conversations I've ever had, because no one had contacted her with a ransom demand. We spoke for an hour and she only departed after I'd agreed to represent her if kidnappers contacted her. I think she had some serious mental problems, and some real issues with her marriage."

"Do you recall any connections between Ryan Martin and Colleen Smith?" Dan asked.

"Let me think for a second about client privilege," the senior Prokop said, and hesitated. "I think we're in the clear since Ryan is dead.

"It was at least a few months later that she made an inquiry about a criminal defense. She told me she'd just been divorced and had gone back to her maiden name, McCarthy. She asked me to represent Ryan Martin, who was being held in the St. Louis County jail. She was also the one who paid my bill."

"Do you have any idea why she was involved?" Dan asked.

"That was a long time ago," Prokop said. "I didn't notice anything at the time, and she claimed her do-gooder obligation, but after a few meetings I got the impression that Ryan Martin had something on her. Their relationship was really tense. He seemed to manipulate her and she was always very uneasy around him. Personally, I thought she was flaky, and I wondered if she had been tied to his drug dealings or something. He may have threatened to expose her unless she protected him with unquestioning loyalty."

"We have some juvenile witnesses that think they saw them having sex when Ryan was eighteen." Dan said. "Would that fit with your observations of their relationship?"

"That wouldn't be inconsistent with what I saw passing between them. I think that they may have each manipulated the other person at times."

"Is there anyone else in the community those two had ties with?" Laurie asked.

Prokop paused. "I'm afraid that information would fall under lawyer-client privilege."

Dan, the sheriff, and Laurie all passed a look. Sepanen leaned forward. "Mister Prokop, this is sheriff Sepanen. If you have knowledge about a crime that may have been committed, you should speak up now."

"I'm well aware of my legal obligations, sheriff. If I had prior knowledge of an upcoming criminal act, I have an obligation to act. If a client shared information about previous criminal acts, those are privileged conversations, and I am bound not to disclose that information as long as the client is alive."

"No matter how many dead bodies are buried in the woods?" Dan asked.

"I can say with a clear conscience," Prokop said sharply, "that I have no personal knowledge of any dead body buried anywhere in Minnesota. I will also add, that I have asked my son to seal all of my old files and not provide law enforcement access to them. I understand that may be a moot point since most of them are under water anyway. I think that I will say goodbye at this point and end our conversation." Those words were followed by a dial tone.

"He was a little defensive," Dan said as he turned off the speakerphone.

"The one tidbit he gave us," Laurie said, "was that there is still someone alive, who he represented, who committed a crime that hasn't been prosecuted."

"We also know that it wasn't a murder," the sheriff added.

"The question is," Dan said, "did it lead to murder?"

CHAPTER 42

Sunday

Floyd explained the investigation as Hennepin County Detective Kline drove another beat up Crown Victoria toward Colleen McCarthy's home in the light weekend traffic. He weaved through the traffic silently evoking a few hand gestures from drivers he passed, and it surprised Floyd that drivers would gesture at was obviously an unmarked police car. After turning off the interstate, Kline stopped at a red light on Chicago Avenue.

"Here's the scenario as I see it," Kline said. "The McCarthy woman is using the Martin kid. He thinks he's got the upper hand because she's stroking his ego and humping him in bed. In reality, she's using him and she gets him to do something that's very illegal, but suddenly he *does* have the upper hand because he's got something on her that's so damning that she can't let it get out. The problem is that he's just as incriminated by it as she is, so although he threatens her with it, he can't really follow through on the threat because it meant both of them would end up behind bars. It takes her a while to figure that out that he can't act on his threats, but once she does, she drops him like a hot potato and he ends up in jail over something else."

Floyd looked at Kline skeptically. "Let's say that's so. Then why didn't he turn State's evidence in return for a reduced sentence when he was busted in Wisconsin?"

"Because," Kline said, "whatever it was that he'd done in Minnesota, was worse than what he got busted for in Wisconsin. Why was he jailed in Wisconsin?"

"Assault."

"So," Kline said, "He must've killed somebody for the McCarthy woman."

"I don't think so," Floyd replied. "The only dead person in that loop is McCarthy's daughter, and I can't believe a mother would have her own kid killed."

Kline pulled in front of Colleen McCarthy's house and turned off the engine. "Maybe she didn't intend for the kid to die. Did she die accidentally?"

"Stab wound to the chest," Floyd said as he got out of the car. "No mother is going to pay somebody to stab their little girl to death, no matter how flaky she is. She got nothing out of it but a divorce. There's no motive."

The front door was open a crack and warm air blew out at them as they stood on the small landing. The door opened further when Kline knocked.

"Sheriff's Department!" Kline yelled into the open living room. "Anybody home?" Kline was reaching for his pistol as he pushed the door fully open with the back of his hand. Floyd followed behind with his own gun drawn.

The living room had been ransacked with every piece of furniture upended, the couch cushions and every chair cut open. The cotton batting and foam rubber were strewn on top of the mess. Kline put his hand on Floyd's arm and they stepped outside. He dialed 911, and asked for back up from the Minneapolis Police.

"Stay here," Kline said. "I'll look around the back."

Before Kline was around the corner of the house, sirens wailed nearby. The house was silent except for the sound of the furnace fan, blowing warm air out the open front door. Kline was back as the first Minneapolis police car pulled up in front of the house. Two more MPD cars were in sight by the time the first officers were on the front steps.

Kline flashed his badge at the first officers, who he vaguely recognized. "We came to question the resident of the house, and found the front door open and the living room trashed. I checked the back door, and it's open too. You two secure the back until we get a patrol sergeant here and enough people to do a secure search."

As the rest of the officers approached the house Kline called his dispatcher and asked her to call the soup kitchen where McCarthy worked. Before he was off the phone, there were four more Minneapolis officers at the house, and Floyd was explaining the situation to them. A patrol sergeant arrived within two minutes. Floyd and Kline watched the team of Minneapolis Police officers enter the house for the search.

"This is incredible," Floyd said. "I call for back up in Pine County and I'll have another officer on the scene in fifteen minutes. On a good day, a third person will be there within half an hour."

"I'd be scared shitless," Kline replied. "Of course, you don't run into a gang very often either." His cell phone chirped, interrupting the conversation.

Kline answered and said, "Okay," several times. "McCarthy just showed up at the soup kitchen. She's on her way back here," he said as he folded the phone back into his pocket.

The MPD sergeant was a middle-aged man, with a belly hanging over his belt. He was talking into a radio mounted on his shoulder as he approached Kline and Floyd.

"The house has been trashed," the sergeant said, "but it doesn't look like anyone was injured. I'd guess that someone was looking for drugs if the décor was a little less flashy. But, given the neighborhood and the furniture, I'd guess that someone was looking for money hidden in the mattress. Since no one was injured, I doubt the captain will want to send a crime scene team in. We'll take a report and leave the homeowner to clean up and file an insurance claim."

"That's it?" Floyd asked. "You don't do an investigation unless there's someone injured?"

"Not usually," the sergeant replied. "There are too many other high priority crimes to chase down burglars. Cruise through the emergency room tonight and see how many stabbing and shooting victims are lined up, then tell me I should spend a lot of time trying to track down a penny-ante house burglar."

A battered Chevrolet Citation, with the exhaust smoking like it was afire, came wheezing down the street. It stopped across from all the police cars and Colleen McCarthy flew out of the passenger's side door. The driver, who appeared to be the lean man who'd checked on McCarthy in the alley, stayed behind the wheel and lit a cigarette without making eye contact with any of the cops.

McCarthy crossed the street with her arms waving. She reminded Floyd of an educational program he's seen where people were trying to train whooping cranes who'd been raised in captivity how to act like whooping cranes.

"What have you done?" McCarthy screamed at Floyd and Kline as she raced across the lawn. "The sheriff's department called and said you'd burglarized my house!" She stopped, nose to nose with Kline, as if she planned to strike him.

The Minneapolis Police sergeant stepped between then, pushing McCarthy back on her heels. "Your house was burglarized before they got here," he said. "Settle down a little."

McCarthy reached over his shoulder and pointed at Kline. "He's been harassing me! This is just the final straw. Arrest him!"

The sergeant pulled down her arm and held it firmly. "I said that you should settle down. Your house has been burglarized. Detective Kline had nothing to do with it."

"He's a jerk and I hate him!" she said, following the oath with flying spittle that landed on the Minneapolis sergeant's uniform shirt.

"All right," he said, spinning her around and pulling her arm behind her back. "We'll do this the hard way." He clipped handcuffs around her wrists. "You're going to sit in my car until you settle down. Do you think that your friend in the car could come over and make the house secure so the local punks don't steal anything that's not already broken?"

"You're all Nazis!" McCarthy screamed. "You can't do this to me! I know my rights and you can't arrest me for spitting at you!"

"That's enough," the sergeant said quietly. "Let's go to the car."

McCarthy let out a scream like a banshee as the sergeant lifted her handcuffed arms and directed her to the car. Several officers showed up at the door to watch the spectacle. While the sergeant was trying to protect her head from bumping on the header over the door she lunged forward and butted him in the chest while screaming that she was being raped.

"That's a woman with spirit," Kline said as he watched the show.

A female, African-American officer came out of the house and ran to assist the sergeant. They finally pushed McCarthy's body into the back seat of the car, only to have her kick viciously at their legs and groins. McCarthy landed a solid kick to the female officer's crotch, which elicited a group groan from the men watching from the porch.

"Glad that was Angie and not one of us," the nearest male policeman said.

"Yeah, but it's going to leave a bruise," Kline added.

Angie grabbed the offending foot and gave it a vicious twist. The scream that came from the back seat was searing, but it stopped the struggle long enough for the sergeant to slam the door. He walked over to talk to the driver of the Citation while officer Angie walked gingerly back to the house.

"Hey, Angie," the youngest officer said, "bet you're glad you're a girl. Any of the rest of us would've been out of commission for weeks after a kick like that."

Angie reached down and massaged her injured tissue. "Let me tell you, it was no treat for me either. I'm not gonna be chasing Norman around the bed for a couple days."

In the back of the crowd a male Hispanic officer said, "I told you Angie had the Cajones to be a cop."

They all laughed, including Angie.

☆ ☆ ☆

Pam Ryan arrived at the nursing home with a bag of Snickerdoodles tucked under her arm. She asked the receptionist to page the head nurse, and offered the teen-aged receptionist a cookie while they waited for a response to the page. The girl was seated behind a high Birch desk, with a phone console mounted on one side. She took the cookie, but gave Pam a curious look.

"Didn't I see you here wearing a dress a few days ago with an old cop?" The young receptionist with bleached blonde hair asked. Pam guessed her to be about sixteen, going on twenty-six. She wore a tight V-neck sweater with a push up bra making the most of her limited cleavage. Her face was much younger than the look she was trying to portray, and the sweater showed a little roll of fat where her waist was forced into a pair of pants too tight for her girth.

It reminded Pam of her own insecurities of six or seven years ago. High school was the high point of her social life, with dates, flirting, and necking. It was the absolute low in terms of self-confidence and self image. Every day she'd felt insecure and unattractive. Now, she could roam the countryside wearing a bulletproof vest under her uniform shirt, and she had no qualms about guys thinking she wasn't buxom, and with enough self-confidence to stand up to a loud-mouthed drunk alone on a dark highway.

Deb McIntosh hustled down the hallway, and gave Pam a discreet wave. She arrived at the reception desk slightly breathless. "You're back to see Grace Palm, I assume. She had a little episode last night where she was short of breath and we had to send her to the hospital. I hope you haven't wasted the trip."

Pam got directions to the hospital, on the outskirts of Mora's south side. The parking lot was mostly empty and the few people moving back and forth were carrying flowers and metallized plastic balloons sporting wishes for quick recovery. Pam suspected that a quick recovery wasn't in the cards for Grace. She got directions to the second floor room from a pert volunteer, who looked like she was keeping busy with public service in her young retirement.

Smells of disinfectant, and the subdued scent of flowers greeted her as she made her way though the brightly lit, beige hallways. The second bed in Grace Palm's hospital room was empty, and Grace was sleeping when Pam arrived. A small green nasal cannula ran under the frail woman's nose and hissed as it released oxygen. Her chest rose and fell slowly as an overhead monitor updated her heart rate and blood pressure continuously.

Pam stood at Grace's side for a few moments, trying to decide if she should wake her. After deliberation, she decided to pull a guest chair next to the head of the bed and wait for Grace to wake up on her own. A nurse, whose nametag said, Gerri, walked in with a chart after a few minutes.

"Have you been waiting for Grace to wake up?" the nurse asked. She walked to the bedside and put her hand on Grace's arm. "Wake up, you sleepy head. You have a visitor."

"Where am I?" Grace's eyes popped open and she looked around the room like she was seeing it for the first time. "And who's the cop?"

"You're in the hospital," the nurse replied. "I have to take your temperature, and this deputy sheriff seems to have brought something in a bakery bag."

Grace tried to push the electronic thermometer out with her tongue, but the nurse was prepared and held her mouth shut until the monitor beeped. "Now you can talk to the deputy."

"Did you bring cookies" Grace asked. "Russian Tea Cakes are my favorite."

"All the bakery had today was snickerdoodles," Pam replied, opening the bag and handing Grace a single cookie. Grace took it with a quivering hand as Pam offered a cookie to the nurse, who politely refused. Grace ate the cookie hungrily, and spilling crumbs and cinnamon on the bedding and her striped hospital gown. She reached for the bag as soon as the last piece was in her mouth.

"I need your help," Pam said, handing Grace a second cookie. "No one can seem to remember some things about the summer camp where you worked. I was hoping you could tell me what happened to the girl who disappeared."

Grace ate the second cookie, chewing a few times, then coughing. She stopped to catch be breath before swallowing. "Could I have another?"

"In a minute," Pam said, switching strategies. "First tell me about Helen Smith."

"She ran off with that boy," Grace said, struggling to catch her breath but carefully keeping an eye on the bakery bag. "I think she got pregnant and they had to elope."

"Which boy did she run off with?"

"That troublemaker. The one who got her pregnant, I suppose."

"Was his name Arlyn Prokop?" Pam asked as she broke a cookie in half and handed a piece to Grace.

"No," Grace replied, as she took the half cookie. "Arlyn was that wimpy lawyer's kid. He didn't get anyone pregnant. I think he was afraid of girls. It was that Martin kid she ran off with." She spoke in short sentences, catching her breath between bursts of speech.

"We heard the Martin kid was seeing some redheaded older woman. Do you know who she was?"

Pam asked, holding the half cookie back, teasing Grace with it.

"I seen them together," Grace replied, reaching for the other half cookie. "A redheaded woman… picked him up at the camp. I never heard her name… but I heard he maybe got her pregnant, too. At least I heard they…were doing it. Maybe she was…some sort of party girl. I heard that…maybe a few of the boys had…done it with her."

"Are you breathing okay?" Pam asked. "Should I come back after you rest a little?"

"I'm just a little tired."

"Who told you about the redheaded woman?"

"It was probably…those lazy girls," Grace said. "You know…those two from Dalbo. They told me… all kinds of gossip." Grace's breathing became more labored with each sentence.

"I talked to them," Pam said, holding the half cookie back. "They didn't know anything about the redheaded woman. Who else would have told you about her? What you told me sounds more like teen-aged boys bragging than girl's gossip."

"It must've been my nephew." Grace reached to take the half cookie from Pam's fingers but dropped her hand to the bed when the effort seemed too great.

"Who is your nephew?" Pam asked.

Grace broke into a coughing fit that sprayed bits of cookie across the bed covers. When she stopped, her face had drained of color. Pam noticed that the heart rate monitor had raced up to 143 during the coughing fit. It was slowly recovering. Grace was struggling to catch her breath.

Grace's eyes closed and her breathing slowed. Pam's frustration at not getting a straight answer was tempered by her concern about Grace's breathing difficulties. Pam's study of Grace's graying face was interrupted by the sound of the automatic blood pressure cuff inflating. She looked up at the overhead monitor and saw the updated blood pressure display: 87/0. She rushed to the nursing station and hailed Gerri.

"Grace had a coughing fit and then fell asleep," Pam said hastily. "Now her blood pressure is eighty seven over zero."

Gerri nodded and walked without rushing to Grace's room with Pam. She checked the blood oxygenation meter, and looked at the new heart rate and blood pressure readings. She gently squeezed Grace's fingers, and not getting a response, she led Pam from the room.

"Are you a family member?" the nurse asked.

"No," Pam replied. "I've been interviewing Grace because she may have information about an old murder case."

"Grace is declining. I can't give you medical details, but let's say she won't be with us long. The family has asked that we keep her comfortable, but that we not resuscitate if…when she goes into cardiac arrest."

"Do you think she'll be..." Pam paused, not wanting to ask a calloused question. "Will she wake up again?"

"She's resting now," Gerri said, looking over Pam's shoulder, at Grace. "She may wake up again in a while, or she may not. Her naps have been getting longer and the periods between less lucid. I overheard her talking to you. You're fortunate. That's the most lucid she's been since she arrived yesterday.

"Tell you what," the nurse said, "grab a cup of coffee in the cafeteria and come back in an hour. Maybe she'll be awake then and you'll be able to talk to her some more. But, don't get your hopes up."

CHAPTER 43

Dan and Laurie were testing theories on each other when the dispatcher paged Dan.

"I'm going to call Jerry Workman's wife while you take this call," Laurie said. "I want to nail down the timeline on his travels last night."

Floyd Swenson's voice greeted Dan when he picked up the phone. "We've got Colleen McCarthy in custody, and we're going to question her in a little bit. But, there are a couple twists that have come up. When we got to her house, it had been burglarized. The place is a shambles. Hennepin County tracked her down at the soup kitchen and she came racing back all in a rage. She assaulted two Minneapolis cops, and they arrested her."

"Why did she attack the Minneapolis cops?" Dan asked.

"I'm not really sure. When she got here she was totally out of control, yelling, screaming, and claiming that the Hennepin County detective and I had ransacked the house. A Minneapolis sergeant stepped in, and she spit on him. He cuffed her, and a female officer helped him put McCarthy into his car. She kicked the female cop in the crotch and things deteriorated from there."

"Where was she last night when the law office burned down?"

"She claims that she was with her boyfriend," Floyd replied, "at his apartment. He didn't refute that, but he seemed like it was more her story than his."

"Any idea who trashed the house?"

"The Minneapolis cops made it sound like it was local thieves. They didn't even call in a crime scene investigation, they said there were too many murders and assaults ahead of this to spend time investigating a burglary where no one was hurt."

"I have another tidbit for your discussion with McCarthy," Dan said. "We spoke with Arlyn Prokop senior this morning. Not only did McCarthy testify at Ryan Martin's war protest trial, she paid for Prokop to represent him on other charges after that. Prokop thought Martin may have had something on her because they acted so strangely together.

"Give me a call back after you talk to McCarthy. I'd like to hear her explanation of the Benson boys seeing her in the streetcar with Ryan Martin."

Laurie was at Dan's door as soon as he'd hung up. "Walker's client meeting was at eight-thirty. His wife was sure he would've done by ten at the latest. I wonder if his girlfriend will say he was with her the whole time from ten until Jack found him at her house."

"I've got a better question to ask than that," Dan said. "Someone was at Workman's house to tell our deputy that Jerry wasn't home. If his wife spent the whole night with a friend, who told us Jerry wasn't home?"

Dan pushed a button to activate the speakerphone and dialed the dispatcher. "Hank," he said to the dispatcher, "check the logs and see who was dispatched to Jerry Workman's house after the fire was discovered. Then, call him at home, and ask who was home at Workman's. If he didn't get a name, have him describe the person to you."

"Are you kidding?" The dispatcher had started a note and then stopped.

"I'm dead serious," Dan replied. "A deputy was dispatched to notify Workman of the fire. If he talked to someone at the house I want to know who."

"You know," the dispatcher said, "that Jerry has a little reputation. Just because there was a woman at his house, it doesn't mean she was his wife."

Laurie and Dan exchanged looks. "We've come to understand that," Dan said. "Just check on this one for me. Inspector Lone Eagle and I are going to Pine Brook to visit the flower shop. Call me on the radio and let me know who came to the door."

☆ ☆ ☆

Brad Kline and Floyd were sitting across the table from Colleen McCarthy inside an interview room. Officer Angie Jackson was standing in the corner, giving McCarthy an evil glare every time she cast her eyes that direction. McCarthy had an Ace bandage wrapped around her right knee, with an ice pack embedded in the wrap so it looked like her knee was basketball sized.

"You will all end up in jail over the way I've been treated," McCarthy said to Angie with venom.

"Not when the lawyers see the dash camera video and the pictures of the bruises on my crotch," Angie replied.

"When's my lawyer going to be here?" McCarthy asked. "I should be in a hospital, not sitting under a heat lamp being questioned by Nazis."

A harried young woman opened the door and stuck her head in. She was short, with neatly trimmed brown hair. "Excuse me," she said, "is this Colleen McCarthy's room?"

"C'mon in," Kline said. "I assume you're from the public defender's office."

The woman stepped into the room. She wore a gray polyester pants suit and her small stature made her look like a teenager. Her one item of jewelry was a silver Timex watch.

"I'm Tina Wess," the public defender said, setting the pile of folders on the table. "I'm sorry to be late, but apparently Miss McCarthy is known to the other people in our office, and they decided it would be better for a new attorney to represent her."

Colleen McCarthy rolled her eyes. Kline smiled and offered his hand.

"I'm Detective Sergeant Kline, from Hennepin County. This is Sergeant Floyd Swenson, from Pine County. In the corner is Officer Angie Jackson, from MPD."

"Nice to meet you," Jackson said, stepping forward and shaking the defender's hand.

"Excuse me," McCarthy said, "I'm the person you're here to represent."

"I understand that you assaulted Officer Jackson during your arrest," Wess said, ignoring the verbal jab from her client.

"It was self defense," McCarthy replied, lifting her knee into view. "She attacked me and injured my knee."

Wess opened the top file and took out a videotape. "One of the police cars had a dash mounted video camera that recorded the whole event," Wess said. "I watched the video. I suggest you cop a plea and hope that Officer Jackson doesn't sue you for assault. It appears that you kicked Officer Jackson before she was forced to subdue you."

"I want a new attorney."

Wess put the video back into the folder. "Sorry. No one else in the office will have anything to do with you. You've done a wonderful job of alienating everyone who's represented you, and you have been up on charges so many times they all know you. Unless you have the cash to hire a private attorney, I suggest you shut up and listen. I realize that would be a big change for you, but it's about time you grew up."

McCarthy's jaw dropped and her eyes grew wide. "I don't have to take abuse like this!"

"Shut the fuck up," Angie Jackson said. "Or didn't you understand your attorney?"

Wess settled into a metal chair and opened the file. "I assume you have a video running?" she asked, nodding to a camera in the corner. "If you're ready, start your questions."

Floyd opened a small notebook and flipped through a few pages. "In a previous conversation," he said, "you told us that you didn't know Ryan Martin, and then corrected your statement to say that you didn't know him well. We pointed out that you had been arrested together and that you'd testified in his trial. Would you care to expand on those statements?"

"I have nothing to say," McCarthy said.

"Tell us why you paid the lawyer to defend him," Kline said.

McCarthy's eyes narrowed. "Like I said, I have nothing to add."

"Ryan Martin was the last person seen with your daughter," Floyd said. "We thought you'd want to provide as much information as possible about this background so we could solve her murder."

Wess's eyes looked at McCarthy with the apparent expectation of an answer. Instead McCarthy looked away without answering.

"We have two witnesses," Floyd said, "who saw you having sex with Ryan Martin in the streetcar he rented the summer, prior to the day your daughter disappeared. That kind of information raises all kinds of questions about your relationship with him."

Wess looked at McCarthy expectantly and then looked back to Floyd. "Excuse me," the attorney said, "I thought this was an assault case. If I'm interpreting your questions correctly, Miss McCarthy's daughter was killed, and you're questioning her about her relationship with the man who was last seen with the decedent?"

'That's correct," Floyd said. "In previous discussions she was evasive, and has apparently supplied us with some incorrect information about her relationship with one of the suspects. We're trying to clarify that information."

"Have you questioned Mister Martin?" Wess asked.

"He was killed in his home a few days ago," Floyd said.

"Are you accusing Miss McCarthy of any crimes related to either of those deaths?"

Floyd shook his head, "No. We're just trying to get straight answers about her relationships with some of the suspects."

"How long ago did your daughter die?" Wess asked, turning her attention to McCarthy.

"Thirty five years ago," McCarthy replied. "She was kidnapped and they killed her when my husband wouldn't pay the ransom."

"Excuse me," Floyd interrupted. "We are not aware that a ransom demand was ever made. If that's the truth, it's new information to us."

"I'm sure they would've made a ransom demand if you cops hadn't screwed up the investigation."

"Can you explain your relationship with Ryan Martin?" Floyd asked.

Tears welled in McCarthy's eyes. "God, I can't believe this shit. She looked at the lawyer and asked, "Do I have to tell them about the sordid details of my sex life?"

"If it's pertinent to resolution of your daughter's death," Wess said, "I would think that you would *want to* share anything that clarified their questions. On the other hand, you don't *have to* tell them about anything that would incriminate you, or that isn't pertinent. It sure seems like they aren't going to let this drop. By giving them misleading information in the past, you have certainly raised some questions in their minds."

"Okay," McCarthy said, composing herself. "I'm not proud of this. I had an affair with Ryan Martin. I did pay for his defense, and we had disgusting sex in that filthy streetcar. Does that resolve your need to know about the seamy portions of my past, or are there other parts of my soul you'd like bared?"

"Where were you last night?" Floyd asked.

"I already told you," McCarthy said. "I was at my friend's house. I had sex with him, too, just in case you wanted to know about my current sex life as well as my distant past."

Floyd's cell phone chirped, and he stepped back from the table. Kline continued the questioning by asking, "You are saying for the record, that you were not in Willow River last night?"

"That's right," McCarthy said without equivocation. "I was not in Willow River last night."

Floyd returned to the table and put the cell phone in his pocket. He looked McCarthy in the eye and said, "That was the Pine County dispatcher. A deputy spoke with you last night at Jerry Workman's house, in Willow River."

Wess put her hand on McCarthy's arm. "I think my client needs to not answer any more questions. The statement she just made was not made under oath, so she has not perjured herself. However, she and I need to confer in private before she answers any more questions." Wess looked directly at the camera in the corner of the ceiling. "And, turn off the camera when you leave. This will be a privileged conversation."

CHAPTER 44

Dan and Laurie walked into Pine Brook Floral after lunch in Hinckley. The shop appeared to be deserted, but Mary Junger's head popped out from the back room before they made it to the counter.

"Hi, Dan. Where's Floyd, and who's your friend?"

"I'm Inspector Lone Eagle with the BCA," Laurie said, reaching out to shake hands with the florist.

"Whew," Mary said. "They send in the 'A' team, who brought reinforcements. Does this mean I'm being busted for plotting all those murders?" Her face beamed with a broad smile.

"Mary told Floyd about all the possible motives she'd have for killing off inconsiderate customers," Dan explained to Laurie. "There are lots of them. Actually, Mary, I have a few more questions."

"Imagine that!" Mary said. "The sheriff's department showed up to ask questions. C'mon back. I just made a fresh pot of coffee and there's a box of doughnuts left over from the morning crew." Mary winked at Laurie. "I know the deputies *LOVE* doughnuts. Floyd could get through two or three in a visit and I swear he could do it without gaining an ounce. He's just skin and bones."

"Cops liking doughnuts is an old wive's tale," Dan said, following Mary into her office. "However, I do eat an apple fritter on occasion."

"Did you peek in the box, or are you that good at detecting? I think there's one fritter left."

Laurie refused the offered doughnuts, but Dan took the one remaining apple fritter. Mary brought three purple Telefloral mugs of coffee to her office from somewhere in the back room.

"Aren't you having a doughnut?" Mary asked Laurie.

"I don't get enough exercise to burn off a doughnut, and I like to fit in my slacks. But, I do appreciate the offer, and I'm sure Dan's consumption will more than make up for my abstinence."

"So," Mary said, "what's up?"

"The mystery just seems to get deeper," Dan said. "A law office burned down in Willow River, and we found a body in the basement after the fire was put out. We think that fire and corpse may be related to the skeleton found in the car trunk."

Mary was suddenly somber. "I heard about the fire on the news. I guess it never occurred to me that the two incidents might be connected. Floyd didn't mention that when he called this morning."

"It's not common knowledge," Dan said, making a mental note that Floyd hadn't been assigned Mary in follow up, but managed to make a call. "I'd appreciate if you didn't spread that news around until you've heard it on television. But we do know that there's a redheaded woman who's tied in to both of these events somehow. Your brothers saw her in the streetcar with one of the renters, and she showed up in Willow River last night, too."

"Floyd mentioned that. So it's not just a coincidence?" Mary asked.

"There are no coincidences in law enforcement," Laurie said. "That's quote number one from the Dan Williams's school of police procedures."

"We assume this woman is involved," Dan said, "but she's just a link. There has to be someone else. We know that Arlyn Prokop hung around the camp the summer the girl disappeared, but we're pretty sure he isn't involved. Is there anyone else who comes to mind when you think back to the summer that Ryan Martin lived in the streetcar?"

"Arlyn Prokop," Mary repeated, "that's a name from the past. Shy Arlyn Prokop, the lawyer's kid. He used to blush when I said, 'hi,' to him after he wrote up the purchase contract for this shop. I don't think he ever partied anywhere with anyone."

"Can you remember anyone else coming out to the streetcar to see Ryan Martin?" Laurie asked. "Maybe you recall someone who had an unusual truck or car?"

Mary stared through the open door. "I remember a bright orange sporty car sitting next to the streetcar. I remember asking the boys what kind of car it was because the kids at school thought it was really hot. It was a GT-something and I saw it there several times."

"Who owned it?" Laurie asked, as Dan stuffed the last bite of fritter into his mouth.

"I don't know," Mary said, shrugging her shoulders. "A guy with light brown, wavy hair; one of the *in crowd.* I was the *out crowd* with the other poor kids whose parents couldn't afford designer clothes. That guy was one of the party people. I think his Dad owned a business."

"Who would know?" Dan asked, as he wiped some frosting from his lips with a handkerchief.

"My brothers might," Mary replied. She hesitated, and then said, "I'll bet Arlyn Prokop might remember. He and this other guy were older, and maybe about the same grade in school. My brothers said it was a cool car. I'll bet it stuck in every guy's mind."

Pam Ryan walked back to Grace Palm's hospital floor after eating a sandwich and drinking three cups of coffee. Gerri was reading a chart at the station and Pam caught her attention with a wave.

"Is Grace Palm awake?" Pam asked.

The nurse closed the chart and came out from the station desk. "Let's check."

The door to Grace's room was closed and the lights were dimmed. Grace's face was a dreary gray, and the monitor over her head indicated her pulse was thirty-four beats per minute. The blood pressure monitor was flashing, "error."

The nurse pushed a button that started an automatic cycling of the blood pressure cuff. She touched Grace's arm gently.

"Grace," she said softly, "there's a pretty young deputy here to see you. Can you open your eyes?"

When Grace failed to respond, the nurse checked the blood pressure reading. It hadn't been able to record a measurement, so she took a cuff out of the drawer and made a manual test with her stethoscope.

"I don't think Grace is going to rejoin us," the nurse said, as she folded the manual cuff and returned it to the drawer. Her blood pressure isn't high enough to profuse her brain with oxygen." Gerri disabled the blood pressure reading on the monitor and removed the blood oxygenation monitor from Grace's finger. Pam watched the scene play out in silence, her eyes fixed on the heart rate monitor - every few seconds the displayed rate would drop another number.

"Shouldn't you do something?" Pam asked.

The nurse gave Pam a weak smile and motioned for her to go into the hallway," Let's talk in the hallway. We find that even comatose patients sometimes come around and repeat things they heard while they were away."

They walked in silence to the nurse's station and Gerri took Grace's chart out of the rack.

"I have to call her relatives again," the nurse said. "That's about all there is to do. Her heart is worn out, and it will eventually slow and stop. Grace has a living will, and it directs us not to attempt to resuscitate her when her heart stops beating. Her family brought it in, and they're all in agreement. They've asked us not to put her on a respirator or to give her medications to artificially elevate her blood pressure. If you'll excuse me, I have to call her niece and nephew to let them know that the end is quickly approaching."

"You could give her something to stimulate her heart."

"To delay the inevitable? That's not what Grace wants, and not what she indicated in her living will. She's comfortable, and she'll pass peacefully."

Pam walked back to Grace's room and stood by her bedside. Tears welled in her eyes as she watched the old woman struggle to draw shallow breaths. Pam touched her paper-thin skin and whispered, "Grace," in the hope her eyes would pop open in response. The overhead monitor showed Grace's heart was beating twenty-eight times a minute. Pam was tempted to sit down and wait for the end, but decided to let the end come without her.

She walked to the nurse's station to say goodbye, but found nurse Gerri on the phone. When she tried to speak, the goodbye croaked out, and she decided on a discreet wave instead. The nurse waved back as someone answered the call she was making.

Pam watched with tears streaming down her face, and powdered sugar from the cookies clinging to her uniform shirt while she clamped the bag under her arm so she could blow her nose on a tissue. The nurse was informing the next of kin that they needed to come quickly if they wanted to say goodbye while Grace's heart was still beating.

"I understand Mister Workman," the nurse said. "I don't think she'll last until you drive from Willow River. We'll take care of things. It will be fine."

Pam blew her nose into a tissue, and then asked, "Who is the next of kin?"

"There are two," the nurse said, "Jerry Workman, from Willow River, and his sister, Ginger Ingebritson, from Wadena. I was just going to call Mrs. Ingebritson now."

Pam's heart skipped a beat. "Grace Palm's nephew is Gerry Workman?"

"Yes, do you know him?"

CHAPTER 45

The message on Dan's desk said, "Call Oresek." He dialed the medical examiner's office in Duluth while Laurie brought cups of coffee from the bullpen. Dan was popping Tums into his mouth, while the speakerphone rang.

"Medical Examiner's office," Eddie Paulson, the medical examiner's assistant, came over the speaker as Laurie closed the office door.

"Eddie, this is Dan with Laurie Lone Eagle on the speakerphone. I had a message to call Tony."

"Hang on. I'll grab him." Within a minute, Eddie was back on the phone with Tony Oresek, the St. Louis County Medical Examiner.

"Dan," Oresek said, "we have some preliminary results from the body in the basement. Eddie really humped this morning and tracked down dental records from the Fond-du-Lac reservation. We have a positive ID. It's as Laurie said, the remains are Angela Little Bear."

Dan watched as Laurie closed her eyes, the pain brought to the surface once again.

"What can you tell me about the cause of death and where the body may have been stored?" Dan asked.

"As we noted at the site, there are apparently two knife wounds; one pierced the aorta and left lung, and the second passing all the way through the lung to strike a rib on the back. In terms of where the body was stored, well that's a little tougher. We're doing some chemical analysis on the tissue, but I can make some observations; There is no trace of formaldehyde, so the body was not embalmed by an undertaker. The tissue is deeply discolored, and the discoloration penetrates fully into the medulla of the femur. The discoloration appears to be tannins, probably from rotting plant matter, so we can surmise that the skeleton has been buried in rotting plant debris for decades, probably since she was killed, and somewhere that would keep the remains from depredation by scavenging animals. Sometimes we can see the etched marks of pine needles and leaves where they rested against the bones, but there's none of that here. It's almost like she was in a compost pile or manure pile where the plant matter had already degraded before it came in contact with the body, but we would've had massive decomposition of the tissues within days in those settings. The only thing that makes any sense at all is that the body has been buried in a bog for the past three decades where the acidity and lack of oxygen let the tannins penetrate and preserve the flesh while keeping scavengers away."

"Dan, this is Eddie. I did a little research on bog bodies this afternoon. There aren't too many that have been recovered in the US, but there are dozens in Europe. Some have been preserved like the day they died for hundreds of years. The tannins in the bog color and preserve the tissues until the body is excavated. I'm trying to get in touch with some people who've actually examined one of the bog bodies, but so far no one has returned my calls."

"Would burial in a swamp meet those conditions?" Dan asked.

"It could be if the body was deep enough so the rotted plants had already broken down into slop so there was lots of acid and no oxygen to feed bacterial decomposition."

"Well," Dan said, "there are only about five hundred square miles of swamp in Pine County. That should narrow down the search a little."

"I looked more closely at the post mortem gash on the victim's thigh. In some disinterments we see damage caused by a shovel, but this damage was more like tearing caused by a coarse saw."

"Why would someone use a saw to exhume a body?"

Laurie grabbed Dan's arm and whispered. "Remember the ugly saw with moss hanging from the teeth in Prokop's garage?"

"Eddie hit on one other hint," Oresek said, "there were microscopic diatoms in the victim's mouth."

"What's a diatom?" Laurie asked, "And what's the significance?"

"Diatoms are microscopic creatures with glass shells. They live in virtually every body of fresh water. The significance is that there are thousands of species, and they each have a specific type of environment they prefer and each species shells are almost as unique as snowflakes. This species of diatoms, and we had to check with a Limnologist at the Duluth EPA lab, are unique to small bodies of still water. They would not be found in a swamp, in a river, or in a large lake. That should narrow the possibilities down about ninety-nine percent. If you bring in samples from some suspicious lakes, we can compare the diatoms in the samples to the ones Eddie found with the body."

Dan held his hands over his face. "So," he said, "I should have the deputies pulling water samples from every little lake in the county and have them sent to you for analysis."

"Start with lakes close to the fire," Oresek suggested.

Laurie lurched forward so quickly that she spilled her coffee on Dan's desktop. "Tony, what would happen to a body if you dropped it in a Tamarack bog?"

"I think the body would look like this one did," he replied. "That's what Eddie was explaining, the bog environment is perfect for preserving bodies. Why, do you have a particular bog in mind?"

"The whole back side of McCormick Lake is a bog," she replied. "And one of the suspects has an ice saw in his garage and a canoe that he could use to transport bodies back and forth. I saw that canoe this morning, and it had just been in the water. As a matter of fact, when it was moved, a few chunks of fresh moss fell out of it and there's moss on the ice saw."

Dan was on his feet before Laurie finished the sentence. "I'm going to see if there are any judges in the courthouse this afternoon," he yelled over his shoulder as he headed down the hall.

"What's going on?" Oresek asked.

"I think Dan just went to get a search warrant," she replied.

"One other thing before you hang up!" Eddie said. "This body has probably only been out of the bog for a day or two."

"How can you tell?" Laurie asked.

"Although bog bodies are well preserved in their buried environment, they decompose rapidly when they're removed. The body here is already changing even though we've got it refrigerated."

CHAPTER 46

Pam Ryan was barely out of Mora when she radioed dispatch and requested a link to Dan Williams. After a few minutes, dispatch said that Dan was out of radio contact and away from his office. Pam left a message for him to call her as soon as he returned.

As she drove highway twenty-three, she called dispatch and asked Floyd Swenson to call her cell phone. After several minutes, Pam's phone rang.

"What's up?" he asked.

"Where are you, Floyd?"

"In Minneapolis questioning a suspect," he replied. "Where are you?"

"I'm on my way from Mora to Willow River," she said. "The nephew is the key. I don't want to mention names over the airwaves. Ask your suspect about Jerry."

"She's talking to her lawyer now, and may not want to share much with us. What's the link?"

"I think there was supposed to be a ransom, but Grace's nephew screwed it up."

"I'll get back to you," Floyd said. "In the meanwhile, call Dan, and don't do anything heroic."

☆ ☆ ☆

Dan and Laurie were standing on Judge Sorenson's front steps explaining why they needed an immediate search warrant for a prominent lawyer's house, garage, and canoe. Sorenson, not known for his flexibility or sense of humor, was the only judge they could find on Sunday afternoon. He had pushed his reading glasses on top of his head, and the cardigan he wore made him look more like a professional golfer than a county jurist.

"What do you expect to find in this search?" he asked. He pulled his glasses down to read the warrant Laurie printed out before they left the courthouse.

He read the warrant, "Bones, bone fragments, hair, teeth, knives, guns, blood, body fluids, body parts, diatoms, a canoe, and an ice saw. What in hell is a diatom?"

"It's a microscopic organism with a glass-like shell," Laurie said. "They are specific to particular lakes, and the medical examiner found some in the last victim we recovered from Arlyn Prokop's office. We suspect we may find some in his canoe that match those recovered from the body."

"So," Sorenson summarized, "this person died like thirty years ago, and all of a sudden we're in a big rush to search a lawyer's house on a Sunday afternoon?"

"We think the body was disinterred within the past twenty-four hours," Dan explained. "We need to make this search before any of that evidence is lost. We don't expect to find any evidence from the murder."

"Tell me about the ice saw," the judge said, referring back to the list on the warrant.

"I saw it in his garage," Laurie said. "We suspect that the bodies were hidden in the bog across the lake from his house and it appears that the body was cut with a coarse saw when it was recovered from the bog. When we were talking to Prokop in his garage, there were bits of bog moss stuck to the saw blade, so we think he used the saw to cut into the moss and hide and recover the bodies."

"You've already been inside his garage?" Sorenson's voice rose as he asked the question.

"He invited Deputy Ryan and I into his garage and his house," Laurie explained. "Actually, I've been in his house twice in the past two days."

Sorenson pushed the glasses back on top of his head. "You mean to tell me that he's invited you into his home twice, and now you want to search it? Don't you think it would be a little odd for a serial murderer to invite you into his home if he were hiding evidence there?" As he asked the question, veins started to bulge in his neck.

Tires squealed down the block and all three people turned to look. The sheriff's unmarked squad braked to a stop in front of Sorenson's house. Sepanen ran up the sidewalk leaving the red and blue lights flashing.

"John," the judge said, "your folks brought me a search warrant for Arlyn Prokop's house. Does this seem reasonable to you?"

Sepanen caught his breath, "Dispatch called me at home. I don't know all the details, but I trust Dan and Laurie implicitly."

Sorenson pulled his glasses down and read through the search warrant one more time. "All right," he said. "I'll sign it. But, for God's sake, do a discreet search. Don't dismantle his house, and try not to piss him off too badly. We may end up eating this paper later." He signed the warrant and handed it back to Dan.

Floyd grabbed Kline by the arm and pulled him away from discussion with Officer Angie. She was showing him a tattoo on the side of her neck and explaining the significance of the oriental characters. Kline had been feigning interest in hope of seeing some of the hidden tattoos that the rumor mongers had been talking about.

"I just got a call from one of our deputies," Floyd explained. "She thinks that McCarthy was in on the daughter's kidnapping. Consider this scenario; McCarthy hires Ryan Martin and a buddy of his to kidnap her daughter for ransom. McCarthy has no interest in the money, but wants to punish her husband, who is making all kinds of tainted money building war machines while she protests the war. Anyway, the kidnapping goes down, but Martin's friend turns out to be some kind of a freak and he kills the daughter so the ransom demand is never made."

Kline smiles and says, "And that's what Ryan Martin had over McCarthy all along. He knew about her role in the kidnapping, and he squeezed her for sex, money, and legal representation. She couldn't turn him in without admitting her own role in the scam. Hey, and maybe she never even knew who the third party was, so it would make it even less believable if she were to tell the cops."

"Let's confront her," Floyd said.

"Not yet," Kline said. "What happens when she asks what brand of dope we're smoking? We've got to have a plan to make her want to admit it. If not that, at least we have to make her want to point fingers.

"I've got it!" Kline announced. "We go to her while her lawyer's still there and we say that we just got a guy who wants to turn State's evidence on her with this story. We ask for her side of it and see if the lawyer can get her to talk a plea bargain to something like conspiracy, in return for putting the killer behind bars. By the way, what's the guy's name?"

"My deputy said it was Jerry."

Kline knocked on the door to the interrogation room once, and then opened it. McCarthy was sitting on the near side of the table, her eyes red from crying. Wess, the lawyer, was sitting across the table, writing on a legal pad.

"We're not through yet," the lawyer said.

"We have some new information we'd like to discuss with you," Kline said, walking into the room. "It pertains to the disappearance of Miss McCarthy's daughter."

Kline walked across the room and turned the recorder video on again, then sat at the table. Floyd stood with his back against the door.

"Miss McCarthy, we have been approached by a prosecutor in Northern Minnesota with an offer. There is a man whose been arrested for a different crime, who claims to have knowledge of your daughter's kidnapping and murder. He has offered to provide evidence that you were a participant in your daughter's kidnapping in return for a lighter sentence for himself on a different crime."

McCarthy's face turned bright red. "That's ridiculous!" she yelled. "I had nothing to do with my daughter's kidnapping or murder. How could you even whisper lies like that?"

"His name is Jerry Workman," Floyd said softly. "He and Ryan Martin were close friends."

The color drained from McCarthy's face, and she took a deep swallow. She looked at her attorney and said, "I plead the Fifth Amendment."

"We think," Kline said, "that you and Ryan Martin were probably unwitting participants. The prosecutor thinks that Workman's story is bogus, and if you, and your lawyer, were to agree to plead guilty to a charge like conspiracy to kidnapping, he would accept that in return for your testimony against Workman in a trial for your daughter's murder."

"Wouldn't you like to get that off your chest and get on with your life?" Floyd asked.

"We'll leave you two to talk this out," Kline said as Floyd opened the door. They walked out of the room together.

Kline grabbed Floyd's arm as he closed the door. "C'mon, the camera's still running."

They watched from an electronic control room down the hall as Colleen McCarthy's tears flowed while Tina Wess went to her side and held her close.

"I can't believe this," McCarthy sobbed. "After all these years the world is falling in on me."

"I need to know if what they were saying was the truth," Wess said. "If they have the evidence they claim to have, you should strongly consider their offer of a plea bargain."

"How can a mother admit that she arranged for her child to be kidnapped?"

"It sounds like you could be charged with kidnapping and being an accessory to murder. I'd have to do some research to see what the penalties were back then, because if you're convicted, you'd be subject to the laws on the books at the time of the crime. Even with today's determinate sentencing, you could be sent to jail for twenty or thirty years. Since you were the child's mother, a judge might consider that egregious, and might double the sentence."

"I didn't want her to die," McCarthy sobbed. "I only wanted to punish her money-grubbing father. He needed to be taught a lesson. I never intended for anything to happen to Helen. Ryan was supposed to hide her in that old streetcar and his friend was going to call in a ransom demand. We weren't even going to pick up the ransom. The money was going to be put into a smoldering barrel and it was all supposed to burn up, and then Helen was going to be found the next day. It all went so badly."

"Are you willing to plead guilty to the conspiracy charge and be a State's witness against the others?" Wess asked.

"What the hell," McCarthy replied. "What else can they do to me? I'm already in jail."

CHAPTER 47

After getting delayed by a car accident on the Interstate at Hinckley, Pam drove up the Willow River exit ramp, and turned toward downtown. At the stop sign she turned south and accelerated the few blocks to the Workman house and announced her location to the dispatcher. It was a one-story rambler style house on a wooded lot. A large field ran to the margin of the back yard and a three-strand barbed wire fence separated the field from the yard. The driveway was empty and the lights were off. The temperature had risen ten degrees as she drove the forty miles from Mora and the sky was darkening as the warm front pushed over the colder air. Thunderheads were starting to boil up as the turbulent warm air was pushed miles into the troposphere.

There was no sign of life anywhere around the house and the curtains were drawn. Pam hesitated, hoping that Dan would've heard her announce her location, and would radio her with instructions. After a few moments, she went to the door and rang the doorbell. The chimes sounded, but there was no sound from inside. She rang the bell again, with the same response the second time.

Workman's house was large by Pine County standards, with a large lot and rows of full-grown White Pines providing seclusion from the neighbors on either side. It seemed like the loneliest place in the world to Pam Ryan as she walked around the perimeter of the house, not entirely sure what she was looking for.

The window shades were pulled on every window, and a knock on the back door brought no response. A row of huge pines shaded the back yard and providing an effective privacy barrier. A carpet of fallen pine needles and moss made the lawn a cushioned carpet as they surrounded the few thin patches of grass. Pam completed her circuit of the house no closer to a plan of action than when she'd arrived. She went back to her squad and told the dispatcher she was back in service, asking to be connected with Dan as a rumble of thunder rolled through the trees.

* * *

Dan was just turning onto McCormick Lane, having limited all discussion of the impending search to hard phone lines, as Pam Ryan was circling the Workman house.

Laurie was riding with him, and she shouted, "Look! He's pulling out of the garage!" Dan, about to contact Pam on the radio, dropped the mike as he swerved to block Prokop's car.

The string of four county squads blocked the end of Prokop's driveway before the Lexus got halfway out of the garage. The lawyer stepped out of the car, amazed to see the sheriff, a BCA agent, and three deputies walk up his driveway.

"What's up?" Prokop asked.

The sheriff stepped forward and said, "Arlyn, we have a search warrant for your house, garage, and surrounding grounds."

Prokop accepted the piece of paper numbly, and looked at Laurie. "I thought we were past that," he said. "Laurie's been in my house a couple times, and I thought I had resolved the questions law enforcement might have about me or the house."

"Sorry," Laurie said. "We got some evidence from the body that was in the fire. It points this direction pretty strongly."

Prokop led the entourage through his garage and into the kitchen. "Have at it folks," he said, stepping out of the way. "Try not to make too much of a mess, the maid doesn't come again until Tuesday." The words were light, but his face was pained.

Dan directed Sandy Maki and Kerm Rajacich to search the basement. "John, will you search the garage? Laurie and I will start the main floor."

"Let's look at the canoe first," Laurie suggested.

"This way is the closest," Prokop said. Leading Dan through the living room, he opened the patio doors to the deck. They went down the short stairs and Prokop knelt next to the bottom step.

"It's gone," he said listlessly. "I suppose the neighbor boys have it over at the bog." One hundred and fifty yards away, across the small lake, the sliver of aluminum was visible against the rich green of the mossy bog.

"I'll talk to the neighbors," Dan said, as thunder rumbled in the distance. Dark clouds were rolling in from the west and the mild breeze turned to a stiff wind as Laurie and Prokop returned to the house.

The sheriff met Dan at the outside corner of the garage. "I thought there was supposed to be a big ice saw hanging on the wall in there," he said. "I didn't find anything of interest: No bones, no bodies, and no ice saw."

"The canoe is gone, too," Dan said. "I'm going over to talk to the neighbors. Prokop said the neighbor kids sometimes borrow the canoe."

Chris Locken was surprised to see the Pine County Sheriff and chief investigator standing at his door on a Sunday afternoon. "Sheriff," he said, "what can I do for you?" His face went ashen as a thought struck him. "Oh God, don't tell me something happened to the kids."

"It's not about your kids," Dan said. "Someone paddled Arlyn Prokop's canoe across the lake. He said your kids borrow it sometimes."

Locken shook his head. "They haven't used it in years," he said. "They used to take it over to the bog and explore, but since Jeremy got his driver's license they like to drive around instead of canoeing." Locken hesitated, and then added, "I did see someone pull it down to the lake a while ago. I didn't notice who it was, but I've seen the same guy hauling it around a couple times lately. He's always wearing a dark blue jacket and a black stocking cap."

"Have you seen him take anything out of the canoe when he comes back?" Sepanen asked.

"I guess I haven't seen him come back," Locken said. "It seems like he's was going out about dusk and I haven't noticed him return."

"What kind of car does he drive?" Dan asked.

Locken shrugged. "I haven't noticed a strange car on the street." He looked up and down the road. "I don't see a strange one now."

The wind picked up, straining against the door Locken was holding. A big raindrop splattered against the sidewalk, and soon others followed.

"You two had best come in before you get soaked," Locken said.

"We'll head back to Prokop's," Dan said. "Thanks for your time."

Dan and the sheriff sprinted the short distance between the two houses as the raindrops grew in frequency and size. By the time they were in the garage the street was soaked and the driveway had a flow of water running to the street. A lightning flash lit the sky, followed immediately by the tooth jarring boom of thunder. Laurie was talking to Prokop in the kitchen, when they stepped in from the garage.

"You two are drenched," Prokop said, "Let me put a pot of coffee on," He hesitated, and then added, "if you're through searching in here."

"Arlyn," Dan said, shaking his head, "you are either the coolest criminal I've ever met, or you're completely innocent."

"Thank you," the lawyer said as he pulled a can of coffee and a box of filters from the cupboard. "Those are the most reassuring words I've heard this afternoon."

The sheriff was standing at the living room windows, watching the torrents of rain pound across the lawn and what could be seen of the lake as the raindrops pounded the surface into a froth. Another rumble of thunder rattled the cupboards, and the lights flickered, but stayed on. Tones sounded on all the police radios and the dispatcher announced a tornado watch for Aitkin, Carlton, and Pine Counties. A tornado had been sighted near Malmo, on the north shore of Lake Mille Lacs.

"I can't even see the other side of the lake," the sheriff observed. "If someone is moving the canoe, we'll never know it until the rain breaks."

Dan walked next to the sheriff and took in the same view. "What idiot would try to take an aluminum canoe across a lake in a thunderstorm?"

"Maybe the same kind of idiot who would kill off women and hide their bodies in a bog," Sepanen replied.

"I assume it's someone who drove here. Where do you suppose he's parked?" Laurie asked.

"There's a narrow driveway that goes down to the public access where the road turns," Dan replied. "It doesn't get much use, because there aren't many fish other than bullheads in this lake."

"Hey, Dan," Sandy Maki said, coming up the basement stairs. He had his cell phone in his hand. "Pam Ryan's been trying to get in touch with you. Your battery must be dead."

"Williams," Dan said, taking the phone from Maki.

"Dan," Pam said, "I've left a note for you at the office when I left Mora and I've tried to reach you on the radio and cell phone since then. My contact in Mora had some information. Are you near a hardwired phone? I'm calling from the Willow River gas station and I don't want to talk on the radio or cell phone about this."

"Hang on a second," Dan said as he walked to the phone in Prokop's kitchen. "Call me at this number." He read off Prokop's phone number.

The wind buffeted the house, and a clap of thunder hit at the same time the lightning flashed. The roll of thunder lingered. Sandy Maki and Kerm Rajacich were drinking steaming coffee from pale blue mugs. Prokop was pouring coffee for Laurie, while the sheriff stood waiting with an empty mug.

"This is the most laid back search I can remember," Kerm said.

"No bodies in the basement, and no signs of a murder scene," Maki said.

Prokop set the coffeepot down and answered the phone. "Dan," he said, "it's your deputy."

"What's up, Pam?"

"Grace Palm said that her nephew knew Ryan Martin. She hinted that he might have helped her run away." The phone crackled as Pam spoke.

"Are you still in Mora?" Dan asked. "Can you ask her to clarify the running away story?"

"Um," Pam said, hesitating. "Grace was dying when I left. She won't be answering any more questions."

"Who is her nephew?" Dan asked.

"She never said. But, the hospital was calling Jerry Workman to notify him of her impending death when I was walking out."

"Jerry Workman?" Dan asked too loudly. All the heads in the kitchen turned and stared at him.

"Yes," Pam replied. "The nurse told him not to bother driving in from Willow River because Grace probably wouldn't live that long. I drove right to

Workman's house, but no one is home. I think the nurse may have reached him on a cell phone."

"Hang on," Dan said, putting his hand over the phone. "Arlyn, what kind of car did Jerry Workman have when you were in school?"

"Huh?"

"In '74 Jerry Workman had a car," Dan explained. "What kind of car was it?"

Laurie smiled, suddenly seeing the connection between the phone call and their conversation with Mary Jungers.

"It was orange," Prokop said. "A sporty Pontiac, I think."

"Pam, stay at Workman's house, and radio if anyone shows up. We're about five miles away, and I'll be on my way in a few seconds."

Dan hung up the phone, refusing the cup of coffee Prokop was holding out. He took a few steps to the living room and looked into the rain. The pounding rain had eased, but the sun, hidden behind the dark clouds, was quickly setting. Dan strained his eyes to see the other side of the lake. The shore was indistinct at best, and he couldn't tell if the canoe was still sitting there or not. Another flash and clap of thunder blinded them and rattled the cupboards.

"Arlyn," Dan said, "do you have a pair of binoculars?"

The lights went out, and the room fell silent as all the electrical devices shut down. There was enough lingering sunlight so Prokop could move around the house. He opened a drawer near the kitchen and took out a leather case. Dan took the binoculars from him and looked across the lake at the spot where the canoe had been beached.

"I think the canoe is gone," he said, handing the binoculars to Sepanen. "I'm going to drive to the public access, to see if Workman's Explorer is parked there, then I'm going to his house and back up Pam Ryan. Sandy and Kerm, you two cruise around First Lake in case he went through the creek and has his vehicle over there."

"I'll stay here," the sheriff said, searching the surface of the lake, "in case he comes here to return the canoe."

Dan, Laurie, Kerm, and Sandy ran for their vehicles through the pouring rain. Dan and Laurie were moving before the others and Dan called dispatch to let them know the plans. They made it nearly to the corner of the road before they encountered the huge pine that had taken down the power and phone lines. Sparks flew from the unprotected ends of the wires trapped under the eighty year old pine tree as the rain pounded around them.

"Dispatch," Dan radioed, "call the power company and have them send a repair truck to McCormick Lane to remove a fallen tree ASAP. The road is blocked, and we got live wires down so we can't get near the tree." He quickly surveyed the limited options for skirting the downed wires blocking the dead end road. The overflowing ditch on the west was as impassible as the row of trees along Locken's lot on the east side.

"We have about ten reported power outages," the dispatcher replied. "It's going to be a while before they get to you. They have a major feeder down in Hinckley."

"Tell them to divert from Hinckley," Dan said. "We have a police emergency here. Everyone but Pam Ryan is boxed in on this dead end. We've got to get this cleared."

Pam listened to the radio conversations between Dan and dispatch with growing anxiety. The wind rocked her squad and the rain pounded down on the top like a thousand hammers. The windows were steaming from all the water running into the air vents, and even with the heater on full defrost it wasn't able to keep the windshield clear. Reports of live wires on the ground and trees lying on the roads streamed from the radio. Time crept by as she waited for the dispatcher to tell her that another unit would be with her any time soon.

The sudden glare of headlights in her back window caused her to reach for her holster. She pushed the car door open and leaned out, one foot on the driveway, to see who had pulled into the driveway behind her, hoping on hope that it was Dan. The headlights went out and she could see someone open the door of a green Explorer. She was drawing her Glock as Jerry Workman raced toward her at a full run.

"Stop!" she yelled, trying to get gun clear of the holster before he reached her.

Instead of fighting off an attack, as she feared, Pam felt a searing pain in her shin as Workman slammed the car door on her leg as he passed. After briefly recoiling in pain, she stepped from the car on her injured leg and fell to the ground as pain shot up her leg. Fighting off the pain, she gritted her teeth and climbed to her feet, hobbling after him with the Glock clenched in her hand. He disappeared through the front door before she could make it past the front fender of her squad. She limped to the front door only to confront a dark, empty entryway that disappeared into darkness. The smell of kerosene from a small space heater tainted the air. She pulled the portable radio from her service belt.

"Dispatch, this is Ryan. The suspect is at my location. I'm injured and I need back up."

She stepped through the front door into the darkened hallway. Feeling for a light switch with her left hand, she held the Glock on the open hallway in front of her. The switch clicked, but the lights didn't come on. She fumbled for her flashlight and brought it into a tactical position, supporting her shooting hand, before turning it on. Somewhere below where she was standing she could hear commotion and the sounds of something being moved followed by metallic clanking.

Pam's radio crackled to life as the dispatcher said, "Ryan, all Pine County units are unavailable. I have a call in to Hinckley and Moose Lake. Williams says to hold your position until I get confirmed backup and an estimated time of arrival."

The commotion in the basement continued, and Pam had visions of masses of evidence being destroyed while she hesitated in the doorway. She limped slowly down the hallway scanning the flashlight from side to side until she found an open door leading to the basement just inside the kitchen. The noises that she'd heard faintly in the hall were distinct and definitely coming from the basement. She caught a whiff of sulfur smell, from a match, and the odor of burning paper. Workman was burning evidence.

"Swenson is backing up Ryan," Floyd's voice coming over the radio allowing Pam to flush with relief. "I'm less than one minute from her location."

With renewed confidence that Floyd would be beside her momentarily, Pam switched off the flashlight and quietly eased though the entryway to the top of the stairs with the Glock extended in front of her. The noises continued and she could hear the sounds of something solid being thrown into a cast iron stove. A siren whined nearby and suddenly cut out, Floyd's red lights flashing like a strobe through the living room drapes. His flashlight quickly lit the hallway and she took a deep breath.

"Have you cleared the upstairs yet?" Floyd whispered.

"I think he's in the basement burning evidence."

"We've got to clear up here first," Floyd said emphatically. "We can't have someone walk up behind us when we run down the stairs. Cover the stairs while I clear the other rooms."

She stood at the top of the stairs, the basement dark except for the apparent flickering of a flame from the left side of the enclosed stairwell. As Floyd worked from room to room the adrenaline subsided and pain shot through her shin. She grimaced, testing to make sure it would continue to support her weight, and then decided she had to tough it out. When Floyd returned he stepped to the other side of the stairwell and looked at the flickering light below.

"Any more signs of activity?" he whispered.

"Nothing," she said as she stepped past him onto the top step.

Floyd put his hand on her shoulder and whispered, "Me first."

Pam shook her head, "I'll go left, toward the light, you go right." They continued down the stairs slowly, with Floyd a step behind.

At the last step she hesitated and set herself so she could step out of the enclosed stairwell with her gun ready to fire, but back from the corner so someone on the back side couldn't grab it. She stepped down, illuminating the area around the corner with the flashlight. Her radio announced loudly, "The power company will have a truck on McCormick Lane in five minutes."

Pam stepped aside to let Floyd pass behind, and then she scanned the area quickly with her flashlight and Glock. In front of her was an empty family room with flames flickering in a potbelly stove near the opposite wall with papers scattered around its base. The walls were knotty pine with a few dark water stains that looked like there had been a leak in the room above it at some time in the past. A television sat in the corner with an aging plaid recliner facing. The television remote sat on the small table next to the recliner. A pine bookcase covered most of one wall and the flashlight beam glinted off several dozen real estate awards and a few bowling trophies. The opposite wall was taken by a green sofa with a fifties-style pattern in the nylon cover.

Floyd was back in less than 30 seconds. "There's a utility and laundry room on the other side, but no one there and no where to hide. It's all open with cement block walls."

They walked back to the family room and shined their flashlights in every nook and cranny. Floyd pushed the sofa away from the wall while Pam held her pistol on the space. "Nothing but dust bunnies," he whispered. "You're sure you heard someone down here?"

"I'm sure I heard some scraping noises and I heard the stove door close." She limped around the perimeter of the room one more time. "I would've bet a paycheck that he ran down here."

"There's a garage attached to the entryway. Let's clear it."

Pam started to back out of the family room with the nagging knowledge that she'd heard sounds from the basement before Floyd arrived. She returned to the Spartan utility room and affirmed Floyd's assessment that there was nowhere to hide. At the base of the stairs she played her flashlight beam across the family room again. There were wet footprints across the dirty, green shag carpet, most were probably from she and Floyd. She studied them, and they noticed a different pattern in the carpeting in front of the floor-to-ceiling bookcase. She moved closer, holding her Glock on the bookcase and her flashlight on the carpet in front of the bookcase.

She reached for her radio and pushed the transmit key with her thumb. "Come back down here, Floyd."

She pushed at the corner of the bookcase where the carpet pattern showed that the bookcase might swing, but nothing moved. Tucking the flashlight under her upper arm, she pulled on the edge of the bookcase with one hand, and it slid open a crack with heavy resistance.

"FLOYD!" she yelled toward the stairwell. "I NEED BACKUP!"

"All right," Pam said, gathering all the confidence she could project, "come out from behind the bookcase. This is your last chance, Workman. Come out,now," she yelled at the open crack.

She set the flashlight on a bookcase shelf and wedged the fingers of her free hand into the narrow opening and pulled hard, while keeping her Glock trained on the edge near her fingers. The hinges were oiled, but the bookcase was heavy at first, and then it swung free until it hit the table with the remote, tipping the table and sending her flashlight and the remote clattering across the floor. The flashlight winked out when it hit the floor. With the bookcase fully open, Pam looked into a cavernous space hidden behind the bookcase. The flickering light from the fire in the potbelly stove didn't penetrate the newly exposed darkness.

She called out again, "All right! Lie down on the floor and put your hands behind your back!" Her voice echoed off the bare walls, but generated no response. The faint smell of paraffin smoke caught her nose, but there was no sign of candlelight.

Pam's heart was pounding, and the pain in her leg stabbed at her nerves with every heartbeat. She wondered if Workman had slipped through some back door as she took a step to the edge of the opening.

"Floyd! Get your butt down here! There's a hidden room behind the bookcase!" She yelled over her shoulder.

She took a step forward with the Glock extended in front of her, crouching down, her eyes straining into the dank, cement block recess, until her toes were at the end of the light cast by the stove. She couldn't see into the darkness to the sides of the narrow bookcase, and no sound reached her ears. She straightened up, and something brushed against her forehead. When she batted at it her hand struck more cobweb-like material and a scream rose in her throat.

The force of the rush hit her full in the chest, propelling her back and then onto the floor. Workman's toupee flopped forward as he fell on top of her, the weight of his body pushing the air from her lungs and his face so close she could smell his sour breath. Her heartbeat pounded in her ears as she realized the gun had been knocked from her hand. She struggled against Workman's attempts to wrap his hands around her throat.

"Stupid bitch! Why are you here?"

Workman's face was a mask of anger and his weight so overmatched Pam that she quickly found it difficult to breath or struggle against his restraint. She turned her face away from him and let out small grunts as she tried to kick at his legs and groin, while she clawed at his hands with her fingernails. Suddenly, the force on her neck released.

At first she thought he'd given up, but then the glint of the steel knife blade caught her eye. She reached her hand up to stop the knife as Workman arched his back and plunged the knife down. The sound of her own scream seemed deafening as the air rushed from her lungs and pain shot through her chest. Workman seemed confused for a fraction of a second when the knife failed to penetrate the bulletproof vest hidden under her jacket. He quickly recovered, raising the knife for a second time while she grabbed at his hands. She stared into his feral eyes, glazed with hatred and his jaw clenched tight. She shrieked in terror as she fought to keep the knife away from her throat and face.

Pam screamed again as Workman pulled the hand with the knife free from her grip. The knife plunged toward her neck and she tried to deflect the blow with her arm as a thunderous sound and blinding flash filled the tiny darkened room. The knife arced toward her neck but struck the carpet next to her ear. The second gunshot was followed by a third, and then Workman's body fell on top of her, his blood spraying into her face as he coughed. In panic Pam clawed at Workman's shirt, trying to get enough of a grasp to push the dead weight off her body. Suddenly, the weight was rolled off away and Floyd's face stared down at her.

She started to shake as Floyd sat next to her on the floor and pulled her into his arms. After a few seconds he pulled a handkerchief from his pocket and wiped the blood from her face.

"Are you hurt?" he asked.

"I … I don't think so, but it hurts when I try to take a breath." Pam pushed herself back from Floyd's arms and touched a tear in her jacket next to her badge and then checked her fingers for blood. "I think the knife was stopped by my vest. He was going for my neck the second time."

"What were you thinking?" he asked. "You can't chase a guy into an empty room without back up."

"I called you for back up!" she yelled before breaking into tears.

CHAPTER 48

Dan and Laurie were standing in Jerry Workman's driveway when sheriff Sepanen pulled behind Dan's car. The sheriff was puffing a large cigar when he approached them.

"How's Pam?" he asked.

"The paramedics took a look one look at her and hauled her to the hospital," Dan said. "She probably has a concussion, and possibly a broken leg as well. She's in no danger, but they transported her for X-ray and observation. I put Floyd on five days of administrative leave because of the shooting."

"Sounds like we were lucky," Sepanen said to Dan.

"Your forensic guys are through with the basement?" the sheriff asked of Laurie.

"The BCA techs did the full shooting investigation and cleared the scene," she replied. "The special agent in charge said that they felt Floyd was justified in the shooting and will offer that testimony at the shooting board of inquiry."

"We'll have to call in Chisago or Carlton County to do the official shooting investigation," Dan said.

Sepanen nodded his assent. "What have we got inside?" he asked.

"We sealed the shooting scene until the BCA completed the investigation," Dan said. "So no one has done anything except collect the physical evidence and remove the body." He handed out purple nitrile gloves. "Let's take a look."

They stopped at the bottom of the basement stairs, staring at the scene marked with a dark pool of blood, string showing the path of Floyd's bullets, and tape outlining the location of Workman's body. A tree of halogen lamps stood in one corner, bathing the area with intense white light. The cloying smell of fresh blood hung in the air, mingling with the smell of burnt gunpowder and oak smoke.

"My God," the sheriff said. "Pam walked into this in the dark?"

"She was standing next to the open bookcase when Workman tackled her and slammed her to the floor, there," Laurie said, indicating a spot on the floor where the strings ended. "When Floyd came around the corner, Workman was lying on top of her, drawing his knife back to stab her. The three strings represent the path of Floyd's bullets, tracing the line from the muzzle of his gun to where they struck. Workman fell on top of Pam, and the taped off area with the puddle of blood shows where his body was after Floyd pushed him clear of her."

The sheriff looked away abruptly. "What else is down here?" He took a step toward the open bookcase. "This looks like a fallout shelter. What are these pieces of orange yarn hanging from a fish line across the door?"

"They're tied where we found braided plaits of hair that we're assuming Workman saved from each victim," Laurie said.

"I can't believe this," Sepanen said, counting the yarn. "I've met Jerry before. I can't see him doing stuff like this."

Dan ducked under the string and walked to a small desk sitting in the fallout shelter. He picked a Polaroid picture from a stack on the desk and handed it to the sheriff, carefully avoiding the fingerprint powder dusted on the surface. "This will change your mind."

"It looks like Jerry sitting next to a naked girl on a bed." The sheriff studied the picture for another second and then looked at the small, military style bed next to the desk. "It's that bed, and she's got a handcuff..." The sheriff handed the picture back to Dan. "This is sick."

"We think the girl in that picture is a runaway from Missouri," Laurie said. "I plan to send pictures of the girls we can't identify around to see if we can close some other missing children cases."

"I've got to get out of here," Sepanen said. "This just turns my stomach."

CHAPTER 49

Monday Morning

Floyd carried an arrangement of cut flowers into Pam's hospital room. "How's your head?" He asked as he set the vase on the windowsill. He was dressed in a gray polo shirt and blue slacks. His hair was neatly trimmed and combed, evidence that he'd just left the barber's chair.

"Actually, my head feels fine. My leg hurts like hell." She carefully tucked the edges of her hospital gown and pulled the sheet up past her waist.

"What happened to your leg?"

"Workman slammed it in the car door when he ran past my squad. The doctor says I have a fractured fibula and he'll keep me in a walking cast for a few weeks. The doctor says I have a concussion, so he wants to keep me here another night to make sure I'll be safe at home." Pam paused and then asked, "Are you retired? I've never seen you in civilian clothes before."

"Dan put me on paid administrative leave until the shooting board convenes."

"I don't know if it was hitting my head or if I've been out of the information loop, but it seems like there are a lot of unanswered questions. What happened?"

Floyd shook his head. "I hardly know where to start. You knew I was in Minneapolis yesterday interviewing Colleen McCarthy when everything broke loose. She was denying everything and anything until you gave me Jerry's name. When I told her Workman was going to testify against her, the public defender jumped in and demanded they talk in private. She spilled everything to her lawyer; from manipulating Ryan Martin, to putting together the bogus kidnapping to extort money from her ex-husband."

"How can you know that? Did she cop a plea?"

"Her rookie public defender didn't ask us to stop the video, so the camera kept running when we left the room and I watched it all."

"So, none of that is admissible evidence unless the prosecutor offers her some sort of plea deal."

"That's the rub. I talked to Kline, down in Hennepin County, this morning. I guess that McCarthy clammed up when she heard that Jerry Workman was dead and couldn't testify against her. But the videotape that ran while she was talking to her lawyer sews it all up pretty well. She met Ryan Martin in Minneapolis, prior to the peace rally. He was a wild spirit, and she apparently thought he could be molded into something more. At one time she was very militant, and she may have seen his wildness as a possible source of violence to promote her anti-war activism. Anyway, she came up with the plot to have Ryan Martin run off with her daughter, and then Martin would call up and demand a ransom. McCarthy thought the daughter would be perfectly safe through the whole thing, because she'd be hiding out with mom's buddy, Ryan. The kidnapping would teach her evil, war-mongering husband a lesson by removing a bunch of tainted money from his wallet."

"Let me guess about the next part," Pam said. "Ryan couldn't handle all the logistics himself, so he linked up with his buddy, Jerry Workman, without telling McCarthy. Little did Ryan know that Jerry had some real problems, including a thing for dark-haired girls. Ryan hands the Smith girl over to Jerry for safekeeping, and Jerry takes her to the streetcar, but gets carried away when little Helen doesn't like him as well as he likes her. Ryan goes ballistic when he finds out the girl is dead and starts making excuses with McCarthy, claiming that he can't find his buddy or the girl. At this point, Mom freaks, because Ryan's lost the girl, and no one is making ransom demands. On the other hand, she can't go to the cops, because she cooked up the whole scheme, and there are two people who can pin the whole thing on her. Best part is she doesn't know who the second guy is, which puts her at an even greater disadvantage."

A gentle knock on the door interrupted the discussion. "Is there room for another cop in there?"

Laurie asked as she walked in with another floral arrangement.

"C'mon in," Pam said. "There's room for anyone who brings me flowers."

"I was just filling in some of the blanks for Pam," Floyd said as Laurie set her flowers next to Floyd's vase. "What we know for sure is that it's several months before McCarthy realizes that Ryan is using her for his own purposes. She finally realizes her daughter isn't coming back and she gets fed up with the threats and just walks on him."

"While that plays out," Laurie says, "Workman starts to get this longing for another dark-haired girl, and then goes through one after another, after another."

"I don't understand," Pam said, "how his wife wouldn't know about all this going on in her basement."

"I talked to her," Laurie said, "They got married after the last of the murders. Jerry was on some medication to deal with anger for years and he stopped taking it a couple months ago. She said he's been so weird since he stopped his meds that she's been living with friends for several months, although I think her departure may be as much related to the appearance of Jerry's girlfriend as it does to his meds. Before that, she said the basement was too creepy to set foot in. She knew there was a fallout shelter, but she'd never been brave enough to look in it … spiders." Laurie gave a melodramatic shiver.

"Apparently," Pam said, "Ryan Martin never told McCarthy who the missing partner was?"

"McCarthy told her public defender that she finally found out that Jerry Workman was the other partner when Ryan Martin called after he got out of prison," Floyd explained. "Martin called her to extort some cash, and in return for the cash he gave her Workman's name and told her that Workman had evidence to implicate her in the kidnapping and murder. She drove to Willow River with her boyfriend to confront Jerry the night of the office fire. Workman wasn't there, but the house wasn't locked, so they decided to go in and check things out. I guess she almost peed in her pants when they heard a knock at the door and found a deputy standing there. When she figured out that the deputy was only looking for Jerry, she quickly recovered, pretended to be Mrs. Workman, and told our deputy that Jerry was out. Once the squad pulled out of the driveway they decided to poke around a little bit, but obviously didn't find the fallout shelter. At some point they decided that it wouldn't be prudent to ransack the house looking for the evidence so they drove back to the Cities empty handed."

"I suppose," Laurie said, "that finding the first body brought everything to a head for Workman. He's been off his meds for a while, apparently at the urging of his new girlfriend who was convinced that they were making him impotent, when suddenly, his crime is thrust into the limelight and he kinda likes making the cops look like fools. At that point he decides to see if he can pull any of the other bodies out of the bog, and then planting them around town to make the cops squirm."

"But why plant a body in your own office building?" Pam asked.

"It was brilliant!" Laurie said. "And we bit on it exactly as he thought we would. He ate lunch with Arlyn all the time, so he knew that Arlyn Prokop's name was showing up on our radar, and that we had Arlyn searching old records for us. If the fire were to destroy all the records before we could get the information out of them it would point more suspicion at Prokop. On top of that, if it looked like Prokop had stashed a body in his own office we'd be hot after him and I'll bet that it gave Workman a big rush to read about it in the newspaper. He's got quite a collection of clippings from all the cases."

"His ploy almost worked," Floyd said, "even with the forensic evidence. We had the search warrant for Prokop's house, and we were going through it when Workman was pulling the third body out of the bog. I suspect that he didn't think we'd act as fast as we did, and if we hadn't beaten him to the punch, there would have been a body in Arlyn's basement for us to find today."

"In all the confusion I haven't had a chance to tell Dan," Laurie said. "I had the State Patrol rush a sample of Workman's hair to the BCA. They confirmed that he had ring hair. It'll take a while to do a DNA match, but they said we can be ninety-nine percent sure that the hair found with Helen Smith's body was from Jerry Workman."

"What about the bog and the creepy ice saw in Prokop's garage?" Pam asked.

"Tony Oresek and Eddie Paulson are working with the department of natural resources. They've recovered five bodies so far," Laurie replied. "They're using some sort of sonar device to find solid spots under the moss in the bog. Tony says the bog is just a mat of moss and Tamarack roots on top of some soupy rotting plants. They use the sonar to identify solid objects under the mat, and then they cut through to see if there's a body there."

"Have they figured out how he put the bodies in the bog?" Floyd asked.

"The ice saw," Laurie replied. "He'd make a slice in the moss with the saw and then he'd just push the body into it. The moss would cover it right back up again, and within a few months the Tamarack roots would knit across the cut and seal it tight."

"I wonder how Workman found the body he put in the law office basement?" Pam asked.

"The DNR guys found slash marks on a couple of Tamaracks near graves." Laurie paused, "Well, since Pam looks healthy, I think I'll head back to the bog to help with the identification of the bodies."

"Floyd, are you really going to retire now the case is solved?" Pam asked.

"I was thinking I might have to run through the numbers one more time and maybe consult my tax guy before jumping to any conclusions."

CHAPTER 50

Tuesday afternoon

Floyd and Dan were finishing hot beef sandwiches with mountains of mashed potatoes at Art's Café in Moose Lake when Floyd's cell phone chirped. He wrestled it free from his the pocket of his Carharrt jacket on the third ring. "Yeah."

"Swenson, you owe a patch to Arnie at the bar," Kline's raspy voice came over the phone with its usual edge. "Since you and that Ryan woman are on leave, at least according to the Strib, I thought this might be a good time to make good on that promise."

"I'm tied up for today," Floyd said, looking at the deer mural painted on the wall.

"Tied up with what, nightmares and self pity? Just put your butt in the seat of the car, pick up the Ryan woman, and drag yourselves down here. When you get to the 694 loop give me a call and I'll meet you at the bar."

"I don't know that I'm up for the bar scene right now," Floyd said, his voice not carrying an air of certainty.

"Get into your uniform and get your butt in that car, or I'll come up there and kick it all the way to Minneapolis."

"Well, if you feel that strongly about it, I guess I can track Pam down." He was talking to a dial tone before he ended the sentence.

"Kline, the Minneapolis Detective, wants us to deliver a Pine County patch to be pinned on the wall in the cop bar in The Cities," Floyd explained as he put the cell phone back in his pocket.

"Have a nice trip," Dan replied.

☆ ☆ ☆

Pam answered the door dressed in a purple Minnesota Vikings sweatshirt that hung nearly to her knees. Her hair looked like chipmunks had nested there, and her eyes were rimmed with red, like she hadn't slept well. She was obviously surprised to see Floyd. "What's up?"

"Put on your uniform and run a comb through your hair," he said as he pushed past her toward a coffee pot he spied on the kitchen counter. "I'll pour myself a cup of coffee while I read the story of your heroism in the Pioneer Press one more time."

"I thought we were on five days of leave," she said as she watched him rattle through the dirty dishes in the sink, searching for a cup. Floyd was never rumpled, but his uniform was freshly pressed and he had a spring in his step.

"We are," He replied as he rinsed a cup under the tap. "But you and I have a request from Hennepin County. Go get your uniform on and I can explain it while we drive to Minneapolis."

He poured a cup of amazingly good coffee and took a sip before running soapy hot water into the sink. He was drying the last of the sink full of dishes when Pam returned. Her uniform was neat, and she'd used gel to tame her wild hair. A thin coat of makeup covered the paleness of her face, but couldn't fully cover the purple bruises that were fading to yellow and green on her neck or the walking cast strapped on her right foot.

Floyd explained his promise to bring a Pine County shoulder patch to the Minneapolis bar owner and Pam responded with skepticism and irritation that he'd dragged her away on such a flimsy pretense. When 35W crossed 694 Floyd called Kline's cell phone and they agreed to meet outside the bar.

The downtown streets were jammed with commuters trying to escape and when Floyd got to Sixth Street, he found that there was no parking on either side of the street during afternoon rush hour. Kline was standing in front of the bar and motioned for Floyd to turn at the corner, and then walked ahead of them while they crept ahead in the gridlock. When they turned the corner, Kline waved them into an opening in front of a fire hydrant.

"Won't this be a problem if there's a fire?" Floyd asked as he locked the squad.

Kline chuckled. "You'll be able to drive back to Pine City in the time it would take a fire truck to get through this grid lock. I'll have one of the uniformed cops listen for the fire chimes on his radio."

"You must by THE Pam Ryan that Swenson talks about all the time," Kline said, offering his hand to Pam as she limped down the sidewalk. "I'm Brad Kline."

"THE Pam Ryan?" she asked, shaking his hand and giving Floyd a dirty look. Kline had a firm grip and his smile seemed genuine. "I hear you fed Floyd some cock and bull story to drag us down here to pin a shoulder patch on the wall of some bar."

Kline shook Floyd's hand. "He promised, and I'm holding him to it."

The bar was jammed with cops who seemed to be from every department in the Twin Cities. Pam nodded to a St. Paul traffic control officer and shook hands with a State Patrol Trooper as they followed Kline who was elbowing his way to the bar. Crumpled doors from police cars hung by wires atop the bar, and every foot of wall space had some sort of police memorabilia pasted, nailed, or pinned to it. A police car light bar was mounted over the top of the bar, flashing blue and red lights. When they reached a set of four by eight foot corkboards at the end of the bar, Pam was amazed by the assortment of patches, representing law enforcement units from coast to coast and from the RCMP, in Canada, to the Costa Rican Federal Police. Floyd took out a new Pine County patch and was looking for a thumbtack when Kline stopped him.

Arnie, the bar owner and a former cop, showed up at the end of the bar with a bottle of brown liquor with a black label and a handful of shot glasses as Kline borrowed a stool and climbed atop the bar with a police whistle between his lips. With the shrill scream of the whistle, the cacophony of voices slowed and stopped as the patrons turned to look.

"Kline, I thought you quit drinking?' Someone yelled from the back of the bar.

"Shut up for a second and listen up," he yelled. "You all read the Strib about the serial killer who got put down in the fight up in Pine County. Well, I've got the two Pine County Deputies who were involved in the shooting. Pam Ryan wrestled the guy to the ground and got stabbed and beaten up pretty well in the process. Floyd Swenson was backing her up, and took the guy down." Kline pointed to them and Pam waved nervously. "They brought a Pine County patch for Arnie's board."

Kline handed Floyd a tack and as he pinned the patch to the board a slender, black, female cop, who was sitting on a barstool next to Pam, stood and started to clap. The applause rippled across the room until every cop was standing and clapping. Arnie set two shot glasses on the bar and poured brown liquor into them. "This is Black Bush. I save it for special occasions," he said as he pushed shots in front of Pam and Floyd.

He poured a third shot for himself and held it high. "To heroes!" he shouted before tilting his glass towards the back wall and downing the shot.

Pam stared at the Irish whiskey and hesitated. The female cop, with a nametag that said, "Blake" was standing next to Pam leaned close and whispered, "Tradition is that you hold the shot glass up to the pictures of the fallen officers on the wall and then take it all in one swallow."

Floyd tipped his glass to the pictures and downed the shot. Pam then looked at the three rows of black and white pictures on the wall. Under each photo was a small brass plate listing the date they'd died in the line of duty. Suddenly aware of how close she'd been to being another picture on that wall, she felt her eyes well as tears streamed down her cheeks.

"I'm not…" Pam whispered to Officer Blake.

"You are," Blake whispered back, followed by a nudge.

Pam tipped the glass and threw back the shot. She was immediately hit with a coughing spell as the whiskey burned her throat and hit her empty stomach like a fireball. The result was a roar of laughter, and a line of cops pounding her on the back and shaking her hand as she gasped and wiped tears on her sleeve. Someone handed her a glass of beer that spilled as she got jostled in the crowd of well-wishers. She looked for Floyd, but he'd been swallowed up in another part of the bar.

"You did well," a female voice said in her ear. Pam turned and found the same trim Minneapolis officer at her side. Her skin was black, which highlighted her sparkling white smile, and her hair was tied back in a bun that exposed her high forehead. "In case Kline forgot to tell you, I'm Donna Blake, and I'm your designated driver and guardian angel for tonight." She held up a plastic bottle of Diet Coke.

"I'm not really a hero," Pam said, whispered back as another group of cops patted her on the back and shook her hand. "I was scared to death."

Donna reached up and folded Pam's collar back, exposing the large blue and green bruises on her neck. "Honey, being a hero isn't about not being scared. It's all about being scared, but having the courage to overcome that fear and to act. The way I heard it, you followed the killer into a house and confronted him while he was trying to destroy evidence even though you knew that your backup was still out of touch. Every cop here respects you for what you did, and we all know that you're a hell of a cop for doing it. THIS is what law enforcement's all about, honey. You have earned the respect of your peers."

"I don't know what to say," Pam said, leaning close to Donna's ear to be heard over the roaring crowd.

"Don't say a thing," Donna replied. "You're among friends, and this is the place where you can let your hair down and not worry about it. You may wake up on my couch tomorrow morning with a hangover, but I guarantee you'll have some great stories about tonight for your grandkids."

EPILOGUE

Thursday morning

"Well, we finally got that missing girl case closed, Ginny," Floyd said, standing next to the headstone in the Pine City Cemetery. The clear blue skies that came in on the heels of the high-pressure front made the morning dew sparkle like a diamond on the tip of each blade of grass. His shoes and pant cuffs were soaked and there was a dark trail where he'd trampled the dew walking from the driveway to Ginny's grave.

"Funny thing; the girl's father was really thankful that we solved the case. There was a big, color picture of him standing next to Sheriff Sepanen on the front pages of the Minneapolis Star-Tribune and the Pine County Courier. The mother, well she wasn't as happy. Seems she was in cahoots with some unsavory characters that staged the girl's kidnapping. Maybe closing the case will let her clear her conscience because she's been doing penance for all the years since the kidnapping by working in soup kitchen's and such."

Floyd worked a piece of driveway rock loose from the sod with his toe and threw it back toward the gravel driveway. "I guess you probably aren't much interested since you never wanted to hear much about my cases anyway. But, I guess … well, I wanted to let you know that I decided not to retire right now," he blurted out quickly. "Truth is, I was thinking about coming to join you, and this case made me feel … full. I contributed and it felt good. It made me realize that I had something to teach those young deputies. I'm not sure Pam Ryan would be alive right now if I'd retired a week ago. She got herself in a bit of a pinch, and I came running to the rescue as this guy was trying to kill her." Floyd hesitated and looked up at the high white clouds that were racing across the sky, pushed by a high pressure front coming down from Canada. He took a deep breath.

"During the investigation I met a widowed lady who runs the Pine Brook flower shop," He said, sniffing back a tear. "Her name is Mary Jungers and I told her I'd stop by tomorrow to take her out for a slice of pie and a cup of coffee. I couldn't bring her to any of the places we used to go, 'cause I'm not quite ready to deal with that, yet. But it was nice talking to someone my own age with values like mine. I know you told me that would be okay before…" Floyd hesitated as memories of Ginny lying in the hospital bed flooded his memory; Ginny trying to be rational about her deteriorating health and him a basket case hoping that a doctor would walk in with a miracle cure for metastatic ovarian cancer. When she'd told him that it would be okay to move on with his life, it was the last thing he wanted to hear.

"I thought I'd better let you know," he choked out as he bent down to run his fingers over the lettering on the headstone. "I'm sure nothing will come of it, but … Oh hell, I hope something comes of it and maybe she can help me fill some of the lonely days and nights."

ABOUT THE AUTHOR

Dean Hovey is the author of two previous Pine County Mysteries, **Where Evil Hides**, and **Hooker.** He finds inspiration in the woods and fields of Minnesota where he spends hours walking with his wife, Julie, and his golden retriever, Summer. He splits his time between southern and northern Minnesota, passing through Pine County regularly.

Made in the USA
Charleston, SC
21 February 2010